NO HEAVEN, N̶

J. T. BRINDLE

PRESENTED BY
HEAD OF ZEUS

Part 1

Hide…

1

'For God's sake, Katherine, are you out of your mind? Aren't you afraid of what might happen?' He visibly shuddered, his voice dropping to a whisper. 'You surely can't have forgotten why he went away?'

The old woman's eyes flickered to a smile. 'No, Cyrus,' she murmured, 'I could never forget.'

In spite of the horror that had driven away her only son, and even through the long lonely years that followed, Katherine Louis had never lost hope that, one day, she and the child she adored would be reunited. She had never apportioned blame, nor did she pretend to understand the awful sequence of shocking events that had aged her before her time.

'I want Jack to come home,' she said simply. 'The parting has been too long, too painful.'

Roaring like a lion in agony, he raised his two fists and slammed them one into the other. 'You don't know what you're saying,' he cried. 'It's been over twenty years. He's probably imprisoned in an asylum somewhere. He might even be dead.' His blue eyes stared at her with intense love – or hatred. 'I can't... *won't* let you do it.'

'Listen to me, Cyrus.' She regarded him with patience, this tall well-built man who, even in middle age, still bore the stamp of youth, and whose bright blue eyes and curly fair hair camouflaged a deep and serious nature. 'You must know I've thought long and hard before coming to this decision.' She saw that he wasn't listening; incensed, she demanded, 'Look at me, Cyrus, damn you!'

At first he deliberately looked away, but there was something so compelling about his sister's voice that he was forced to return her gaze. For a long moment he looked into her eyes, soft brown eyes that had seen so much tragedy, eyes that had laughed and wept, and at times closed in unbearable anguish. Katherine Louis had survived seventy years. She was a handsome woman, with a wonderful smile and quiet charm. Her small features were strong and sharp; her long silver hair, which had once been vibrant with the flaming auburn of her Irish ancestors, was swept into a coil, like a sleeping snake nestling in the nape of her pale slim neck.

Her brother devoured her with his eyes. All their lives he had admired and loved this creature with a passion that had never died. Katherine was always a tower of strength. It was she who had carried them through the nightmare that had threatened to engulf all of them; she who had kept their sanity intact; she who had suffered most, yet shouldered the burden with immense courage.

In her countenance there was no sign of the awful things she had endured. Her aged face maintained its mesmerising beauty. Her sense of honour rose from within; her generous heart endearing her to all who knew her. She was clever, and shrewd, and possessed of a remarkable perception. Yet still she blamed herself for not seeing the tragedy unfold. She had not seen the madness that came into their lives – only when it was too late; only when there was no stopping it.

Now, while they regarded each other, Katherine grew impatient. Tall and serene, in the high-backed red-leather chair, with her pale hands folded like gossamer on her lap, she seemed impossibly exquisite. She wore a black dress, and at her throat a large blue cameo brooch – the only beautiful thing her mother had left her. Katherine cherished the brooch, and, in spite of everything, held fast to the memory of the woman who had worn it close. Even so, there were times when her own skin would cringe at its touch.

As she continued to stare at him with those all-seeing eyes, he respected the proud dignity that raised her above other mortals. 'I love him as much as you do,' he insisted, 'but I have a real bad feeling about this. Bringing him home would be like raising the past.'

'Don't fight me on this,' she warned. 'I understand your fears and I too am a little apprehensive. But my mind is made up. I have to find him.'

There were times like now, when he would have given his life for her. 'I'm sorry,' he muttered. 'It's just that I've never been able to put the horror out of my mind. I'm afraid…' His voice trembled and he could not go on. Instead he shook his head and hung it low, his heart turning with fear. 'If you mean to search him out, there's little I can do.'

'Do I have your blessing then?'

Raising his head, he gave her a stony look. 'I'm sorry, Katherine. I can only pray you never find him.'

She put out her hand, and he clasped it in his, warming to her touch. Wishing he could hold her hand for ever. She nodded her head with a certain grace, acknowledging his dilemma. 'It wasn't Jack who did those terrible things.'

'Can you ever be sure of that?'

Gently shaking his hand, she said, 'In my heart I *have* to be sure. For too many years I've been uncertain, made myself bitter against him for running away… leaving me alone when I needed him most. In all that time I never really thought of him, of how *he* might have felt, or of how much he might need me. I'm older now, and wiser. I long to see him.'

'Wouldn't it be better to let sleeping dogs lie?'

'Sleeping dogs can be dangerous too.' She sighed from deep within. 'I asked you to look at me, Cyrus, but you don't, not really. You see what you want to see, you always have.' She was loath to hurt him, but he had to face the truth. 'I'm seventy years old. Every breath I take brings me closer to the maker.'

He would have protested, but one kind glance silenced him. 'Soon it will be too late. I don't mind that. In many ways it will be a relief to leave the cares of this world behind, but I have to see him, just once more.'

'Why now? Why didn't you decide this long ago?' He couldn't understand women. Above all, he could never understand Katherine.

'Lately I've begun to think about how he might feel... lonely like me... afraid... wanting to come home. I still love him. I always will.'

'*I'm* here. Don't you love me?' He felt like a child again. When he was a child, and stranded in the apple tree, Katherine had rescued him. She was young then. Now she was seventy and her heart was young and brave as ever. He envied her that. All his life he had wanted to be like her. He had never married. Now he never would.

'That's emotional blackmail, Cyrus.' She stood up and her presence filled the room. 'Of course I love you. You're my brother.'

As she moved away, his dogged gaze followed her. 'What do you want me to do?'

'I want you to stop questioning every decision I make.' At the door she paused but didn't turn. Suddenly she felt old. Her head was heavy on her shoulders and her bones ached with the weight of many years. 'When Maureen comes in from the kitchen, ask her to bring the tray to my room... and to remember the plasters for my foot.' Stepping forward, she winced slightly.

'No better?'

'Worse if anything.'

'Maureen will take care of it. I have to go soon. Remember I have an appointment with the accountant at nine.' He felt irritated. Normally Katherine would see to that side of their affairs, but lately she had her head too full of finding Jack.

She turned to observe him, amused at his surly expression. 'I know you'd rather be playing golf, but business has to come first. You'd best make a start. You know he doesn't like to be kept waiting.'

He walked across the room, smiling at her now with affection. 'I'm sorry if I've said anything to offend you. Jack did the best he could in the circumstances, and I know he took it badly, as we all did. It's only natural you want to find him. I have no right to interfere. It's just that... well, how can you hope to trace him after all this time?'

She returned his smile. 'Don't make the mistake of underestimating me.'

He nodded. She was right, of course. She had always been one step ahead of him, always knowing what he thought, what he planned, how his mind worked. He smiled secretly. She always read his mind. *Except for that one time all those years ago.* He was sweating, inexplicably afraid. 'I have to go. We'll talk later.'

'We've talked enough, I think.' Her features stiffened. 'Don't keep him waiting, and while you're there, make another appointment for the two of us. I'm still not satisfied with the terms offered on that proposed investment. I know we can do better. In fact, I've been giving it some serious thought. Maybe we should make a bid for that fast food company after all?'

He shook his head with wonder. 'I won't argue,' he said. 'I'm happy to go along with whatever you decide. You're never wrong.'

'Exactly!' She gave him the strangest look. It unnerved him.

With that she took her leave, shaking her head and softly chuckling as she walked towards her private rooms. 'Oh Cyrus! Cyrus! Why can't you find a decent woman and make a home for yourself?' But he wouldn't. She knew that. It was another source of anxiety to her.

Her footsteps were muffled by the deep, luscious pile of the carpet and, as always, her appreciative gaze rested lightly on each painting as she swept by: there was a beautiful Parisian scene by Monet; a study of still life by an artist she had taken to when he was barely making enough to live, and who now commanded astronomical sums for his work. There was a splendid portrait of an old man with the most mesmerising, weathered face, and a small gallery of paintings depicting generations of Katherine's family; one in particular which she could never pass without pausing awhile.

She paused now, her eyes raised upwards to meet the stare of the woman in the painting. 'I don't know if I can ever forgive you,' she whispered harshly.

For the briefest moment she half expected those red-painted lips to part and say how sorry she was, how she never meant for any of it to happen. But the face remained immobile, half smiling, its beautiful features set like stone on the canvas, the unexpected mass of Titian hair and the dark eyes spellbinding in their beauty. This was the face of Virginia Louis: Katherine's late mother.

The portrait had been painted many years earlier. There had been another portrait of her, showing an older woman, still beautiful, but the eyes were already changing, darker somehow, glittering with a kind of madness. After the trial, Katherine had burned the painting on a pyre in the garden. She might have burned this one also. But it was too magnificent, too filled with youth and life, betraying nothing of the wickedness beneath.

As she gazed into the eyes of her late mother, Katherine was haunted by the memories: of sunny days in Central Park, of her mother setting out the picnic while she and her father played a very bad game of baseball. She smiled at the memory. It did her old heart good to remember. She recalled how very much in love her parents had been, how they would walk back home hand in hand, watching her while she skipped along in front and occasionally glanced back to make sure they were still there. Such warmth. Such a passion for life! Where did it go? How could it have ended the way it did?

Other memories assailed her then. Memories of what they had found. Unbelievable carnage. Crimson on white... etched on her mind for all time.

Bending her head she gave out a deep, withering sigh. 'Help me, Lord,' she pleaded. 'Help me to find him.'

Raising her eyes she stared at the portrait. It was more than she could bear. Reaching up, she took hold of the frame and swung the picture over. In all these years this was the first time she had turned the face of her mother to the wall. Yet it gave her no pleasure. Instead, it made her feel uneasy.

Katherine was resting in the chair when she heard the familiar tap on the door. Her face broke into a ready smile. 'How many times have I told you, there's no need to knock!'

The door inched open and a woman's face appeared: a round, surprisingly unlined face, with a mischievous grin and twinkling blue eyes. 'And haven't I told ye I was brought up not to barge in unannounced?' She came into the room and closed the door.

'I'm glad you're here, Maureen.' Katherine's voice was tired. 'I'm feeling sorry for myself this morning.' She let her old eyes rest on the homely figure, and it gave her a warm feeling.

Maureen Delaney was a tonic. She had never married, and Katherine thought that was a great pity, because she was convinced Maureen would have made a wonderful wife and mother. She was a little absentminded at times, bless her, yet, in spite of her dumpy figure and old values, she was young for her age. This morning she had a certain gleam in her eye. Her brown permed hair was thick and bouncy, and she wore a pretty Laura Ashley dress which wiped the years away. It made her look like a young country lass, fresh from the green fields of old Galway.

'You're looking bright and perky this morning,' Katherine told her. 'What mischief have you been up to?'

'Huh!' Maureen came to stand before her. 'I'm thinkin' it's *you* who's been up to mischief.'

'Chance would be a fine thing.'

Maureen would not be drawn into a meaningless conversation. It was obvious Katherine had guessed what she was about to say, and was trying to avoid the confrontation. 'Sure, I saw ye turn that portrait to the wall.'

Katherine looked down. 'You shouldn't spy on me.'

'Why did ye do it?' This time her voice was kinder.

'I don't have to answer to you. I don't have to answer to anyone.'

'I didn't say ye did. I only want to know what ye think it will solve by turning the portrait to the wall.'

'I felt like it.'

'Has it made ye feel any better?'

'No.'

'Do you want me to burn it?'

Katherine sat up straight in the chair. *'Don't you touch it!'*

'Ye still love her, don't ye?' Gentler now, sensing the pain beneath.

Katherine's eyes grew moist. 'She was my mother.'

A long, agonising pause. Maureen knew her every thought. 'I took the liberty of turning the portrait back again.'

Katherine's slim fingers reached out, grasping the other woman's hand in friendship. 'Thank you,' she murmured, her eyes raised in a smile.

The mood had passed. Outside the sun began to shine. It flooded into the house, into that room, bathing the expensive furniture, lightening the dark corners. Fear and terror had subsided – for the moment.

Dipping into her skirt pocket, Maureen took out the most amazing number of items; a small pair of scissors, a bag of cotton wool swabs, a packet of plasters, a tube of ointment and a small bottle of red liquid, all of which she laid on the footstool directly in front of Katherine's chair. 'Been giving you some gyp has it, me darling?' Planting a kiss on Katherine's forehead, she stood a moment, hands on hips, her wise blue eyes watching the old woman's face. 'An' don't be telling me no lies.'

Katherine's face lit with a beautiful smile. 'Would I do that?' she teased.

'I know very well ye would! Sure ye've led me a merry dance these past forty years, and God willing, ye'll lead me a merry dance for the *next* forty.'

'I don't know if I want to live that long.'

'I'm insisting on it.' Her chuckle was like a ripple of water tumbling down the mountainside. 'If ye should decide to pop off, who's gonna pay me wages, that's what I'd like to know?'

'So it's my money you're after, is it?' Katherine loved these little games. 'Shame on you, Maureen Delaney.'

Maureen's eyes opened wide with feigned surprise. 'Well now, it's *you* should be ashamed, so it is! After yer money indeed! How could ye think that of a poor old thing like meself?'

'Poor old thing be blowed. You're as sharp as a wagon-load of monkeys, and anyway, what are you... fifty-one? Fifty-two?'

'Is yer brain addled, or what? I'll be fifty-nine years old next month, and well ye know it.'

'That's no age at all, and anyway, you look disgustingly healthy to me.' She scrutinised the other woman affectionately. 'Look at you,' she murmured, 'your skin's as clear as milk, and your cheeks rosy as the summer's day when you stopped me on Fifth Avenue, looking for work, you said... run away from home to seek your fortune, you said.' She couldn't help smiling.

'Sure I did an' all! And haven't I found me fortune with ye? Aren't we the best of friends? Didn't ye give this poor little wretch a home, and aren't I forever grateful?' She screwed her face up in the way Katherine had come to know so well. 'Ah, but yer a grand old lady, Katherine Louis, an' I'll strangle anyone wit' me bare hands if they say different.'

Katherine studied her a while longer, until in a voice heavy with regret she said, 'I don't know if I did you any favours by taking you home with me.'

'Sure ye had no choice. Big as an elephant ye were. Be Jaysus, I thought, the poor lamb's gonna drop the young 'un on the blessed pavement, so she is. What! If I hadn't got yer in the taxi an' raced it all the way home, ye'd have been a right spectacle for all an' sundry, sure ye would. As it was, ye'd only been inside the door half an hour before yer waters broke.' She raised her face and laughed out loud.

The conversation had taken a turn which led Katherine straight back to the bad things. 'You'd best look at my toe, and then get back to your work,' she said icily. 'I'm sure there are a thousand and one other things you could be doing.'

Maureen was smitten with guilt. How could she have been so stupid as to raise the issue of the other place? And whatever possessed her to mention Katherine's late husband? 'I'm sorry,' she muttered, positioning herself on the other footstool. 'I never did know when to keep my mouth closed.'

Katherine wanted to say it was all right, but it wasn't. So she kept quiet, though she felt sorry to have spoken in such a cold voice. Maureen had been with her right from the start. She had been with her on the day Jack was born, and every day since. It was right what Maureen had said just now: she wasn't just her companion and housekeeper, nor was she a mere servant. She was a *friend*, and that was a very precious thing.

While Maureen cleaned her toe with the antiseptic, Katherine let her mind gently roam back over the years, to that summer's day when she first met Maureen. 'You were just a child,' she murmured now. 'Nineteen years old. A little Irish colleen, lost on the streets of Manhattan.'

Maureen chuckled softly: her mistress never could stay angry for long. 'I'm *still* lost when I take to the streets,' she admitted. 'I know New York was designed on this marvellous grid system, which is supposed to help me find my way round without any trouble, but, so help me God, I can't even go shopping for a cabbage, without ending up down some dark narrow alley, scared out of me wits in case some drunken down-and-out takes a fancy to me.'

It was Katherine's turn to laugh out loud. 'Where's the map I drew you?'

'I threw it away. It only got me more confused.'

'But it's so simple!'

'Not to a simpleton.'

'You're no simpleton.'

'Oh? And what about yesterday?' She peeled off the remnants of the corn plaster. One piece in particular refused to budge, so she gave it a little sharp tug.

'Jesus Mary and Joseph!' Katherine rolled forward in agony, clutching at her foot, and glaring at Maureen through narrowed eyes.

Maureen was not impressed. 'Cursing will get ye nowhere,' she declared. 'Sit still, or I'll take me bag o' tricks an' be gone.'

Katherine reeled back, her eyes closed in pain. 'Be quick then.' She could feel the cool liquid being swabbed against her skin. It felt good. 'What did you mean... about yesterday?'

Maureen wasn't sure whether to tell her or not. She decided it was easier to confess, than to undergo an inquisition every time she showed her face. 'Well, it's just that I was lost for nearly an hour. I thought about going into a shop and asking directions, or even flagging down a policeman, but, well, I didn't want to make meself a laughing stock.'

'Oh, Maureen!' She really was the limit. 'So what did you do?'

'I got into a cab.'

'Good thinking, but why didn't you go to a phone booth and telephone me?'

'Because I knew ye'd laugh.'

'I wouldn't do that... well, not *really* laugh.' She was trying not to laugh now. It was hard not to laugh at Maureen and her little adventures – especially as they had been going on for the best part of forty years.

'Did you tell the cabbie you were lost?'

'Of course not.' She reddened in the face. 'But he knew it anyway.'

'Oh? If you didn't tell him, how could he know that?'

Maureen bent her head and scrubbed at the sore skin, ignoring Katherine's protests.

'I asked you, how could the cabbie know you were lost?'

Maureen took her courage in her hands. 'Because he picked me up two doors away, that's why. When I gave him the address, he collapsed with laughter.' With her two thumbs she squeezed the centre of the corn. 'Nasty man!'

When the whole foot began shaking, Maureen feared she might have squeezed too hard. She looked up and realised that Katherine had covered her face with the palm of her hand, and was trying hard not to let the smile break into a gust of laughter, but the telltale tears ran down her face as she rocked backwards and forwards. Maureen was horrified. 'Ye bugger!' she cried. 'Ye're laughing at me again!'

Katherine couldn't speak. She shook her head from side to side, opened her mouth to apologise, and that was it. Try as she might, she couldn't suppress it any longer. 'I'm sorry,' she blurted, and was convulsed.

Maureen gave her a stern look before she too could see the funny side. In a minute she had flung her arms round Katherine, and the two of them were helpless. 'I'll have to set a car on for you,' Katherine gurgled.

'Ye'll do no such thing!' Maureen declared. 'Where's that drunken down-and-out gonna find me then?'

The following afternoon, in his plush office on the eighteenth floor, Eddie Laing waited patiently for the phone to ring. Leaning over his desk, he had his arms stretched out in front of him. The slim cigarella, drooping from his bottom lip, had fizzled out long since, and now his fingers were tapping out a medley on the blotting pad. His office reeked of success. His suit was tailor-made, and his shoes of the finest leather money could buy. He was neat and clean shaven, and his dark hair expertly groomed. His brooding eyes, one blue, one green, fascinated women, and his tall, gangly figure had an easy way of moving that stirred their secret desires. The only disappointing feature about Eddie Laing was his nose, which was ever so slightly bent, a legacy from Brooklyn, where as a homeless urchin he stayed on top by fighting. In those days you got nothing for nothing, and if you didn't live by your wits, you died in some filthy gutter.

He'd come through all that. Now, in his prime, at the age of forty-two, he was a top detective with a fast-growing reputation. Living rough on the streets had taught him a certain cunning, a shrewd knowledge of the underworld, he had learned how to track down an enemy, and there wasn't man nor woman who could match his talents for sniffing out a frightened soul who had gone into hiding. There were times when he'd been real bad. Times when he'd done things he was now ashamed of. He'd been locked up in the slammer more times than he cared to remember, but even in there he'd learned a few tricks that stood him in good stead.

It took a woman and a soured affair to set him straight. When he decided to change his lifestyle, it seemed natural that he should set up as a private eye. Though he said it himself, he was a natural! Success after success brought him new clients, and now, less than ten years on, some of the wealthiest and the elite of New York were among his clients. He was a man of consequence: wealthy, living the life of Reilly, and loving every minute. He had his regrets. But then, who didn't? His biggest regret was the broken bone in his nose. Women didn't care for it. Lately he'd been toying with the idea of having it surgically straightened. Since his divorce, the idea was becoming more and more attractive.

He had got out of his chair, gone to the mirror on the back wall, and was examining the nose, when the phone rang. Swinging round, he snatched at the receiver, a little irritated. 'Yeah?' A pause, then he nodded, his homely features lifting in a grin.

Tucking the receiver on his shoulder, he located a notepad and made copious notes. After a few minutes, he replaced the receiver and began to pace the room. The nodding continued, interspersed with satisfied grunts and the occasional click of the tongue. He was very pleased with himself. Very pleased indeed. He returned to the mirror and looked at his nose again. 'You want it straightened, but you ain't got the guts.' He shook his head in disgust. 'Laing, you're a cowardly bastard!'

He glanced through the window, across the skyline of New York. It was awesome, a panorama of skyscrapers touching the clouds. The sky was darkening fast. Soon the whole city would be lit like the fourth of July. Going to the door, he flicked the light switch. 'God! I hate winter,' he moaned.

He was a man who wore his overcoat right up to the month of June, a man who had never picnicked in Central Park, not even when the sun was so hot it could fry eggs on the pavement. His ex-wife had complained that he was too thin to hold the heat. However, she could be right. Maybe you have to have a thick layer of muscle to keep out the cold. One of these days, when he had the time, he would go to the gym and thicken his biceps, maybe broaden his back and build up his thighs too.

'Too much like hard work, Laing,' he muttered. 'What's more, you'd have to shop for a whole new wardrobe.'

The thought of using up his precious spare time in the gym was not attractive; neither was the prospect of spending money on a new wardrobe, when he had a perfectly adequate one right now. 'Forget it!' he told himself. 'Who needs muscle when they've got brains?' He tapped his temple, and smiled wryly. 'Got it down below too.' He winked and clicked his tongue. 'More than enough to go round. Working out in the gym? Naw. Forget it, Laing. It was a crazy idea anyway.' But the nose? He tweaked it and stroked it and was irritated. Keeping the torso he had was fine by him. But the nose was a different matter, and one which he had to tackle, like yesterday.

At the desk, he thumbed through the blue ledger until his finger came to rest on a name, then on the number beneath. Keeping his eyes fixed on it, he dialled patiently, waiting until a female voice answered, a distinctly Irish voice.

'Louis residence,' it said. 'Can I help ye?'

He nodded again. Using the voice he cultivated especially for the Katherine Louises of this world, he replied, 'This is Eddie Laing.' Taking out a new cigarella, he bit the end off and spat it ever so gently into the ashtray. He didn't light it. He was trying desperately to give up the habit. 'I need to speak with Mrs Katherine Louis.' His smile broadened. 'If you could please tell her I have the news she's been waiting for.'

Maureen held on to the receiver. She wanted to put it down. To tell this Eddie Laing that Katherine didn't want to speak to him, or that she had died in her sleep last night, or that the news she had waited for was no longer important – but Katherine would never give up. If it wasn't this detective, it would be another, and another, until Jack was found. 'I'll give her yer message,' she said. 'Please wait.'

Katherine took the call in her study. She switched on the desk lamp, locked the door and drew the blinds. Her calm manner and quiet dignity belied her fast-beating heart, and the rise of panic in her stomach. 'Thank you, Mr Laing,' she said. 'You've done your job well.'

During the two hours she spent locked in the study, she was aware of Maureen's voice calling her name. She was also aware of the gentle taps on the door, and that kindly soul's anxiety. 'I'm all right,' she replied. 'I'll be out shortly.' She had much to think about.

Katherine was grateful when Maureen left her alone, but the silence in that room was eerie. The news she had received was eerie. The journey she was about to embark on was something she had long dreamed about, something she had to do – whatever the outcome.

Two hours later when she emerged, she voiced the questions that had troubled her. Maureen listened patiently, anticipating each and every one. Katherine was brimming with excitement, yet deeply apprehensive. Had she done the right thing? Would Jack thank her for setting a detective on his trail? Would he refuse to see her? Had he changed? Was he still marred by the things that had happened all those years ago? Was he married, or single? What kind of life had he built for himself?

Maureen set the tray on the side table and sat beside her. 'It's a bit late to be getting the jitters now,' she said, pouring the coffee. 'Yer doing what ye have to do. Whether he'll thank ye for it remains to be seen. As for his wellbeing, and the other things yer curious about, surely the detective must know?'

'I didn't want him to tell me over the phone. When he said he'd found Jack, I couldn't think straight.' Knowing Jack had been found was enough. Even that was a shock. 'Mr Laing is coming here tomorrow. I'll know everything then.'

Maureen was indignant. 'What in God's name made yer ask him here… to yer home? Wouldn't it have been better for ye to go to his office? I would have come wit' ye.' She handed Katherine a cup of coffee and made a disapproving face. 'Detectives in yer home… sitting in yer best chairs! Whatever next?' Sipping at her own coffee, she gave Katherine an odd, sideways glance.

Katherine read her mind. 'I know what you're thinking,' she murmured. 'You're remembering the last time we had detectives crawling all over the old place, but it's different this time.' She drank from her cup. 'This time the gentleman is invited.' Replacing her cup on the tray, she leaned back in her chair. Maureen had raised an issue best left alone. 'Switch on the television.'

Sighing noisily, Maureen did as she was bid, remaining by the set ready to switch it off again. If she knew anything, it was that Katherine soon tired of watching television. 'It's the news.'

'Leave it. Come and sit down. You make me nervous, hovering in front of the set like that.'

Again Maureen did as she was told, turning her eyes to the set and listening intently. The news was bad. A plane had crashed after hitting a bridge over Potomac. Reports were coming in that seventy-eight people had lost their lives.

'Jesus Mary and Joseph!' Maureen made the sign of the cross.

Katherine was speechless for a moment, then in a slightly trembling voice she said, 'Please. Turn it off.' Her heart went

17

out to the families who had lost their loved ones. Suddenly the bad memories were overwhelming.

'I want you to know something.' Katherine's voice hardened. 'If anything happens to me, you'll be well taken care of. I've left instructions.'

Maureen glared at her. 'Sure I don't want to talk about such things.'

'I just want you to be sure I wouldn't leave you destitute. You must know I love you like a sister. What *do* you want to talk about?' There were many times when Katherine preferred to be alone. This was not one of them. Sitting here in the chair, with the warmth of the room enveloping her, with her good friend close by and the knowledge that soon she might be reunited with her son, she felt a sense of peace she had not felt in a long time.

'I'd like to ask about Cyrus.'

Katherine was surprised. 'What about him?'

'Is he happy, d'ye think?' Maureen had her own good reasons for wanting to know.

Katherine thought for a moment. 'I *think* he is. But you know Cyrus as well as anyone. He keeps himself to himself.' Curiosity prompted, 'Why do you ask?'

Maureen shook her head, looking away for a moment, as though she had been caught stealing. 'It's just that lately he seems to be…' She searched for the right words. 'I don't know… miles away.'

Katherine knew what was wrong. 'He doesn't approve of me contacting Jack. He believes I'll be opening a Pandora's box.'

Maureen had known this family long enough to speak her mind. She spoke it now. 'He could well be right. In fact, ye know how I feel about it.'

'You're as bad as he is. If we're ever going to have peace of mind, we have to forget what happened.' But it wasn't easy. It never would be.

Maureen sighed and groaned, and fell back like a deflated balloon. 'Aye, yer right o' course, but, well…' She tightened her lips and shook her head, and there followed an awkward silence before she went on in a hushed voice, 'I pray to God yer doing the right thing… for *all* our sakes.'

'It's something I have to do.'

Sitting up straight, Maureen poured them each another cup of coffee, grimacing when she sipped at her own. 'Leave it be,' she advised with a shudder. 'It's stone cold. I'll make us another.' She would have got to her feet, but Katherine stopped her with a wave of her hand.

'I don't want another,' she said. 'I want to know why you're so concerned about Cyrus.'

'Because he was only a bairn when I first came to this family, and because I worry about him, like I worry about you.'

Katherine's smile was filled with love. 'You were only a bairn yourself when you came to this family.'

'I was nineteen! What's more, I knew how to take care of myself. Cyrus was only ten, and he was always a little lost soul.'

'And you were a little mothering hen.' She chuckled. 'You love him very much, don't you?'

Maureen blushed a bright shade of pink. 'I love you all,' she answered. 'But I've seen Cyrus suffer more than any of us. I'll never forget the day they put her away… the agony he went through after he lost the father he idolised. But he survived it all, thank God. I watched the child grow into a man. I saw him fall in love, and I cried in the church when he got wed. I cried when their bairn was stillborn, and later, it broke my heart when that wife of his threw him aside for another man. Now he has no real home, and all the life he has is what ye make for him. He dotes on ye, and has no room in his heart for anyone else.' She threw out her fat little hands. 'God love us! He deserves better!'

Katherine sat like stone throughout the other woman's tirade. Something she had said triggered off a reservoir of hate within her so bitterly strong that she had to wait a moment before speaking. Then, in a cold, stern voice she said,

'Sometimes, my dear, I think you overstep the mark.' Pointing to the tray she said, 'Take it away. I know it's early, but I'm going to my bed. Make sure I'm up at seven, won't you?'

Maureen was mortified. When would she learn not to let her tongue run away with her? Collecting the tray, she made a funny little bow. 'Don't worry,' she said humbly. 'I'll have your breakfast ready by eight.'

'And don't spill the tea. You know I can't eat from a sloppy tray.'

'Don't worry.' Maureen was used to the old lady's habits. 'Goodnight then.'

Katherine nodded, but did not reply, nor did she raise her eyes.

Only when the door closed behind Maureen, did her stiff body visibly relax. She knew Maureen had meant well, but sometimes the wrong word could bring down an avalanche. 'It isn't your fault, my dear,' she murmured, staring at the door. She recalled Maureen's fighting mood and chuckled. With a long, deep sigh, she thought, We're a pair of daft old buggers, you and me. All we have is each other, and still we play these silly games.

As she leaned forward to call Maureen back, the door inched open, and there she was, peering round the door, asking with a sheepish look, 'D'ye want me to give yer toe another going over before ye take yourself off to bed?'

Katherine rolled her eyes in anguish. 'I'm sorry,' she apologised, bringing her penitent gaze to rest on Maureen's homely face. 'I want my tongue cut out, speaking to you like that.'

The other woman's face broke into a grin. 'Cutting out yer tongue seems a bit drastic,' she replied in a relieved voice. 'What d'ye say we kick each other's arses instead?'

'Goodnight, Maureen.'

'Goodnight, me ol' sunshine.'

Katherine had a bad night. Sleep seemed elusive and thoughts of her parents wouldn't let her be.

It was exactly five minutes to eight when Maureen arrived with the breakfast tray. 'The eggs are sunny side up, and the toast oozing with butter. The tea's piping hot – no spills,' she said mischievously, 'and would you believe it's like a summer's day outside?'

Fitting the legs of the tray over Katherine's lap, she went to the window and flung back the curtains: the sun flooded in. 'I had a word wit' the man up there.' She winked, flicking a thumb towards the heavens. 'Let the lovely Katherine wake up to a bit o' sunshine, Lord, or she'll be crotchety and impossible all the day long.'

'That's not true, you old devil.' Katherine was in a brighter mood. The eggs were delicious and the aroma of fresh cooked toast filled the air. Better still, her toe felt unusually comfortable.

'Hey! Not so much of the old, if ye don't mind.' Feigning indignance, Maureen gripped the hem of her pinny to flick a speck of dust off the windowsill. 'What time's yer man coming?'

'Nine thirty.' She bit into the toast and the butter trickled down her chin. Embarrassed, she wiped it away with the napkin. 'As usual you've buttered the toast too thickly.'

'Aw give over! If I didn't put at least three layers of best butter on it, ye'd have me guts fer garters, sure ye would.' She came to stand by the bed. 'Are ye sure ye want to meet this fella?'

Glancing up, Katherine appealed to her friend. 'I've come this far, and there's no turning back now, but I must admit I am a little nervous.'

'Get away wit' ye!' She hurried to the door. 'I've never known the day when Katherine Louis was nervous. Anyway, I've got things to do.' She grinned. 'I bet ye mean to sit the poor beggar in the high chair, don't ye?'

'I might.'

'Yer a wicked woman, sure ye are.'

21

'Don't I deserve a little pleasure at my age?'

'Will I come back for yer tray in fifteen minutes?'

When Katherine nodded, she breezed out, singing at the top of her lungs: 'I'll take you home again, Kathleen, to where the fields are fresh and green…' As Maureen swept past the window, she looked out to see the traffic jammed below, with myriad people crushing sidewalks, and not an inch in which to twirl about. 'One o' these days I'll cross the seas to the old country,' she promised herself. But then she had promised herself the very same these past twenty years, ever since… since… She couldn't let herself think about that. So she took a deep breath and broke out in song once more, going about her work in a dream. The ol' country. Always the ol' country. When she sang she cried, and when she cried, she cursed herself. All her family were long gone. What was there to go back for?

Eddie Laing was on time, looking smart and businesslike, in a grey suit and long dark overcoat. 'Shouldn't have worn this,' he remarked, handing the coat to Maureen. 'Whoever thought it would turn out to be so damned warm?'

Katherine was ready for him. Bathed and dressed in a white blouse and straight navy skirt, she looked quite formidable. Her silver hair was meticulously coiled at the nape of her neck, and when she spoke it was with a clipped voice that hid her anxiety. 'Sit down, Mr Laing.' Gesturing to the chair in front of hers, she waited for him to be seated. Her chair was low and relaxing, while his was upright and hard. It was a technique she had seen on an educational programme, and one which gave the interviewer an advantage. She had tried it on the bank manager and it worked a treat.

Maureen brought tea. As she came in she noticed how Eddie had been confined to the high chair. While his head was bent over his notes, she wagged a discreet finger at Katherine and went away sniggering.

'Your son is living in England,' Eddie said. 'He's changed his name from Jack Louis to Jack Lucas.' He paused there, waiting for her reaction. Somehow he believed the news would infuriate her.

It didn't. 'Go on,' she urged, her features betraying nothing of her disappointment.

'Your son is married, with two offspring – both girls, one fifteen, the other seventeen. Very close they are… born within two years of each other.'

'The way you talk, they might as well be dogs.' Katherine interrupted him icily. 'Do they have names, these "off-spring"?'

He coughed and smiled, and cursed his mistake. 'Of course. I'm sorry.' He glanced down at his notes. His hands were trembling. Only this morning he had unearthed the background to Katherine Louis' family. It had been riveting, and shocking.

The sweat began to trickle down his forehead. 'Would you mind very much if I sat there?' he asked boldly, glancing appreciatively at the inviting leather couch. 'Only I feel conspicuous perched up here. It's like I'm being interrogated.' He wasn't really warm, just extremely uncomfortable.

Surprised and amused by his honesty, Katherine turned away to smile. Maureen would be amused too, she thought. Clearing her throat, she answered with great dignity, 'Oh, I am sorry. Of course.'

Visibly relieved, he moved to the couch, shuffling his notes as he went. 'The younger girl is named Lianne,' he continued. 'Her elder sister is called Virginia.'

He didn't see the colour drain from Katherine's face, but he heard the small sharp gasp, and looked up, thinking she had said something.

Katherine was shocked by the name of her son's eldest daughter, but had learned from experience not to show her deeper emotions. Returning his gaze, she asked calmly, 'And what about my son's wife?'

Again he consulted his notes. 'Her name is Elizabeth. She's thirty-five years of age.'

'So! She was not yet twenty when she had her first child.' She felt a strange comradeship with this young woman whom she had never met; this woman who had borne her son's children.

'What sort of work does my son do?'

'He owns a small bakery, supplying to the local shops and restaurants.'

That was good news. 'Following in his grandfather's footsteps,' she remarked proudly, then realising she was thinking aloud, she quickly added, 'I'm sorry. Please go on. Whereabouts in England do my son and his family live?'

Flicking through his notes, he found the necessary information. All the time that her eyes were on him, he felt sure she was examining his nose. Once or twice he covered it with his hand, until she asked impatiently whether he needed a tissue. That made him feel more conspicuous than ever. 'The address is Heath and Reach,' he said, with an inward sigh of relief, 'in the county of Bedfordshire. According to my information, the house is a huge rambling place... in the Second World War it belonged to the British army.'

'Thank you, Mr Laing. Leave me now.' She felt emotionally exhausted.

For a moment he was confused. She had dismissed him so quickly, he didn't quite understand. 'If there's anything else...?'

'There is nothing else, except for you to send in your bill. Oh! And leave the notes for me.'

'Of course. I brought the report, all neatly typed.' God! What the hell did a woman like Katherine Louis know? With her money and privilege, she had only to click her manicured fingers. It was only poor sods like him who knew how hard it was out there. Look how difficult it was proving to get himself a decent secretary. The last one had left to work in a burger bar, and he still hadn't managed to replace her. It took him three nights, and four baskets filled with discarded paper, to type this particular report. Christ almighty! The tips of his fingers were still aching. And all she could say was, 'Send in your bill.' If he didn't soon find a secretary, he'd have to type *that* as well!

'The notes, please, Mr Laing.'

Suddenly she was standing beside him. Her nearness was oddly disturbing. Quickly now, he reached into his briefcase and withdrew a bound copy of his report. 'You'll find everything in there,' he reassured her.

Taking the folder, she walked with him to the door. 'My housekeeper will see you out,' she said.

As he stepped into the hallway, Maureen was already waiting.

'She's some lady, ain't she?' he said with admiration.

Maureen pushed him out the door. 'Ain't she?' she quipped. But her smile was genuine, because, much to her surprise, she found she had taken a liking to him.

When she came into the study, Maureen was astonished to find Katherine at her desk. 'I want you to take a cab, and send this letter airmail,' she said, handing her a long white envelope.

Curious, Maureen took the letter and also took the liberty of reading the address. In her beautiful handwriting, Katherine had addressed the letter to 'Mr Jack Lucas, The Lodge, Heath and Reach, Bedfordshire, England'.

Maureen was puzzled. 'Jack *Lucas*?'

'He changed his name.'

'I see.'

Katherine's face softened with pride. 'He has two daughters.' Then her voice stiffened. 'One of them is called Virginia.'

Maureen was incredulous. 'Virginia, you say? Dear God above! Why would he do that?'

There was a pause, before Katherine answered softly, 'That's just one of the things I shall have to ask him.'

'Why don't ye leave him be?'

'I can't.' There was a strange desperation in her voice. 'When you come back, we'll begin the travel arrangements. I told you I had made provision for you in my will. At present

25

my brother Cyrus is the main beneficiary. I have no plans to make changes just yet. Not until I've seen Jack and spoken with him.'

Maureen stared at her. 'I'm still not sure yer doing the right thing.'

'It's too late for all that, my dear. I have a son, and I have two granddaughters.' Her words were chilling. 'How could you expect me to stay away?'

Cyrus stayed in the doorway for the briefest moment, then he turned away. He had heard enough, and now he felt it in the pit of his stomach. *It was all going to happen again.*

2

Jack sat hunched over the bar. The Red Lion was always busy, but tonight it seemed as if the world and his neighbour had poured in. Every now and then he would glance round the room as though expecting someone... something. He shivered. Even in a room filled with people, he felt oddly alone, frightened. The cold rippled through his body as though a tap had been turned on.

Highly nervous, yet not knowing why, he clutched his pint jar, gently rolling the cool glass between his sweaty palms, and occasionally wiping his finger up the rim to scoop up the over-blown froth. 'Christ, Lenny, you tight-arsed bugger.' Licking at the froth, he visibly shuddered. 'It's freezing in here. Are you trying to save on the heating, or what?' He was so cold. So very cold. Behind him he could feel the warmth from the radiator, but he was chilled to the bone.

Lenny the barman gave him one of his shrivelling looks. 'Get your missus to buy you some long johns. That'll keep your balls warm.'

Jack chuckled. 'You're a crude bugger.'

'And you're out of your mind if you think I'll turn up the heating.' The sweat was dripping from his forehead. 'If you need to warm up, get behind this bar and serve a few customers. Sal's had to go out and I'm run off me feet.'

Jack took a moment to consider. 'I can give you half an hour. But then I'll have to be away. I promised Liz I'd be back before the girls went to bed.'

Lenny took the cap off a bottle of Coke and mixed it with a measure of rum. 'That's a nice little family you've got.'

Jack groaned. 'Liz rang me at work. Ginny's been in trouble at school again, and I'm supposed to come the heavy father with her.' Beads of sweat stood out on his forehead now, but his back was icy cold. He made himself wonder about the trouble at school. What was it this time? Ginny had always been his favourite, but the older she got, the less he understood her.

The barman looked at him enviously. He and his wife had never been blessed with children. It was the biggest regret of his life. 'It'll be something and nothing,' he consoled. 'You know what kids are like… fighting one day, and fast friends the next.'

'That's the trouble. She's not a "kid". In a few weeks' time she'll be eighteen.' His mood brightened. 'Thank God she'll be leaving school soon. She's got herself an apprenticeship at one of the big hairdressers in London.'

'A commuter, eh?' There had been a time, many years back, when Lenny had travelled backwards and forwards to London. He wouldn't do it again. 'That's not an easy life,' he said dryly. 'You're in danger of ending up like a bloody zombie.'

'She'll cope.' He was proud of his girls, and it showed in his voice.

'Hmm.' He served a packet of crisps and ten Rothmans. 'She'll not be carrying on with her studies, then?'

'Not altogether, though the apprenticeship means her going to college three days a week, and if that's what she wants –' he turned his hands over and made a grimace – 'it's fine by me.'

A threatening voice yelled from the other end of the bar, 'Hey! Let's have some service down here!'

Harassed, Lenny put up his hand in acknowledgement before turning to Jack. 'That's one trouble. Get yourself over here,' he pleaded, 'before the buggers lynch me.'

'Half an hour, that's all… or it'll be *Liz* lynching *me*.'

'Half an hour will save my life.' He glanced up at the clock. It was half past ten. 'By that time the bar will be half-empty anyway.'

Swilling down his drink, Jack wiped the froth from his lips and, much to the amazement of the onlookers, vaulted the bar. 'Right, mate,' he grunted, addressing the burly fellow who had yelled for service. 'Where's the fire?' He had served behind this bar enough times to know that the big man's bark was worse than his bite. All the same, he was prepared to deal with him if need be.

The big man took one look at Jack's capable physique and at the determined glint in his green eyes, and wisely decided to be sensible. 'Give us a pint, mate,' he pleaded, licking his rubber lips. 'I've a raging thirst on me.'

The next half hour was frantic, with customers queuing three-deep to be served, and money spilling over the counter like it had gone out of fashion. 'I thought times were hard,' Jack remarked, when he and Lenny found themselves side by side pulling the pints.

'Maybe,' Lenny mused aloud. 'But if a man can't afford his pint, his newspaper, and a woman in his arms, life isn't worth living.'

The time went by unnoticed and, just as Lenny had predicted, so did half the customers. 'That's me finished.' Jack served his last pint and rinsed his hands under the tap.

'I owe you.' Lenny winked. 'Off to face the music, are you?'

'I don't mind admitting, I hope they're all in bed asleep by the time I get home.'

Outside was pitch black. January was always a dark month. The days were short and the nights long, and in between it was grey and cold. 'G'night, mate.' The voice of a passerby sang through the air. 'Too cold to piss, ain't it?'

Jack nodded. He wasn't in the mood for strangers. He needed to think, to get his head together before he faced Liz. She was a good woman, warm and loving, the kind of woman a man met just once in his life. But, like any woman, Liz wasn't all sweetness and light. When occasion demanded it, she had a quick and fiery temper. She was in a temper when they first met: he had bumped into her as they alighted from the train at

Waterloo. He was in such a hurry that he didn't see her, until he sent her flying along the platform; the high heel broke off her shoe, she lost all her shopping on to the track, and she split three fingernails. It took him twenty minutes to calm her down, during which time a crowd gathered to enjoy the show. It also took him two cups of tea and a salmon sandwich to earn her forgiveness.

She was in the same fiery temper when she rang the bakery earlier, and he had no doubt that she would still be in a temper when he got home. It was usually Ginny who set her off. He stopped in his tracks, astonished at the brutality of his own thought. What in God's name made him think that? In fact, wasn't it true? Wasn't it always Ginny who set her off? Always Ginny who came between them? And lately, wasn't it happening more and more? He wasn't thinking straight. He was angry. Angry with himself for doubting Ginny's goodness.

The rain began to fall, and the heightened wind cut through his clothes. Pulling up the collar of his overcoat, he sighed. What the devil was wrong with him? He told himself to look on the bright side... in a few months' time Ginny would be working. In a few years both she and Lianne would be married and off his hands. He chuckled. The chuckle turned to a serious mood. The trouble was, he didn't believe there was a man alive good enough for his precious Ginny. He was flushed with guilt. Or Lianne, he chided himself. Don't forget Lianne.

He crossed the road and hurried along the narrow path. Feeling something squelchy beneath his shoe, he swore out loud: 'Dog shit!' Leaning against the wall, he examined the sole of his shoe in the light from the street lamp. The dark lumpy stain confirmed his fears. 'Bugger it!' That's all he needed... to take the stench of dog shit in with him.

Going to the edge of the path, he vigorously wiped his foot up and down the grass verge, again and again, until he was satisfied. Can't blame the dogs, he thought, quickening his footsteps home. It was the bloody owners who wanted their noses rubbed in it.

He paused outside his house. He always did. It gave him a great sense of pride just to look on it. The house was much too big for his needs; it was old and dilapidated and if he worked his arse off from here to doomsday, he would never earn enough to restore it to its former glory. Even in the rain it was imposing, a glorious relic of a former time. It had a skyline all of its own, with a multitude of chimneys, different roof levels and quaint dormer windows; there was even a battlement at one end. The front windows were huge, with small panes and attractive stone mullion surrounds.

All manner of climbing shrubs festooned the front of the house. There was a long meandering drive up to it, and a pair of wrought-iron gates ten feet high, fronting the pavement. To keep out the ghosts, he thought as he opened them now. The rain had brought a kind of warmth to the night, but still he trembled, like a frightened child.

'Stay away, you bastards!' He swung round, his voice rising above the pattering rain, above the night and beyond the stars, into the darkness that went on for ever. *'You stay away from me!'* The rain ran down his face and mingled with his tears. The tears ran into his mouth and he could feel himself choking. 'Bastards!' He went up the drive muttering beneath his breath.

Suddenly he was running, crashing through the porch and into the house, as though the devil were on his heels. Once inside, with the great door closed behind him, he fell against the wall, gasping for breath, the rain dripping from his nose and the clothes on his back sticking to him like clingfilm.

One minute he was frantic, the next he was laughing out loud. 'You're a bloody coward!' he cried. 'Still afraid of the dark.' He glanced out of the window. The wind was howling. The rain was lashing the door, making a fascinating melody as it split itself into a billion particles and sprayed them at the house, *his* house. 'But you're not after the house, are you?' he whispered harshly, pressing his nose close to the pane. 'It's *me* you want, isn't it?' With a boldness he didn't really feel, he made a sign with his two fingers. 'Well, you won't get the satisfaction, so piss off!'

'Who's chasing you?'

The voice made him swing round. 'Liz!'

She came forward, her soft voice soothing the turmoil inside him. 'Don't tell me Lenny's chasing you for the price of a pint?' she teased.

Grabbing her to him, he held on tight: she was his anchor in the storm. 'I'm sorry I'm late,' he apologised, 'only Sal had to go out and Lenny was on his own. He couldn't cope, so I offered to help behind the bar.'

Pushing her hands into his chest she raised her head and glared at him. 'Did you do that on purpose?'

'What?' He was puzzled.

A little smile played round the corners of his mouth. 'Look at me!' She drew away. Her clothes were dark with damp. 'I'm soaked through!'

He rolled his eyes to the ceiling, then he looked at her and grinned, the same way he had grinned when he sent her sprawling on that platform, a shy helpless grin that showed his embarrassment. 'Sorry,' he said. And he was.

His eyes coveted her. She was so lovely, slim and small like a doll, with round hazel eyes and a mop of brown hair that never looked tidy; she was pretty and fun and, besides Ginny, she was everything in the world to him. Oh, and Lianne! He cursed himself. Mustn't forget Lianne.

'Well?'

'Well what?'

She sighed, but didn't pull away. 'I said you've soaked me through, you sod.'

He kissed her, then in a whisper reminded her, 'When we stood in front of that altar, didn't we vow always to share everything?'

She nodded cautiously. 'Hmm.'

'I'm soaked to the skin, so why shouldn't *you* be soaked to the skin?' He winked and kissed her again. He could feel himself hardening. 'We could take a shower together?'

'Maybe.' She was deliberately hedging.

'Oh? Turning me down, are you?' Easing her away he held her at arm's length. 'I thought we just agreed to share everything?'

She smiled wryly. 'There are some things I refuse to share.'

'Oh? And what are they?'

'My favourite perfume, chocolate Digestives and...' She hesitated, wrinkling her nose.

'Go on! And?'

Her gaze dropped to his feet. 'Whatever it is that's stuck to your shoe and stinks to high heaven.'

He burst out laughing. 'Dog shit.'

She glared at him. 'Get them off before you take one more step into this house.'

His eyes shone with mischief. 'Get them off, eh?' He began undoing the belt on his trousers. 'Can't wait to ravish me, is that it?'

She was already on her way across the hallway. 'Throw them into the front porch!' she ordered. 'With a bit of luck some old tramp will cart them away.' There was a chuckle as she disappeared into the drawing-room. It wasn't the first time he'd brought home an obnoxious smell. A few weeks ago Lenny gave him a pair of dead pheasants. They'd been hanging in his shed, 'maturing' he called it. Jack had come home like a puppy with two tails. Unfortunately the pheasants were past rotten and stank the house out for a week.

'Am I forgiven?' It was only a minute before Jack stood at the kitchen door, looking like a drowned rat.

'I'll think about it,' she said. 'You'd best get a shower, but be quiet. The girls are asleep.' She switched the kettle on and gave him a dry glance. 'I thought I asked you to come home before they went to bed?' Leaning with her back against the sink she continued to look at him, secretly admiring him, wanting him as always.

'Sorry, sweetheart.'

'You're always saying you're sorry.'

'That's because I'm always messing up your plans.'

'I know.'

He gazed at her, noting how the top of her blouse was open, showing the gentle rise of her breasts. 'I want you,' he murmured.

'I know that too.'

'Want to shower with me?'

'I've just put the kettle on.'

'Switch it off.'

'Persuade me.'

Slowly he took off his wet coat, then his trousers. His dark blue socks were hopelessly wrinkled and the tail of his shirt hung low over his thighs. She softly laughed, putting him through every agony. 'I hope the girls don't come down. They'll be having nightmares for weeks.'

'Are you persuaded?'

'Maybe... maybe not.'

His smile was devastating. 'I can see you're weakening.' Next came his shirt. His broad, bare chest was glistening wet, the long dark hairs clinging to his skin like black meandering rivulets. The rain had driven right through to his underpants. Wet and flimsy they clung to his body. The shape of his thick hard penis was clearly visible, poking out, raising his briefs into a grotesque shape. He stripped off his socks and held out his arms, his eyes heavy with desire. 'Well?'

Unable to refuse him, or herself, she walked across the room and slipped her hands into his. Without a word he gathered her into his arms and carried her upstairs. In the bathroom he couldn't bear to let her go. Stepping out of his briefs he gently stripped her naked, his mouth on hers, his hands caressing her breasts, the warm sticky triangle between her legs. He kissed her, and held her, and she clung to him with a passion that only fired him the more. Together they moved into the shower, forced into each other by the confines of the walls. Skin and moisture deliciously merged as the warm water sprayed over them. He played with her for a while, teasing and tormenting while she leaned against the cool tiles, legs thrust open, arms wide, wanting him, aching for him.

He was on his knees now, his tongue tickling the crevices of her navel, licking at her skin like a dog might lick at a bone, lovingly. Possessively.

Half-blinded by the tumbling water, he looked up from beneath dripping lashes. She was so beautiful. Her smile enveloped him. Her small hands reached down and drew him up. His thighs tightened, he grew so hard he thought he would burst. She was wonderfully open to him. The water showered down, exhilarating.

Wrapping his arms round the small of her back he felt her small tight buttocks. Pressing them towards him he slowly entered her. The water entered too, silky smooth and luxuriously warm. She made a soft, guttural cry. Filled with delicious agony, he pushed deeper, deeper still, into her very soul. Frantic now, all foreplay done with, the rhythm quickened. Unbearable pleasure, heightening with every stroke. Like a storm it exploded inside them. Their cries merged one with the other as together they slithered to the floor.

Even when it was over, it was not. Tangled in a heap of skin and limbs, the pleasure lingered, slowly ebbing. 'Want some more?' he teased. Because of the girls their laughter was subdued.

'Get your fat arse off me!' she moaned, pushing at him. But even while the words left her mouth she secretly coveted his neat tight buttocks. On that first day when he had bumped into her, he was wearing jeans. She saw then how his round tight buttocks fitted into them like a hand in a glove. She smiled at the memory. His long legs and the strong lithe shape of his body were still a powerful turn-on.

'Fat arse, eh?' Suitably offended he chided her. 'Just like any hussy,' he said, 'you only want me for what I've got.'

All the same he let her scrub his back. Then he scrubbed hers, and when they were dressed in their terry-towelling robes, she enticed him downstairs, where she made two cups of cocoa.

Sitting opposite him at the round pine table, she told him worriedly, 'We have to talk. It's the third time in as many weeks that the school has been in touch about Ginny.'

He glanced anxiously at the half-open door. Getting up he went to the door and softly closed it. 'Have you ever thought it could be the school's fault, and not Ginny's?' He knew he was clutching at straws, but he couldn't, *wouldn't* believe she was beyond the saving.

She groaned, reminding him impatiently, 'We've gone through all that, and no, I don't think it's the school's fault. Lianne attends the same school and she stays out of trouble. Why can't Ginny?'

'Maybe it suits one of our daughters and not the other.'

'And maybe you look at Ginny through rose-coloured spectacles.' She sat up straight and stared at him, anger in her voice. 'It's no good, Jack. You're going to have to face the fact that we have a problem on our hands.'

He sighed and covered his head with the palms of his hands, but there was no shutting out the truth. 'All right. What's she done this time?' Raising his head, he looked at her through tired green eyes. 'Something shocking, was it? Did she molest the maths teacher?' He shook his head. 'No, of course not. He's old as Father Time, and wrinkled like a prune. A daughter of mine would have better taste.' He chuckled. 'Maybe she was caught in the bike shed with the caretaker. Is that it? Are she and Old Tom having an affair?'

Liz got up from the table, went to the sink and poured the entire contents of her cup down the drain. 'If that's all you have to say, I might as well go to bed.' She was boiling with rage. For what seemed an age she remained at the sink, her back to him, her shoulders hunched, and her knuckles white where she was gripping the draining board. 'Bastard!' she muttered. 'What's the point?'

He came up behind her. Slowly his fingers covered hers. 'I'm sorry, sweetheart. You're right, I *am* a bastard.' He rubbed his head against her shoulders and kissed her neck.

'There you go again,' she said in a calmer voice, 'saying sorry.'

'That's because I am.'

She turned to look at him. He was so damned handsome, such a good man, and she loved him fiercely. If it weren't for Ginny, always coming between them, always souring their relationship, life would be so much easier. 'Will you talk to her?'

'First thing in the morning.'

'And don't let her twist you round her little finger.'

'You mean like *you* do?'

His grin was a tonic to her. Ever since that phone call from the school, she had been on edge. Ginny had a way of doing that to her. 'This time I want you to punish her.'

'What did she do?'

'I'd rather *she* told you.'

'Okay. Now, do you want me to get you another cup of cocoa?' He stared down the drain with a woeful expression. 'What kind of woman throws away a perfectly good cup of cocoa?' he asked mischievously.

'A woman at her wits' end.'

The tone of her voice pulled him up sharp. He knew then that whatever Ginny was supposed to have done, it must be bad... worse than before. His heart sank inside him. 'I'll talk to her.'

'She's getting impossible. Can you handle it?'

'Of course I can handle it. She's not a monster after all.'

'If you say so.'

He smiled at her, but Liz wasn't smiling.

As they passed the girls' rooms on their way to bed, she whispered, 'I love her as much as you do, Jack, but she won't talk to me about the things that worry her. What makes her do these shocking things?'

'Are they so shocking?'

She considered it for a while, recalling the story she had been told by the headmistress. In a softer voice she gave Jack his answer. 'She worries me, Jack. I can't help feeling there's something very wrong.'

He turned to look at her. God almighty! She was echoing his own fears. 'I think you'd better tell me what you mean.'

For no reason that she could think of, a well of anger rose up in her. 'I don't know what I mean!' she snapped. But she knew all right, only she dared not say it. There were times when she believed Ginny was insane. There were also times when she was actually afraid of her own daughter. 'I'm sorry,' she said deceptively. 'You're probably right. Ginny's at a difficult age, neither woman nor child. I expect it's just high spirits and mischief.'

Before he closed his eyes to sleep, he reassured her, 'Don't worry, sweetheart.' He recalled what Lenny had said and he repeated it now. 'It really will be something and nothing. Trust me. I promise I'll get to the bottom of it.'

Liz was quiet for a moment, then in a hushed voice she told him, 'I hope so, Jack, because your daughter is far more devious than you give her credit for.'

'Oh, so now she's *my* daughter.' He leaned up on one elbow and kissed her full on the mouth, asking with a little grin, 'Do you want me to ravish you again?'

She kissed him back. 'I'm too tired.'

'Okay. I'll go along with that.' In fact he was bone-weary. The bakery was thriving, thank God, and orders from shops and supermarkets were pouring in. But there was a price to pay for running your own business. The long punishing hours and the never-ending struggle to rise above the competition somehow drained a man.

Liz turned away. 'Goodnight then.'

'Goodnight, sweetheart.' He lay on his back and drew the quilt up to his chin. The radiator wasn't too far away and he could feel the heat on his face, but he was dreadfully cold, shivering as though he had just stepped into a bath of freezing water. It was a strange kind of chill though, because there were no goosebumps on his skin, and it didn't feel cold to the touch. It was almost as though the chill was radiating from inside out. A rush of terror coursed through him. The shudder rippled from his head to his toes and left him clasping the blanket, his fingers gripping it so tight he didn't even realise the material was tearing apart.

Liz stirred. 'Are you all right?'

'I'm fine,' he answered. 'A bit cold, that's all.'

'Snuggle up then.' Her arm reached out and cradled him, but she didn't turn round. He was a man easily aroused and she was on the verge of slipping into a warm and cosy twilight.

Jack didn't sleep well. When he did fall into a fitful slumber he found himself immersed in a terrible nightmare. He was in a big house, much like his own home. There were bodies all around. The walls were splattered with blood: bright crimson stains from floor to ceiling. Furniture was tossed about like a child's playthings; the remains of blue velvet curtains hung from the windows, shredded into strips as though many cats had torn into them with long, jagged claws. Every picture was ripped from the walls; every mirror shattered into a million fragments. And the stench! Dear God! Look around! The carnage. As though a savage beast had been let loose.

In his nightmare, he could sense someone behind him. He turned and what he saw was too horrible, too real. He could hear himself screaming.

He was still screaming when Liz woke him. The girls came rushing into the room. 'Go back to bed,' Liz told them. When they were gone, she held him closer. 'It's all right,' she murmured. 'It's all right.'

But it wasn't all right. It never would be. Desperate to protect his family, he had never spoken of the dread that followed him. Above all else, he must keep his family intact, safe from all harm. Lately he felt he was losing control.

That was what frightened him. The fact that Ginny and Lianne were growing up, growing away from him. Because of what had happened all those years before, the thought of his family being split up again was more than he could bear. He couldn't think about it without coming out in a cold sweat. In spite of having distanced himself from the horror. In spite of praying it could never touch him again, he still couldn't believe he was free. After all these years, it still haunted him.

'Why does he keep having these awful nightmares?' Unnerved by her father's screaming, Lianne followed her big sister into her bedroom.

Ginny gave her a scathing glance. 'How should I know?'

'Is it all right if I stay in here with you tonight?' She flung herself forward, on top of the double bed. 'I don't want to sleep on my own.'

'Aren't you worried what people will say?' Virginia went to the mirror, where she began brushing her hair. Short and thick, and burnished with autumn hues, it shone like gold in the overhead light.

Lianne lay on her stomach, her chin resting between the cups of her hands as she stared up with astonishment. 'I don't know what you mean,' she said simply. 'Why should people say *anything*?'

Ginny continued to brush her hair. She brushed it up and down with great tenderness, then she began stroking the brush from top to bottom. The mass of hair bounced and glowed, framing her face with fire. Ignoring Lianne's question, she asked one of her own: 'Do you think I'm beautiful?'

Lianne sighed, her gaze growing with wonder as she spoke. 'I think you're the most beautiful person I've ever seen.'

Ginny turned to look at this creature who was her sister. She could never understand why Lianne was not as splendid as herself. After all, she was from the same parents. Oh, Lianne was pretty enough, with her petite figure and golden hair. Her nicest features were her eyes, darkest green like her father's, and such lovely lashes too, long and luxuriantly thick, but she was not unusually attractive, not in a special way.

Deep down though, Ginny secretly envied Lianne's sweeping lashes. They had always irritated her. They irritated her now. It showed in her voice as she snapped, 'Go to sleep!'

'Are *you* going to sleep?'

'No. I have things to do.'

'I want to watch you.' Even though there were times when she wished Ginny was not so cruel, she still adored her. Ginny was her sister, and had never really hurt her... not like she hurt other people.

'You're always watching me!'

'Will Daddy die?' It was something she had been worried about ever since she first heard him cry out in his sleep.

Ginny laughed. 'Don't be stupid. You can't die just because you've had a nightmare.'

'It frightens me.'

'You're too easily frightened.'

'Aren't *you* frightened?'

'Why should I be? It isn't *my* nightmare.'

'Don't you love him?'

'I don't let myself love anyone.'

'Not even me?' There was pain in her voice.

Ginny watched her through the mirror. She saw how small and vulnerable Lianne was. 'I must love you a little,' she lied, 'because I look after you, don't I?'

Lianne was satisfied. '*I* love *you*... better than anyone in the whole world,' she said, blushing with embarrassment. 'It's all right for me to say that, isn't it?'

Ginny continued brushing her hair. 'It's all right for you to say *anything* if you really want to,' came the haughty reply.

'I couldn't say the things you say.'

'What things?' The tone was icy.

'You know... those bad things you said to the teacher today.'

A small harsh laugh. 'Oh! You thought they were bad, did you?' She glowered. 'And I suppose you think *I'm* bad?'

Lianne didn't like it when Ginny looked at her in that hateful way. 'Sometimes you *are* bad,' she answered truthfully.

Ginny's dark eyes smiled on her. Replacing the brush on the dresser she took off her robe. 'Do you think I could be a model?' She twirled around before facing Lianne again. 'You said yourself I was the most beautiful person you'd ever seen.'

Lianne had seen her sister in the nude before, under the showers after a game of volleyball at school, and here at home, because she loved to walk around naked when their parents were out. 'You know very well you'd make a wonderful model.' She let her gaze rove over the tall slim figure, over the long shapely legs and the small pert breasts. Ginny was very special, and she adored her, looked up to her, wanted to be like her. Except when she was bad.

'Do you think I'm changing?' Ginny stood before her, legs apart, arms dropped to her thighs. 'Am I different, do you think?'

Disturbed by Ginny's nearness, Lianne raised her gaze to look into those dark malicious eyes. 'Different?' She knew what Ginny was getting at, but she didn't like to say. Instead she feigned ignorance. 'How do you mean?'

Ginny stepped nearer. 'You know very well what I mean... I'm not a girl any more. I'm a woman, so tell me how I'm different!' she insisted angrily.

Lianne hated her when she was like this. But then her hatred soon went and the love flooded back. She had always clung to Ginny, in a way she could never cling to anyone. Ginny was strong. That was comforting. 'Your breasts are bigger.'

'What else?' She eased her legs open, so brazenly close to her younger sister that the warmth of their bodies mingled.

Lianne visibly cringed. If she had stretched out her hand she could have touched Ginny's private. As it was, she could see it, pink and wet, half-hidden behind a curtain of dark curly hairs. 'You're like that woman in the picture Tom Wright showed us.'

'Don't call him Tom Wright.'

'What should I call him, then?' She was confused. Not knowing how to please and not knowing how to escape. When she set her mind to it, Ginny could make her feel very uncomfortable.

'Call him the caretaker. Because that's what he is.'

'He'd get the sack if Miss Routledge knew he'd shown us dirty pictures.' She giggled.

'You wouldn't tell though, would you?'

Lianne's smile fell away. ''Course I wouldn't tell. I don't want him to get the sack.'

'Good. Because if you told, I might have to punish you.'

'I don't want to listen when you say things like that.'

'You said I was like the woman in the picture he showed us.' Her slow-revealing smile was like the moon settling over a dark sky. 'Tell me what you mean.' She thrust herself forward, tantalising, slowly curling the hairs round the tips of her fingers. 'Tell me, Lianne,' she insisted. 'I won't go away until you tell me.'

'I've already told you… your breasts are bigger.'

'What else?'

She hesitated. 'I don't know.'

'Yes you do, you little liar!' Grabbing a hank of Lianne's blonde hair she yanked her head up, forcing Lianne to look at her. 'The woman in the dirty picture was having sex with a man. Just like I had sex with Stuart Dickens… in the changing rooms, after everyone else had gone.'

'I don't want to know.' Lianne's features were contorted with pain. 'Please, Ginny. Let me go.'

'Not until you say it.'

'All right! You're different because you've had sex, and I haven't. Now let me go.'

'I should still punish you, but I won't. Not yet anyway.' She moaned as though in ecstasy. 'Oh, it was wonderful, Lianne.'

Thrusting Lianne aside she went and sat before the dresser, admiring herself and trembling with passion at the memory of her encounter with Stuart Dickens. 'You should try it,' she suggested. Swinging round she gave her sister a fierce look. 'But not with Stuart. He's mine. Any of the boys in the sixth form would be glad to lay you.' Her mood calmer now, she deigned to administer a smile. 'If you want it, I can always arrange for you to have sex.'

Lianne rolled over to stare at the ceiling. 'I've told you before, I don't want to have sex.' Closing her eyes she let herself think of the one person she might want to have sex with. Dave Martin was a tall good-looking sixth former who had moved into the neighbourhood only four months ago. Though they hadn't yet spoken to each other, Lianne had been attracted to him from the start. He liked her too, she could tell.

Ginny's voice cut through her fanciful thoughts. 'You're a liar, Lianne Lucas! I bet you'd enjoy sex with Dave Martin?'

Lianne was shocked. Lunging round she demanded, 'How do you know I like him?' It was almost as though Ginny had read her mind.

'I just know, that's all.' She patted a blob of cream into her hands and spread it ever so gently over her slim, high cheekbones. 'Dave Martin is smitten with you. I'm sure he'd cut off his right arm to frig you.' She made a sound like a laugh, but it was too low, too angry. 'I'll talk to him.'

'*Don't you dare!*' Leaping off the bed she confronted her sister with a courage that astonished them both. 'You leave him alone!'

'My! My! I didn't realise just how much you liked him.' She scowled. 'I bet you even flutter those long thick lashes at him, don't you?' Lianne had lovely eyes but it was the lashes that made them special. It gave her an idea. A wicked spiteful idea.

'I don't want to sleep in here. I'm going back to my own room.' With that Lianne ran out, leaving her sister to cream her skin and pamper herself a while longer.

It was almost two o'clock. The house was quiet and dark, and everyone was asleep – except for Ginny. On tiptoes she crept along the corridor towards Lianne's room. In one hand she carried a pencil torch. The light from the torch was reflected in the small metal instrument in her other hand. Her footsteps whispered on the carpet, quickening as they neared Lianne's room. Softly she went inside; holding the torch low she directed the light to the floor.

Lianne was asleep, curled like a kitten to one side of the bed and, like a kitten, her eyes were closed, the thick, rich lashes dark against her cool skin.

Fascinated, Ginny gazed at her, at the sleeping face, at the protective manner in which that small figure was tightly curled. It made her smile. 'What a strange little thing you are,' she whispered, gently touching a hank of blonde hair. 'All curled up like a dormouse, afraid something's coming to get you while you sleep?' She grinned. In the half light it was a sinister thing. 'It can't be *me* you're afraid of,' she whispered. 'Why would you be afraid of me?'

Carefully placing the torch on the bedside cabinet she opened the tiny scissors and leaned down. Gently pushing aside a lock of hair from Lianne's forehead, she set to work. Lianne stirred only once, and that was to paddle the air with her arms, as though fending off an attacker. Ginny merely switched off the torch and waited. When her sister was still once more she finished the delicate task.

Afterwards she shone the torch on her sister's face. Not close enough for Lianne to wake, but close enough to see the results of her own handiwork. Lianne's face was different, cleaner somehow, more childish. 'That's much better,' Ginny sighed. 'Now we can both sleep.'

Leaning down she gently blew on her sister's face. Just as she planned, the thick shorn lashes showered down on to the pillow, scattered dark fragments against the white background.

The same way she had tiptoed out of her room Ginny tiptoed back again. Once in bed she silently congratulated herself on a good night's work. Afterwards, she slept like a baby.

Jack was up early. He had a great deal on his mind and wanted to get it over with. 'Kids!' he mumbled, as he went about making a pot of tea. 'Who in their right senses would have 'em?'

'They put you away for talking to yourself.' Liz came across the kitchen and gave him a good-morning kiss. 'Have you thought what you're going to say to her?' Dipping her hand into the bread bin, she drew out two slices. 'How many toast?'

'Three,' he groaned. 'Being a father gives you an appetite.' He popped four tea-bags into the pot and took out two mugs from the cupboard. When he saw Liz looking at him with that expectant expression he had come to know so well, he told her with a shake of the head, 'No, I haven't thought what I'm going to say.' The kettle whistled. Grateful, he turned away, deliberately keeping his back to her while he poured the boiling water into the pot. 'First I'll listen to what she's got to say.'

'If she says anything at all, that is.'

'Oh, she will. I can promise you that. She will!' He chewed nervously at his bottom lip, suddenly not feeling so confident. 'Are you sitting in?' he enquired hopefully.

She gave him one of her dazzling smiles. 'Sorry, sweetheart. I have to go into Leighton Buzzard this morning. The market's on and I need some curtain material for that back room.'

His heart sank. 'Can't it wait until Monday?'

She sang the reply. 'There's no market on a Monday. Only on a Saturday.' She felt relieved now that Jack was taking control of the situation.

'I really would like you to sit in.' He felt like a coward. What man was ever afraid of a girl not yet eighteen? Him! That's who.

Cruelly, she reminded him. 'Last night you said you could handle it. Are you saying now that you can't?'

With her pretty hazel eyes challenging him, he couldn't let it be known that he was shrinking inside. The thought of Ginny's dark eyes quietly beseeching him while he ranted and raved was not a pleasant prospect. To be honest he didn't know what all the fuss was about. 'Of course I'm not saying I can't handle it. When did you hear me say that, eh?' he demanded with a show of outrage. 'When did I say I couldn't handle it?'

She nodded with satisfaction. 'Good.' When the toast popped up she grabbed the two slices, put them on a plate and thickly buttered them. She laid the plate on the table in front of him. 'Do you want eggs?'

'No, thank you. I do not want eggs.' He felt peeved, angry with himself. It was all Ginny's fault, damn and bugger the girl! When she got down these stairs she'd be sorry she'd ever made a nuisance of herself!

'Bacon then?'

'No, I do not want bacon… nor sausages, nor tomatoes, nor marmalade on my toast.' He poured out the tea and fetched the mugs to the table, where he resumed his seat, lifted a slice of toast from the plate and bit out a big chunk. Talking with his mouth full he told her, 'Get off to the market then, and take Lianne with you. I'll be better on my own anyway.'

'Don't talk with your mouth full.' The next lot of toast burned so she went to the sink and began scraping it.

He gulped the mangled food down. 'Sorry.'

'And don't say sorry.'

'Okay, I'm *not* sorry. Who said I was sorry?' He looked round with big surprised eyes.

The toast came flying across the room and hit him on the side of the head. 'Stop acting the fool, Jack. I want you to be serious this morning.'

Whether it was the toast smacking into his head, or whether it was because Liz was not in a playful mood, he didn't know. All he knew was that he suddenly felt like fighting the world. 'She'd better not keep me waiting too long,' he grumbled. 'I've got better things to do on a Saturday morning.'

The next ten minutes were spent with Liz on one side of the breakfast table and Jack on the other, and a dark explosive atmosphere between them.

Upstairs, Lianne sat before her dresser and sobbed until the anger had mellowed. She touched her eyes and stroked the short stubby lashes with delicate fingers. 'Oh, Ginny! How could you?' she cried. 'How could you do that to me?' She knew it had to be Ginny. No one else would do such a terrible thing.

After she was more composed she gathered the fallen lashes into the palm of her hand and dropped them unceremoniously into the waste bin. Then she ran out of the room and sped along the corridor.

Dressed in a burgundy tracksuit, Ginny was putting on her plimsolls when the door was flung open and Lianne stood there, red in the face from crying and visibly shaking with temper. Or fear. Remaining at the door she stared into those dark malicious eyes. She spoke just one word. 'Why?'

Ginny merely smiled and continued to tie the laces on her plimsolls. 'Because you needed punishing. Remember I told you that?'

'It's *you* who needs punishing.'

'Really, Lianne. Don't make such a fuss. They'll grow again I expert.' Collecting her duffel bag from the wardrobe, she dragged it along the floor. 'I expect you'll tell on me… go crying to Mummy, like a big baby.' She pushed her face into Lianne's and made a childish cry.

'I would never do that.'

'Only because you know I'd have to punish you again.'

'I hate you.' Rage sped through her, leaving her breathless. Bringing her arm high into the air, she swept it down, slapping her hand into Ginny's face, the sharp sound cutting through the air like a knife. 'I'll never forgive you,' she cried.

Reeling from the shock, Ginny stared at her, then kissing Lianne full on the mouth, she admitted, 'You're right. It was a wicked thing to do.' Her eyes filled with tears. 'Don't hate me.'

Still seeming penitent, she quickly took her leave, impossibly arrogant, exquisitely beautiful. A devil in angel's disguise.

Lianne watched her go down the stairs. When she could no longer see her, she flattened herself against the door jamb, banging her clenched fists so hard into the wood that the knuckles bled. Plump blinding tears tumbled down her face. 'I *wish* I could hate you,' she said through bared teeth. 'Why can't I hate you?'

As Ginny came into the kitchen, Liz went out, calling up from the bottom of the stairs, 'If you're coming with me to the market, Lianne, you'd better get a move on.' When Lianne's voice called back to say she wouldn't be long, she returned to the kitchen where she told Ginny in a hard voice, 'Your father wants a word with you, my girl.'

Jack saw the animosity that passed between the two. It touched a chord inside him, triggering off a deep, buried memory, though he couldn't quite understand it. 'There's time enough,' he chided. Turning to Ginny, he suggested, 'Get your breakfast first.'

Ginny looked from him to her mother, then back again to him. In a syrupy voice she replied, 'I haven't got time for breakfast.' Pointing to her duffel bag she explained, 'I'm due at the centre in half an hour.' But she sat down all the same, her dark eyes smiling into his, melting his heart, filling him with all kinds of regrets.

Liz stepped forward, eyes blazing. 'Well, you'll just have to be late, won't you? You have a few questions to answer, I think. You won't talk to me, so perhaps you'll talk to your father.'

Ginny fell back, slouching in the chair, a look of innocence on her face as she turned from Liz to her father. 'What's all this about?' She knew very well what it was all about. But it suited her to make them squirm.

Before Jack could answer, Lianne came in. Her knuckles were washed and soaked in ointment. Luckily the damage was limited and not easily detected. Still, as she took one step from the doorway, she kept her hands behind her back.

'You'd best have a cup of tea and a slice of toast,' Liz told her. 'We'll be too busy to stop off for anything. I have to get back and see to the washing. There's a pile a mile high in that bathroom.' Going to the sink she filled the kettle. 'I'm amazed at how it seems to mount up.'

Dropping two slices of bread into the toaster she quietly addressed Ginny. 'You might as well have something too, especially if you're going to be swimming all morning. You'll come out of there starving otherwise.'

'Are you trying to kill me?'

Startled, Liz swung round. 'Whatever do you mean, child?'

'I'm not a child, mother, or haven't you noticed? And I didn't mean anything in particular, except that you should never swim on a full stomach. It could cause cramp and you might drown. Is that what you want?'

'Don't be ridiculous.'

Lianne's voice intervened. 'I won't have anything either.'

'Oh? And what's the matter with you, then?' Liz asked anxiously. 'It isn't like you to go without your breakfast. Would you rather have some cereal?'

Lianne made no effort to enter the room. Instead she stayed near the door. 'I don't really want to go into town either.'

Liz looked closely at her. 'What's the matter with you? Are you ill?' She came across the room to stand before her. There was something different about Lianne, she thought curiously. 'What's the matter with your eyes?'

'Nothing.'

'They're all red.' Glancing sideways at Ginny, who was slyly watching, she studied that arrogant face for a minute before returning her attention to the younger girl. 'Have you been crying?'

Lianne shook her head. 'I was brushing my hair and accidentally poked myself in the eye. They watered a bit that's all.'

Liz looked closer. 'They look… I don't know… odd.' There was something peculiar but she couldn't decide what it was.

Jack intervened. 'I'd appreciate a few minutes with Ginny if that's all right?'

The business of Lianne's eyes was forgotten. 'Get yourself ready,' Liz told her. 'By the look of you, it'll do you good to get some fresh air.' Her parting words to Jack were a plea for him to get to the bottom of it as he had promised. 'We'll talk later then.'

Returning her kiss he winked aside. 'Later,' he confirmed.

A few moments passed and he was alone with Ginny. They heard the front door close and the house was deathly quiet for what seemed an age before Jack prompted, 'You're in trouble again, I gather?'

'She asked for it.'

'Who asked for it?'

'Miss Warren.'

'The one who takes the swimming class?'

Ginny nodded. 'She takes science sometimes as well, when Mr Arlington is away.' She wrinkled her nose. 'She's not very good at it though. Mr Arlington is a trained science teacher. Miss Warren doesn't even know how to light the burners properly.'

He chewed his bottom lip. 'Oh, I see.' He forced himself to half smile. 'Miss Warren got on the wrong side of you, did she?'

'Sort of.' Ginny's face broke out in a sinister grin. It shook him to the core.

'And how did you pay her back?'

A moment to think, to wonder whether her father should be told. But he was not a threat. It was her mother who was the real threat. 'I let the rats out.'

He jerked as though someone had jabbed him in the back. 'You *what*?'

'In the science lab. I let all the rats out of their cages, and I put one in Miss Warren's locker.' Her face crinkled with glee. 'It bit her on the leg.'

For the first time since she had been born, Jack wanted to slap her. 'Jesus Christ! That was a bloody stupid thing for you to do!'

'It's all right. She can't prove it was me who did it.'

'What in God's name were you thinking of?'

'How did you know about it?'

'Apparently, Miss Warren rang your mother, asking the two of us to go in and see her. She said the matter was serious.' He grimaced. 'And she was right, wasn't she, eh? By God she was bloody well right. The rat could have been infected... could have poisoned her.'

'Mr Arlington's rats aren't infected.'

'You weren't to know that!' He was bubbling with anger. 'What if you get expelled? You're taking your exams this year. For Christ's sake, Ginny, what if you get expelled?'

'I won't get expelled. Miss Warren might be a pain, but she's not a tell-tale. She won't report me until she's spoken to you and Mother. Even then she might be afraid to tell the headmistress.'

'Oh? And why's that?' He was rapidly losing patience.

'Because it was she who left the locks undone on the cages. Mr Arlington always locks the cages when class is over and everyone's gone.' She sighed impatiently. 'No one saw me let the rats out. Everyone else had made their way to the cloakroom and Miss Warren was working at her desk. It was easy. Anyway, she can't say it was me because she doesn't know for sure.'

'What else have you been up to?'

Ginny was startled. 'Nothing. Why?'

'According to your mother Miss Warren has several matters she needs to discuss, and all concerning you.'

'She's lying!'

'No, Ginny. It's *you* who's lying, and I expect we'll have to wait until Monday to find out how much. Now, get off to your swimming practice before you're in trouble there as well.' He stood up and turned his back on her. A moment later the door banged shut. Weary at heart, he leaned on the table and dropped his head to his chin. 'You're right, Liz,' he admitted, 'I couldn't handle it.'

It wasn't so much what Ginny had done, though that was bad enough. It was the way she smiled at it all. The way she seemed to enjoy other people's terror. *That* was what he couldn't handle.

By the time Ginny got to the corner the school bus was already waiting. Miss Warren was pacing the street, and growing more agitated by the minute. 'Where *is* that girl?' She glanced up and saw her coming, sauntering down the street as though she had all the time in the world. 'Quickly!' she shouted, waving her arms about. 'We've only got the pool for an hour. We'll be late as it is.' Miss Warren was a homely sort, but girls like Ginny wound her up to fever pitch.

Ginny pretended not to hear. Instead she deliberately slowed her steps. Suddenly, above Miss Warren's frantic voice could be heard the entire school team. They were shouting through the windows, counting down as Ginny came closer: 'Ten, nine, eight, seven, six…' and so on, until Ginny finally stepped on to the bus and a crescendo of cheering caused Miss Warren to shout them down and give them a little lecture. After that, she seemed to have lost all control. For the remainder of the journey she sat in the seat beside the driver, sweat pouring down her face and her eyes closed as the laughter from behind drowned out her loathsome thoughts.

Twenty minutes later the bus pulled into the leisure centre and the girls piled out. Miss Warren had them back under control, her face set like stone as she ordered, 'No one to go into the pool until I arrive.' What she lacked in the knowledge of science she made up for in the water. In her youth she had been a champion swimmer. When she dived, her back straight and her slim figure entering the water without making a ripple, she was a magnificent sight. Every girl under her supervision, including a reluctant Ginny, admired and respected her considerable athletic accomplishments.

The girls were a little more orderly now, though obviously excited at the prospect of practising their swimming skills. Miss Warren had already warned them they would have to work extra hard if they were to beat St Roach High School in the forthcoming competition.

Leaving the girls to change, Miss Warren went to the office. 'You've lost five minutes already,' the bespectacled clerk told her.

'Don't I know it,' she replied, hastily gathering the locker keys and bidding him cheerio.

Being well practised in the art, it took her just a minute to change. When she appeared at the pool, slim and muscle-taut in her plain black costume, with her long hair scraped back into a plait, the girls were waiting, all lined up at the deep end and raring to go.

'Are we swimming in twos like last week?' one girl asked eagerly.

Miss Warren considered that for a brief minute. Swimming in twos was a favoured exercise of hers. It taught the girls how to keep their distance. It showed them how to work as a team, yet gave them a strong idea of swimming in competition. Today though, the girls were all too excited by what had happened earlier on. One or two of them were giggling, whispering about the daring of Ginny Lucas.

Miss Warren turned her head slightly to glance at the culprit. Ginny was standing at the corner of the line, looking for all the world like a complete innocent. She gave Miss Warren a warm, affectionate smile. 'I'm sorry for what happened, Miss Warren,' she said in a clear voice that carried the length of the line. 'It won't happen again.'

Miss Warren appreciated the gesture. But she was not convinced. 'I'm glad to hear it,' she answered, while muttering bitterly, 'You have a lot to answer for, you little bitch!'

The girls were waiting for instructions. She quickly made her decision. It was a decision which was to cost her dearly. 'I think we'll warm up first,' she told them. 'A five minute free swim, to loosen the joints and ease the stress.' God only knew how she had been put through the wringer with Ginny Lucas!

'Can we use the whole pool, Miss Warren?' It was the same girl who had previously voiced a question. She smiled at the eager face. Amy Burton was a born organiser.

'Not yet. I want you all to use the bottom end of the pool.' Indicating the halfway mark, she explained, 'No one to come past that marker, and you're all on trust while I go through a short diving programme.' For her, it was the best way of all to relax. Besides, the girls were all accomplished swimmers and fairly responsible. They would come to no harm for five minutes. 'Right, girls, into the water… up to the far end.' As they dived in one after the other in sequence the way she had taught them, she called out in a louder voice, 'No tomfoolery, and no diving. It might be a good idea to practise your crawl across the pool width. Five minutes' free time, that's all we can afford.'

She watched them for a moment, monitoring as they entered the water, and mentally assessing their potential as champions. Of all the pupils she had ever supervised, there was only one who possessed outstanding qualities, and that was Ginny Lucas. She saw her stretch out now, arms high and figure tucked in the way she had been taught. She entered the water at just the right angle, sleek and magnificent. When she swam away to join the others, Miss Warren envied her. You have youth and talent on your side, she thought. You have it in you to be the best one day. As she climbed to the top diving board she caught a glimpse of Ginny cutting through the water. Strength and speed, you have it all, young lady. What a pity you have such a cruel nature.

From the top of the diving board she looked down. That vast pool looked so small from up here, yet it was a sight that always filled her with great excitement. Her eyes turned to where the girls were swimming across the far end of the pool, practising their crawl as she had suggested. Carefully now, she walked to the very tip of the diving board; it gently bounced beneath her feet. With her entire weight finely balanced, she stretched out her arms, up on the balls of her feet, head tucked down. Ready now. This was the moment. One quick flick, a powerful thrust, and a ripple of exhilaration as she launched herself into the air.

Down below, deep, deep down where no one could see her, someone waited, calculating the area where Miss Warren would cut through the surface.

For the briefest moment Ginny hesitated. It seemed so cruel, such a wicked waste. Beneath the water the uplifted features took on a devilish look. Miss Warren had told tales. On Monday she would tell a whole lot more. That must not be allowed to happen.

At the moment of entry, when Miss Warren sliced through the water, the figure bided her time, waiting until that lithe figure curved upwards to begin the ascent. With the frightening speed of a fish born to water, it darted forward. Miss Warren never knew what happened. She felt the tug on her long thick plait. She experienced a sudden vicious sensation of shock as she was drawn upwards and, by the time she realised her hair was being sucked into the machinations of the filter, it was already too late.

With legs and arms flailing the water, she fought and screamed in vain. The more she struggled the tighter she became entangled, and the more she screamed the more the water rushed like a tidal wave into her lungs, crushing the air from them, taking her life.

In that moment before Miss Warren took her last breath, she saw the figure swim away. Realisation dawned. But, God help her, it was too late now.

'Stop mucking about, Ginny!' Amy Burton gave a loud cry as Ginny swam towards her. 'I'll tell Miss Warren you're tomfooling,' she threatened. But still Ginny came at her, up and down, in and out, breaking the water with the agility of a dolphin.

'I'm not tomfooling,' Ginny protested. 'I've been swimming backwards and forwards across the pool for ages, and I'm fed up.'

'I'm fed up too,' remarked another girl. 'I wish Miss Warren would hurry up. Five minutes, she said.' She glanced towards the diving boards. 'Where is she, anyway?'

Ginny turned her attention to the top diving board. 'The last time I looked she was diving from the top.'

Now everyone was looking, all asking the same question. 'Where is she, then?'

'She should have surfaced by now.'

'Maybe she's gone to the cloakroom.'

Nobody wanted to express concern. Miss Warren was a powerful swimmer. But their incessant questions and the hysteria in their voices betrayed their deeper fears.

In a matter of minutes the girls were gathered into a tight circle. Ginny made an uncharacteristic offer: 'Shall I go and look in the cloakrooms?' The anxious expression on her face belied the amusement in her wicked heart.

She climbed out of the pool. One of the class prefects went with her. They ran to the cloakrooms and searched high and low. 'That's strange,' Ginny remarked. 'I could have sworn she'd be in here.'

'Well, she's not,' the other girl said, 'and look, there are her things.' She pointed to the towel and flat shoes beneath the slatted bench.

When they returned, it was a scene of chaos. Amy Burton had volunteered to check the deep end of the pool. When she saw Miss Warren's lifeless body, her screams brought everyone running. With as much astonishment as everyone, Ginny ran to the top end and dived in. It was she who yelled for someone to fetch help. 'And some scissors! Her hair's caught in the filter. *Hurry up*!' Feigning horror and seeming to put herself at risk, she appeared to be frantically trying to free the lifeless body, and twice she surfaced, gasping for air. But she knew. In her black heart she knew the life had ebbed away. And she could hardly contain her delight.

By the time help came, there was little anyone could do to save her.

When the lifeguard shook his head, Ginny climbed out of the water and lay on the edge of the pool, tears rolling down her face. 'I can't believe it,' she cried. 'Poor Miss Warren.' Such was her show of compassion that she had the other girls sobbing, clinging to her, thankful that she too had not been drowned while trying so valiantly to save their teacher.

Later, when Miss Warren was taken away in an ambulance, everyone was questioned about the incident. The girls were brokenhearted. They were all treated with the utmost tenderness.

The clerk was in a state of shock. With a white, stricken face he explained to the police inspector, 'A smaller budget forced us to cut back on the lifeguard's hours. He weren't due to report for duty until ten o'clock, when the younger children use the pool, but he turned up a bit early today… only just got through the door when the girl came running in, screaming how her teacher were caught up in the filter.' He covered his face with his hands. 'He did his best,' he muttered, 'but it were too late. The poor bugger were already drowned.' He couldn't understand it. 'In her day she were a champion, you know. She told me that herself… proud of it she were.' An angry tear threatened. 'It'll not happen again, by God! She'll be the first and last to drown in this pool, I can tell you. The authorities will have to redesign the filtering system, and bugger the budget!'

After treatment for shock, the girls were collected and kept safe at the school, while their parents were notified about the tragedy. 'Please come and take your children home,' they were asked, and in no time at all the children were gone, some sobbing, some talking too much to make sense, and others very quiet, unbelieving.

Ginny Lucas was one of the quiet ones. She shrugged away all help, while being secretly thrilled that Miss Warren had got the punishment she richly deserved.

3

Though nearly a week had passed since the tragic accident, the whole community was still subdued by the shock. Miss Warren could not be laid to rest until after the inquest, and according to the coroner that would not take place for some weeks.

At a meeting at the school where she had taught for many years, sombre-faced dignitaries paid tribute in the packed assembly hall. The headmistress stated in a breaking voice, 'Miss Warren was highly regarded by both members of the teaching profession, and the parents whose children she taught. She was dedicated and caring, and we have suffered a terrible loss.'

A representative of the local authority deeply regretted the tragedy, but was quick to reassure everyone that all filters at the pool had been made safe. He was a good man and spoke from the heart; however, he was secretly relieved to know that Miss Warren had no family and so the department was not likely to be caught up in a writ for compensation.

Amy Burton had sat close to Ginny during the meeting. She had seen how Ginny and Stuart Dickens glanced longingly at each other. She was painfully aware of how strongly attracted he was to her, and it had caused her many sleepless nights. From the moment Stuart Dickens had set foot in the school, the plain-faced Amy had vied for his attention. He never gave it to her, but gave it willingly to Ginny Lucas. Amy could not forgive him for that. Nor could she forgive Ginny. That was why she always watched.

That was why she was watching on the day Miss Warren drowned.

Ginny sat through it all with straight expressionless features. All around and to one side sat her peers. On the other sat her family. After the gathering was over, everyone trudged outside to make their way home through last night's heavy snowfall. Ginny made the excuse that she wanted to be alone for a while.

'Let her be,' Jack said when his wife expressed the intention to go after her. 'She'll be home when she's ready.'

'She's been far too quiet for my liking,' Liz replied. Since the awful accident she had hardly slept, afraid to dream, afraid of her own dark suspicions. For the sake of her sanity, and her family, she dared not let herself think too deeply about the events of these past few days. With immense effort, she deliberately closed her mind to the gruesome fate of Miss Warren.

'Give her space to breathe, Liz,' Jack pleaded. 'It's been a terrible shock.'

'All the more reason why we should deal with it as a family.' She blew into her hands before putting on her woollen mittens. There was something about Ginny she couldn't forgive, and yet there was no reason why she should feel that way towards her own daughter. It was obvious that Jack adored his eldest child. Was that the reason? Was it nothing more than jealousy? She couldn't, *wouldn't* believe that of herself. 'It's been a shock for all of us,' she muttered. 'She shouldn't shut us out.'

Jack thought she was being a little harsh. 'I know that,' he patiently conceded. 'But Ginny was there. We weren't, thank God.'

Addressing Lianne, who had her own suspicions about the incident at the swimming pool, he suggested, 'Go after your sister. Watch her. You know how impulsive she can be.' He felt out of his depth. Just as he had felt out of his depth all those years ago.

Lianne chased up the street after Ginny. 'Wait for me!' she called. But that only made Ginny walk faster. She didn't want anyone with her just now, least of all Lianne. Lianne had a conscience. That was a dangerous, pitiful thing.

Undeterred, Lianne pursued her. 'You might as well wait for me,' she cried, 'because you know I'll find you anyway.' She had followed her beloved sister too many times not to know her every hiding place.

'I've never known two sisters to be so different.' Mr Clayton was the history teacher, and had been a close confidant of Miss Warren's. His gaze lingered on Lianne's departing figure. 'She has a delightful nature, that one,' he murmured, almost as though to himself.

Jack took offence. 'Are you implying that Ginny *doesn't* have a delightful nature?' Even as he spoke he knew what the answer, was. 'I'm sorry,' he added. 'That wasn't a fair assumption.'

Mr Clayton shrugged his shoulders. 'I meant no offence,' he assured him. 'Ginny has a different nature, that's all. She's far more confident and outspoken than her sister. They're both intelligent, capable human beings. Ginny though is highly perceptive and bristling with ambition, while Lianne is more content, more approachable, if you know what I mean.' He gave a little wry smile. 'Of course you know your own daughters better than anyone. In my experience no two people are alike. We each have our own strengths and weaknesses, and we each want different things from life. Which is just as well, don't you think?'

'I expect so.' Jack glanced at his wife. Seeing her shiver with cold, he put a protective hand on her shoulder. 'If you'll excuse us?' he apologised, gently propelling Liz away.

'Of course. It's too bitter cold to hang about chatting.'

Mr Clayton didn't immediately return to his colleagues, who had sought each other's company inside the school building. Instead he watched Jack and Liz walk away. 'Far be it from me to say,' he muttered, 'but your eldest daughter has the makings of a monster.' He hunched his shoulders against the biting wind, thrust his hands deep into the cavernous pockets of his overcoat, and returned to the confines of the assembly hall. Like Miss Warren, he had a sneaking dislike for Ginny Lucas.

But he was professional enough not to let his personal feelings spill over. He had learned to keep his opinions to himself. That was his way, and so far it had kept him out of trouble.

As they walked away, neither Jack nor Liz was aware that Mr Clayton was regarding them with interest.

'You go on,' Liz said as they came on to the lane. 'I need to stop off at the grocer's.' Threading her arm through his she pressed close. The breeze was whipping up and it was bitterly cold. 'Lianne used up the last of the marmalade this morning. I can't abide my toast without marmalade.'

'Can't you get it in the morning?'

'No. It's Saturday.'

Giving her a curious glance he remarked, 'I know that, sweetheart, but they are open on Saturdays, aren't they?'

She nodded but didn't look up. Her gaze was fixed to the ground, drawn by the fresh snowfall, so white and virginal. In a short time it would be smudged with dirt, violated by the footprints that ground it down.

'Right. And they sell marmalade, don't they?'

She looked up. 'What?'

He groaned, then smiled, and his smile lit the morning. 'The shop... on Saturday... they sell marmalade, don't they?'

Snuggling closer she arched her back against the cutting breeze. ''Course they sell marmalade!' she answered indignantly. 'It wouldn't be much of a grocer's if they didn't.'

'So! Why can't you get your marmalade in the morning?'

She tightened her grip and gave him a squeeze. 'I'm not getting into all that. It only gives you an excuse to argue.' With wise eyes she gazed up at him. 'Anyway, you're only a man,' she said beaming. 'You wouldn't understand.'

He shook his head with frustration. 'Try me.'

She looked up into his green smiling eyes and as always he triggered off a need in her. 'What? Right here and now?' she laughed suggestively.

Bending his head he kissed her on the mouth, a long lingering kiss that chased out the cold and fired their blood.

'Slag!' he muttered. 'I believe you would.'

She grimaced. 'I don't think so.'

He glanced down the lane. It was deserted, almost as though they were the only two people left alive in the whole world. 'You don't think so, eh? Might I ask why not?'

'Because there's a foot of snow on the ground and my arse will freeze.'

Laughing, he kissed her again. 'I suppose that's as good an excuse as any.'

'Have you ever known me make an excuse?'

'What about last New Year's Eve?'

'Not fair! If I remember rightly, I'd just spent two hours having my hair done for the dance. We were about to go out the door, half an hour late as I recall, and I was dressed in a skintight dress that took me ages to pour myself into.'

'It was the skintight dress that did it.' He winked mischievously, his handsome features crinkling into a boyish grin.

'You get your marmalade,' he said, 'and I'll drop in on the workforce… make certain they're not wasting my time and money.'

'Slave driver.'

'Pays for the marmalade.'

Before they parted company he reminded her, 'You never said why you couldn't go to the grocer's in the morning.'

'Because the village shop is always packed on a Saturday morning and everyone wants to stand and talk. Besides, Martha Knowles has just got a job on the cheese counter and you know how she gossips. It will take me half an hour just to get away from *her*! It's all very well, but I can't spare the time. I need to go into Leighton Buzzard market to get some material.'

'I thought you got that last week?'

'I did, only, well, when I got it home I didn't like it, so I'm taking it back.'

'That's the second time, isn't it?'

'The third. I do so want the curtains to blend with the settee, and it isn't easy getting the match.'

'Why not snip a piece of material off the settee covers?'

'You must be mad!'

He gave a beleaguered smile. 'Like you so rightly pointed out, sweetheart. I'm only a man.'

'See you at the bakery?'

'No, darling. It's best if you go straight home. I don't know how long I'll be.'

'I'll have something waiting to warm you up,' she answered.

'That sounds tempting.'

Her laughter lifted his heart. 'I meant a cup of tea.' Casually blowing a kiss she pushed open the door of the grocer's shop and was instantly waylaid by the dreaded Martha Knowles.

Still chuckling to himself, Jack strode on up the lane and into the alley where his bakery was situated. 'If I live to be a hundred I'll never fathom the mind of a woman,' he sighed.

Suddenly he was made to think of another woman, and his flesh crawled.

The bakery was over a hundred years old, a big square red brick building with long narrow windows and big wooden doors. When he bought the premises some years back, they were run down. The business was sadly neglected, and the ovens had given up the ghost. It took a frightening bank loan, a lot of guts and an iron determination to build it up into the thriving prosperous concern it was today. Jack and his family got a good living from the bakery, and with the fair wages set by Jack, so did the four hand-picked men who now worked for him.

'Morning, Jack.' Fred Stacey's cheerful voice emerged from the bowels of the earth. 'Come to check up on us, have you?'

Lurching round, Jack peered across to where one of the vast oven doors was swung open. Sprawled beneath it was a man of senior years, his two arms reaching inside the huge oven and his round familiar face looking up, grinning as usual, displaying a unique pair of wide pink gums. Fred was proud to declare they were 'all my own'.

'What in God's name are you doing down there?'

'The bugger's playing up again.' Getting off his knees and groaning, he explained, 'Spoiled a batch of bread this morning, she did.' Above the smutty face his thin grey hair stood on end. His overalls were covered in flakes of burned segments. 'I've had it to pieces and for the life o' me I can't see where the trouble is.'

'I expect the flue's blocked up.' Jack glanced down the room, along the stone walls and down towards the other men: Arnie was drawing a dozen loaves of bread out of the far oven; Tony was putting the finishing touches to his latest creation – wedding cakes were his speciality – and John was busy loading the pallets with freshly baked currant buns. The pallets were almost ready to be loaded into the van and delivered to the local shops.

'A hive of industry,' Fred observed proudly, taking up a place beside his boss. 'The business is growing all the time.'

Jack frowned. 'As long as it doesn't grow bigger than the men who run it.'

The older man stared at him. 'I can't understand you, Jack. You could have the biggest bakeries in Bedfordshire, yet you're happy enough with what you've got.' He clicked his tongue. 'By! If I were you, I'd not be satisfied.'

Jack's mood darkened. 'Don't ache for what you can't have, Fred,' he advised. He knew from experience that money didn't necessarily bring happiness.

'Don't you want to be a millionaire, then?'

'It's not one of my priorities, no.'

Fred displayed his pink gums in a grimace. 'Being wealthy can keep a lot o' nasty fellas from the door. Only last week the bailiff called at a neighbour's house and took away all his furniture because he hadn't paid his wife's maintenance.' He chuckled. 'Mind you, it were a real surprise to me. He never said he were married.'

'Wealthy people have skeletons in their cupboards too.'

Fred wasn't listening. He was dreaming of being a millionaire, lying on the beach with a bikini-clad beauty and having a yacht moored in the harbour. 'You don't want too much out of life d'you, Jack?'

'Not too much.'

He looked at him then, curious, not understanding. 'A man like you… still young, and with a shrewd business head on your shoulders. What *do* you want, then?'

'The need to survive in a mad world.'

So profound and unexpected was the answer to his question, and given in such a soft intimate whisper, that Fred was momentarily struck silent. When he spoke again it was in a quiet, thoughtful manner. 'How did it go this morning?'

Jack mentally shook himself. He was letting his thoughts wander. That was a dangerous thing to do. 'It was just as you might expect,' he answered, being suddenly more attentive to the old man's chatter. 'She was well thought of, that was obvious.'

The old man shook his head. 'By! That were a bad thing. A real bad thing.' He took off his cap and scratched his head, then rubbed his old eyes and put his cap back on again. 'The filings from inside the oven are the very devil,' he explained. 'They get everywhere.'

Jack was sympathetic. 'It's Friday. The others can cope. You take yourself off home.' He smiled at him, thinking what a poor old sod the other man was. His hair was fast receding, his teeth had dropped out one after the other. Last year his wife upped and left him for a man half her age and lately he had begun talking to himself. But he was a man of the old breed, a worker who earned every penny of his pay packet. Jack valued him more than he would ever know. 'I'll not stop your pay if that's what's worrying you,' he promised.

Fred was indignant. 'I weren't thinking that.'

'Go on then. Get off home. Take your old dog for its daily constitutional, then put your feet up for the evening.'

'You're a good 'un.'

'I know that.' Jack's grin reassured the old fellow. 'Now get out before I change my mind and ask you to strip that oven down to the bone.'

'I will if you want?'

'I don't. We'll call Dickens in tomorrow. What he doesn't know about big ovens isn't worth knowing.'

'I'm off then.' He waited, as though for some new instruction. When none came he went away, merrily whistling, and wondering how long he could go on working. He was coming up seventy after all. Jack had kept him on as long as he could, but there must come a time when it all had to end. It was a sobering thought.

An hour later, the old fellow was walking his dog through the woods. 'The snow can't get in here,' he told the scabby old terrier. 'The trees are too tall, and the branches act like an umbrella, d'you see?' He pointed up, where the watery sun was trying to filter through, silhouetting the veins in the leaves and creating beautiful spidery patterns.

He followed his usual route, along the bracken path and down by the disused RAF barracks. 'See that?' Pausing, he brought the mongrel's attention to the long Nissen huts. 'At one time them huts were bustling with activity.' His memories took him back over forty years. 'I were a soldier then, fighting for life and country. These 'ere woods might seem peaceful enough now, but during the war they were alive with Air Force personnel.' His old eyes grew moist. 'There were a lot o' good lads lost in the war, God bless 'em.' Feeling suddenly old and useless, he tugged on the mongrel's lead. 'Come on, you bugger,' he said sharply. 'Best not to linger.'

Inside the Nissen hut Ginny lay still as a mouse on the grimy stone floor. 'Has he gone?' she whispered to her companion.

Easing himself away from her warm body, Stuart Dickens peered through a crack in the wall. 'It's all right,' he answered with a sigh of relief. 'He's out of sight now.' A slim, hard young man with wonderfully straight shoulders and a shock of blond hair any woman would be proud to own, he laid himself over her again. 'Christ, Ginny! What if he'd come in here and seen us?' He was hot and bothered, staring at her through astonished blue eyes, and bitterly frustrated at being interrupted just when he was about to climax. 'It's put me right off,' he groaned.

He was ready to leave it for another day, but Ginny had other ideas. Clinging to him, she clutched his small round buttocks in the palms of her hands. Reaching her tongue inside the pinkness of his mouth she whispered softly. 'Love me.'

And he did. With all the fire and exuberance of youth, he pushed himself inside her. Again and again with increasing force, bruising and delighting her, while she tore at his back with sharp fingernails, moaning and whispering, urging him on, firing his every sense until he thought he would go insane.

Afterwards, they lay together exhausted, their naked bodies welded by sweat, a grotesque shape that rose and fell with every frantic breath. Suddenly Ginny started giggling. The giggling erupted into a crescendo of laughter.

'Shut up, you bloody idiot!' He slapped his hand over her mouth, but the laughter crept out between his fingers, a weird muffled sound that made him afraid. *I said shut up!*

She stopped then, her furious dark eyes looking over his fingertips. He took his hand away and her smile was magnificent, alluring. 'I want you to do it again,' she whispered.

'Can't.' He was embarrassed.

Her hands slid down, caressing the used penis. In her hands it was soft and pliable, empty now, momentarily contented. 'Yes, you can.'

'I have to get home... got a hockey match tonight.'

She didn't answer. Instead she continued to stroke the tip of his hardening penis. Opening her legs she took hold of his hand and guided it to the inside of her thighs. 'I won't let you go,' she softly threatened. 'I wasn't satisfied.'

His blue eyes flickered. 'Liar!'

'Once then. You know that's never enough.'

There was no resisting her now. He gazed at her breasts. In the half-light they were like two perfect fruits. 'You'll be the death of me,' he moaned. But when he slid into the warm inviting crevice he was beyond all reason.

Lianne had lost sight of her sister, but she knew where to find her. Pushing through the undergrowth she paused and looked around. The long dark shape of the Nissen hut was straight ahead. 'You sod, Ginny Lucas!' she grumbled, going towards it. 'You don't get rid of me that easy.'

As she approached, a noise coming from inside the hut stopped her in her tracks. It was a cry of sorts, but not a cry of pain. Anger surged through her. 'I know you're in there!' she cried, rushing through the door. 'If you're trying to frighten me, it won't work.' But she *was* frightened. The noise was high pitched, like the moan of a ghost.

In the gloom she narrowed her eyes. The noises continued. 'Ginny, stop it.' Her voice was trembling. Now she saw: her sister lying stiff and open on the ground and on top of her was Stuart Dickens, thrusting into her, his hands pawing at her breasts. Ginny was still making that weird noise, her whole body drawing him in, eating him up. They were both too far gone to know, or care, whether anyone was watching.

In a rage it was over, and Ginny turned her head. Her face was flushed. 'Did you see?' she asked the shocked Lianne. '*Now* do you want it?'

Stuart turned, but Lianne was already gone, running through the spinney and away from that place. '*I hate you!*' she called. But it wasn't hate she was feeling. It was envy, and a certain, wonderful need that was growing stronger all the time. Stronger than her. Stronger than anything she had ever known.

Amy Burton was a loner. She often took long walks through the spinney. In that great peace and quiet she could think, and after the untimely demise of Miss Warren she had plenty to think about. Now, though, she was astounded to see Lianne running from the Nissen hut. Curious, she hid behind an old storehouse. It was only a matter of minutes before Stuart Dickens emerged from the hut, along with Ginny. They were holding hands, he smiling down at her and she looking up with a kind of possessive adoration. It was obvious what had taken place in that hut, in the dark.

Amy shuffled out of sight. As they passed, so close she could feel their footsteps trembling against the earth, she heard Ginny suggest, 'Do you want to do it again tomorrow?'

'If you like,' he answered casually.

Ginny laughed, shifting her glance sideways. When her eagle eyes spotted Amy hiding near the shed, she could hardly contain her joy.

First she allowed Stuart his moment of feigned indifference, before she drew him to a halt, jolting him with the question, 'Have you ever done it with Amy Burton?'

'That's not fair.' A young man of his calibre could have any girl he wanted. He wanted only Ginny, but he dared not let her know that. It would give her a terrible power over him.

'Have you?' she insisted.

'No.'

'Do you want to?'

'No.'

'Why not? Don't you find her attractive?'

He grinned. 'Like I find a dormouse attractive.'

'That's cruel.' She sniggered. 'It's a good job she can't hear you.'

He laughed. 'I daresay *someone* finds her attractive.'

'But not you?'

'Don't be silly.'

Snuggling up to him, she asked slyly, 'How would you compare her to me?'

Just for a moment he forgot his vow never to let her know how strongly he was attracted to her. He gazed at her rich burnished hair and those compelling dark eyes, and the need rose in him again. 'Beauty and the beast,' he said. 'That's you and Amy.' Although at times he was never quite sure which one was the beast.

'Walk me to the end of the path,' Ginny suggested, urging him on. 'I'll make my own way home from there.' As they walked on, she dropped her gaze to the ground, secretly smiling, quietly satisfied the other girl had heard every word.

Flattened against the tree, Amy clenched her fists and waited for them to pass her by. Afterwards she slid to the ground and cried like a baby.

Liz was at the window. For almost an hour now she had been watching out for Jack to come home. When she saw his tall familiar figure turn in at the gate she gave a little smile. 'You're still the handsome bloke I married,' she sighed. Even though they had their ups and downs she could never live without him. She watched him now, playfully kicking up the snow with the tips of his shoes. 'You're like all men,' she laughed. 'Just a little boy at heart.'

As he came nearer she saw his brows were furrowed in a frown. She noticed how he kept glancing back over his shoulder, just as he had done many times before, as though expecting someone, or something, to be lurking behind him. 'What is it, Jack?' she whispered. 'What are you frightened of?'

Instinctively she moved out of sight, though she remained close to the window, still watching and wondering.

Before stepping into the porch he paused and looked around, staring at the gate for a while, his green eyes hostile and wary. Seeming satisfied, he skipped up the steps, took his key from a trouser pocket, and let himself into the house.

'I'm home, sweetheart!' His voice echoed down the hallway. 'Liz! I'm home!'

The aroma of freshly brewed coffee wafted from the kitchen. Not realising how thirsty he was until then, he quickly threw off his shoes. Hanging up his scarf and coat he almost ran down the hallway. When he came into the kitchen he was amused to see Liz seated at the table, grandly sipping her hot drink.

'I don't suppose there's one for me?' he asked impishly.

Liz didn't reply. Instead she glanced up and swivelled her gaze to the opposite end of the table. Jack followed her look, his face breaking into a grin when he saw the second mug of hot coffee placed in front of the chair opposite to Liz.

'Just what the doctor ordered,' he remarked. Coming round the table he kissed Liz on the forehead. 'Sorry I was so long,' he apologised, 'only I got talking to the old fella. I sent the poor old sod home… worn out, he was.'

'I know how he feels.' She took another sip of her coffee. 'Are you sitting down or what?'

Puzzled at her strange mood, he went around the table to the other side. 'What's got you?' he wanted to know. When she didn't immediately answer he sat astride the chair and took the mug of hot liquid into the palms of his hands. It was wonderfully steaming, the delicious vapour floating up to his nostrils and making him feel cosy. He sipped slowly, eyes closed, savouring every mouthful.

'Nothing's got me,' she answered. Her voice said one thing. Her attitude said another.

He opened his eyes and quietly studied her. She looked angry. No, not angry. Something else. 'What did you mean just now?'

'When?'

'When I told you the old fella was worn out, you said you knew how he felt.'

'I do.'

'Are you saying *you're* worn out?' He regarded her with concern. She looked pale, he thought. That worried him. 'Are you concerned about the girls? I mean this business with Miss Warren. Are you afraid it might play on their minds?'

'Are you?'

'It's rude to answer a question with a question.' What was she playing at? What the devil was wrong with her?

'It's Lianne I'm concerned about.'

He scowled at that. 'Not Ginny, then? You're not concerned about how Ginny might be taking all this?'

'Virginia can deal with it.'

He dropped his gaze to the table, his strong fingers playing on the mug. 'What's she done this time?'

'I don't know what you mean.'

'Yes you do!' Frustrated, he stamped his fist on the table. 'You said "Virginia". You always call her by her full name when she's done something to anger you. She's done something bad, hasn't she? You might as well tell me.' He was keyed up inside, wound up like a clock spring, ready to fly off in all directions.

Liz cursed herself. Why did she keep allowing Ginny to come between her and Jack? But she didn't allow it, did she? It just happened. And kept on happening. 'Sorry, sweetheart,' she answered. Leaning back in the chair, she stretched the palms of her hands over her face and rubbed her eyes. 'She hasn't done anything bad.' No, that wasn't exactly true. Ginny was always up to something, and none of it good. 'Well, nothing that I know of,' she hastily assured him.

'Come here.' He stretched out his arms and she went to him. 'Don't let's argue.' Gently, he pulled her on to his knee. 'I know she isn't the best daughter in the world, but, well, she's not the worst.'

'I know, and I'm sorry.' Still, there was something about their eldest daughter. Liz couldn't describe it, but it was a deep-seated fear, a premonition she'd felt right from that first moment when she held Ginny in her arms. *Evil!* No! No! Don't say that.

'Did you get your marmalade?'

'What?' His soft voice penetrated her anxious thoughts, visibly startling her.

He frowned. 'Are you all right, sweetheart?'

'Sorry. I was thinking, that's all.' She could never tell him what she was thinking. Never. 'Yes, I got the marmalade.' She pointed to the dresser where it stood.

He chuckled. 'I saw you get waylaid by that awful woman.'

Playfully she punched him on the chest. 'I know you did, and I saw you laughing, you heartless devil.'

He was silent for a moment, content just to be close to another human being. Liz was warm and soft in his arms, and he needed that right now.

'I watched you come up the drive, kicking at the snow, you were.' She stroked his face. 'Just like a little boy.'

'Spying on me, were you?' It panicked him to know she had been watching. 'It was the snow,' he said softly. 'The snow always reminds me of… when I was a child.' Without him realising, his voice had dropped to a whisper. 'I suppose that's what you saw when I was kicking the snow just now… the child in me.' He was shivering again. The memory washed over him, raged through him, and drowned everything he had created to keep it out.

Astonished, Liz sat up. Turning her face to his, she remarked in awe, 'Do you realise what you're doing?' When he didn't answer she tugged at his shirtsleeve. 'You're talking about yourself. In all the years I've known you, you've never talked about yourself.'

He gulped hard, desperately composing himself. 'Did you pay the electricity bill?'

'God almighty, Jack, you're trembling!' Even as she looked at him, the sweat stood out on his forehead like swollen pearl drops.

Easing her away, he stood up. 'I must have a chill coming on,' he lied. 'That man… Tom, isn't it? The caretaker at the school? He was coughing and sneezing all through the meeting. No consideration for others, that's the trouble.'

Without ceremony Liz went to the kettle, switched it on and while it was boiling emptied a flu powder into a cup. When the boiling water was poured over the powder she gave it to him. 'Drink this,' she ordered.

Between sips he glanced at the clock over the mantelpiece. 'It's nearly three o'clock, time the girls were home.'

'They'll be gossiping I expect. Don't worry.' She returned to her lukewarm coffee, toying with it a while before asking in a changed voice, 'Why don't you ever talk about yourself, Jack?'

This was what he'd been dreading. Just now, when he said about the snow taking him back… he knew he must have awakened old curiosity. 'You know why,' he reminded her. 'Nothing to tell.'

'What about the snow?'

'What about it?' Jesus Christ! Why couldn't he stop trembling?

The hazel eyes appraised him. 'You said it brought back memories of you as a child.'

'I don't remember saying that.'

Suddenly it was there, like an old movie flicking through his mind. He was a boy again, just a boy… kicking the snow as he went up the path to that beautiful old house. The snow… deep pools of crimson… spidery trails making a pattern beneath his feet… the horror when he opened the door. He could see her now, staring at him through wild dark eyes. It was so real, so vivid. Dear God! He raised his eyes and looked on his wife's face. She was still waiting. Waiting for the answer he could never give.

'There's nothing to tell!' he yelled. In his terror he leaped from the chair and fell like a dead weight against the table. When he looked up again, Liz was watching him, a puzzled expression on her face. All the anger ebbed away. It wasn't her fault. 'I'm sorry,' he murmured.

She forced a smile. 'There you go again, saying you're sorry.' She came to him, comforting. 'It's me that should be sorry. When I first asked you about your family and you told me how you'd been orphaned after a car accident, I promised never to raise the subject again. It was what you said just now, about being a child. For one precious minute I felt so close…'

Taking a deep breath he straightened up and slowly flexed his shoulders. For some reason he hurt all over. 'The past is gone,' he told her. 'All we need be concerned about is the future… Ginny's future.'

Bristling she reminded him, 'You have *two* daughters, Jack.'

'I'm well aware of that, sweetheart.' Though it was only Ginny he was concerned with. Ginny who gave him the worst nightmares.

He glanced towards the window. 'These past few days,' he remarked, changing the subject, 'have you seen anyone new hanging about? A stranger?'

'What? Round here, you mean?'

He nodded, his eyes raking the window. 'Round the house… in the street outside?'

'No, I don't think so.'

'What about the girls? Have they seen anyone?'

'If they have, they haven't mentioned it to me.' She regarded him with curiosity. 'Why do you ask?'

He needed to allay her suspicions. 'Oh, it's just something the old fella said,' he lied. 'Apparently somebody raided his chicken shed last night… made off with a prime rooster.'

She rolled her eyes to the ceiling. 'If you mean old Bandy Clegg, he's so forgetful he's probably sold it or cooked it for his own Sunday lunch.'

'All the same, if you see a stranger near this house, I want to know.'

'You worry too much.'

'Give us a kiss.' He grabbed her to him. 'Did I tell you you looked gorgeous today?'

'Tell me now.' Raising her face she parted her lips, melting when he bent to kiss her.

Ginny's voice sailed across the room. 'I should have thought you were past all that,' she said cuttingly.

Breaking apart, they seemed embarrassed. 'Hello, you.' Jack came towards her. 'Where the devil have you been?' He noticed with some trepidation that she was not only dishevelled, but that her shoes were caked with mud. He was about to question her when Liz stepped forward.

Irritated by Ginny's untimely intervention, she demanded, 'What have you been up to?'

Ginny's dark eyes enveloped her. 'Honestly, Mother, why do you always think I've been up to something?' Her sly, challenging attitude only served to infuriate her mother, but that was what she intended.

Like always, Liz was goaded. 'Just look at yourself. Anyone would think you'd been in some bloody pigsty.'

'Leave it, Liz,' Jack pleaded. He had seen how these two could rile each other, and it was never a pleasant encounter. 'I'll deal with this.' Turning to Ginny with a stern face, he told her, 'Get your shoes off and go upstairs. Take a bath. Afterwards you can explain why you've come home in such a state.'

As she walked away, head high and defiant, Liz called out, 'Where's your sister?'

Without turning, Ginny coolly answered, 'How should I know? I'm not her keeper.'

It was half an hour later when Lianne arrived home. Having taken the time to calm down and clean the debris off her shoes, she breezed in with a smile. 'Hello, everyone. Sorry I'm late, but I got talking to Amy Burton.'

Liz was relieved, but angry. 'You might have let us know you were going off after the meeting.'

'Didn't mean to,' came the reply. Crossing the room she came to the table. Liz was stirring a cake mix. Lianne watched for a moment before asking in a more subdued voice, 'Is Ginny home?'

Liz stirred the mix with more urgency. 'She came in looking like she'd been in a fight, and there was mud all over her shoes. Your dad sent her up to get a bath.'

'Where did she say she'd been?' With more calm than she felt, Lianne reached out and dipped a finger in the cake mix. All she got for her trouble was one quick lick and a rap over the knuckles with the wooden spoon.

'She didn't. You know Ginny, close lipped and secretive. Your dad means to talk with her when she comes down.'

'Where's Dad now?'

'In the other room, reading his paper, I expect.' Pausing in her stirring, she gathered a mess of mix on to the spoon and dropped it into the bowl to test its consistency. Regarding Lianne with suspicion, she asked, 'I don't suppose *you* know where she's been?'

'Nope.' Taking advantage of the moment she scraped her fingers round the bowl rim. 'One minute she was there and then she wasn't.'

Liz shook her head. 'That girl will be the death of me.'

'Don't be so dramatic.'

'And don't you follow her example. The truth is, Ginny's grown very hard. She doesn't seem to care about anything these days.'

Lianne leaped to her sister's defence. 'You and Dad are partly to blame.'

Liz dropped the spoon into the bowl. 'You'd better explain that, my girl.'

Straddling the chair, Lianne seemed reluctant to talk about it, but seeing how her mother would not be satisfied until she replied, she told the truth as she saw it. 'You shouldn't keep nagging her.'

'I don't know what you're saying. We don't nag her.'

'If you just leave her alone she'll sort herself out.'

'I doubt it.' Going to the cupboard Liz took out a deep cake tin. She dropped the mixture into it and began spreading it to the corners. 'Never mind your sister. Have *you* any thoughts about what you want to do? I mean, you're fifteen. You ought to be thinking along career lines.'

'I don't want a career.'

'Oh?' She went to the oven and slid the cake tin inside. Closing the door she set the timer and returned to the conversation. 'If you don't want a career, what do you want?'

'I want to work in the supermarket for a while. Then I want to get married to the boss and have a dozen kids.'

Laughing out loud, Liz rounded the table to hug her. 'If only life was that simple,' she said. What she thought was, Why can't Ginny and I talk like this? Why does she never make me laugh? And, as always, she vowed to be more understanding of her eldest child.

When Ginny came out of the bathroom, Lianne was waiting for her. 'I ought to tell on you,' she whispered. 'I ought to tell them that you and Stuart did it in the Nissen hut. I ought to tell them you were like a mad thing.' She followed Ginny back to her room. Lying on the bed while Ginny brushed her hair she was mesmerised.

Ginny's smile was enigmatic. 'If you did tell them, what would you say?' She always brushed her hair in the same way, long slow strokes, over and over, until the hair shone like fire.

Lianne thought very carefully about her answer. 'I'd say you were both naked, and that he was on top of you.'

'What else would you say?'

Lianne thought again. 'Mmm… I'd say he had these lovely long legs and they were hairy too. I've never seen a boy with hairy legs before.'

'That's because he's past being a boy. Stuart Dickens is a man now.' She bestowed a wonderful smile on her young sister. 'What else?'

'Nothing.' She blushed a deep shade of pink. 'I wouldn't tell them anyway—'

The last word was caught in her throat as Ginny flung herself at her, grabbing her by the shoulders and shaking her like a rag doll. 'If you did tell them, what else would you say, bitch?'

Lianne tried to shrug her off. 'I would never tell!'

'What if I *wanted* you to tell them?'

'Leave me alone!'

'Answer me. What if I *wanted* you to tell them how me and Stuart did it in the Nissen hut? What if I *wanted* them to know what a dirty little cow they've got for a daughter? That's what you think I am, isn't it... a dirty little cow. You'd like to tell them that if I asked you to, wouldn't you?'

'No! No! I don't think that. I don't.' Terrified, she hit out. Her terror increased when her nail scored across Ginny's cheek and drew blood. 'I'm sorry, Ginny,' she cried, 'I didn't mean it.' But she did! She loved her... loathed her. In her deepest heart she believed there was goodness in Ginny. She also needed her, as much as she needed the life blood in her body.

For the longest moment of her life she curled into a ball, covered her head with her arms, and waited for Ginny to punish her.

'Get up!'

Slowly she uncurled. Lifting her face to look into Ginny's she saw with a sinking heart that she was not forgiven. The long deep scratch on Ginny's face was raw. 'I didn't mean to do that.'

'I want you out of my room. *Now.*' Standing upright beside the bed, with her arms folded and a grim expression shaping her handsome features, Ginny seemed formidable to the cowering girl.

There was a moment of empathy between them, a surprising intimacy, and then a hatred so foul it was like a presence in the room. Without another word Lianne scuttled away.

When the door was closed, Ginny resumed her seat at the dresser, where she began brushing her hair, this time counting the strokes aloud: 'One... two...' three Sheer pleasure showed on her face. Through the mirror she glanced at the closed door and smiled, and carried on counting, contemplating the moment when Lianne would return, as she always did.

Five minutes later, there came a knock on the door. 'Ginny. Are you ready to talk now?' It was Jack. He would have preferred to forget, but Liz had sent him up to demand an explanation.

'It's all right. You can come in.' In fact, Ginny had been waiting for him. Dressed in a clean tracksuit and white trainers, she was standing by the window.

'Your mother needs to know where you went,' he said, closing the door behind him. 'You know how she worries.'

'I went into the spinney, into one of the Nissen huts. You can hide in the doorway and watch the little creatures… it's so beautiful in the spinney.' She saw no reason to lie.

'That was a bloody stupid thing to do, wasn't it?'

'Why?' Head high, always arrogant.

'Because there have been reports of a stranger lurking about, that's why. For all we know he could be hiding out in one of those deserted huts.'

'I didn't see any stranger.'

'You're not to go there again.'

'I can't promise that.'

'I'm not asking you to promise. I'm telling you. You're not to go there again, do you hear me?'

'I hear you.'

His whole body relaxed. 'Good. Then we understand each other.'

With that he slammed out and stood for a while on the landing. I don't know who he is, he thought, but I have the feeling he's watching us… me… my family. The sweat ran down his face. On quickened footsteps he went to the bathroom, ran a measure of cold water into the sink and dipped his face into it. Afterwards he went down to tell Liz what Ginny had said, and that he had told her she was never to go there again.

Ginny heard her father go downstairs. She gazed out of the window at the melting snow. 'Sorry, Father,' she murmured. 'You can order me to do whatever you like, but I can't promise. *Won't* promise.'

It was midnight when Lianne crept along the landing and into Ginny's room. 'Ginny.' Gently shaking her sister she knelt by the bed. 'Ginny, wake up.'

Dark eyes opened to stare at her. 'I'm not asleep. What do you want?'

A doubt. Then a smile and a request. 'Can you really get Dave Martin to do it with me?'

'If that's what you want.'

'It is.'

'Go away.' Turning over, Ginny made it clear the conversation was at an end.

'I want him to do it with me in the Nissen hut, just like you and Stuart.'

Ginny made no response.

'It won't hurt, will it?'

Still no response.

'Goodnight, Ginny.'

When the door softly closed, Ginny smiled to herself. 'I knew you'd be back,' she murmured. Then she began scheming as to how she might bring Dave and her sister together.

As the night deepened, the rain started, drizzling at first and then increasing in strength until it was a downpour. The stranger had been watching the house, but now he turned up his coat collar and ran to the waiting car. Once inside he took a notepad and pen from the glove compartment and scribbled a few words. Replacing the pad, he started the engine, shifted it into gear and drove off, the rain still dripping down his neck.

'There must be a better way to earn a living!' he groaned. But he couldn't think of one. What was more, he loved his work. Especially when he got to see two young things thrashing about on the ground, going at it like there was no tomorrow.

4

New York was alive and vibrant all year round, but in the cold month of February there was a strange quietness about it. Today there was a cruel wind blowing. The skies were grey and angry, and the streets unusually deserted.

Warm and cosy in her magnificent centrally heated apartment, amongst her beautiful, expensive artefacts, Katherine Louis was desperately unhappy. 'I can't understand it,' she told her devoted companion. 'Why didn't he reply? Even if only to tell me he never wanted to see me again… why didn't he answer my letter?'

Casting her sorry gaze to the plush red carpet, she fell silent, stubbornly calling up thoughts of long ago. The thoughts were not comforting. Instead they only made her feel sad, and afraid. Some days she felt old. Today she felt older still. Old and worn, and lonely for the son who had deserted her.

Maureen sat before her, her blue Irish eyes bright with compassion. Having listened to her mistress and sympathised with her, she now had to be strong for her. 'It's no good making yerself miserable,' she announced sternly. 'He hasn't replied to yer letter, so it's plain as the nose on yer face that he doesn't want anything to do with ye.' She loathed hurting the old lady, but could see no better way. 'Oh, look now, I don't mean to be spiteful, ye know that, me ol' darling, but ye can't go on the way ye are.'

Keeping her gaze on the carpet, the old lady shook her head. 'I know you mean well, my dear, but I can't put him out of my mind.'

'What has that fella, that Eddie Laing got to say for himself?'

'He only told me what I suspected, that my son is getting on with his life as usual. He runs his business, and he takes care of his family, and outwardly, according to Mr Laing's man on the scene, nothing has changed. Everything appears to be the same.' She looked up now, and there was a glimmer of fear in her eyes. 'Except She gulped and sat back in the chair. There was... *something*...' She swivelled her gaze to the ceiling and fell silent, afraid to go on.

Maureen leaned forward, urging, 'What *something*?' She hated half a tale.

Katherine lowered her gaze and sitting up in the chair she revealed, in a voice so soft it was almost inaudible, 'There was a tragedy.' Now her gaze was harder, more intense, never leaving the other woman's face.

She watched as Maureen's expression changed from curiosity to confusion, then to fear. 'What kind of tragedy?'

'A teacher by the name of Miss Warren. According to Laing, she was at the pool with a group of girls, when there was a terrible accident. She was found with her hair enmeshed in the pool filter. When they got her out, she was already drowned.'

A moment then, while each woman pondered on the shocking news. It was Maureen who spoke next. 'Ye say she was with a group of girls?'

'That's right.'

'If ye were given this information, it must mean that one or both of Jack's daughters were involved?'

'Just one.'

Maureen's eyes closed momentarily. When she opened them again it was to see Katherine's face drained of colour. She knew then, but needed confirmation. 'Was Virginia at the pool when this woman was drowned?'

Katherine nodded, at the same time clenching her fists as though she might fight the monster that was once again growing in their midst.

'Jesus, Mary and Joseph!' Making the sign of the cross on herself, Maureen then clambered out of the chair. Pacing the room she nervously wiped a podgy hand across her face. 'Ah, but we mustn't jump to conclusions,' she declared in a brighter voice. 'Accidents will happen, more's the pity. And just because he named the daughter after the grandmother, it doesn't mean the badness was passed on as well.'

Katherine smiled, the same slow smile that never reached her eyes, the same smile that said, Don't tell me lies, because in my heart I know the truth.

The silence was almost unbearable. While one woman stood, shoulders bent and a look of disbelief etched on her face, the older one remained seated, deep in thought, her bony hands clasped on her lap, and the all-knowing smile etched on her features. They remained this way for what seemed an age until, in a broken voice, Maureen said, 'I've something to tell ye.'

Katherine answered, 'I know,' and the smile disappeared. She never liked being lied to. Especially by someone she trusted with her very life.

Maureen swung round, her eyes large with contrition. 'How did ye know?' she demanded. '*When* did ye know?'

The smile returned. 'Just now. The minute you realised Virginia was there when that poor woman drowned.' Her face stiffened. 'That was when I knew you had not posted the letter.' Her face darkened. 'That was unforgivable, my dear. By rights I should punish you.'

Maureen was filled with remorse at having deceived the old lady, but she still held fast to the reason for not posting that letter. 'I don't want ye to go,' she cried. 'That's why I didn't post it.'

'What are you afraid of?'

'That yer son might not want anything to do with ye. I couldn't bear it if he hurt ye again.'

'That's not good enough. What are you *really* afraid of?'

Clutching at her breast with both hands, Maureen stepped closer. 'All right. If ye must know... I'm frightened.'

'Of what?'

Her voice rose to hysteria. 'You *know* what!' When Katherine put up a hand to calm her, she dropped her voice to a whisper. 'Ever since ye contacted that detective, I've been afraid. Afraid ye'll wake the sleeping monsters. Afraid it might not be over. Afraid because he's named his eldest daughter after the grandmother he idolised. At night I lie awake and I think about it… what she did… the evil things she uttered as they led her away.' Quickly making the sign of the cross on herself again, she moaned as though in great pain. 'Dear God above! Don't pretend with me. Ye know why I'm frightened, because aren't ye frightened in the very same way? Don't ye feel nervous about the things ye might uncover? Can't ye see with yer own eyes what ye're doing?'

'What would you have me do?' There was no fear in Katherine's eyes. In her heart there were no regrets. No second thoughts. No reservations. Whatever the consequences, her mind was made up.

Maureen's fear though filled the room like a physical presence. 'Leave it be, I beg ye,' she pleaded, 'especially now we know about the accident. Ye said yerself the girl was there when the woman drowned. If he's created his grandmother in his own daughter, there's nothing ye can do. Let him deal with it. Don't put yerself in danger. Please, Katherine. Ye mustn't go.'

The old lady stood up. Touching her hand against the other woman's hair she answered with dignity, 'My mind is made up.'

She walked across the room, tall and stately, a proud but foolish woman, driven by a mother's love, and the desperate need to cherish what was left of her family.

'Please, Katherine. Will nothing change yer mind?'

'Not even if heaven and hell were to fuse.' She said the words lightly, but they did not appease the other woman.

Maureen had to make the old lady share her own terror. 'We're not talking about the places we know by name,' she argued. She paused, glancing about the room as though ensuring there was no one listening. Returning her brooding gaze to the old lady, she went on in a quiet voice, 'We're not talking of heaven or hell. We're talking about the dark space between… where there is no heaven and no hell.'

Katherine merely nodded, her features set hard. 'My mind is made up,' she repeated with conviction.

On determined footsteps she made her way to the table in the hall. Here she searched through the directory and afterward scribbled a telephone number on to the notepad. That done she took up the telephone receiver and dialled the number. 'This is Katherine Louis,' she announced grandly. 'I need you to book reservations on the next scheduled flight to London. Oh, and I'll need a chauffeur-driven car on arrival at the airport. I will also require a suite at one of the top hotels.' There was a pause while the clerk verified the details. Katherine turned her head to glance at Maureen who was standing by the door. 'No, I'm not certain how long I need to stay.'

'Don't expect me to come with ye.' The Irish voice was adamant.

Katherine gave her the warmest smile before continuing with her instructions. 'Oh, and there will be two of us… myself and a Miss Maureen Delaney.'

Cyrus had been upstairs in his room and was on his way down. 'She still means to go, then?' he asked, coming face to face with Maureen.

'She's obsessed with the idea of seeing Jack again. I've already argued that he may not want to see her.' Drawing a long breath through her nose, she held it awhile. When she exhaled through her mouth the words came out in an angry rush. 'I know I'm not family, and I know I really shouldn't interfere, but, well, can't ye make her see sense?'

He gave her a broad reassuring smile. 'You're as much family as any of us,' he said. 'As for Katherine, unfortunately she has always believed she knows best.' Turning his soulful eyes towards his sister, he muttered harshly. 'This time, though, I'm afraid she must learn the hard way.'

5

Liz was at the end of her tether. Rushing to the foot of the stairs she called up, 'I won't call you two again! If you're not down in five minutes I'll throw your breakfast in the bin and you can go to school hungry.'

She waited a minute, hoping her threat would bring them running. When it didn't she hurried angrily up the stairs, stopping halfway to yell, 'Don't think I'm bluffing. I've got a hairdresser's appointment at nine thirty. Lorraine's the only one who can do my hair properly, and she's only there on Monday mornings. I'm not missing her for the sake of two lazy girls who can't get out of their beds.'

Silence.

'I mean it. I'll throw your breakfast away.'

Unnerving silence.

'Are you coming down or what?'

Defiant silence.

'Right!' She spun round, making her way downstairs again. 'When your father comes home tonight, you can explain why I've had to throw perfectly good food away. Food that he works hard to provide.'

In the kitchen she began clearing the table. 'Bloody kids! Who needs them?'

'That's not a very nice thing to say.' Virginia stood at the door, regarding her mother with dark unsmiling eyes. 'Why didn't you call us earlier?'

Liz gave an impatient snort. 'I've been calling you for the past hour.'

Coming into the kitchen, Ginny sat herself at the table. 'I'll have coffee this morning,' she declared sleepily. 'Two sugars.'

'Whatever you want, madam.' Making a subservient little bow, Liz glared at her. 'But you can damn well get it yourself. The pair of you have made me late.' Pointing to the grill she explained, 'I've done scrambled eggs and sausages. If you want anything different you'll have to cook it.'

'Then *we'll* be late!'

'You should have thought of that.'

Lianne came in, her face falling when she realised there was an argument going on. 'You're in a bad mood, aren't you, Mum?'

Liz ran into the hallway and grabbed her coat. Throwing it on, she returned to the kitchen. 'You're right, I am in a bad mood,' she confirmed, 'and is it any wonder? I have two grown daughters who can't come in of an evening when they're asked to; can't get up in the morning; would rather throw their used clothes on the floor than put them in the wash-basket where they belong. They have an opinion on everything from pop to politics, and think they know how best to rule the world... yet they're too proud to ever admit they're wrong, and bold enough to expect their breakfast put before them.' Stretching her neck she glared at them. 'In case you hadn't noticed, this is *not* a restaurant, and I am *not* the waitress. It's also *not* a hotel where you can place a call to get you up in the morning, and then choose to ignore it.'

Astonished, Lianne looked from her mother to her sister and back again. She felt like piggy in the middle. She also felt ashamed. Blowing out her cheeks she let the air lazily escape. 'Sorry, Mum.'

'So you say.' Fastening the buckle of her belt, Liz went out of the room. 'And don't leave the kitchen like a pigsty!' she called. A moment later the front door slammed and she was gone.

'Blimey!' It took a moment for Lianne to gather her wits. 'I don't think I've ever seen her in such a foul mood.' Coming to the table she slid into the chair next to Ginny. 'What did you do to rile her?' The whole upsetting scene had touched an angry chord inside.

Ginny's smile was the tiniest bit sad. 'I don't have to do anything,' she declared.

'What do you mean?' When Ginny was in this kind of mood, Lianne was always apprehensive.

'You mean you haven't noticed?'

'Noticed what?'

'Mother seems to have taken a dislike to me.' The dark eyes flickered with a kind of hatred, boring into Lianne as though *she* was to blame.

Disturbed, Lianne looked away. 'You're imagining things.'

'If that's what you want to believe.'

Lianne had to get up, get away from the influences that made her afraid. Going to the cooker, she asked brightly, 'I'm having toast. Do you want some?'

'No.'

'What then?'

'Coffee. Strong and black.'

'Must you?'

'Make the coffee and don't start nagging.'

'Dad says it's bad for you.'

'He should have known better than to tell me that.'

'Why?' Having boiled the water, she made the coffee and presented it to her sister.

'Because if he hadn't said it was bad for me, I probably wouldn't have wanted it.'

Bringing her orange juice to the table, Lianne had another question. 'Is that why you let Old Tom show you the dirty pictures, because Dad would go spare if he knew?'

Dark eyes flashed. 'I look at the pictures because I like to. Not because I want to spite anybody.'

Thoughtfully, Lianne sipped at her orange juice. 'I think he's just a dirty old man.'

'Who... Dad?' She was smiling now, irritatingly confident.

Lianne laughed out loud. 'No, silly... I meant Old Tom.'

'He's harmless enough.' She nudged Lianne in the side. 'Although...' She hesitated. 'No, I don't think I'll tell you.'

Frustrated, Lianne argued, 'You'll have to now.'

'All right then. But you mustn't tell anyone.'

'You know I never tell.' Leaning towards her sister she urged, 'Go on, then. What's Old Tom done now?'

'It's not what he's *done* exactly. It's what he would like to do.'

'Oh? And what's that, then?'

Ginny stared into her sister's face. It was worried; small creases of anxiety around the eyes and mouth. Ginny liked that. She took great delight in causing anxiety. Smiling warmly, she pushed her face closer to the other, anticipating its reaction. '*Me!* Old Tom would like to do *me!*' She watched while the face reddened to the shade of a ripe tomato. Beside herself with glee she asked in a whisper, 'Haven't shocked you, have I?'

Lianne squirmed uncomfortably. 'Ugh! He's old and smelly.' Shock and disgust showed in her every feature. 'You wouldn't let him, would you?'

Throwing herself back in the chair Ginny laughed until she was breathless.

'You *wouldn't*, would you?' Suddenly Lianne was on her feet, glaring down at her sister with amazement.

Composing herself, Ginny looked up. There was a strange softness in her face. 'I wish you wouldn't worry about me,' she said. 'You're worse than they are.' Glancing towards the door through which her mother had departed, she grimaced. 'Don't be like them,' she snapped. 'I couldn't stand it if you were like them.'

'Promise you won't let Old Tom do it to you?'

'Look!' She pointed to the grill. 'Your toast is burning.'

'I don't want it now.' Going to the cooker she took out the blackened slices and threw them into the bin, afterwards licking her slightly burned fingers. Glancing up at the clock she remarked impatiently, 'If we don't hurry we'll be late for concert rehearsal.'

'So? They can't hang us, can they?' Shrugging her shoulders she finished her coffee at a leisurely pace. 'I'm not too bothered about the concert. I didn't want to be in it anyway.'

'Oh, Ginny! How can you say that? There's no one in the whole school who can sing the way you do.' She was bursting with pride. 'If anyone should have been left out it's me. There are any number of girls who can play the flute better.'

'Ah! But they wouldn't religiously turn up for rehearsals the way you do.' There was scorn in her voice. 'Go on. Own up… you only auditioned so you could keep an eye on me.'

'I wish you wouldn't make fun of me.'

'And I wish you wouldn't follow me everywhere.'

Fifteen minutes later when they were ready to leave, Ginny was incensed to see Lianne wiping the cooker down. 'Leave that,' she ordered. 'It'll teach her a lesson for yelling at us.'

'No. It isn't fair. You go on. It'll only take a minute.'

'Please yourself.' She went out the front door and down the road with quickening footsteps.

As good as her word, Lianne caught her up before she reached the bottom of the lane.

Liz was racked with guilt. 'I was a bit hard on them,' she told the young woman who was doing her hair. 'You know what it's like. You have a bad night, get up late and fly round doing all the things you should have done yesterday. Then you take it out on the nearest person who happens to be there.'

'Oh, I shouldn't bother,' the young woman consoled. 'If your daughters are anything like I was at their age, they probably didn't listen to you anyway.' Her smile was crooked but homely. 'My mother used to say I had skin thicker than a rhinoceros.'

There was a short span of silence while she parted Liz's pretty brown hair in the middle. Sweeping it back with a flick of the comb, she teased either side into two deep waves that fell loosely over the temples. 'You have beautiful hair,' she told the bemused Liz, 'and this style really suits you.' Cupping the thick short hair in the palms of her hands she bounced it up and down until the lie of the hair fell naturally into place. 'What do you think?' she asked eagerly. She held up a hand-mirror, occasionally moving it so that Liz could see herself from every angle.

Liz scrutinised herself. 'You don't think I've let you cut too much off?' Somehow it had turned out different to what she expected. Better, but different.

'I think it suits you.'

'You don't think I look like mutton dressed as lamb, then?'

'No, I do not.' Liz was not the most attractive lady who frequented these premises, but the young woman thought her pretty, and very likeable. 'If I could get away with wearing my hair like that, I'd have it done tomorrow,' she said honestly. Her own blonde hair was long and straight, while Liz had a natural spring to her brown locks. The short bouncy style framed her face perfectly, and yes, it did make her seem younger. But then she *was* young... mid-thirties maybe.

At the till, Liz spied a set of rollers on the shelf. 'I never seem to keep the shape once I've washed it,' she groaned. 'Would it help to put in rollers?'

The young woman handed her the change. 'You don't need rollers,' she said, shaking her head. 'All you have to do after it's washed is make a clean parting down the middle, then run the tips of your fingers through to lift it from the roots... like I showed you.' Leaning forward she put a hand either side of her temples and spreading out her fingers she pushed them upwards, flicking the hair out and letting it settle back naturally. 'It doesn't work well for me because my hair is thick and straight,' she admitted, 'but you have light bouncy hair that will go where you want it.'

Liz laughed at that. 'You could have fooled me,' she said. All the same, she never fussed with her hair and somehow it always seemed to look respectable.

'Had it styled for a special occasion, have you?'

'That all depends,' her hazel eyes sparkled mischievously, 'on whether I can persuade Jack to whisk me off to Paris for a naughty weekend.'

'Really?' The young woman's face lit with delight. 'If you manage that, I'd like to know the secret. I can't remember the last time my old man took me somewhere romantic.'

Liz giggled like a schoolgirl. 'I'm only teasing,' she confessed. 'Jack's run off his feet right now. But I'm working on it for next year.' She patted her hair. 'I've had this done for the school concert. I thought I'd get it cut now so I can get used to the idea. All the mums will be there in their best bib and tucker and I don't want to be the odd man out.'

'When is it?'

'Two weeks from Friday. My eldest girl has a beautiful singing voice, she's been given a solo spot. Lianne is playing the flute as part of the backing orchestra, and by all accounts it's going to be a wonderful evening with a bigger programme than ever, and a buffet interval.'

'Sounds very grand.'

'That's because Miss Baker retired last year, and the new music teacher thinks he's Andrew Lloyd Webber.' Counting her change, she sorted out a coin and gave it to the young woman. 'I'll ring you for another appointment.'

Dropping the coin into her pocket, the young woman thanked her. Then she ushered the next client in, giving her the same warm smile she bestowed on everyone. It was a tiresome chore that went with the job. 'Nice now the snow's almost gone,' she said for the umpteenth time, 'though it's still sloppy underfoot.'

Jack was in the office. Bent over his desk he didn't hear her come in. For a while she stood and watched him, enjoying the fact that he was totally unaware of her presence. Long and lean, dressed in his white coat and with his dark hair tousled, he was oblivious to everything but the ledger he was poring over. So intent was he on the task in hand, there could have been an earthquake and he probably wouldn't have noticed. He touched her heart with love. 'Shall I go away and come back again?' she asked cheekily.

He slewed round so fast he almost fell off the chair. 'Liz!' Regarding her with a mixture of curiosity and admiration, he covered the space between them in a rush. It was only when he raised his eyes from her face that he realised there was something different. 'You've had your hair done,' he remarked, and from the tone of his voice she couldn't tell whether he liked or hated it.

Her anxiety melted when he kissed her on the mouth and held her close. 'It suits you,' he murmured.

'That's what Lorraine said.'

Holding her at arm's length he made a mock-serious face. 'I'm sorry, sweetheart, but you've really ruined my schedule.'

'What are you talking about? How could I have ruined your schedule?' She glanced at the pretty watch he had bought her last birthday. 'It's only midday. Be here by twelve thirty, that's what you said. Now are you saying I'm late?'

'No. I'm saying I can't allow you to drive a baker's van with an expensive hairdo like that. Our customers will think we're doing too well and expect a cut in prices.'

When she saw his face crinkle into a smile she slapped him on the chest. 'Swine! For a minute you had me worried!'

He kissed her again by way of an apology. 'Fancy a cup of Jack's coffee?' He was in a devilish mood.

'Will it poison me?'

Her question was given in the same vein of humour. But the effect on him was astonishing. His smile fell away. The green eyes momentarily closed, and by the way he stiffened, it was as though someone behind had taken him by the shoulders and stretched him upwards.

'Jack?' She wasn't certain whether he was still playing the game. 'Are you all right?'

He bent his head to her and grinned. 'Just teasing,' he answered. But his pale drawn face told another story.

'You get on with your accounts, and I'll get the coffee,' she said. Stripping off her outdoor clothes she went to the cupboard. On top stood the percolator, bubbling away, its strong warm aroma filling the room. Beside it stood a tray containing a number of cups, teaspoons, a sugar bowl and a jug of milk. 'Is there a problem?' she asked, bustling about.

'What makes you ask that?' Seated at the desk, he paused in his work to stare at her. He was afraid again: afraid she might guess; afraid he had revealed his worst nightmare. She must not know. There were things in his life she must *never* know.

Shrugging her shoulders, Liz put his fears at rest. 'Just now when I came in, you seemed very intent on your work... as though you were struggling with a problem.'

'The only problem I have here is too much work.'

'That doesn't need to be a problem.' Handing him a cup of strong coffee she sat on the edge of his desk. 'All you have to do is extend the bakery at the back, take on a couple more high class bakers, two more vans and drivers...' She raised her cup and took a sip before continuing, 'You've built the business up as far as you can with the limited facilities you've got. The orders are pouring in, and you said yourself you could cover the whole country if you were to let the business have its head. Maybe it's time, Jack... time to let it grow.' She tickled him under the chin. 'You're a born businessman, Jack Lucas. You could corner the supermarkets and all the main outlets. Spread your wings abroad. Nothing's impossible with you. In no time at all we'd be millionaires. We could have the old house renovated... open the world to the girls, and,' she chuckled, 'I wouldn't mind a swimming pool and all the trappings that go with serious money.' While she waited for his response, she took another sip of her coffee.

Jack's coffee was left untouched. For a long moment he kept his head down, his gaze resting on the pages of his ledger.

The figures ran into one, and he could feel his blood rising. 'Have you ever wanted for anything?' he asked, raising his gaze.

'No.'

'Needed anything I couldn't give you?'

She knew what he was getting at, and wished she had not broached the subject. 'You've always looked after me and the girls, Jack. I'm not disputing that.'

'And I'm not expanding the business. I've told you before... it's not what I want. I'm content with things the way they are. We'll get the house done bit by bit as we agreed. I don't want to make a million, and I certainly don't intend to spread my wings abroad.' Even here he never felt really safe. The idea of going abroad terrified him.

'All right, Jack. It's your business and I shouldn't interfere. I only want you to be recognised for the man you are.'

'I have my family and my work. As long as we all have enough for our needs, we can't complain.'

Realising she had resurrected a prickly argument, she was quick to promise, 'I won't raise the matter again. Forget I ever mentioned it.' Sliding off the desk she gulped down a measure of coffee before rinsing the cup under the tap. 'Where am I delivering?'

'Two drops. Leighton Buzzard and Bedford.' He stood up, his coffee still untouched. 'I'd better go and check whether the van's loaded.' He went out of the office, running down the short flight of steps that led directly into the bakery.

From the doorway, Liz followed his familiar figure. 'What is it with you, Jack?' she murmured. 'Sometimes I get the feeling you're shutting me out.' She took a long deep breath. The air was pleasant with the smell of fresh baked bread. Looking along the bakery floor she could see rows of shelves packed with cakes of every description, rolls, loaves of bread in their many varieties – long tin, plaited, cottage, farmhouse – all risen to the right degree and done to perfection. Like Jack, she took great pleasure in this place. Unlike Jack, she would have liked to see it break the boundaries he imposed on it. 'What's wrong with being a millionaire?' she sighed.

Jack started his way back. Her face lit up. 'You're right, sweetheart,' she murmured. 'There are more important things in life than being filthy rich.' All the same, she would dearly have loved the house to be renovated. As it was, it might take another five years to complete the work.

Skipping up the steps two at a time he told her, 'Ready when you are.'

Needing to lighten his mood, she quipped, 'Is that an indecent offer?'

He smiled, then grinned, and in a moment was laughing out loud in that delightful boyish way she loved so much. 'Don't tempt me,' he whispered, pushing her back inside with the weight of his body, 'or I might just forget where we are.'

'I won't tell if you don't.' She began playfully toying with his shirt.

Neither of them heard the old fellow at the door, until he made a very polite cough and gave them a look like they were children misbehaving.

Red in the face, Liz excused herself and pushed by. 'I'll be off then,' she said, going down the stairs chuckling to herself.

'Drive carefully!' Jack called. Then he dealt with Fred's query and returned to his desk, where he too had to chuckle. 'God I love that woman! I hope to God nothing ever spoils what we've got,' he mused aloud.

But he hadn't reckoned with the mother he had left behind all those years before. Unbeknown to him, the badness he yearned to forget was already reaching out to harm him.

Katherine Louis hobbled to the waiting car; her corn was more painful than ever and she was not in the best of moods.

Maureen followed behind, edgy and irritated, subdued by the long flight from New York the day before. Terrified of being up there in the clouds she had not altogether forgiven Katherine for insisting that she accompany her to England. 'I hope ye don't regret what ye're doing,' she muttered as the two of them came to the kerb edge. 'Cyrus was right... old wounds will never heal if ye insist on probing them.'

All she got for her trouble was a gentle prod from Katherine's brass-handled walking stick. 'Stop moaning, my dear. You moaned on the plane, then grumbled all evening through dinner, and here you are on a morning filled with sunshine, and I'm blessed if you're *still* not moaning.'

While Maureen sulked, the chauffeur opened wide the door and waited for his elderly passenger to embark. As he leaned out to assist, he was treated to a sharp rebuke: 'I am quite capable, thank you!'

Maureen gave the driver a smile. 'Her bark is worse than her bite,' she consoled with a wink.

Katherine's voice sailed from the interior of the car. 'Stop loitering out there. Give the driver the address and look sharp. Every minute is precious.'

Rummaging in her handbag, Maureen found the piece of paper with the address written on. 'Heath and Reach,' she remarked, peering at the address through narrowed eyes. 'D'ye know it?'

The driver was a small man, with white hair and grey rubbery skin. He screwed his face into a painful grimace, then rubbed his chin with the tips of his fingers. He suggested, 'Could I take a look?' indicating the paper in Maureen's possession.

When Maureen stretched out her hand he took the paper and perused it with deliberation. 'Heath and Reach, Bedfordshire.' The grimace relaxed. 'I've a good idea,' he said. 'If you'll climb in, I'll take a minute to check the map.' He cupped his fingers beneath her elbow and this time his offer of help was graciously accepted.

A few minutes later with the two passengers comfortable in the rear and the driver up front, the car was still stationary. Impatient to be on her way, Katherine slid back the glass partition, demanding in a shrill voice, 'Are we going to sit here all day?'

Visibly startled, he hurriedly folded his map. 'Just checking, ma'am,' he stuttered. 'We're on our way.' Settling into his seat he released the handbrake, thrust the car into gear and eased it forward. The traffic had built up all morning and now there was hardly room to manoeuvre. 'London traffic gets worse,' he complained, making conversation.

Suddenly there was a gap in the flow of traffic. Shooting forward he slotted in between a bus and a taxi-cab. 'All right back there?' he enquired dutifully, at the same time observing Katherine through the mirror. He had been a driver for many years, pandering to the rich and famous, bowing and scraping to those who were no better than himself. He searched the old lady's face; a face of faded beauty, with its full mouth, high cheekbones and expressive brown eyes. It was easy to see that she was an aristocrat, used to money, used to having her own way.

Suddenly Katherine caught him looking at her. For a riveting moment their eyes met. Embarrassed, he looked away, returning to his thoughts, wondering about her. She was American. Staying at one of the most expensive hotels. That was nothing new to him. Most Americans seemed to be wealthy, at least the ones he drove about. What! The hire of this car and himself for a day was more than he earned in a month.

His present passengers were a puzzle to him. It was obvious that the Irish woman was beholden to the other, maybe a companion, a friend. No. More than a friend, he reasoned. He put his foot down. The car surged forward in a rush of power. Settling now, he let it cruise along at seventy. Glancing into the mirror he saw how his two passengers were still deep in conversation. The Irish one was leaning forward, seeming to argue a point. His gaze fell on the older one. A haughty face, but kind. He sensed the urgency of her journey and, a moment ago when she had glanced at him, he felt the sadness behind those pretty brown eyes. His anger melted. 'Rich or poor, we all have our troubles,' he murmured compassionately. Though with all his experience of mankind, he would never have guessed Katherine's troubles, not in a million years.

It was almost five o'clock when Liz came into the house. 'I'm home!' she called. Throwing off her outdoor clothes she went straight into the kitchen. It was tidy enough, but there was no sign of the girls. She ran upstairs and tapped on Ginny's bedroom door.

No answer.

'Ginny? Lianne? Are you in there?'

Still no answer.

Opening the door Liz looked inside. The room was empty and there was no sign that anyone had been home yet. 'Okay,' she conceded, 'as long as you're home before your father.' She didn't want another row. On the other hand neither did she want the girls thinking they could do exactly as they pleased.

Suppressing the niggle of anger she went to the bathroom. Here she splashed her face and washed her hands and returned downstairs to the kitchen, where she washed four sizeable pork chops, laid them in the casserole, and covered them with sliced vegetables and a sauce. That done she replaced the lid and put the dish in the oven, switching it to cook at a moderate heat.

Three times she went to the front door, hoping to see the girls on their way home. Each time she was disappointed. Going into the lounge she switched on the television. 'That's all I need,' she groaned, tuning into a lecture by Margaret Thatcher on the importance of family unity. Even so, she could see the irony of it. Glancing at the mantelpiece clock she noticed it was nearly five thirty. She sighed. Jack would be home any minute, and there was still no sign of the girls. She looked out of the window and her anxiety increased. The daylight was already beginning to fade, and it would soon be dark.

She toyed with the idea of going out after them. She even put on her coat, then took it off again. I might go one way and they could be coming home another, she reasoned. God knows what Jack would think if he got home to find the house empty.

'If you don't want to, I'll understand.' Dave Martin leaned against the wall in the caretaker's room. Some three years older than Lianne, he was tall, of medium build and darkly attractive. With his mop of black hair, cocoa-coloured eyes, easy smile and a soft friendly voice, he drew girls like a magnet. Dave Martin was intelligent and compassionate, a young man with ambition, and a deep liking for Lianne Lucas. 'You shouldn't let your sister talk you into doing things you don't want to.' He made no move. Instead he remained by the door, leaning on the wall and regarding Lianne with some concern. 'She did talk you into it, didn't she?'

Lianne was seated on a chair by the window. The only light in the room was from a small lamp standing on the tool cupboard. Her face was in shadow as she looked up. 'I have a mind of my own,' she murmured. 'If I didn't want us to do it, I wouldn't be here.'

'Are you sure about that?' He made no attempt to close the door.

'Are you calling me a liar?'

'I don't want to fight with you, Lianne.'

'Do you want to make love to me?' Her voice came in a whisper. He was right. She was frightened. Trembling all over.

He closed the door before answering softly, 'Ever since I first saw you, I've wanted nothing else.'

In the half-light, with his dark eyes plucking her out, she could hardly breathe. 'Will it hurt?'

'I won't let it.'

The silence was like a wall between them. Lianne's fear was marbled with excitement. *His* only fear was that she might turn him away. But he would accept that. He had never taken a girl against her will, and never would.

The tap on the door startled them both. It was Ginny. 'If you're going to do it, you'd best get a move on. Old Tom might be back any minute.'

Lianne's fear was tenfold. 'I'm not sure,' she murmured, her green eyes raised upwards, appealing to him, to them both. 'What if we get caught?'

At that moment Dave stepped forward. Stooping before her, he took her two hands into his. 'I don't want you to be frightened,' he murmured. His soft smile was reassuring. 'If you're that worried, maybe we should do it another time... in another place.' Glancing round he wrinkled his nose. 'If you mean to lose your virginity, it shouldn't be in a stinking rat-trap like this.'

'I really like you, Dave.' She felt like a child, when she so longed to be a woman.

Leaning forward and keeping her small hands in his, he bent his head and covered her mouth with his own. It was a wonderful kiss, a long and passionate declaration of his deeper feelings for her. As long as that wonderful kiss lasted, Lianne's heart was like a fluttering bird in the middle of her chest, entrapped, desperate to be free. Like her. Like emotion she had never experienced. 'We'll do it when *you* feel it's right,' he whispered drawing away. 'And remember this...' He gently moved his head from side to side, his dark eyes enveloping her. 'I would never hurt you.'

Before she could get her breath, he was gone, leaving her hands feeling cold and her heart empty. 'I couldn't do it,' she told Ginny. Her voice broke. 'I just couldn't do it.'

Ginny would not be consoled. 'You let me down,' she hissed. 'I set it up, and you turned coward on me.'

'Why should you care anyway?' Lianne stood up, anger taking the place of regret.

'Because I wanted to watch, that's why.'

Brushing past her, Lianne gave her a stabbing look. 'Old Tom's turned you into a pervert,' she growled. 'Somebody should set fire to this place.'

Ginny's laughter echoed across the school playground. As suddenly as it started it stopped. Grabbing Lianne by the shoulders, she warned, 'You want to be careful what you say. He could be listening right now. *Anybody* could be listening. If this place was ever to burn accidentally, you might be the one to get the blame, and you wouldn't want that now, would you?'

'Why do you enjoy frightening me?'

'Because you're like them... always worried, always fearing the worst. If I'm bad, it's because you make me bad... you and them.'

'I'm not worried now, I'm just sorry.' The ghost of a smile washed over her features. 'He's very handsome, isn't he?'

'Hmm. And I'll bet he does it really well.' Draping one arm round her younger sister's shoulder, Ginny propelled her into the cold night air. 'This is just a setback,' she promised. 'Next time we'll find somewhere safer for you and Dave. All right?'

'All right.'

'And you won't keep him waiting too long, will you?'

'No.' The cold air struck her flushed face. It was a welcome relief from being closeted in that awful smelly room. There was something very disturbing about Old Tom's work-place.

'I like him. He's nice.' In fact he was more than nice, she thought fondly. He had strong hands, and warm loving eyes that seemed to smile from deep inside. She wished now she hadn't been so frightened. 'No, Ginny, I won't keep him waiting too long.' She couldn't get him out of her mind.

'Good girl!' There was a hug by way of reward, and then the instruction, 'We'd better get a move on. I expect they're wondering where we are.' Without waiting for her sister, Ginny ran on. It was only a moment before Lianne caught up. 'Don't tell them where we've been,' she pleaded breathlessly.

'As if I would.' A short burst of laughter, then only the sound of their feet hitting the sloshy snow.

It was a long time before they spoke again. But in between their minds were locked into the same thought. Dave Martin.

And how long it would be before Lianne got up the courage to let him take her virginity.

It was Maureen who spotted them from the car window. 'Shall I ask those girls where Leighton Road is?' she suggested, tapping Katherine on the knee. 'They look like they live round here.'

Peering out of the window on Maureen's side, Katherine's attention was drawn to where Ginny and Lianne were waiting for the car to pass before crossing the road. At once, she leaned forward and banged on the glass partition. When it slid back, she said, 'Stop the car. We've been going round in circles long enough. Those two girls will put us right.' She pointed to them. 'Quickly, man, before they're gone.'

In a minute the car was brought to a halt and the driver was making his way towards Ginny and Lianne. 'Look!' Lianne followed his progress. 'He's coming to speak to us.'

Ginny's gaze was on the car. One day she would have a limousine like that, and a chauffeur to drive her about.

As he approached, the toes of his heavy shoes scooped the sloppy snow like great shovels. 'We're lost,' he said, taking off his cap. 'I'm looking for Leighton Road.'

It was Ginny who answered. 'You're miles away,' she said, indicating behind him. 'Go back to the main road, turn left and carry straight on for about three miles. Leighton Road is right opposite a big garage. You can't miss it.'

'Thank you very much.'

'You're welcome.'

Replacing his cap he gave a polite little nod and returned to his precious car.

Lianne was dumbfounded. 'Why did you send him back in that direction?'

The two of them strolled on, taking their time now, knowing they were in trouble whether they ran or walked.

'Because he's made us late with his silly questions, and because you've already put me in a bad mood.'

'But you've sent him the wrong way!'

'Serves him right for making us late.'

Lianne couldn't help but giggle. 'The poor man will be going round in circles looking for a garage that doesn't exist. I don't know *what* he'll think when he eventually finds Leighton Road and realises he was standing right next to it.'

'He'll think we're a pair of shits.'

'*I'm* not!' Playfully punching Ginny on the arm, she accused indignantly, 'It was you who told him a pack of lies.'

'You could have stopped me.'

'I wouldn't dare.' Something occurred to her then. 'Why do you think he was looking for *our* street? I mean, what would somebody like that be doing round here?'

Ginny wasn't listening. 'Did you see the car?' she asked dreamily. 'One day I'll have a car just like that.'

'Give over! It must have cost a fortune.'

'The best things in life don't come cheap.'

'Where would you get that kind of money?'

'I'll get it, don't worry.' Some inner instinct pushed the words out. 'I was always meant to be rich.'

Lianne's heart fell. She had visions of Ginny stepping out in furs and jewels, laughing wickedly as she drove off in her limousine.

Unbearable loneliness swamped her. Ginny was the devil. But, for reasons she might never understand, she loved her. Loved her more than anyone else on this earth. 'If ever you do get rich, you won't want me, will you?' she murmured. No. Ginny wouldn't want her then. She would never want her again. The loneliness was like a crushing weight inside her.

Unwilling or unable to put Lianne's mind at rest, Ginny told her, 'I do intend to be rich. Don't ever doubt that. I'll have more money than I know what to do with.'

Lianne followed her, sulking but fascinated. 'But where will you get so much money?'

'I might steal it.' Quickening her steps she momentarily left Lianne behind, her voice rising excitedly as she mused aloud, 'I might even marry a wealthy man.' She glanced at her sister. In the glow from the street lamp her eyes glittered like wet coal. 'Go on! Say it, bugger you. You don't believe I could do it.'

''Course I do.' Lianne had no qualms where this beautiful young woman was concerned. A great sadness came over her as she softly answered, 'I know you can do anything you like.'

'So can you if you set your mind to it,' Ginny remarked sharply. She was still angry deep down because she had been cheated out of a peep show.

'No, I can't. I'm not like you.'

Ginny pushed her in through the gate. 'If you're saying I'm the one with the good looks and the guts, and you're the plain one who's also a coward, then you're absolutely right.'

Her cruelty knew no bounds.

But then she laughed and joked, and made Lianne forget. As she always did.

Not surprisingly, it was Lianne who took the blame for being late home. 'I spilled a pot of glue in the art room, and had to stay behind to clean it up,' she lied. 'Ginny stayed to help me.'

Jack didn't know whether to believe her or not. Swinging Lianne round he snatched at the hem of her skirt. 'And did you spill a can of oil while you were at it?' he demanded, glaring from one to the other.

Lianne feigned ignorance. 'I don't know what you mean.'

He yanked his fist upwards and her skirt with it. 'I mean *this!*' he yelled. 'There's oil all over your skirt.'

Lianne swallowed hard. The dark glutinous stain must have come from Old Tom's work-bench. 'I don't know where that came from,' she said lamely.

Jack dropped the hem of her skirt. Ginny had been smirking in the background. Infuriated, he caught hold of them both and forcefully drew them forward. In a voice that was low and shaking, he told them, 'In future, when your mother tells you to come straight home from school, you're to do just that.

Do you understand? Not two hours later, looking the worse for wear, and with your hem covered in oil.' Addressing the next remarks to Lianne, he appealed to her good sense. 'When I came in ten minutes ago your mother was sick with worry. The streets aren't safe these dark nights, and there's talk of a stranger lurking about.'

Indignant, Ginny interrupted, 'Anybody would think we don't know how to take care of ourselves.'

'Don't get clever with me. I've had a hard day. Two of the big ovens packed up, and half the day's work was burned to a crisp. When I get home I find your mother in a rage and you two out, God knows where.' Releasing them now, he stretched out both hands and passed them over his face, as if to erase the weariness.

It wasn't just the bad day, or Liz complaining the minute he stepped through the door. Nor was it the girls being late, though he worried for them every minute of every day. No, there was something else eating away at him, something gnawing at his reason and sending him half-crazy. If he knew what it was, he might be able to deal with it, but he didn't. All he knew was that he sensed something fearful ahead. Something he had not felt for many, many years. An almighty, indestructible sense of evil.

'If you've had a bad day, you still shouldn't take it out on us.' Sensing a weakness in his armour, Ginny pushed in front of her sister. Facing Jack with an expression as stern as his own, she told him, 'It's not our fault if your ovens have gone wrong. You're supposed to be the businessman. You should be prepared for these eventualities.' She prided herself on being educated. Speaking down to her father gave her a great sense of satisfaction.

Jack couldn't believe his ears. 'What was that you said?'

Smirking, she glanced at Lianne before returning her attention to her father. 'I said, you're supposed to be the businessman. You should be prepared for eventualities like the ovens breaking down.'

Suddenly she was reeling backwards, her lip bleeding where he had hit out blindly with his fist. For a moment they stared at each other: she with her hand up and the blood trickling through her fingers, and he with a look of horror that only matched the horror in his darkest memory. For one terrible minute he was back there. In that house. With her. And all around was the smell of death.

'I hate you!' she whispered, yet her voice was so penetrating that she might have been shouting from the rooftops.

He couldn't move. He wanted to say he was sorry, to tell her it was not meant. He could never hurt her. He loved her too much. *Loved her too much*. That was his terrible sin. *Virginia*. Not this one. The other one. The one from his memories.

His heart turned over as he saw the hatred in his own daughter's eyes. Was that why he smothered her with love? With his fear? Dear God! Oh, dear God.

Sensing something beyond her understanding, Lianne moved sideways. Standing beside her sister, she too stared at him. 'You shouldn't have done that,' she chided, looking at the bloodstains on Ginny's blouse. She wanted to hit him, to hurt him like he had hurt Ginny. 'She hasn't done anything wrong.' Oh, but she had. Yet she couldn't help it, because she was bad. Ginny was bad, and there was nothing anyone could do about it.

'I know,' he admitted. Still he couldn't bring himself to say he was sorry. He was not sorry. He was angry and confused, and his whole life seemed to be falling apart.

The sound of the doorbell rang through the room, shattering his nerves. Beyond the room he could hear Liz's voice, and the voice of a stranger, a woman. Yet it wasn't a stranger, for he thought he recognised the woman's voice. Then Liz was saying, 'If you'll wait in here; I'll fetch him.'

In charge once more he ordered the girls, 'You'd better go upstairs. Get washed and changed. Your mother will call you when she's ready.'

As the girls went out, Liz came in. 'There's someone to see you,' she announced. 'They're in the lounge.'

'For Christ's sake, Liz! I don't want to see anyone. What made you invite them in when you know I've a mountain of paperwork to get through?'

A cheeky smile curved the corners of her mouth. 'They look like they're worth a bob or two,' she whispered. 'I shouldn't be too quick to turn them away.' Like Ginny, she had nothing against being wealthy.

Jack would have questioned her further but she hurried out of the room. 'I'll make some tea,' she called. Then she was gone.

Ginny lingered on the stairs. 'Come here.' Plucking at Lianne's sleeve she drew her back. 'Shh!' Crouching on the stair she bade Lianne do the same. With her slim finger she pointed to the lounge, her voice filled with awe as she whispered, 'Look there.'

Lianne leaned forward. The lounge door was open. Straining her neck to see inside, she regarded the two women with interest; the older one with the stern expression, and the other a coarser-looking woman, but with a kinder, softer face. 'Who are they?' She examined Katherine with interest. 'She looks like Miss Havisham from *Great Expectations.*' Certainly, with her stiff regal posture, snow-white hair beautifully coiled at the nape of her neck, and slim hands clasped over her lap, Katherine made a very formidable figure. 'Wonder what they want with our dad.'

Ginny was bewitched. 'Didn't you see them before?' she asked wondrously, her dark eyes intent on Katherine. 'Didn't you see *her*?'

Afraid she might be punished, Lianne regarded Katherine with renewed interest. 'No, I've never seen her before.' Inching away she remarked, 'Why? Have you seen her before?'

Ginny nodded. 'Just now. These are the two biddies in that chauffeur-driven car.' Pointing to Katherine, she suggested,

'She's the important one.' Her whole face lit up as she whispered excitedly, 'She's the one with money.'

Something about her sister's smile, about the way she couldn't take her avaricious eyes off that old lady, was very disturbing. 'We'd better go upstairs.' Beginning to move away she did her best to persuade Ginny that it was folly to remain on the stairs. 'If Dad sees us here, it'll start him off again.'

Long slim fingers reached to press her down. 'Shut up and stay where you are. I want to listen. I have to know why they're here.'

Frightened as a mouse, Lianne remained close, hiding behind her sister, hoping they would not be seen, and silently praying there would be no more trouble.

They watched Jack stride across the hallway. From his set face and purposeful manner it was obvious he was still angry.

Outside the lounge door, Jack cleared his throat, straightened his tie, painted a smile on to his unhappy features and, pushing open the door, stepped inside.

At first his mind couldn't take in what his eyes were seeing. The moment he stepped into that room he was surrounded by everything he had striven for so long to shut out: the past and all that went with it. But now it was here. Like a malevolent presence it wrapped itself round him, suffocating, squeezing the life from him. In one split second the smile had gone from his features and in its place was a look of disbelief. He stared at Katherine for what seemed an age.

'Mother?' It had been so long. So very long, he couldn't be certain. Only his instincts told him the truth.

Katherine was on her feet now, walking towards him. 'I'm sorry, son,' she was saying, 'I had to find you.'

As she came near, he backed away, his insides cringing. His voice was oddly like that of someone else, a young man, not much older than Ginny was now. 'I don't want you in my house.' The words issued through gritted teeth, his head making small violent movements from side to side. *'I never wanted you here!'* Hysteria spiralled inside him, threatening to take his reason.

'Jack?' Liz's entrance had a calming effect. 'Is everything all right?' Looking from one to the other, she laid the tray on the coffee-table.

Maureen stood up, her face wreathed in a smile. 'I'm Maureen Delaney,' she offered in her warm Irish accent. Extending her hand for Liz to shake she diffused the atmosphere with her quick tongue. 'Katherine Louis and meself have travelled all the way from New York to met yer good selves…' In that inimitable, endearing way she rolled her pretty Irish eyes. 'I don't mind telling yer I hated every minute on that blessed aeroplane. What's more I'm dreading the journey back, so I am.'

Liz shook her hand. She was puzzled and intrigued. 'Why would you come all the way from New York, just to meet us?' This time she was looking at Katherine, expecting an answer from her. 'Is it to do with Jack's business?' she wondered. 'Have you a proposition? Is that it? But then, being so far away… how would you know about Jack?' Fear trickled through her and her whole manner changed. 'Who are you?'

It was Jack who answered. For Liz's sake he put on an act. 'In a far bigger way, this lady is also in catering,' he said. It was not altogether untrue. His family had been in catering all their lives. Maybe they still were. He didn't know. 'The company is looking to expand its business abroad… franchises, that kind of thing. I've already told Miss Louis I'm not interested.'

Somewhat subdued by his apparent dismissal of her, Katherine remained quite still, her brown eyes intent on her beloved son.

Just a little flustered, Maureen dropped her gaze to the floor. 'We shouldn't have come here,' she muttered.

'I asked who you are,' Liz said again, 'and I would like an answer.' She looked at Jack and knew he was lying. 'I'm no fool, Jack. Your story doesn't ring true. There's talk of franchises, and making a special journey from New York. Obviously, you would like me to believe these people are in business in a big way. It doesn't seem feasible that they should contact you, a village baker, excellent yes, and with the ability to build your own business in a way you adamantly refuse to do. Yet if by some fluke your name really has been brought to the notice of a bigger company, I believe it would make better sense if that company appointed an agent to contact you.' Flashing an angry glance at each in turn, she saved the most scathing for Jack. 'Somebody is lying here. Is it you, Jack? Or is it them?' She gave Katherine a withering look. 'I don't pretend to know what's going on, but someone had better tell me. And this time I want the truth.'

Feeling his strength drain away Jack crumpled into the chair. 'I should have told you,' he admitted. 'I wanted to, but God help me, I couldn't.'

Liz visibly stiffened. She looked at his handsome face that was now white as chalk. She noticed how guilty he seemed, how small and frightened, how pitifully vulnerable, and her heart ached for him, for herself also. 'Is this about another woman?' she asked pointedly, switching her question to Katherine when he seemed not to have heard. 'Are you here because he's been seeing another woman… has he broken her marriage? Made her pregnant?' She smiled coolly but her blood was burning. 'Is it your daughter? Or granddaughter maybe?'

Jack sat up straight. 'Don't be so bloody stupid!' He wanted to laugh. How could she think he would even look at another woman? Well, maybe he might look. That was any man's privilege. But he would never want another woman over her. God! How enlightening! Here she was thinking he'd been poking his dick where it shouldn't be, when all the time he was battling with his sanity.

Liz knew him well enough to know that now he was telling the truth. Whatever the reason for the strangers being here, it was not because of Jack having messed with some other woman.

'You'd better explain.' Without a word, she gestured for the two women to be seated. Then, without betraying the slightest emotion, she poured the tea, handed each one a cup and offered milk and sugar. That done, she offered the same to Jack. When he abruptly refused, she took her own cup and saucer and sat in the big chair, from where she had an excellent view of everyone. 'Now. The truth, please.'

Katherine felt it was not her place to betray her identity. That was for her son to do. Convinced that she had conducted herself in a proper manner throughout, she now remained silent.

Seated beside her and keeping her own counsel, Maureen Delaney felt like an intruder. Embarrassed and overtaken by circumstances, each quietly and deliberately sipped their tea, while Liz stared expectantly at her husband, waiting for the truth. The atmosphere was tense. The truth too terrible to speak it aloud.

Everyone's attention turned to Jack, and for Jack it was all too much. With a moan he leaned forward, his big hands covering his face for a moment. When the moment was over, he sprang out of the chair and began pacing the floor.

Coming to the fireplace he paused, his arms stretched wide, long strong fingers gripping the mantelpiece as he leaned his whole body weight forward. His sorry eyes raked the empty grate. In the ensuing awful silence, he took the time to think, to deliberate on what to do, when to start, how much to reveal. Like a man torn in two, there was one half of him here, in this room with his mother and his wife, and there was the other half, shocked and afraid, back there in New York. In that house where it all happened. And afterwards, when there seemed no end to the nightmare. Could he tell? Should he? No. Not all of it. He could never tell it all.

Liz's voice cut through his mind. 'I'm waiting, Jack.'

A moment longer. Gathering his thoughts. Gathering his strength. How to start? How to start? What to tell? Not all of it. Some. Just some.

He hung his head, not daring to turn, not wanting to see their faces. It was Liz he cared about. Not the strangers. They didn't belong here. He opened his mouth and a groan escaped his lips. A deep agonising groan that only the strangers understood. Sucking in a long breath he stretched himself to full height. Even now, he dared not turn round.

In a small voice, he told her, 'I'm sorry I lied, sweetheart.' He gave a lopsided grin. 'There I go again, saying sorry.' It seemed such a small thing, unimportant. Why shouldn't he say he was sorry? The idea that Liz might have been tempted to correct him brought him closer to her. It was comforting. In the chaos of his mind, it seemed wonderfully normal.

'Go on, Jack.' Her voice was firm, yet encouraging. It gave him hope.

'I've known our visitors for many years,' he confessed. 'Long... oh, long before I ever knew you, sweetheart.' His chest was tight. He could hardly breathe. He tried desperately to press the words back into that dark terrifying place where they had been hidden away for too long. But they played in his mind, making pictures, flicking through his memory like the remnants of a film. Now the words were on his tongue, and suddenly, without him consciously speaking them, they were out in the open, uttering themselves as though they had a life of their own. 'Maureen Delaney has known me since the day I was born,' he confessed. 'The lady with her is Katherine Rachel Louis.' A pause. Regrets. Then, turning, he raised his gaze to mingle with Liz's quiet one. 'Katherine Louis is my mother.'

There! It was said, and it felt as though a sword had been drawn through his insides.

He saw the shock in her face. He saw how her brows furrowed with confusion, and the pitiful way her hands clung to the chair edge. Ashamed, he closed his eyes. He heard the quick intake of breath and the long gasp when it was exhaled. He felt Liz's disbelieving stare on his face, and knew there was no going back. There would never be any escape. Not now. All these years, and now it was almost over. He felt an immense sense of relief. Even though he knew he would have to pay the price. They would *all* have to pay the price.

The listeners on the stairs were momentarily struck dumb. Like her mother, Lianne gasped aloud, slumping with shock. Ginny's mouth fell open, but soon she was smiling. 'She's our grandmother!' she murmured. 'That wealthy old lady is our grandmother.' Pressing her hand to her mouth she stifled the bubble of laughter that threatened to burst. With her dark eyes peeping over the top of her fingers she laughed at Lianne. 'Don't you see what that means?' she demanded through her fingertips.

Lianne edged away. 'I don't want to know.' She had seen that look in her sister's eyes before and it struck the fear of God into her.

'It means I'll be rich after all.'

'No, it doesn't. Even if she is our grandmother, and even if she's wealthy, it doesn't mean to say you're going to be rich. Even you can see that Dad doesn't want her here. He's never told us about her, has he? We've never known her. We don't know her now, do we? So it isn't likely she'll ever want to leave her money to any of us.'

'You heard what that Irish woman said. Katherine Louis... our grandmother... has come all the way from America to see him.'

'So?'

'So! She's probably ill, dying maybe, and means to leave him everything in her will.'

'That will make Dad rich. Not you.' Lianne didn't like where this conversation might be leading.

'You're right. But he would make a will leaving everything to Mum, and when she dies, it will all come to us.'

'Maybe. When you're as old as they are now.'

Ginny softly laughed. 'You're so innocent.' Rage infused her features. 'Be quiet now. I need to listen.' She also needed to think, and scheme.

Moving stealthily down the stairs, the two girls dared to remain within earshot.

White and shaken, Liz spoke to Jack in a calm dignified voice. 'Please ask them to leave now.'

It was Katherine who spoke next. 'I'm sorry if this has been a shock to you. I had hoped Jack might have told you, but obviously I was wrong.'

Jack's voice intervened. 'My wife wants you to leave, and so do I.' There was regret in his voice. For one blissful respite he had faced the past and found a certain strength. But it was short lived, because once the two women had gone, he would be put through an interrogation. Maybe not as horrifying as the last time, but an interrogation nevertheless.

As the four people emerged from the lounge, the two young women on the stairs pressed back so as not to be seen. From their vantage point they could see everything: their parents, apart now, Liz leading the entourage towards the front door and Jack bringing up the rear. Neither looked at the other but kept their eyes straight ahead, Liz staring at the door as if it was a means of escape, and Jack staring at the tall regal figure of Katherine Louis, with the shock still etched on his face. The smaller, plumper person of Maureen Delaney ambled between, a benign smile on her face and the occasional concerned glance at her elderly companion.

At the door, Katherine offered her apologies. 'But I can't say I wish I hadn't come.' She addressed her remarks to Liz. 'Jack is my son. I'm old, and time is running out. I had to find him. You do understand that?'

Liz was in two minds. She had taken a liking to Katherine. But she could not forgive Jack for lying to her. 'I suppose any woman would have done the same.'

'Can we be friends, do you think?'

'I have nothing against you,' Liz told her, 'and maybe in time we could get to know each other better. But right now I really would like to be alone with my husband.' Opening the front door she stepped aside and waited for them to leave.

Jack said nothing. He too wanted them to leave. He wanted them never to come back. He wanted Liz to smile at him, and tease him in the way she always did. He needed that. He needed to feel that nothing had changed. Please God! Don't let anything change.

Katherine's voice gentled into his thoughts. 'Forgive me, Jack,' she murmured, 'but I have never stopped loving you. In all the years when you were gone, I wanted to find you. Time and again I would have tried, but I know how much you needed to be away from me… from everything. Now I want you back. I have to make up for all those lost years, for us both. I yearn for us to be mother and son again, and when I die, I want you to have what is rightfully yours.'

Jack's face was like stone. 'I want nothing from you.'

'Don't be so unforgiving, Jack. It was a very long time ago. Let me make amends.' Her brown eyes seemed bulbous, streaked with tiny blood vessels. The meeting with her son had left her weaker, emotionally drained. In him she saw his father. The same handsome features, the same wonderful green eyes, the same strong build. It only made her all the more determined that they should never again be parted from each other. 'Don't let me leave without a word of love from you,' she pleaded.

For a moment he was mesmerised. When he left her twenty years ago, she was vibrant, stunning to look at. Now she was weary. And so very old. For the briefest heartbeat he felt the smallest compassion. But it soon passed.

He appealed to Maureen. 'I wish you had never found me,' he said coldly. 'I have a life of my own. There is nothing I want from any of you. Make her see that.'

Maureen's smile was like a lifeline to him. 'I tried to stop her. But she so wanted to find ye.' Her smile flickered. 'Ye haven't changed,' she said fondly, 'still the same Jack. Handsome as ever. Ah, sure it does me old heart good to see ye.' Aware that Katherine was hanging on her every word, she pleaded, 'Try not to be too harsh with yer mammy, because when all's said and done we all make mistakes. She only wants to make amends.'

'It's too late for that,' he said regretfully. A shiver ran down his back. He glanced up to see Ginny hiding in the shadows. 'Take her home,' he urged softly. 'You mustn't stay here any longer.' He could feel Ginny's dark eyes staring at him. His fear heightened. She must have heard everything. Gently propelling the two women towards the door he warned them in a whisper, 'You should never have come here.'

Katherine would not be so easily dismissed. 'I've travelled a long way to see you, Jack,' she declared. 'We're booked in at the Wayside Inn in Leighton Buzzard. I'll wait for your call. You see, I have no intention of leaving until we've resolved our differences.' She reached out to touch his hand but he moved away. Continuing in a faltering voice she revealed, 'We have a great deal to talk about, you and I. Besides, how can you ask me to leave without first meeting your daughters?'

Panic surged through him. Surreptitiously glancing towards the stairway he demanded, 'How do you know about my daughters? How did you find me?' Even as he spoke, realisation dawned. 'Of course!' Throwing back his head like a man reprieved from the gallows, he accused harshly, 'You put a private detective on me, didn't you?' His smile was a mixture of relief and loathing. 'Christ almighty! And I thought it was some bloody lunatic skulking about.' He thought about the way he had made the girls stay in, terrified that they were being stalked, marked by some awful monster from his youth. He recalled the dreadful rows in this house these past few months, and the awful pressure he had been put under, the times he'd sensed he was being followed; the shadowy figure who lurked by the gate at all hours. Jesus! He had even believed he was going insane. In that moment of realisation, he could easily have killed her. 'For pity's sake, have you any idea of the worry you've caused me?'

'I didn't intend that.'

'Just go. And don't ever come back.' Unable to look her in the eye any longer, he stormed away.

Liz was a little more gentle. 'It's been a shock,' she explained. 'You're a stranger to me. I didn't know.' For the first time, Liz felt pity for her. 'He said he had no family… that you were dead.' She had so many questions. 'Why would he say such a terrible thing?'

Katherine knew, but said, 'I can't answer that. You must ask him.'

'Goodbye, Mrs Louis.' Giving the women a moment to negotiate the steps, Liz couldn't help but admire Katherine's courage. After all, she had not received a welcome from her son. Instead she had been turned away. It took a strong woman to bear such cruelty.

While Katherine made her way to the car, Maureen lingered at the foot of the steps. In a low voice that was meant only for Liz's ears, she imparted, 'I'll do me best to make her see she's not wanted, but I'll not promise anything. She's a stubborn old bugger, so she is.' She gave a parting smile.

The smile froze on her lips as she caught sight of Ginny seated on the stairs. For one devastating moment it was not a young woman crouching there. It was an old, old creature, with wild eyes and the look of madness in her face.

Liz couldn't understand. She saw the growing horror in Maureen's eyes. She heard her mutter something unintelligible while making the sign of the cross on herself. Shaken, she looked round. All she saw was an empty stairway.

Afraid but not knowing why, she turned again. She would have spoken. She might have asked if the woman was all right, because she had seemed so disturbed. But Maureen Delaney was already climbing into the car. In a moment it was gone, with the two women closeted in the back. Each was silent. Each struggling with her own secret thoughts.

Jack was waiting in the kitchen. With his back to the cooker, long legs apart and a look of fire in his eyes, he looked set to do battle. 'I know! I know!' Taking a long deep gulp of air he blew

122

out his cheeks and rolled his eyes to the ceiling. 'I haven't been honest with you, and I'm every kind of a bastard.'

Remaining by the door she stared him out. 'You said that, Jack. I didn't.'

'And now you want some answers?'

Her tone was cutting. 'I think so. Don't you?'

He sighed and nodded. Then he swallowed hard and feared the ordeal to come. 'They're on the stairs,' he said.

She frowned. 'Who?' Anger rippled through her. '*Who's* on the stairs?'

'Your daughters. They heard everything.'

'Oh, I see.' It always niggled her, how he called them her daughters, whenever they had done something to displease him. 'Would you like me to call them down? Do you want to explain how they've always had a grandmother and you never even told them?'

'Send them upstairs.'

'Are you sure about that?' She wanted to hurt him the same way he had hurt her, hurt his daughters.

'For Christ's sake, woman! Send them upstairs!' He felt he would go mad. *She* had been here, in his house. She had looked at him and asked for forgiveness. His mother wanted to forget… behave as though it had never happened. Even now he couldn't believe she had actually stood in his house. Katherine Louis belonged to that part of his life he had left behind. Left behind for ever. Why did she have to come here? Now it was all spoiled. Everything he had worked so hard to achieve. His family. The pitifully short measure of peace he had found. Now nothing would ever be the same again.

He could feel her staring at him, hating him in a small way. 'Please Liz.'

She stared at him a while longer. Loving him. Hating him. Wondering how she could ever have imagined she knew him. 'All right,' she murmured. 'If that's what you want.'

Gratitude shone from his eyes. 'Thank you,' he said. Then he watched her go and waited. And the wait seemed like the longest time of his life.

Liz was surprised when the girls went without protest. 'Tomorrow,' she promised, 'we'll talk it through.'

When she returned to the kitchen, Jack was seated at the table, his body leaning forward, his head pushed into the palms of his hands. He looked like a man devastated. 'I should have told you,' he conceded, raising his eyes to hers.

Drawing out a chair Liz seated herself opposite him. 'Tell me now, Jack.' The tone of her voice hardened. 'The truth, mind.'

It took a moment for him to gather his thoughts. 'To be honest there's little to tell. You knew I came from New York. I never kept that from you.' When she merely nodded, he went on, 'What I didn't tell you is that my family are wealthy. The money came from my Irish grandfather's side. He started out much like I have… a small bakery, then he went on to open a chain of foodstores right across the States. Eventually he sold them off and played the stockmarket.' He grinned. 'Turned out that was where his real talents lay. He made millions in the first year. After that he went from strength to strength.'

His expression changed from pride to despair. 'After a while the odds turned against him. He made a bad investment… bought an ailing company and poured a fortune into propping it up. It all went wrong and the strain became too much for him. One day he was a tower of strength. The next he was gone. Struck down.'

Anguished, he wiped his hands over his face. He wanted to tell her the whole truth, but he couldn't. What really happened to his grandfather was so horrible that even he could not come to terms with it. How could he ever expect Liz to understand? She must never, never know.

'What do you mean? How was he struck down?'

Quick, Jack! Think. Think. 'He had a massive stroke.' God forgive me for lying.

'What about the family?' Though still angry because he had not confided in her, Liz was entranced by his every word. 'What about his wife? And your parents.'

Beneath her intense hazel gaze, he feared she might see right inside his soul. He gulped, stared at the table and saw his life enacted there. 'I never knew my father.' Bracing himself against another terrible lie he went on, 'Soon after he and Mother met, she got pregnant. He left and was never seen again.' But he *was* seen again. Not as you might expect, and maybe it was a fitting punishment. But he was seen again, if only for a very short period of time. Before it happened. Before the carnage. And afterwards. For one shocking moment. That moment was woven into his nightmares for all time. His mind began to wander. Was he mad? Was he really mad?

'Jack?' Liz saw him hesitate. Saw him tremble, while beads of sweat tumbled down his face. Sensing there were things he was not telling her, she hoped he would tell her now. There was a note of urgency in her voice. 'You were saying?'

Startled, he seemed to visibly shake himself. With his fists clenched together and his head dropped low, he continued, 'Shortly after Father disappeared, Mother went to live with my grandparents. I was born in their house.'

'Was your mother an only child?'

'No. There was a brother… Cyrus. When Grandfather died, Cyrus believed he would inherit what was left of the business. He was bitterly disappointed when it went to my mother. Of course he was given a sizeable income, but it was a blow. However, he always loved Katherine, so he got over it. Besides everything else, Mother had inherited Grandfather's shrewd business acumen. In all his career, Grandfather made only one mistake. It cost him dear.'

'What? Money, you mean?'

'Not just money.' He groaned from deep inside. 'If I've learned anything at all Liz, I've learned that there are more important things than money.'

'Is that why you've never let your business expand? Because you're afraid of what happened to your grandfather?'

He looked at her then, a strange little glance and a wry little smile. She didn't really know what she was saying. She could never understand the awful implications of her words. 'Yes.' His answer was deliberately vague. 'Because of what happened to Grandfather.'

'What happened when he died?'

'Katherine took up the remains of his company and vowed to turn it around. She did that, and more. And all the time she looked out for her brother, Cyrus. Apparently he was never very stable... respectable, I mean. He had a habit of drinking, gambling, that sort of thing. After Grandfather died, he went completely off the rails for a while. My mother took him into the family home and cared for him. She gave him back his self-respect. Then she gave him equal partnership in the company. Later he met someone, got married, and all seemed fine for a time. Then it went wrong. Mother stood by him. She was his mentor through every step of his life: marriage... the loss of his child... divorce.'

The memories were vivid now. Closing in on him. He felt his chest tightening and took a deep breath.

'You still haven't explained why you lied to me.' This was the real issue with Liz. 'Why did you say your family were dead? What made you break with them? I have to know, Jack. If I'm ever to trust you again, I have to know it all.' Even now, she was not certain whether she could ever forgive him.

'I was nineteen. I had a life to live.' He couldn't tell. He mustn't tell. Instead he fabricated. 'It was the usual thing... family arguments. Mother trying to make me do what I didn't want to do.'

'Force you into the family business, you mean?'

'She wanted that, yes.' He was telling the truth now, and it felt good, but he must be careful not to let his tongue run away with him. 'It was Katherine's dream... that her only son would eventually take over the company.'

'But you didn't want that?'

He shrugged his shoulders. 'Things didn't turn out that way,' he said cautiously. 'Things never turn out the way you expect.'

'I can sympathise with your mother.'

'Oh?'

'Well, I'm a mother myself. I know how infuriating it can be. One of these days it wouldn't surprise me if Ginny took off… just like you left the family. Only I hope she doesn't bury us before our time.'

A dark rage rushed through him as he grabbed her hand, so hard her features grimaced with pain. 'What do you mean, bury us before our time?' It wasn't rage now. It was terror. Sheer terror.

'What in God's name do you think I mean? I hope she never tells anyone we're dead while we're still alive and kicking. Like you did, Jack! Like you bloody well did!' With one mighty effort she freed her hand from his. 'You're the one at fault here, not me. Just remember that.' Thrusting the chair away she went to the window where she looked out across the dark night. It had never frightened her before. It frightened her now.

'How could you leave your family, Jack? How could you just walk out like that?'

'I was nineteen, for Christ's sake! I had a whole life to live.'

'What about your mother? How do you think she felt… all those years without a word from you.' She tossed her head in anger and felt a shade better. 'You're a bastard, Jack!'

He hung his head, softly muttering, 'You don't know.'

'What did you say?'

'Nothing! I said nothing.' He wanted to hurt her. God help him, he wanted to hurt her before she hurt him.

Liz was calmer now. Hopelessly intrigued. 'Where does the other woman come into this? The one who came here with your…' The word 'mother' stuck to the roof of her mouth. Somehow she couldn't say it. 'With Katherine?'

'Maureen Delaney, you mean? Oh, she was always there. Katherine found her on the streets of New York and took her home. It was she who raised me. Maureen's a good soul. She's been Katherine's maid, housekeeper, friend and confidante for as long as I can remember.'

Liz thought she knew her husband. Only now did she realise that she had been living with a stranger. 'I can understand why your grandfather couldn't leave his business to an only son who drank and gambled. But why would he leave it to his daughter? Why not to his own wife?'

This was it. This was the one he had hoped she might not ask. But she had, and now he would have to be careful. 'Grandmother had no head for business,' he answered. 'She was very beautiful. Bewitching, some said. She could spend money in every conceivable way, but she had no idea how to earn it.'

'You didn't like her, did you?'

Unaware that she had seen the repugnance on his face, he was shocked to the core by her questions. 'What a thing to say!'

'It's true though, isn't it? You didn't like her.'

What he didn't like was being drawn in, and Liz was already drawing him in deeper than he intended to go. He had answered with too many lies. Now he gave her a glimmer of the truth. 'My grandmother was everything to me,' he murmured. 'She was kind and warm and I adored her more than I can ever say.' What he had felt for his grandmother was very special. A once-in-a-lifetime relationship which not even death could destroy.

Expecting an altogether different answer, it was Liz's turn to be shocked. 'Was she Katherine's mother?'

'Yes.'

'Does your mother look like her?'

'Katherine inherited Grandmother's long slim limbs. Other than that there is no likeness... not in feature, nor in nature. Katherine has brown eyes while Grandmother had the most magnificent midnight eyes. Her hair was thick and rich. In the moonlight it shone like fire. She was aloof. Mysterious. A thinker.' Suppressing the other, bad things, he smiled at her memory. 'She was secretive... devious even. No one ever knew what she was thinking. She was beautiful and she knew it. Men danced attendance on her, and she led them on.' He laughed aloud. But just as quickly the laughter subsided and he was sad. 'When she died, it was as though someone had drawn a dark blanket over the sky.'

Liz was shocked. Crossing the room she sat before him, her voice incredulous. 'Jack, do you know what you're saying?'

He stared her in the face, his dark brows furrowed in puzzlement. 'You asked me a question and I answered it.' The frown hardened. 'What more do you want?'

In a hushed voice, Liz brought him back to that answer, to the vivid description of his grandmother. 'Just now, when you were telling me about your grandmother... you could have been describing Ginny.' It seemed uncanny. It seemed perfectly natural. So why did it make the hairs on the back of her neck stand up?

Again she had touched on something hideous. 'You're right,' he confessed softly. 'I've always thought Ginny inherited my grandmother's great beauty.' And what else, he feared? What else had been passed down?

Liz was curious. 'What was your grandmother's name?'

He took a moment to compose his thoughts before coolly answering, 'Virginia. My grandmother's name was Virginia.'

'I can't believe it!' She stood up and her fury towered over him. 'You really are a bastard! *You* chose her name. She was our firstborn and you so wanted to choose the name. How could you give our daughter your grandmother's name, and not tell me? All the time... in the hospital when I held her in my arms and we said how beautiful she was... at the church when she was baptised... *Our* daughter was given your grandmother's name, and I didn't even know.' She hit him then, punching him so hard that he reeled backwards. 'What other secrets are you keeping from me, Jack? What else do you know that I don't? All these years I've been married to a stranger.' At first she was crying for herself, then she was crying for him. And the sadness crept through her heart like cold cruel fingers.

Jack scraped back his chair and stood up. Unable to look her in the face he stared over at the door, then he stared at the ceiling, biting his lip until he could feel the salty taste of blood beneath his tongue. 'I'm sorry if I hurt you, sweetheart,' he murmured softly, at last bringing his troubled gaze to her pretty face. 'You know I would cut off my arm before I'd hurt you.'

Returning his gaze, she thought about what he had done… about the strange secret he had kept, and the even stranger reason why he had kept it. She didn't feel satisfied with his explanation. She felt unsure. A little afraid without knowing why. And she wondered how to cope, how to accept this unexpected intrusion into their lives without too much disruption. He had a mother, and an uncle. He had a whole existence she had never suspected. Right from the first he had deceived her. He had no family, he had told her, and she had believed him, when all the time he was lying. Not only did he have a family, but they were filthy rich. He had had a grandmother too. Judging by the look in his eyes when he spoke of her, he must have adored her. Suddenly she was jealous. Insanely, stupidly jealous. This grandmother, who sounded like the mirror image of Ginny, had known Jack's love, had seen him grow, had been there when she was not. The jealousy grew until it felt like a hard stone inside her. Damn you, Jack! How could you give your precious grandmother's name to our firstborn without confiding in me? He was sorry, he said. He *should* be sorry.

Unaware of the turmoil going on in Liz's head, Jack waited for some sort of forgiveness. There was anger in him too. Anger because his mother had rooted him out from a safe hiding place. But she had always been able to do that. When he was small and didn't want to be found, it was always she who found him. He loved her. He hated her. Jekyll and Hyde. He could never tell who was who.

While he waited, Liz waited also, her fingers drumming on the tabletop, jarring his nerves, the rhythmic sound echoing in his fevered mind, louder and louder until he thought he would scream.

When he could bear it no longer he reached out and silently closed his fingers over hers. His gaze bathed her face. Growing softer. Pleading. Her fingers were still beneath his now. Small and warm, and still. And hopelessly trapped.

Astonished at his silent gesture, Liz made no effort to release her fingers. There was something wonderful about his long hard fingers coveting hers. His hand was warm and protective. She liked that. The quick pulse of his blood danced with hers, and she was fired to passion. He could have taken her then, any way, and she would not mind. But there was something else between them now, something she did mind. Something that had to be settled.

'What about the girls?'

'Later,' he promised wearily, 'I'll deal with that later.'

He lifted his hand and the cold rushed in. Liz silently chided herself for spoiling the moment. When he spoke again, she bristled.

'Leave the girls to me,' he said, 'especially Ginny. You have a knack of getting on the bad side of her.'

Snatching away, she retorted, 'Oh, I see! So it's me that's in the wrong, is it? Sod you! How do you always manage to turn the fault on to me?'

'Just leave them to me, that's all I ask.' He had no idea how he would tell them, or even how much. But tell them he must. There was no option.

'They were on the stairs.' She took wicked delight in telling him that.

His face whitened. 'When?'

'Just now. They were listening... watching.'

'How much do they know?' He didn't want them to know only half a tale. Nor did he want them imagining things.

'I'm not sure. They must have heard most of what was said.'

131

They were startled when Ginny's voice intervened. 'We heard enough to know we have another family.' She waited until she had their attention, before continuing in accusing tones, 'I don't care how you fell out with your family all those years ago. It doesn't even matter to me whether you loathed the sight of your own mother. The truth is, you had no right to deprive us of grandparents.'

Lianne stood a little way back, half-hidden behind her sister. Her face was expressionless. Though her eyes surveyed the scene with interest, she remained silent.

Jack stiffened. 'Don't tell me what rights I have where you're concerned. You know nothing of your grandmother, and you know nothing of the circumstances that drove me away.'

Ginny stood her ground, head high and equally scathing. 'You lied to us. We should hate you for that.'

Jack was out of his depth. He wanted to slap Ginny's beautiful, hostile face. Conversely he wanted to take her in his arms and make amends for cheating them. But no! He hadn't cheated them. He may even have saved them. Yes! That's what he'd done. He had saved them. The day might come when they would thank him for that.

'I want you to bring her back, so we can talk, all of us, as a family.' Like a dark stranger, Ginny's voice crept into his thoughts.

Something snapped inside him. 'That will never happen,' he roared. 'Katherine Louis will never again step foot inside this house.' Already she had tainted it. The smell of death was everywhere. Just like before.

'Then we'll go to her.' Defiant. Always defiant.

He realised then, and smiled. 'Ah! I see now what you're really after.' There were times when Ginny was so like his own grandmother it was unnerving.

'I don't know what you mean.' The eyes were deep as the darkest ocean. The mind also.

'Don't play games. You heard her say how she meant to leave me what was rightfully mine.'

'I still don't know what you're getting at.' She half-turned when her sister moved a little closer. The feel of Lianne so close, so nervous, was grossly irritating.

'You like the idea of being wealthy, don't you, Ginny? You think if you get close enough to your grandmother, she might leave you a sizeable chunk of her fortune?'

This time it was Lianne who spoke. Emerging to side with her beloved sister she declared, 'There's nothing wrong with wanting to have money, is there?'

His face hardened. 'Hmm! So now she's got you thinking the same way.' He gave Liz a wry little smile. 'See what mercenary creatures we've bred?' Without waiting for a reply, he strode across the room and, brushing past the girls at the door, he snapped, 'I need some fresh air. The old crow's left a nasty taste behind.' Moreover, Katherine had left part of herself behind, and it was that which he feared above all else.

The night was black and forbidding. Long, thin slivers of cold reached inside him, toying with his senses, making him curl into himself. He shivered aloud, shrinking his neck deeper into the collar of his coat. He couldn't get warm. So cold. He couldn't think straight.

Ramming his hand into his pocket he groaned with relief when his fingers touched the hard metal keys. 'The bakery,' he muttered. By now everyone would have gone home. It would be silent as the grave, and warm. Hours after the ovens were turned off they still emitted a degree of warmth. Yes. He would go there, where he could get his mind in some sort of order. There was so much to think through. He felt overwhelmed by all that had happened. His mother was here and, like before, he was afraid.

The ghost of a smile lifted his stony features as he changed direction. A cat scuttled across his path. 'Black cat for luck,' he noted aloud. But it would take more than a black cat to change the tide of events.

With grim face he hurried to the door of the bakery, slid the key in the lock and let himself inside the building. The warmth struck home and he felt a little easier.

Just for a moment he remained by the door, his ear cocked to the rafters. Silence greeted him. Then the smallest sound, like the scraping feet of a rat. Better not be rats in here, he thought, or the health authorities will have me out of business before I can turn round. He waited a minute longer, but the sound never came again. 'It's the old timbers moving,' he muttered, walking towards his office. 'Wouldn't surprise me if this place wasn't haunted.'

Liz couldn't sleep. Four times she got out of bed, and each time she glanced at the clock. First it was half past eleven, then midnight. Then the third time she'd gone to the window it was four minutes past one, and now it was almost two a.m.

'You bugger, Jack.' She wondered if she'd nagged him too much – or not enough?

She was trying desperately to give up smoking, but now the craving was too much. Going to the dresser she dug deep into the drawer, sighing aloud when her fingers touched a pack of ten. Plucking them out she searched another drawer for a lighter, lit a cigarette up and drew long and hard on it. You're weak, she told herself. Her eyes instinctively turned towards the door. You're weak and Jack's a liar. Ginny's right. You're a bloody pathetic pair. Fine example you are to your daughters.

She paced the floor again, angry, afraid, wanting to go after him, but not wanting to. 'Where the hell are you, Jack?' She blamed herself for not being sympathetic. What kind of wife are you? she demanded of herself. Your husband's mother turns up out of the blue and all you can do is give him a hard time.

She sat on the bed, her mind racing. Where was he? Jack wasn't the kind to desert his family. But you never knew. Suddenly she was filled with panic, pacing the floor again. What would my life be like if Jack walked out on me? The thought brought her only despair. The trouble was, in spite of his faults, in spite of everything, she loved him.

She stubbed out the cigarette in a pot-plant: 'Filthy habit,' she muttered with shame. She then sat on the edge of the bed, picked up the receiver and dialled a number, muttering, 'Probably the only time in his life when he needed me most… and I turned on him like a mad dog.' Pressing the phone to her ear she listened to the clicks as the number rang through, then the clear tones as it echoed out. She let it ring for a long time. No answer. 'Damn it!'

She paced again, and sat down again, redialled the number, and still there was no answer. She had dialled that number so many times she knew it by heart. Instinct told her there would be no answer. Either he wasn't at the bakery as she thought, or he guessed it was her and wouldn't answer.

She tried once more. She imagined him there, then he was not. In her mind's eye she saw the office with its tall cream and brown filing cabinets in the corner; the old leather-topped desk, strewn with papers and paraphernalia; a faded carpet that had seen better days; and the windows, sparkling clean. Jack had a thing about being able to see out, as though he was caged. A young lady came in twice a week and cleaned the windows. She emptied the wastepaper bins and vacuumed the faded carpet. She wasn't pretty, thank goodness, or Liz might have been just the teeniest bit jealous.

There was an emptiness to the ringing of the telephone, a certain echo that told her the place was empty. 'I should have sided with you against the girls,' she told the receiver. 'If I don't stand with you, who else will?' Back came her own answer. 'No one.' All she had was Jack and all Jack had was her. It was obvious he wanted nothing to do with that old woman… that stranger… his mother. She shivered as though cold water had just poured down her back. With a slow, extravagant gesture she dropped the receiver into its cradle. Who was she to tell him what he should and shouldn't do?

The sight of the girls came into her mind then. For one awful minute she hated them both. I wish we'd never had any children, she thought forlornly. I'm sorry, Jack, but somewhere along the way I seem to have lost you.

Unsettled, she threw herself into the chair and prepared to wait. It was no good going to bed, because she wouldn't sleep. I've slept with you for too many years, she mused. When you're not beside me, when I can't feel the warmth of your body, I can never sleep. But she was tired, so very tired. It wasn't long before she closed her eyes and drifted into a shallow, restless slumber.

In her room, Ginny sat on the floor, cross-legged, with her outstretched hands resting on her knees. Her eyes were closed. There was a serenity about her face that fascinated Lianne, who was lying on the bed face down with her legs bent into the air.

'Ginny?' Her voice was tremulous. Unnerved and restless after the events of the evening she needed her sister's company. 'Ginny? Please, Ginny, don't go to sleep.'

Slowly, Ginny opened one eye, a dark seeing thing that gave no comfort to the watching girl. 'Be quiet.' The voice was soft, curiously invasive. The eye closed, and all was silent.

Lianne had a knack of reading her sister's mind. She read it now. 'No, Ginny. I don't want you to kill her.'

The one eye opened. 'Kill who?'

'You know who.'

The eye closed.

'You won't kill her, will you?'

The eye opened. 'Go to your own room.'

'I'm afraid to.'

A low wicked laugh. 'You're *always* afraid.'

'It's you that makes me afraid.'

'Stop talking.'

The eye closed. Muscles stiffened. Hard and unyielding. The mind also.

For what seemed a lifetime, Lianne lay on the bed, very still, powerless to speak yet wanting to scream; powerless to move, yet wanting to run. Ginny was in one of those strange, frightening moods. When she was like this there was no reaching her. Still fascinated in spite of herself, Lianne lay motionless, her face turned towards Ginny. There was something uniquely compelling about that ramrod-straight figure, with its perfect, uplifted face. Even though the eyes were closed, they saw. They saw everything.

After a while, Lianne's tired eyes rolled upwards towards the small carriage-clock on the dresser. It was almost two a.m. Sleep threatened to engulf her. But she mustn't sleep. This was Ginny's bed.

Keeping a watchful eye on Ginny, she waited. It could be a minute or it could be an hour. No matter. She would wait. She had waited many times before. Eventually, Ginny would visibly relax the stiff posture. She would stretch her arms high above her head and sigh. She would smile that bewitching smile, and everything would be all right. It was always all right when Ginny smiled.

She settled into the bedspread. Comfortable now. But so tired.

The eye opened. It turned its dark light towards the bed and smiled. 'Don't be afraid,' the voice whispered. 'I'll let you sleep peacefully.'

Silently now, Ginny rose from her disciplined position and went on soft footsteps out of the room. Carefully, she turned the doorknob and shut the door behind her.

Pausing outside her mother's room, she pressed her ear to the door. She had heard her mother pacing the room, but now all was silent. Satisfied, she continued downstairs where, lingering only to put on her outdoor clothes, she took a moment to recall snippets of a conversation: 'Leighton Buzzard. Wayside Inn.' A long, satisfied sigh. 'Grandmother.'

As she went into the night, the purpose of her journey made her smile. Her smile was incredibly beautiful.

When the knock came on the bedroom door, it was Maureen who opened it. 'I'm sorry it's so late,' she told the bleary-eyed clerk. 'It's just that we can't sleep and, what with one thing and another, sure we've had little to eat all day.'

The clerk was a little man with a big headache. He had a family of four and a pitiful wage. He hated rich privileged folk, and he didn't take kindly to being summoned by two ageing biddies at this hour of the morning. 'It's no trouble at all, ma'am,' he lied. Swallowing his resentment he placed the tray on the table between the armchairs. 'Enjoy your snack,' he said, backing away.

'We won't disturb ye again,' Maureen promised, discreetly pressing a five-pound note into his hand.

'That's very generous. Thank you.' Just for a minute, he hated himself for hating them. 'If you need anything else, just ring.' Stuffing the note into his trouser pocket he hastily retreated.

Katherine looked very gracious. Swathed in a cream silk robe she was seated in the tall-backed wicker chair. Her long silver hair was brushed smooth, and her hands shook as she stroked one against the other. 'I'm sorry, my dear,' she apologised. 'It was wrong of me to wake you.'

Maureen rebuked her. 'Aren't we friends?'

'We are.'

'Then what are friends for?'

'All the same, you were deep asleep when I came in just now.'

Chuckling, Maureen warned, 'Yer very fortunate I didn't lash out when I saw ye standing by me bed, though.' She chuckled. 'Sure, I'd forgotten we each had a key to that door.' Glancing at the door which linked the two rooms, she explained, 'I fell asleep after watching that late-night ghost film, and suddenly I'm woke by a figure with long silver hair and a sorry white face, standing by me bed and whispering in me ear.' She blew out her cheeks and rolled her eyes to heaven. 'Lord preserve us, I almost knocked ye from one end of the room to the other. Be Jaysus, ye gave me a bloody fright, so ye did!'

'I didn't want to be alone. Suddenly my own room seemed too big and lonely. Suddenly *life* seemed too big and lonely.'

Maureen affectionately patted her hand. 'Then ye did right to wake me, so we'll hear no more of ye being sorry.' She began to pour the chocolate. 'We'll sit and talk a while. Then we'll finish this little lot and get a good night's sleep. Sure we'll feel all the better for it in the morning.' She poured Katherine a good measure of the hot chocolate. 'Get that down ye,' she ordered in her bossy, inimitable way.

'You're right.' Katherine felt better already.

'Aren't I allus right?' Maureen declared cheekily.

'You were right about Jack, too.' Katherine lapsed into a quiet mood. 'He doesn't want me here.'

'Does it surprise you?' Taking her own cup, the Irish woman sat in the chair opposite.

'He's my son. He should never forget that.'

'Mebbe. But aren't ye forgetting something?'

Katherine frowned. 'That it's been twenty years?'

'There is that, yes.' Her eyes surveyed that old face and her love swelled. 'Then there's the other business. Have ye forgotten that?'

'You know I could never forget.'

'So what makes ye think yer son should forget?'

'Because he's young. Because his life is ahead of him, while mine is almost past.'

'That isn't the issue here and ye know it.'

Katherine smiled then, a wry little expression that spoke volumes. 'It's obvious you have something on your mind, my dear, so you might as well say what you're thinking.'

'I'm probably thinking the very same as yerself.'

Weary, Katherine put down her cup and leaned back in the chair. Suddenly she felt old as time itself, old in every bone of her body, old and feeble, and despairing of life itself. 'Oh, Maureen, it was all so long ago.'

'It might as well have been only yesterday, and well ye know it. Ye can't forget and neither can I. Cyrus… Jack… we all remember every detail vividly. Jack more than any of us, for wasn't it that poor lad who walked into the nightmare? Wasn't it he who got the blame, when all the while the poor soul was as innocent as you or me? Wasn't it yer own darling son who was nearly locked away, could have been executed even, for something he didn't do? And yer own brother Cyrus, so affected by what she did that he spent two whole years in a home for the insane.'

Katherine's eyes filled with tears as she defended the brother she loved. 'Cyrus was deeply affected by what happened. He had a breakdown. He was never insane.'

'Aw, sure don't I know that, me darling?' Quickly now, she made the sign of the cross on herself. 'Lord love and preserve us, it's a wonder we didn't all lose our minds. But d'ye see what I mean?' She sighed and folded her hands and bent forward, her head drooping; her pretty, soulful eyes locked into Katherine's pitiful gaze. 'Ah, look now, I know how ye must feel, but we should never have come here. Can't ye see what ye've done? Jack was trying to put it all behind him, and now ye've delivered it all to his doorstep… the badness and the pain.' She hesitated, not wanting to hurt or apportion blame, but it had to be said. 'Ye wronged him twenty years ago when ye believed he might have done all those dreadful things. Now, in coming here, ye've wronged him again.'

She reached out to touch the old lady's hand, her voice dripping with sadness when the touch was refused. 'Let's go home before it's too late. Before the badness is let loose again.'

'It won't be.' There was a rush of loathing in the old one's face as she stared at the other woman. 'You disappoint me, my dear. I hoped you would understand.' The sigh came from her soul. 'I'm too old to worry about right and wrong any more. I need my family about me. I need my son. And my granddaughters.' Her face softened. 'I saw them sitting on the stairs. Oh, it will be good to have young people close again.'

A look of horror flitted over Maureen's features. 'I didn't think ye'd seen them.' She lowered her voice intimately. 'The older one. Did ye get a good look at her?'

Katherine nodded, but couldn't meet her gaze. 'I saw her.'

Maureen's eyes grew wide with fear. 'In the light from the landing, did ye see how her hair shone… like fire? Did ye see the dark glint in her eyes, like the glint of a devil in moonlight?' Her voice grew incredulous. 'Did ye see? *Do ye know what it means?*'

'I don't want to talk any more.' Making no effort to leave, she deliberately sipped at her chocolate. Back there, in Jack's home, she had seen everything just as Maureen described it. The young woman whom she assumed to be Virginia. The one who carried her own mother's name, the consequences of which she dared not think about. Maureen had seen, and now she was in terror. Katherine was duty bound to hear her out because, like it or not, Maureen was the echo of her own conscience.

'Virginia by name. Virginia by nature.' The implication was chilling.

'Your imagination runs away with you.' Anger. And the smallest, unmistakable terror. 'I won't listen!'

Undeterred, the Irish woman painted the picture in the other one's mind. 'The same fiery hair. The eyes that could be yer own mother's. *The eyes of a madwoman.*' Taking a deep, shuddering breath she went on relentlessly. 'The same tall, stately build. A smile that destroys while it caresses. And the name. *Her* name.' She shook her head frantically. 'Knowing what he does, why would he give her your mother's name?'

'You know how much he loved my mother before… before…' It was on the tip of her tongue, but to utter the words would make it seem too alive, too real.

'Say it, why don't ye? Before she went mad. Before she slaughtered so many innocent souls.'

'*No!* I don't want to hear it.'

But she had to, because Maureen would not be silenced. Desperate to make her see how they should leave well alone and get the next flight to America, she insisted, 'What if she really is like her great-grandmother? Oh, ye might say, what does it matter if she has the same hair and eyes, the same build and the same name. She's of this time and yer mother was of the past. Ye might say there are generations between. *Jack's daughter is not insane!* Ye might say that. Ye might even believe it. But can ye be sure? Can ye really be sure she isn't yer mother all over again?'

'It's you that's being wicked now. Jack's daughter can't help inheriting her great-grandmother's features.'

'Ye have to listen to me, Katherine. This young woman has taken so many of yer mother's genes. Outwardly she's so like yer mother it makes my skin crawl. What about *inside?* Is she the same? How can we know whether she has a killer's instinct? Is she mad too? What about the teacher... the one who drowned? Jack's daughter was there. Did she drown that poor woman?'

'It's you that's mad.' Rage kindled in her.

'Listen to me, Katherine. All I'm asking is, can ye be sure? When ye looked at the girl, did ye see beyond the face, beyond the image of yer own mother? Did ye see the badness? Did ye feel a sense of horror? Because, God help me, I did.'

'You won't frighten me.' Over the years Katherine had come to realise how her old Irish friend had developed a sixth sense. In her heart she too believed that Jack's daughter was the essence of everything evil. But she could not turn a blind eye. Not this time. 'I don't agree with what you're saying,' she lied, 'but if, and I'm only saying if, the girl is bad, then it's all the more reason for us to stay. We didn't see it coming last time. This time we can watch and be ready.' She looked at Maureen in the strangest way. 'I would never let it happen again. Believe me. If, as you say, she is evil, then I will simply have to deal with it.'

Momentarily taken aback by the malign glint in the old lady's eyes, Maureen couldn't believe what her mind was telling her. 'What do ye mean… deal with it?'

For one unnerving moment, Katherine's smile was uncannily like that of her own mother as she softly answered, 'I would have to kill her, of course.'

Subdued and nervous, Maureen could not speak. For the very first time she wondered whether the madness had risen in Katherine. Maybe it was always there and, because she idolised the old lady, she had never seen it. Frantically, she cast her mind back, to the time when Katherine's own mother had shocked the whole of America, and the world, with her heinous crimes. Her heart turned over. Surely to God Katherine was not involved. Her mind was doing somersaults. It wasn't possible. But it was! It was!

The sound of sobbing brought her back to the moment, to the room, and the pitiful creature before her. 'Please, Maureen. Don't let's assume the worst. We've crossed an ocean to be here with my son and his family. I beg you, don't spoil it for me.' Taking a dainty frilled handkerchief from the cuff of her robe she dabbed at her eyes. 'Anyway, the girl is as normal as you or I.'

'We see what we want to see. I looked into those beautiful eyes and I saw something terrible there.'

'You're wrong.'

'I want to leave here.' More so now she had detected something odd in Katherine. She began to wonder whether she herself was affected. Or was it Jack's daughter? Was the evil already touching all of them?

Turning her head Katherine stared into the fireplace. The coals were dying. Life… flickering away. Like those other lives long ago. So many lives. 'No one will hurt us,' she murmured. 'There is nothing to be afraid of.'

'Oh, but there *is* something to be afraid of!' Fearful now, Maureen sprang out of her chair and hurried through the adjoining door. A moment later she returned with a small valise.

Katherine sat bolt upright. 'That's mine. What do you think you're doing?'

'I know what ye carry about in this case. What I don't know is *why* ye carry it about.' Laying the valise on the table, she withdrew a sheaf of papers. Clutching them in her fist she demanded, 'How can ye say there's nothing to be afraid of? And what do ye mean to do with these? Will ye show them to Jack? Is that it? Do ye want to send the poor man right over the edge?'

Grey faced, Katherine defended herself. 'I would never do that.'

'Then why have ye brought them?'

'Because they belong with me.'

'No!' Bending over the old lady, her voice little more than a whisper, Maureen declared, 'They're wicked and evil.' Raising the papers to her face she sniffed at them. 'They reek of death. They don't belong with ye. They belong with the Devil.'

'Put them back!'

'When I've made ye see sense. When ye tell me we're going home. When ye promise to leave Jack and his family alone. That's when I'll put them away... for good. But, until then, I want ye to know what ye're carrying around with ye. Not fond memories. Not a cherished keepsake of loved ones. What ye've kept is evil. It's corrupted us all. It's corrupting us now. Something terrible is happening here. We'll end up suspecting each other. The badness is not dead. Can't ye see that? It's here. It's in these papers. Everywhere we turn it will follow us, for the rest of our lives.' Her voice softened. 'It's time to let go.' Brandishing the papers, she pleaded, 'Let me burn these. Let's leave this place and go home. Right now.'

She made a move towards the fireplace, but the old lady's hand moved quicker. Like iron it gripped her, held her there. 'If you do, I'll kill you!' Sitting on the edge of her seat her eyes looked bulbous, jutting out from her face like small stabbing beacons.

The other woman stared hard at her, searching for something she might easily recognise. In a small scathing voice she asked, 'What's happening to us, Katherine?'

'You!' The word spat out. 'What right have you to go into my private papers? Interfering. Always interfering! What I do is my own affair, and I'll thank you to mind your own business. You're nothing to me. You're not a relative. You have no family, so how can you possibly understand how I feel? I lost part of my family through no fault of my own and I want it back. I don't want you. You make me feel guilty. You frighten me, *just as she did*.' Her face contorted with grief and pain, she went on mercilessly, 'I'm beginning to hate you. I ought to send you packing. Throw you out on to the streets where I found you!'

Incensed, Maureen could hardly contain herself. 'Do it then, why don't ye?' she cried. 'Happen I'd be glad to get away from ye an' all. Happen I've had enough of yer spoiled ways and selfish manner.' It was too late to hold back. The words tumbled out before she could stop them. 'Just now, I saw something in ye that reminded me of yer mother. Mebbe ye're insane too. But it doesn't matter to me any more. I would have died for ye, Katherine Louis. Now I don't care what happens to ye. So, go on! Throw me out on to the streets. Or maybe I'll save ye the trouble.' Swinging round she would have stormed out, but Katherine took hold of her, pressing her down, staring into those pretty blue eyes that were now alive with malice.

'I'm sorry,' she whispered. The bulbous eyes paled. The tears ran down that aged face, following the creases and folds, meandering to her chin and dripping to her chest. 'I can't let you destroy them.' Grabbing the papers she clutched them to her heart, a world of pain in her voice as she murmured, 'They're all I have left of her.'

Composed now, and moved by the old lady's plight, Maureen gently caressed her. 'No, they are not all ye have left, me darling. Ye have yer memories,' she consoled. 'Before, when ye were small, when she was yer mother, and you her daughter.

When everything was as it should be. These were the good times. These are the memories ye ought to keep.' Tapping her chest, she murmured, 'In here. Keep the good memories safe in here.'

The old lady clung to her. In Maureen's arms she felt safe and secure, just as she had when she was a child, when her mind would be crushed by awful, merciless headaches, and her mother would hold her, just as Maureen was holding her now, and yes, they *were* the good times. When there was no premonition of what would happen later. *What might happen again.*

But she dared not think on that. There was too much fear still. Too much that would finally destroy them all. Maureen was right to be afraid. Deep down, in her darkest heart, she too was afraid. She wanted the papers destroyed. Oh, the many times she had yearned to burn them, but how could she do that, when the faces of her loved ones stared back at her? *Destroy them!* she silently pleaded now. *Keep them!* The struggle never ended.

'I'll put them back, shall I?' In the face of such sadness, Maureen relented. There would be another time. A time when the burning of those papers would not be so painful.

The old lady stirred in her arms. 'I'm so tired.' Tired of living, she thought. Tired of being afraid.

'Come on then, me darling.' Astonished at how light and frail the old lady seemed, Maureen helped her to her bed. 'See, I'm putting them back where I found them.' Replacing the papers in the valise, she then returned it to the top shelf of the wardrobe. 'Get off to sleep now. If you want anything ye know where I am. Otherwise I'll join ye for tea in the morning.'

But it was not to be.

Never again would the two women sit across a table and talk of things close to their hearts.

The evil was close. Already the room smelled of death.

Heavy eyed, and drained by the bitter exchange, Katherine watched her old friend leave. She heard the familiar click as the door was pulled to and the lock rammed home. 'Goodnight,' she whispered. 'In the morning I'll make it up to you.' There had been times before when she and Maureen had crossed swords, but there had never been a time when she could so easily have taken the other one's life and watched her die with a sense of satisfaction. She sighed. It was those papers. If only she could find the strength to burn them. The truth was, Katherine did not have that much strength left in her. Not now. It was all used up twenty years ago, back there, when her mother was strapped into the electric chair and paid for her foolishness.

Raising her face to the ceiling, she smiled, a wicked sorry gesture that made her feel ashamed. You did wrong, Mother. I'll never really know why you did it. But love makes us do strange things, don't you think? The smile fell away and in its place came such despair that it was too much to bear. *Life* was too much to bear. Sleep was impossible.

She lay quiet for a moment longer, after which she got out of bed, tiptoed across the room and put her ear to the door. 'You've a nasty streak in you, Maureen Delaney,' she chuckled, 'but I expect it serves me right for taunting you.'

Satisfied she would not be disturbed, she went to the wardrobe and got out the valise. 'They're mine,' she muttered sourly. 'I won't burn them, ever!'

Climbing into the bed she took the valise with her, cradling it as though it were a baby, stroking it and softly singing, 'Rock-a-bye baby in the tree-top... when the wind blows the cradle will rock...' She was a child again, and her mother was singing to her.

Suddenly she was silent, jerking her head up like a sparrow in fear. 'Who's there?' Silence. Unnerving silence.

She listened intently, her heart beating so fast she could hardly breathe. The silence was nerve-racking. From the street below, the low throaty sound of a car horn was startling. Reassured, she softly chuckled, mentally shaking herself.

'Maureen's right,' she muttered nervously, 'we could *all* be going mad.'

A quick glance about, then she took out the papers, lovingly caressing them as she feverishly laid them on the bed. There were fourteen in all. Each one a newspaper cutting. Each one yellowing with age, dog-eared where she had fingered them time and time again. In a straight, uniform line at the top she placed the larger ones. Beneath, she set out the smaller articles. Each article depicted a face, and as she touched them she visibly trembled.

In the low light from the bedside lamp they made an eerie sight. 'Oh, Mother! Mother! Why did you do it? *Why did you do it?*' All these years later she still had not discovered the reason. It haunted her. Her mother haunted her. The faces that stared up at her now, normal faces, smiling, happy faces. They haunted her too. And one face in particular, a handsome face with green eyes and brown hair, and a full laughing mouth which she had often kissed. That was the face that tore at her heart more than any other. That was the one that gave her sleepless nights and burned her up with guilt. And love. Oh, so much love.

Tenderly she traced the contours of his face. 'Why did she do it?' The murmur was heartfelt. 'How could she do such a frightening thing? And you! Oh, I loved you so. I love you still.' She bent her head to kiss the mouth, her features filled with the most wonderful emotion. 'Jack's made a fine figure of a man,' she told the face. 'He's built up a thriving business too. You should be proud of him.' Her smile deepened. 'Like father, like son.'

She gingerly perused the articles. Occasionally, when she could hardly bear what she read, she covered her mouth with the flat of her hand, as though stifling the cries that threatened.

When she could no longer go on, she opened the valise. Taking up the first article, she gazed at it a moment longer, her heart tightening with hatred for herself. 'One day I must let Maureen burn you,' she hissed. 'One day we will *all* burn... in hell. Like my mother.'

She opened the corners of her mind to let the images emerge; awful, horrifying images that would stay with her for all time. Something else too. Something so terrible that at times she thought she would go mad. 'Leave me be,' she murmured. 'Why won't you leave me be?'

Emotions rushed through her, leaving her breathless. Closing her eyes she thought of her mother. She thought of the broken bloody bodies, of many eyes, empty, marbled with terror and disbelief. She saw the look on her mother's white face, a wild, frightened look. Like the look of a cornered animal. She thought of all this and, like so many times before, it was too much to bear. She loved her mother still. Nothing would ever change that.

Repulsed by the cuttings, she began to replace them one by one, in order as always. The first victim. Using only the tips of her fingers she plucked the offending article from the bed and slid it towards the valise. It was only half inside when she heard the softest sound, somewhere at the far end of the room.

Jerking her head in a sparrow-like movement, she softly called out, 'Maureen? Is that you?' Knowing what she did, having only just pushed the terrible images away, she wondered... feared. Her voice shook. 'Who is it? Answer me!'

From the gloom, the figure half-emerged, tall and stately, with a certain grace and a face that spoke of madness. 'Hello, Katherine,' it whispered, 'I've come to talk with you.'

The effect on the old lady was devastating. Inarticulate with fear, she rolled her eyes downwards, to the cutting that echoed the face before her now; a proud face, darkly beautiful, with eyes like midnight. Shaking through every limb she slowly raised her gaze, trying desperately to see into the shadows but unable to move a single muscle. Her breathing was laboured, her face agonised. 'Mother. Is it you?' In the harshest whisper she asked again, *'Why did you do it?'*

There was a rush of laughter, soft and wicked. The shadows came alive, lunging, pinning her to the bed, long strong fingers holding her down.

As the light faded and blackness threatened to overwhelm, Katherine realised. In her terrified mind she believed her mother had come for her.

In the adjoining room, Maureen's slumbers were plagued by dreams. Fretting over the harsh words she and Katherine had exchanged earlier, she turned and rolled, and it wasn't long before she was wide awake, sitting up in bed, wondering what it was that woke her. 'Who's there?'

As she strained to listen, the sound came again, like the patter of scurrying feet. 'Lord love us, there's mice in the room!'

Indignant, she swung her legs out of bed. 'Country hotel indeed! No bar. No central heating. And now we've got vermin. Well, you've come to the wrong house, me little friend, because I'll have yer head off yer shoulders sure I will!' Taking her slipper by the toe she held the heel like a weapon.

Following the sound to the door, she almost jumped out of her skin when the door flew open and Katherine crumpled at her feet. 'Jesus Mary and Joseph!' Dropping the slipper she fell to her knees. Cradling Katherine in her arms, she was convinced the old lady was beyond help. All the same she yelled and screamed, and it was only a moment before help came.

Afraid to move her, Maureen covered the old lady with a blanket. While some merely stared and others fussed, she went discreetly to the old lady's bed and picked up the valise. When she caught sight of the article hanging halfway out, she assumed the others were safely tucked away. Hastily she stuffed the offending paper inside. Then she locked the valise and slid it beneath the bed. Soon she would destroy it.

A surprisingly short time later the doctor arrived. After a swift examination, he declared that Katherine had suffered a fit of sorts and would be removed to hospital immediately.

To the astonishment of the doctors, Katherine survived for almost a week. For reasons known only to herself she found a new lease of strength. There were things she needed to do; confessions to make before she was called to account.

Cyrus was contacted. Maureen told him only that his sister was very ill and he must come to England at once. She said nothing about having found Jack and his family. Nor did she contact Jack. Katherine was not long for this world and there was nothing he could do. She might have wished things could be different, but now there was nothing any of them could do.

Cyrus was devastated. 'I blame myself,' he said, looking down on Katherine's frail white face. It was so still, sleeping but not peacefully. There was a strained look about the face. The eyes twitched beneath the lids and the mouth moved as though it was speaking to someone. Cyrus swallowed his grief. 'I should never have let her come here. The journey was too much for her.' He turned to Maureen and was amazed by the composure in her homely features. 'God forgive me, but I should have stopped her.'

Maureen's smile was enigmatic. 'You could never have stopped her. Sure, none of us could. She has a will of iron, you know that.'

Heavy with grief, they left her for a moment, to walk the grounds and talk of the one they loved, and how they would live without her.

They did not speak of the horror etched into her face when she crumpled at Maureen's feet. They did not discuss her purpose for coming to England; nor Jack; nor the newspaper cuttings. Nor did they speak of the atrocities that took place twenty years ago. There were secrets. Awful, dangerous secrets that must never be spoken aloud. *These two knew.* And Katherine. Katherine knew everything.

While they walked the grounds, breathing the fresh air and coming to terms with another disaster in their tormented lives, there was another, a cruel young woman, who wondered only how she might benefit from her grandmother's passing.

'I'll do the talking,' Ginny ordered as she and her sister came to the desk.

Lianne was frightened and it showed. 'I don't want to see her,' she protested.

'You'll do as you're told.' The nurse at the desk was approaching. 'Shh! Be quiet.' Digging Lianne in the side, Ginny gave her a glance that warned of retribution if she was crossed.

The nurse was pink faced and flustered. The morning had been one of the worst she could remember. Every ward was full to bursting; a number of nurses had fallen victim to a flu virus, and only ten minutes ago there had been a mass admittance after a serious traffic accident.

True to her training she greeted the sisters with a wonderful smile. 'Can I help you?'

As instructed, Lianne kept silent. Ginny feigned sadness. 'Our grandmother is ill. We've come to see her,' she said.

'What name?'

'Mrs Katherine Louis.'

'I'm sorry. She already has visitors.' In truth, with the old lady on her last legs she couldn't see that it mattered, but the new consultant was a stickler for rules. 'I'm afraid I can't allow more than two at a time.'

Ginny was insistent. 'But she's our grandmother. We have to see her.'

The sister came forward. Calling at the desk for a batch of files, she couldn't help overhearing. 'Are we talking about Mrs Louis?' she enquired. When the nurse nodded, she looked at Ginny, thinking how beautiful she was. Then she glanced at Lianne and saw something in her face, a kind of fear, that made her relent. 'It's all right, Nurse,' she told the other woman. 'Mrs Louis' visitors have gone out for a breath of air.' Giving Ginny a stern look she conceded, 'All right. You can see your grandmother… but only for a few minutes.'

Tired and irritated, though trying not to show it, the nurse led the way down the corridor. 'She's very ill,' she said. 'I think you should know she doesn't recognise anyone.' She recalled how the brother had cried because the old lady had opened her eyes and seemed to look right through him.

The private rooms were situated in the west wing. After a smart walk along stark-white corridors, they came to a row of well-polished doors. Ushering them through the nearest one, the nurse reminded Ginny, 'Just a few minutes, then I'll be back to fetch you.'

As she walked away, the corridor echoed to the sound of the nurse's footsteps. 'Please, Ginny. I don't want to go in.' Though Ginny had vehemently denied her intentions, Lianne feared she was lying. Like she always lied when it suited her.

Without a word, Ginny grabbed her. 'I want you with me. The old hag would expect the both of us.'

'All right. But, if you harm her... I'll tell.' She clenched her teeth, more from fear than determination. 'I mean it, Ginny. This time I really will tell.'

Her words choked in her throat as Ginny locked her hands round it. 'I couldn't let you do that,' she muttered.

Tearing at the strong fingers, Lianne pleaded, 'You're hurting me.'

Suddenly the fingers relaxed, and Ginny's face was wreathed in a smile. While Lianne drew a long frantic breath, Ginny put her arm round her. 'I don't want to hurt you, sis,' she softly lied. 'You're my best pal.'

'I don't believe you.' Lianne had neither the strength nor courage to face her down.

Ginny knew this and, as always, she played on it. 'You know I love you more than anyone,' she insisted. 'You and me. That's all that matters, isn't it?'

Lianne was won over. 'I suppose so.'

'It's only right that we visit our grandmother together.' That way Ginny would have Lianne on her side if questions were later asked.

She cursed the fact that the old lady had somehow managed to survive. It only made things more difficult.

However, because she had laid her plans well, she didn't expect there to be any questions.

In her deepest dreams, Katherine heard the voice. For one fleeting heartbeat it sounded like the voice of her mother: 'We've come to see you,' it said. Strange. When she heard the voice before, it had said, 'I've come to talk with you.' But it was the same.

She heard her own voice answer. 'Please don't trick me, Mother. How can I be sure it's you?'

Ginny took hold of her hand. Leaning forward she bent her head to the old lady's ear. 'It isn't your mother,' she murmured. 'It's your grandchildren… Lianne and Ginny. We've come to see you.'

Ever so slowly the eyes opened. When they stared into Ginny's face they opened wider, unbelieving, astonished. 'You! It was you all the time!' Katherine knew then. She knew it was not her mother who had visited her before. It was the Devil.

Ginny's smile enveloped her. 'Yes. It was me,' she said. 'I came to see you then. I've come to see you now.' Her face was twisted with hatred.

Katherine felt the life draining from her. In her mind's eye she could see the newspaper cuttings just as she had seen them on the bed. It came to her then. She had had no time to put them away! In the smallest whisper, she accused, 'You saw them, didn't you?' A tear fell from one of her eyes. 'I never meant you to see them.'

Ginny was merciless. 'Yes, I saw them, and now I understand.' Her smile was wicked. 'I'm like her, aren't I? Inside and out… I am the reincarnation of my great-grandmother.'

Now Katherine's hatred matched that of her granddaughter. 'You may look like her, but you will *never* be the woman she was.' Cursing her weakness, she demanded, 'Why are you here?'

'I heard you tell Father how you want him to have what's rightfully his. That means you've made a will in his favour.'

Katherine was tempted to reveal how she had not yet changed her will, and that it still left everything to her brother, Cyrus. And Maureen. Oh yes. Maureen must be repaid for her unswerving loyalty. That disturbing row the other night was already forgotten. It was merely a flicker in a long and mutual friendship.

But this one. Jack's daughter. *She* wanted her dead. Suddenly she was back there. In that house. With all those people. All those corpses. 'Did your father send you? I know he wants me dead too.'

'It's very simple. You die, and leave everything to Father. He dies and leaves it all to Mother.' Her wickedness was tenfold. 'If Mother and Father have an "accident", everything will come to me. Isn't that so?'

Lianne stayed by the door. Because Ginny was bending so low to the bed she could not hear what was being said. 'Can we go now?' She hated it here, in this room, with these two. The presence of evil was overwhelming.

Ginny rounded on her. 'Look in the corridor. See if it's all clear.'

'No!' Taking a step towards the bed, she was unusually defiant. 'I won't let you hurt her.'

Enraged, Ginny stumbled across the room. When Lianne barred her way, she thrust her aside. 'Coward!' she snarled. 'You want her dead as much as I do.'

'Don't, Ginny. She's just an old woman.' The thought of being rich didn't drive her as it did her sister. The thought of killing someone like Katherine for money was unthinkable.

'Get out of my way!' With an almighty swipe of her arm she sent Lianne flying across the room. As Lianne stumbled and fell, only the bed came between her and the array of instruments that kept the old lady alive.

Dazed and humiliated, Lianne glanced at the old lady. 'I won't let her hurt you,' she promised.

Knowing that her time had come, Katherine wanted to wipe the slate clean, to confess the things she knew, but she was afraid. Even now, with her soul in jeopardy, she shirked the truth. 'Your sister is right,' she began. 'She is the reincarnation of your great-grandmother. The same magnificent dark eyes and wild beauty. She's right, too, when she says she's inherited the evil. *But she's not the same.* She could never be the same woman as my mother.'

Lianne's tears fell on to the old woman's face. 'She doesn't mean to be wicked,' she murmured.

Katherine saw the love in Lianne's pretty eyes and her heart went out to her. 'You love her very much, don't you?'

'I have to.'

'I do understand.' Katherine knew all too well that when you loved someone, it didn't matter if they were bad. 'Sometimes, when they're bad, you have to love them all the more.' Grabbing Lianne's wrist, she croaked, 'Help me, child.'

As Lianne ran for help, she heard what sounded like a door closing behind her. In flight she glanced round.

All was quiet.

6

On the first day of March 1982, the family of the late Katherine Louis gathered in the coroner's offices.

It was market day in Leighton Buzzard. Outside, the sun was shining. The streets were packed. People went about their lives in a particular order, up one row of stalls and down the other. In and out of the many shops, always with a purpose.

Inside the courthouse, the coroner's rooms were cold, forbidding, with empty rows of seats and high ceilings that trapped every sound, every thought, coveting them, keeping their secrets. The long bench at the head of the room was littered with official documents. Nearer to the people's benches was a wooden podium, decorated with a splendid crest and angled so that its occupant was clearly visible to both the people and the coroner.

On the narrow hard benches outside the room, the family congregated. Wary and unsure, they each clung to their nearest and dearest, making two little groups, each separate, each wishing they were some place else: Jack and Liz with their daughters on one bench; Cyrus and Maureen on the other.

Ginny sat slightly apart from everyone. Head high, eyes raised to the coroner's door, she waited for it all to be over. 'How much longer?' she asked impatiently. Nudging Lianne she gave her a warning glance and lowered her voice. 'Remember what I told you. One word from you about how she died, and you'll live to regret it.'

In a harsh whisper, Lianne retaliated, 'I've a good mind to tell how you threatened her.'

Jack glanced round, staring disapprovingly at the pair of them. 'Ssh!' His serious gaze went from them to his uncle and Maureen. They were painfully silent. Their features set like stone as they stared at the ground: Cyrus with his legs apart and arms folded, and Maureen with tears in her eyes as she stared at the ceiling. Not knowing what to say or how to pacify these people who were now little more than strangers, Jack vented his irritation on Lianne. 'Remember where you are, and stop arguing!'

Ginny smiled sweetly. 'Sorry, Father.'

While he turned his attention to Liz, Ginny resumed her exchange with her sister. 'I shouldn't have threatened you,' she said. It infuriated her that Lianne was becoming immune to her threats. Moreover, she had been surprised and worried when Lianne took the death of her grandmother so badly.

Realising she would be in deep trouble if there was the slightest suspicion the old lady's death was anything more than an accident, Ginny promised herself she would have to treat Lianne with the utmost consideration. 'I know you always wanted grandparents,' she whispered, feigning affection. 'Even when you were little, on Christmas Eve with our presents all lined up under the tree, you always used to say how it would be nice if Father Christmas could bring us a grandma and grandpa.'

The memories filled Lianne with bittersweet emotions. 'All *you* ever wanted was the biggest parcel, and the prettiest things,' she remembered aloud. 'You laughed at me when I said I wanted grandparents.'

'That's because I knew we would never have them. Anyway, they would only have come between us, just like our parents do.'

In her pain Lianne lashed out. 'You were wrong! We *did* have a grandmother, and now we haven't.'

'We don't need her. We don't need anyone.' Her eyes were smiling, but her heart was bitter. She was glad Katherine Louis was dead. It wasn't only the will, or the money that she hoped would come to her. It went deeper than that, though she herself could not understand it. From the moment she set eyes on Katherine, and for no apparent reason, she hated her. Now that the old lady was dead, she felt as though a debt was paid. As though she herself was released. It was an odd feeling. A strange, exhilarating feeling she could not explain. 'You're right. She's gone. But it wasn't me,' she reasoned. 'You saw what happened. I never touched the old biddy.'

There was hatred in Lianne too; in her trembling body and accusing eyes. 'You *frightened* her to death.'

'I never touched her.' Yet she had. Not with her hands, but with her soul.

Lianne lapsed into silence, reliving the awful scene in that hospital room. Ginny was right. The old lady had taken her own life. Why? The question rose to her lips. 'Why would she do that?'

Jack leaned over to touch her on the shoulder. It was just as well he couldn't hear the conversation. 'If you can't stop chattering, perhaps you'd better wait outside.' He was restless. He hadn't wanted to attend, but Liz insisted. 'I shouldn't be here,' he told her now. 'She meant nothing to me, and I have work to do.' Oh, but there was a time, a lifetime ago. When he was a boy, he had loved her more than anything else in the world.

Awed by her surroundings, Liz had remained quiet and thoughtful, unable to understand the vehemence that Jack held for his own mother. Now, when Jack spoke, she was made to answer. 'We're here to find out what happened,' she said. 'It's your place to be here, Jack. She was your mother.'

'I should be at work.'

'No, Jack. What happened between you and your mother all those years ago doesn't matter any more. Surely you can see that?'

'You're wrong, Liz,' he answered softly. 'It will always matter.' To the end of time, it would matter. Long after he was gone and they were all rotting in the ground, it would matter.

'I never knew you were such an unforgiving bastard.' She loved this man so much it hurt. But lately, since Katherine Louis had stepped over their doorstep, their lives had changed.

He had changed. They hadn't made love since that night, and she wasn't sure she even wanted to. When they went to bed, he would turn his back on her and she hardly dared touch him. He never held her in the way he used to. Sometimes he would wake up, sobbing like a child, eyes tightly shut as though if he opened them he might come face to face with the Devil. During the day he was oddly distant. Jumpy. Unable to look her in the eye. But then he had cause, she remembered with bitterness. He lied to her. Lied to his daughters.

Jack had kept too many secrets.

A tall balding man in a grey suit opened the door to address them. 'We're ready for you now,' he said. Standing aside he held open the door. 'If you'll sit there please.' He gestured to the front row.

Cyrus was the first to rise, then Maureen, leaning heavily on his arm as they went side by side down the aisle and into the row, where they seated themselves, solemn faced and apprehensive. 'Don't worry,' Cyrus comforted her. 'It will soon be over.'

Jack and Liz were next. Jack would have left a number of empty seats between himself and the other two, but Liz nudged him on. Reluctantly he seated himself beside Cyrus. They exchanged nods.

'I'd like to talk with you before we leave,' Cyrus whispered.

Jack gave a half-smile, but said nothing.

Lianne held back, remaining in her seat and visibly trembling. There were other people going in now. She recognised the nurse who escorted them to Katherine's room. 'I don't want to go in there,' she told Ginny. 'Why can't I stay out here?'

'Because you may be called on to say what happened.'

'I won't lie.'

Lianne's forthright statement shook Ginny to her roots. Thinking quickly, she knew bullying would not help. Not this time. Placing her hand over Lianne's she asked, 'What will you tell them?'

Lianne couldn't look at her. Keeping her eyes fixed on the stairway she answered in a whisper, 'I'll tell them how you frightened her. I'll tell them you threatened her, and that she said you were evil. She knew you meant to kill her. That's why she knocked the tubes out.' Recalling her grandmother's words, she recounted them to Ginny now. 'She said I wasn't to let you destroy me. She said I mustn't suffer because of you.' Suddenly it was all very clear. 'That's why she killed herself. Because she knew you would do it if she didn't, and that I would be blamed as well.'

'Do you really mean to tell?'

'Yes.'

'You've never told before.'

'You killed our grandmother.'

'She was a stranger.'

'I hate you.'

'If you say all those things… in there –' she nodded towards the door – 'they might take me away.'

'Good.'

Ginny was beginning to panic. She had never known Lianne be like this. Her calm voice belied the rage inside. 'You know I'm innocent. I did not kill that old lady. If you say all those things, and they think I was responsible, you may never see me again.'

Lianne hadn't thought that far. She was made to reflect on it now. Never see Ginny again? That would be like having her heart torn out.

Sensing the trauma going on in Lianne's head, Ginny appealed to her. 'You wouldn't let them take me away, would you? Especially when I'm innocent.' Caressing Lianne's fingers in her own, she infused her voice with emotion. 'Please, Lianne. I couldn't bear it if I never saw you again.'

'You were cruel to her.'

'I admit I shouldn't have said the things I did,' she schemed.

'If I do as you ask... if I say she knocked the tubes out herself, how do I know you won't be bad again?'

Ginny managed to squeeze out a tear. 'Because I'll make you a promise. I'll try my hardest never to be bad again.' It was only a half-lie. She never wanted to be bad. It just came to her. Now, she didn't want to be good. 'Good' was Lianne. And her mother. Not her father. He had badness in him too.

Still uncertain, Lianne looked into her sister's dark eyes. As always she saw only what she wanted to see, and what she saw was remorse.

'I couldn't bear it if they took you away,' Lianne murmured.

Leaning forward, Ginny kissed her. 'Tell them she was asleep. She had a kind of fit. That was when she knocked out the tubes and you ran for help. It was an accident.'

'An accident. Yes.'

'Good girl!'

'Ginny?'

'What?' A careless hint of impatience. Quickly suppressed. 'I'm sorry. It *will* be all right in there. I won't let any harm come to you.'

'You do love me, then?'

'You know I do.' She hugged her and loathed doing so. 'You and me, sis. Looking after each other. Just like always.'

Jack appeared at the door. 'You two.' Thumbing towards the room where the others were seated, he ordered sharply, 'Inside if you please.'

As they passed him, Ginny gave Lianne a sideways glance. It said, 'My life is in your hands. Don't let them send me away.'

Lianne merely nodded. It was enough.

The inquest lasted three quarters of an hour. The doctor explained how the old lady was in a critical condition following a massive seizure. He said it was not unknown for a sedated patient to half-wake in a panic, sometimes violent... enough perhaps to dislodge the instruments that kept them alive. Everything humanly possible had been done to save Katherine Louis but it was too late. As it was, she would not have lasted more than a few days, if that.

The nurse corroborated his story. Ginny said it was exactly as the doctor had described: their grandmother woke in a start, thrashed about and caught the tubes. 'My sister ran for help, while I stayed with our grandmother.' She sobbed a little, and the coroner took pity on her. 'Sit down, my dear,' he said gently. 'We've heard enough.'

He saw how Lianne was perched nervously on the edge of her seat, wide eyed and anxious while she waited for her turn. 'It's all right,' he assured her, 'there won't be any need for you to give evidence.'

He didn't realise how near she was to admitting the truth. How her sister had threatened to kill their grandmother, and how, to save an innocent from being implicated, the old lady had taken her own life.

After certain deliberation, the verdict was given that Katherine Louis died because of an unfortunate accident. 'Misadventure.' Everyone agreed. Except Liz, whose curious gaze was drawn to Ginny.

Others held their own opinions, but remained silent. Cyrus believed that Jack, by one means or another, may have speeded his mother's exit from this world.

Maureen believed the same. She and Cyrus had cause to suspect Jack. But there was nothing to be gained from opening old wounds. Katherine was gone. Jack would be left in peace. Maybe it was all for the best.

Everyone stood for the coroner to leave. Afterwards, they filed out of the room. Jack would have hurried away, but Cyrus cornered him. 'I never wanted her to trace you in the first place,' he confessed, 'but you know your mother. You know how she is.' He was shocked to find himself referring to Katherine as though she was still with them. *'Was,'* he corrected, 'you know how she *was*.'

Half-expecting Katherine to suddenly appear through one of the doors, Jack glanced round the room. Satisfied that she was safely out of the way, hopefully for ever, he returned his attention to the other man. 'She's dead now,' he said in a strange flat voice. 'That's how it should be.'

Maureen could not let that go without comment. 'Shame on ye,' she reprimanded. 'Ye're a bitter, unforgiving man.'

Liz drew her aside. 'What happened between Jack and his mother?' she asked. 'I need to know.'

Glancing furtively to where the two men were still talking, Maureen answered, 'Sure, it's Jack's place to tell ye.'

'He's told me they had a fierce argument... that she wanted him to join the family firm and tried to run his life. He's told me all that.'

Maureen gave a sigh of relief. 'Well, then?'

'I think he's holding something back.'

'I don't know what ye mean.'

'Neither do I,' Liz reluctantly admitted. 'It's just that he told so many lies. I don't know if he's telling the truth now. I don't know if I can trust him any more.'

Katherine was strong in Maureen's mind just then. Her heart was saying, 'Oh, Katherine! Katherine! Ye have a great deal to answer for.' Her voice was issuing reassurances: 'Ye must believe Jack,' she begged, telling her only what she wanted to hear. 'Everything he's told ye is the truth. Even to the very end, Katherine Louis was a strong-minded woman. But in her younger days she was a formidable creature. Jack is much like her. They were always pulling two ways. I believe there was a little jealousy there too. Though Jack was always at odds with his mother, he adored his grandmother.' Here she paused, her mind reliving the crippling memories. Her heart turning with horror. 'That's possibly why he named yer firstborn after her.'

'Was that for love of his grandmother, or to spite his own mother?'

Maureen laughed softly. It was a mirthless sound. 'A man has many reasons for doing what he does,' she said vaguely. A woman too, she thought. There was no more complex and terrifying mind than that of a woman.

Liz recalled the things Jack had told her. 'He spoke of his grandmother. I believe she was very beautiful?'

'Virginia was the most beautiful woman I have ever seen. Intelligent too.' And dangerously impulsive, she thought, her pretty eyes hardening with a kind of rage. 'She was also her own worst enemy.' Visions of twisted and tortured bodies came to mind. She shuddered. It was all too late now. For the victims. For the murderer. There was no denying it. Katherine's late mother must have been deranged to do what she did.

Aware that Liz was scrutinising her, she went on in a brighter voice, 'It grieved me to see how mother and son drifted apart. I loved Katherine like she was my own family. But she was not the easiest person to live with.' She chuckled. 'She could start an argument from nothing, make ye feel thoroughly miserable, and it would be *you* that ended up apologising.' Thoughts of their last row rippled through her mind.

'You'll miss her.'

'Like ye'll never know,' Maureen answered. Yes, she would miss her. But, unlike Katherine, she refused to dwell in the past. Now, to save Jack more heartache, she had to tell half-truths. Not the whole truth, for that would never do. 'I've never met such a stubborn woman,' she said. 'Katherine was determined Jack would go into the family business. He, on the other hand, was just as determined she would not rule his life. They clashed badly. In the bitter feud that followed, Katherine publicly disowned him.'

Liz was astounded. 'That's a terrible thing for a mother to do to her own son.' Now she was beginning to understand. Still, there was a little nagging doubt.

Maureen went on, eager to mend a rift that was already appearing between Jack and his wife. Fear was a terrible thing. And hatred. And love. Maureen had seen it all before, and she knew, better than most. *If history was to repeat itself, it would be a tragic thing.*

'I believed the bad feelings between Jack and his mother could never be healed,' Maureen explained, 'but old age has a way of mellowing things, so it has. Well now, it was only a matter of time before Katherine relented. When she said she meant to find Jack, I told her then it was wrong. I warned her that Jack may not have forgiven her.' Her eyes closed with sorrow. 'I was right, wasn't I?'

Liz bowed her head. 'He didn't even want to attend the inquest.'

'Then I don't suppose he'll travel an ocean to attend the funeral.'

'Of course. You'll want to take her home to be buried.'

'Her brother would want that.' She glanced towards Cyrus. 'I think we should say our goodbyes now,' she suggested.

As they rejoined Jack and his uncle, Jack's voice rang out: 'It doesn't matter to me whether she's changed her will or not. I wanted nothing from her twenty years ago, and I want nothing now!'

In an effort to calm him down, Liz threaded her arm through his. 'Lower your voice, sweetheart. The girls are listening.' Lianne was seated on a nearby bench. Ginny was pacing the floor, head down, seeming not to be listening, while all the time her avaricious soul swallowed every precious word.

Comforted by the touch of Liz's hand, Jack turned to gaze on his wife. His features softened at her encouraging smile. She had called him 'sweetheart' for the first time since his mother knocked on their door. 'Let's go home,' he suggested. 'We don't belong here.'

Cyrus put out his hand. 'Can't we at least part friends?'

For a moment Jack was unsure. Though Maureen and Cyrus were no more responsible for the atrocities than he was, he did hold them responsible for invading his life. 'You knew I needed to escape,' he accused in a low harsh voice. 'All I ever wanted was a life of my own. Yet you allowed her to find me.' His eyes conveyed a message only they could understand. 'Now you see what's happened?' What had happened was that the killing had started all over again. What had happened was his mother was dead. And he did not believe it was an accident.

It was Maureen who spoke then. 'Jack. Calm yourself.' Addressing a half-smile to Liz, who was feeling out of her depth, she told them both, 'Cyrus and I have to make arrangements to take Katherine home. If ye feel able, we would dearly love to see ye before we return.'

Jack was astonished by her intervention. Maureen seemed suddenly to be taking charge. Cyrus was the master, Maureen the servant. Yet it was she who spoke with greater authority. 'Are you speaking for my uncle?' he asked coolly. When he was small he had loved Maureen. Now he was afraid to trust any of them.

'Sure, I'm getting above myself.' With the flicker of a smile she stepped back a pace, giving Cyrus leeway.

'Maureen only says what we both feel,' Cyrus confirmed. 'This family has suffered enough. It's time to build bridges, don't you think? Your mother wanted that, and so do I.'

'Then you'll be disappointed.' His manner was threatening. 'You know why I ran, and you know why I can't go back.'

'I'm not asking you to go back. All I'm asking is that we stop being strangers.'

Jack would have liked that too. He would have liked for them to be a family. In all the years he had felt only half a man, as though something very precious was missing from his life. Now he just wanted to forget. If only he had not been born. Never known his grandmother. Never seen what he had seen. Never been the son of Katherine Louis. 'Go home,' he murmured bitterly. 'Take your sister with you, and don't come back.' He was happy she was dead. Sad too. It was a lonely feeling. 'As long as I live, I never want to see you again.' His green eyes bored into Cyrus' face. Then he looked at Maureen, and saw that she knew he would never forgive. '*Either* of you,' he said. These were the last words he would ever speak to them.

Cyrus appeared hurt by Jack's hostility. 'I warned your mother, but, as always, she wouldn't listen. But now that you're found, I don't want you to cut us out of your life again, Jack.' His gaze wandered to where Ginny and Lianne were waiting. 'You have a delightful family, and with your blessing I'd like to get to know them.'

It was Liz who answered. 'Let Jack think on it,' she said. 'How long will it be before you leave?' She had taken a liking to Cyrus. In an odd way, he reminded her of Jack.

'I'm homesick already,' he confessed. 'We'll be leaving just as soon as I can make the necessary arrangements… a few days, a week at the most, I think.' His face fell. 'I never wanted to take my sister home in such sad circumstances.' But he knew. Right from the moment she revealed she had found Jack, he had a premonition she would not return alive. He momentarily closed his eyes. 'Unfortunately, Katherine believed she was invincible.'

Jack stiffened. Taking Liz by the arm, he turned and walked briskly away. She was intrigued when he softly giggled, 'She of all people should know none of us is invincible.'

The two older ones watched as Jack collected his family and hurried them down the stairs. 'We won't see him again,' Cyrus said forlornly.

Maureen shook her head. 'Ah now, don't be too sure,' she declared in her broad Irish accent. 'Ye've offered them a fortune, sure ye have. Yer nephew Jack may not be interested.' Tapping her nose she smiled at him. 'But his pretty little wife, and the one named Virginia? These two are another kettle of fish altogether.'

His face brightened. 'You may be right.'

'We'll see, won't we?' she said. 'Now, will ye take a poor old soul for a cup o' tea and an English muffin? Jaysus! Me feet are killing me!'

As they walked towards the stairs, she chuckled aloud, 'The bugger may be gone, and let's hope it's to a better place, but I swear she's left me a legacy of her blessed corns.'

On the way to the car park, Lianne and Ginny hung back. Still disturbed by the events of the morning, Lianne was riddled with guilt, unsure as to whether she might have told the truth if the coroner had questioned her. 'I was wicked not to tell,' she murmured.

'No, you weren't,' Ginny scolded. 'You must never tell. What happened is a secret for ever. Between you and me.'

'And Grandmother.'

Amused, Ginny gazed up at the sky. It was a bright sunny day, unusually warm, yet invigorating. Her dark eyes shone with excitement. 'All right,' she conceded, 'it's a secret between you, me... and Grandmother.' Wrapping her arm in Lianne's she whispered wickedly in her ear, 'But *she's* not likely to tell anyone, is she?'

'She might haunt you.'

It was a moment before Ginny spoke, and when she did it was with a curious satisfaction. 'Won't bother me if she does.' Shrugging her shoulders, she smiled darkly. 'I've been haunted before.'

There was little said on the journey home. Everyone was obsessed with their own thoughts. Jack was seething inside, hating everything, musing whether he should uproot his family and make a new life somewhere else. It was the last thing he wanted. Yet it might be the answer. He had done it before and found a semblance of peace. Here in Bedfordshire, in that proud old house with Liz and his daughters, he had begun to heal. He wondered if he could do it again. Wondered, over and over until he could hardly think straight.

Liz felt lost. Everything she had cherished was falling apart around her. The only real thing was her love for Jack. Whatever he had done, however much she detested him for deceiving her, she could not deny her love for him. It ran through her every thought, throbbed with the beat of her heart, and flowed with her life blood.

She loved her daughters, but not with such ferocity. If she never saw them again it wouldn't really matter. With Jack it was different. He was everything to her. She glanced at him now, at his strong hard-set face. She couldn't even begin to fathom his thoughts. Somewhere deep down, she was afraid. His mother's death was not the end. In a way, she felt it was only the beginning. But... the beginning of what? If only she knew.

That night she and Jack made love. He didn't want to. It was she who made all the advances. A little caressing, a tender touch in the right place, a nibble of the ear, and he was like putty in her hands. 'You're a witch,' he murmured as he took her in his arms.

She didn't argue. If she had to be a witch to turn him on, then that's what she would do. 'Don't use a rubber,' she whispered. 'Let's make love like we used to.'

He was incredulous. 'Don't you care if you get pregnant?'

She smiled. In the half-light she looked like a child. 'That's the last thing I want,' she said. 'It's just that I need to feel you. Your skin against mine.'

'Dangerous.'

'Not if you do what we did before we had the girls.'

'Withdraw, you mean?'

'Hmm.'

'You can never be sure.'

'Be careful then.' Opening her legs she drew him to her. It was like the first night they were married. Wild and turbulent. Deep frantic strokes. Long passionate kisses that reached right into her soul. It was young love rekindled, the two of them locked together for all time, shutting out the world and its badness. When it was over, she loved him all the more.

Drained and exhausted, they slept like kittens. Tomorrow might bring its own troubles. Tonight, and for a time at least, they had each other.

'We'll have to kill them.' In the darkness Ginny had entered her sister's room, and now the two of them were seated on the bed, Lianne propped against her pillow and Ginny lounging across her feet. Her hair was dishevelled. She was naked. In the halo of light from the bedside lamp, she looked half-mad.

Horrified, Lianne pressed her hands over her ears. 'I won't listen.'

In a quick vicious movement, Ginny wrenched her hands away. Holding them in her own she pushed her face close. 'You *will* listen!'

'I don't want you to hurt them.' Her face was ashen. Tears ran down her face and smudged.

'You want to be rich, don't you?'

'Even if you hurt them, we wouldn't be rich. Daddy said he would never touch any of Katherine's money.'

'You're stupid!' Ginny retorted. 'It doesn't matter whether he wants it or not. Cyrus said he was putting a lot of money in the bank... in Father's name. If he and Mother have an accident, the money will legally belong to us.'

'I don't want it!' Cringing, she began sobbing. 'Leave me alone. Leave me alone or I'll tell!'

'Calm down. I'm only fooling.'

'Honest?' Her smile was pitiful.

They hugged. Ginny tucked her up in bed. 'You're a little fool,' she chided, 'thinking I really meant to hurt Mum and Dad.'

'Sorry.'

'I should think so.'

'Goodnight, Ginny.'

'Goodnight.'

Outside the door she leaned against the wall. 'You're all the same,' she whispered, 'and I don't need *any* of you!'

The two figures seemed like any other couple out for a stroll. The moon was low, the night black as tar. 'Are you certain we won't be seen?' Cyrus was nervous. 'It wouldn't do if we were stopped and questioned.'

'Now, why would anyone stop and question us?' Maureen gently chided. 'Sure we're doing no harm.'

'But it's so late.'

'Pretend we're lovers,' she giggled.

Before he could answer, she tugged at his coat sleeve. 'Here,' she whispered, dragging him to the side of the bridge, 'this seems a likely spot. It'll be deep enough here, I reckon.'

Peeping over the bridge, Cyrus stared down into the waters below. 'Makes me go cold,' he shuddered, 'especially when I know what's in this bag.' Holding the valise high for her to see, he glanced about, highly nervous, wanting to do the deed and run from that place. To run and run so he would not have to think about what had brought them here, to the darkest and deepest part of the lake.

'Throw it over,' she urged, 'quickly. Before anyone sees.'

He hesitated. 'Are you certain all the cuttings are inside?'

'You have my word on it.'

'I'm not doubting you,' he assured her, 'but I know how devious she was. How can you be certain she didn't have others hidden away?'

'Because I've searched high and low. There are no more. If there had been others, I would have known.' A fondness crept into her voice. 'She kept nothing from me.'

He glanced at her then, silently accusing. 'There was *one* time,' he reminded her.

She bowed her head and leaned forward, sagging on the wall like a deflated balloon. 'Katherine told me everything,' she answered. 'I knew when she defied her parents in order to see

Jack's father. I was one of the first to know when she was pregnant with Jack.' She enjoyed shocking him. 'Katherine and I had no secrets,' she taunted, 'ever!'

'What if this valise is found?'

'It won't be. This is not a tidal river.'

'We should look inside. Make certain they're all there.'

Impatient she snatched it from him and swung it high in the air. It smacked the water and was sucked from sight. 'We don't need to look inside,' she told him. 'Katherine had already put them back the night she collapsed.' The images were powerful in her memory. 'There was one jutting out. I crammed it back myself, and the valise has been well hidden since then. No one else has touched it.'

Leaning over the wall he peered down. 'She should have destroyed them long ago.'

'She wanted to. They were all she had left.'

'But why?'

Maureen shrugged. Touching him tenderly on the arm, she murmured, 'To remind her of her mother. Of what she had done.'

'Let's go back.' He couldn't bear it here. He had only ever seen those cuttings once, and they were burned on his brain. 'I don't ever want us to talk about this,' he pleaded.

'We won't, then,' she promised. 'Jack will go his way and we'll go ours. That's the way it should be.'

'Are you sure?'

'Never more so.' Like Jack, she suspected that Katherine's death was no accident. One name sprang to mind. *Virginia*. A name that echoed down the ages.

They stayed a moment, solemn and grieving, as though they had buried something close to their hearts. 'I couldn't bear to take them back with us,' he groaned.

One more moment, while they quietly watched the waters, hoping they would keep their secret. 'Let's away,' Maureen said, and together they crept away, as silently as they had arrived.

The hotel was only a short walk away. When they returned the clerk gave them their keys and wished them a cheery goodnight. But it wasn't night. It was morning. Yet he understood. Like he said to the porter later, 'What with the inquest and all, it ain't surprising the poor sods can't sleep.'

Maureen was restless. First it was two a.m. then three. And now it was four in the morning. Outside it was still dark. She thought of the case, and the papers in their watery grave. She thought of Katherine and her loneliness was overwhelming.

Softly she crossed the floor. Going to the door that separated her from what had been Katherine's room, she listened. There was no sound. Slowly, carefully, she turned the knob, opened the door and went in. Except for the thin yellow halo from a night-light, the room was in darkness.

She made no sound as she walked across the room. Nor when she slithered out of her nightgown and climbed in beside him. He stirred, saw her in the half-light and smiled. 'I've been waiting for you,' he whispered. Then he slid his hands down the bed and caressed her. 'I've missed you,' he said.

'I knew you would,' she sighed. So she stayed. Until the morning.

On Monday morning, Ginny and Lianne arrived at school, only to find all the pupils already assembling in the hall.

'Some thief has broken into our science lab,' the headmistress announced. 'There will be no biology or science lessons today. Instead, timetables will be altered, and all pupils will report to cookery class.' There was a loud collective moan. 'I understand your disappointment,' she called out, 'but there has been a great deal of damage, and the police will need to make investigations. It's likely they may want to talk to some of you as the day progresses. Please give them all the help you can,' she said, gesturing to a uniformed officer she introduced as Constable Wilson.

A big round-faced man with twinkling eyes, Constable Wilson was a family man. He prided himself on being able to talk to young adults in a way that didn't get their backs up. 'Good morning, everyone,' he began. 'This is a nasty business. I know how annoyed you must be about having your timetables disrupted.' He wasn't too surprised at the little sniggers and the tight grins as everyone sneaked a look at the person next to them. 'All right,' he conceded, 'it may have been a long time ago, but I was a teenager once. And I daresay I wouldn't have been too worried about missing my science lesson.'

A ripple of laughter told him they were on his side. 'Your timetable is not all that's at stake here,' he explained in a sombre voice. 'We need to find out who broke into these premises, and we need to find out before he... or she... decides to do it again. I'll be talking to most of you during the course of the day. I'll want to know if you saw anything. Overheard anything. Do you know of someone with a grudge?'

The headmistress stepped forward. 'If you do know anything then you must speak out,' she insisted. 'Even the smallest piece of information will be useful. That will be all. Thank you.' With that she walked briskly across the stage and down the steps. As she made her way out, there was a formidable silence. Once she had left the room, the excited chattering became almost deafening until the deputy angrily called them to attention.

'Leave the hall one row at a time,' he ordered. '*Quietly!*'

The front row was made up of prefects and girls who were in their last year before college. Ginny was among them. As always this row was the first to depart the room.

Two rows behind, Lianne kept her eyes on her sister. She had a sneaking suspicion that Ginny might know something about the break-in. As Ginny approached, their eyes met. Ginny was smiling intimately. Nervous and guilty beneath her sister's probing gaze, Lianne turned away. When she looked again, Ginny was smiling. In the moment before she was lost to sight Ginny dared to wink. It was then that Lianne's suspicions were confirmed.

The day went quickly. A round of never-ending lessons and lectures. A day when all Lianne wanted to do was go home. Ginny wanted the same. During the lunch break, when the sisters were alone in the dining hall, Lianne asked the question that had been on her mind since assembly: 'It was you who broke into the school, wasn't it?'

Ginny was wonderfully coy. 'What a thing to say.' She then got up and strode out of the room, leaving Lianne more frustrated than ever.

That evening, the two of them sat at the dinner table with their parents. It was an unpleasant experience; Liz had burned the crust on the shepherd's pie, and Jack was moody, pensive, toying with his food.

'Why don't you say it?' Liz was on edge. 'The meal's ruined. Not fit for pigs.'

'It's not the meal,' he said kindly, 'it's me. I'm not hungry, that's all.'

He lapsed into a deeper silence. She sulked. And there was an atmosphere you could cut with a knife.

The meal ended. Jack insisted on the girls doing the washing up. Liz insisted on doing it herself, and for the next hour, could be heard crashing and banging about in the kitchen.

When eventually she came into the sitting-room, she had a face like thunder, and a temper to match. Switching off the television, she told a disgruntled Ginny, 'Your father and I have to talk. Alone.'

'Miserable cow!' Ginny led the way out of the room and up the stairs. 'She knew I wanted to watch the James Bond film.'

'I expect they've got a lot to talk about.'

'I expect they have. He wants rid of his family, and she wants to bring them all together.' She laughed cruelly. 'He doesn't want his mother's money, and she does.'

'I think *he's* right.' Lianne wished that none of this had happened. She wished Katherine Louis had never found them.

Ginny shrugged, singing a little as they went along the landing to her room. When she and Lianne were inside she said cruelly, 'Soon it won't matter anyway. Because they'll be with Katherine, and the money will be ours.'

'I shan't stay if you talk like that.' Anxious, Lianne remained by the door.

Smiling sweetly, Ginny threw herself on the bed. 'I won't say another word about it,' she promised. But that was all she could promise. Her plans had not changed.

'I hope Mum hasn't forgotten our birthday party.'

'She hasn't.'

'How do you know?'

'Because yesterday I heard them talking about it. You'll be pleased to know the cake is already made and it's being kept at the bakery.'

Lianne's eyes shone. 'I'd like a peep.'

'Hmm! That's because you're still a baby.'

'Don't be stupid! I'm not a baby. I'll be sixteen on Friday, and anyway, you're only two years older than me.'

'And of course I'd forgotten. You've got a young man now.'

Lianne blushed. 'If you mean Dave Martin, I haven't talked to him since... since... you know.' She had looked at him though. And he had looked at her. Time and again. At every opportunity. But they hadn't talked, because she was too embarrassed.

'*I've* talked to him.'

'Who? Dave Martin?' In spite of a rush of anger, she couldn't help but smile.

'Who else?' Languishing on the bed, she rolled over, scrutinising Lianne from upside down. 'I hadn't realised how handsome he was,' she purred. 'In fact, if you don't want him, I might even take him myself.'

Lianne visibly bristled. 'He doesn't even like you.'

177

Ginny's handsome features broke into a grin. The grin deformed her face. Upside down it seemed as though her teeth were in her forehead. 'That's a spiteful thing to say,' she chided. Mimicking Liz's voice, she wagged a finger. 'You've got a bad streak in you, my girl!'

'What did he say?' Eager for news, Lianne sat on the edge of the bed, impatiently tugging at Ginny's blouse. 'Go on! What did he say?'

'Who?'

'You know who!'

'Old Tom, you mean?'

'Bitch.'

'Tut tut. What language.'

'Please, Ginny. What did Dave say?'

Ginny rolled over to sit up. 'You're a strange one. First you're terrified he'll frig you. Now you're terrified he won't.' Lying across the bed she opened her legs provocatively. 'Perhaps he should frig me instead.'

'I'm *not* terrified.' The only thing that terrified her now was the prospect of Ginny luring him away.

'So you wouldn't mind if I told him you wanted to see him again?' Getting off the bed she went to the dresser and took out a packet of cigarettes, then a lighter. In a slow aggravating drawl she taunted, 'Next time you'll have to go through with it.' She lit the cigarette and took a long deep drag. Returning to Lianne she leaned close and exhaled the smoke into her face. 'If you let him down again, he won't want to know you. Men are like that. They don't like getting all wound up for nothing.'

Irritated by the warm acrid smoke, Lianne drew away. 'Dave's not like that.'

'*All* men are like that.'

'Did you tell him I want to see him again?'

'It's what you want, isn't it?'

'I wanted to tell him myself.'

'And pigs might fly.'

'*Did you tell him?*'

'Now, now. Temper, my dear.' She was in no hurry to reveal what she had said to Dave Martin. In fact, she was enjoying herself too much... delighting in her sister's discomfort.

When Lianne turned to leave, she realised she had gone too far. 'All right,' she said, catching her by the hair and yanking her back. 'He's coming to the house on Friday night. I've invited him to our birthday party.'

'You had no right to. *I* was going to ask him.'

'When? Next year? The year after? Well, I've saved you the trouble. After the party, he can pretend to go home with the others, but we'll sneak him upstairs where he can give you the best birthday present of all. You'll have the bedroom all to yourselves, and no one will ever know.' She sucked her bottom lip. 'Except the three of us,' she lied.

'What about Mum and Dad?'

'Don't worry about them. They should sleep through it.' Smiling devilishly, she whispered, 'Unless you yell and scream and make a fool of yourself when he breaks the skin.'

The thought of physical pain was too much for Lianne. 'I'm going to bed.'

'I hope you'll like my present better than his.'

'What is it?'

'It would spoil the surprise if I told you.'

'You're a tease.'

'All you need to know is this... I've got you something really different. No one else will have anything like it, and it's cost me a great deal of work and effort.'

'You shouldn't spend your pocket money on me.'

Ginny kissed her earnestly. 'It's no good you lying awake trying to figure out what it is, because you would never guess in a million years.' She then pushed her out and locked the door.

Admiring herself in the mirror she murmured, 'Your present cost me sweat and trouble. But it didn't cost me a single penny.' She fell on the bed laughing. 'You'll see. It's all a girl could ever want.'

7

'Mother! Will you please stop fussing?' It had been a painfully long week. Friday was here at last, and all he could think of was Lianne.

Meg Martin was a big likeable woman, with huge brown eyes and a mass of jet-black hair; her son David had inherited his mother's colouring and his father's quiet temperament. 'I can't help being nosy,' she answered boldly. 'What mother wouldn't? When her favourite son rushes home from school, has a bath without being nagged at, puts on his new silk shirt... for the first time since his mother bought it for him last Christmas, and now, would you believe, he's actually wearing shoes instead of trainers!' She shook her head, eyes wide with astonishment.

Dave would not be drawn, but his humour was as bright as hers. 'I'm sorry, Mum, but I think I'll have to leave home. It's too hard being an only child.'

His father lowered his newspaper. 'Know what you mean, son,' he said. 'It was the same when I was at home. You're forever under the spotlight, eh?' He hissed through his teeth, 'Many was the time I wished I had a brother or sister to draw the attention from me.'

Grabbing his coat from the chair Dave slung it over his shoulder. 'So! I'm wearing shoes for a change. What's the big deal?'

In a hurry to get back to his newspaper, Dave's father felt obliged to make a comment. 'No big deal,' he remarked, 'it's just that your mother and I were beginning to think them old trainers had grown to the soles of your feet.'

'Whose side are you on anyway?' Dave demanded.

'Why, yours, of course,' came the tongue-in-cheek reply. Chuckling merrily he regarded his son with pride: the way he held himself; the thick mop of shining black hair and handsome dark eyes; the attractive manner in which he wore the brown cords and blue silk shirt. 'You look good, son. There was a time when your dad looked as handsome.' Truth was, he had never been as handsome. Dave had his mother's dark colouring. It stood him out from the crowd.

Suddenly his son had matured into a man. The realisation momentarily filled him with pride, and a little envy, because if his son was a man, he himself was an older man. The pride outshone the envy. 'You go and enjoy yourself,' he encouraged. 'Take no notice of your mother.' He gave his wife a naughty wink. 'She always was a nosy old bugger.'

Meg wasn't amused. 'Hey! Not so much of the "old"!' she complained. At forty years of age she might be too plump, too homely, and not as bothered about her appearance as she used to be. But she didn't feel old. She hoped she never would.

Unperturbed, he returned to his precious newspaper. Neville Martin had three loves in his life: his wife, his son, and the news. Morning and evening, he read the newspaper word for word, and, much to the frustration of wife and son, he watched every news bulletin on the television, constantly switching channels in case he'd missed something important. 'I knew it!' he exclaimed from behind his paper. 'The US are about to ban Libyan exports.'

'Your father's right,' Meg told her son. 'You do look good.' She stretched up to sniff at his face. 'Your new aftershave smells good, too,' she commented ruefully. 'One thing's for certain. This girl... whoever she is... won't be able to resist you.'

Dave kissed her on the forehead. 'Don't wait up,' he told her. 'Like I said, it's a mate's party. Last one before college, I expect. Come the summer, we'll all be going our different ways.'

'I can't believe you're eighteen,' she sighed. Time carries us all away, she thought.

'Anyway, some of the lads might decide to stop the night.'
He thought of Lianne and the thrill ran right up his neck. If all
went as planned, *he* might stop the night. Nobody else. Just him.
With Lianne.

Anticipating his mother's next words, he assured her,
'Don't worry. If I decide to stay, I'll ring and let you know.'

'Make sure you do,' she called as he went down the street.
'Be good now. And if you can't be good, be careful.'

Embarrassed, he hurried away.

Jack unloaded the last of the food from the van. 'There's enough
here to feed an army,' he muttered. A party was the last thing on
his mind. He had been thinking of Cyrus and Maureen.
Tormented as always.

Liz had been thinking, too. 'Why don't you ring the hotel?'
she asked as they came into the kitchen. 'Surely you want to
know whether they're still here?'

'No, I do not want to know if they're still here.' He wanted
them gone. Out of his life for all time.

Liz was persistent. 'If they haven't gone back yet, you could
invite them out to dinner with us.'

'I could,' he agreed, 'if I *wanted* them with us. Which I
don't.'

'Your decision,' she said. 'I just think you're wrong, that's
all.' She began unpacking the fairy cakes, arranging them in
circles on the cakestand.

Thinking aloud he muttered, 'You don't know half.'

She paused, waiting for him to go on. When he didn't, she
suggested quietly, 'Why don't you tell me, then?'

'Dear God!' Slamming the tray of pork pies on to the table,
he wiped his hands down his face. When he looked up, the tips
of his fingers were digging into his mouth, dragging it into a
grotesque shape. His voice was horribly distorted. 'I've told you
everything,' he lied. 'Anyway, I thought we'd agreed not to talk

about it? I thought we were going to have a romantic candlelit dinner? That's what you wanted, wasn't it?'

'Take your fingers out of your mouth.' As though he was a child, she tapped him on the hand. 'All right. I promise I won't mention it any more.'

There was a long awkward silence while the two of them emptied the food pallets. They filled the plates and trays, they piled the cakestands high, and soon there was a spread fit for a king. 'Now it's their turn,' Liz announced. 'Give them a shout, will you? They're in the sitting-room, blowing up balloons.'

As Ginny and Lianne came into the kitchen, Jack and Liz made their escape. 'We're off to get ready now,' she told them. With a sideways smile at Jack she added, 'Your dad and I want to be away before the party-goers arrive.'

Noting how pleased Lianne and Ginny appeared to be, Jack was quick to assure them, 'But we're not going yet. And we could be back at any time during the evening, so mind you behave.'

'Don't we always?' Ginny said innocently.

'We won't wreck the house or anything,' Lianne promised, 'so you can enjoy yourselves.' She was delighted they had decided to go out. She had seen them kissing earlier. It was beginning to seem like old times. Except for Ginny. Except for the bad things.

Up in the bedroom, Jack was thoughtful. 'Penny for them,' Liz teased, pulling off her dress.

'I was just wondering,' he confessed, 'do you think it's wise to leave them to their own devices?' Slipping his shoes off he started on his socks. 'There are still parts of this house that aren't safe.'

Naked now, Liz shrugged her shoulders. 'Lianne's sixteen today. Ginny's eighteen. If we can't trust them now, when *can* we trust them?'

His eyes raked her slim supple form, the dark triangle between her thighs, the perfectly shaped breasts. He wanted her. 'You're a very sensuous woman.' Unbuckling his belt he let his trousers fall. His swollen penis made a huge bulge in his underpants.

A cute little smile lifted the corners of her mouth. 'Put it away,' she said casually. 'No woman's safe when you're around.'

'Have we got time?'

'Nope.' Strolling past him to the bathroom, she reached out to tickle him. 'But we can make up for it later if you like?'

He caught her hand and kept her there. 'Brazen hussy.' His mouth warm against hers, he caressed her skin. Sighing with pleasure as he felt his loins tighten. Sighing with agony as she drew away.

It was an hour later when they walked into the sitting-room. There was no sign of anyone. 'Now where are they?' Jack was still not happy about leaving them.

'I expect they're in the old hall.'

Going through the big oak door that led from the back hallway, Liz led the way along dark narrow corridors and through draughty rooms to the great hall. Like many other rooms in disrepair, the hall was not yet renovated. The old house swallowed money faster than Jack could make it.

'I can't understand why they wanted the party there,' Jack commented. 'It's cold and draughty, and it wouldn't surprise me if there were rats in the rafters.'

'Suits me,' Liz said. 'Saves the carpet and furniture. You should be grateful their birthdays are so close that it's only once a year instead of twice. Kills two birds with one stone.'

'You're a mercenary creature.'

'And you're a man, so you wouldn't understand. Anyway,' she reminded him, 'it was Ginny's idea to use the great hall. Lianne agreed, and I personally don't see what's wrong with it. You've made the place safe. There's electricity.' She laughed. 'There's natural ventilation where the windowframes have come away from the walls. There's even a lavvy. They'll come to no harm, so stop worrying.' Aware that he would give up the evening for half a reason, she wanted him to be satisfied that for a few hours at least, his daughters were more than capable of looking after themselves, and the house.

Lianne covered the sandwiches with cling-film. 'That should keep the dust off until we're ready to eat,' she said.

Ginny had swept the stage, and now she was checking that everything was in order. It was. 'We should have done all this yesterday,' she moaned. 'Now we'll have to rush about getting ready.'

They were about to leave, when Liz and Jack came through the door. 'Well, I never!' Jack was amazed. The great hall looked as he had never seen it before. The old beams were covered in huge colourful posters, depicting rockers and pop stars, and half-naked couples. The ceiling dripped with balloons, and the makeshift tables groaned beneath the weight of a feast. The stage was already cleared for the group to set up their instruments, and the main floor was ready for dancing on. 'You've worked hard,' he told them. 'It must have looked something like this in its heyday.' His admiring eyes roved the rafters: huge timber beams high above his head, intricately interlaced, much like the plait of a cottage loaf. Beneath them he felt small and insignificant. 'I'm half-tempted to take Cyrus' money,' he murmured. 'This house deserves it more than he does.'

But he never would take Cyrus' money. He couldn't take it. Because that would be like exonerating them. It would be like erasing the guilt. Like saying it didn't matter. But it would matter, for as long as he lived, and even after that.

'No fooling around,' he told the girls. 'I'm trusting you to be sensible.' His remarks were general, but his eyes were drawn to Ginny. It was she who gave him nightmares. She who had taken his grandmother's features, and her manners, right down to the way she smiled. It was Ginny he loved most of all. And hated. And feared.

He could be wrong. He prayed he was. Last time was easier somehow. When the others had known. This time only he knew, and he must bear it alone.

'You two look really nice.' Lianne had always been proud of her parents. She was proud now. With Jack in his best dark suit and Liz in a red two-piece, they made a handsome couple.

'Thank you.' Liz smiled appreciatively.

Recalling how he'd offered himself to Liz only a short time ago, Jack was self-conscious. 'I'm sure you two will put your mother and me in the shade,' he said lamely.

'I hope so,' Ginny interrupted. 'After all, we're young and you're old.'

Jack laughed, but he felt slighted. Turning to Liz he bent his back like an old man. 'Now are you sure you're up to an evening out, dear?' he joked. 'We can always stay in if you're too tired. I'm sure you have a whole bagful of knitting to catch up on.'

Liz hit him with her handbag. 'Don't try that on me, you artful bugger,' she laughed. 'You're taking me out to dinner, whether you like it or not.'

Protecting himself by raising his arms, he shouted, 'Help! Don't beat me. I'm only a poor old man.' When she dropped her arm, he grabbed her. 'You're a devil when you're all fired up,' he chuckled, kissing her soundly on the mouth.

'And you're a silly sod.' She loved it, though. This was like the old Jack. This was the way it should be.

Since Katherine had found him, Jack had gone through a gamut of emotions. He had been the son, the grandson. He had been a child, then a young man. He had been the silent witness all over again, reliving the young years. The child, the youth. *The witness.*

Now, he was the husband again. The father.

Turning to the girls, he warned, 'Remember what I said. No fooling around. And no candles.'

A romantic at heart, Lianne groaned. 'Oh, Dad! Why can't we have candles?'

'Because these old timbers would go up like matchwood, that's why.' His eyes travelled the room. The thought of what could happen made him shudder. 'So, if you intended using candles, forget it. Do you hear what I'm saying?'

Ginny was indignant. 'If you say so.'

'I do say so. What's more, I hope you've made it clear to your cronies that there will be no alcohol?'

'Give us credit for some sense.'

'That's exactly what I am doing,' Jack told her. 'Crediting you two with some common sense, so your mother and I can have an enjoyable evening without having to worry about what's going on back here.'

She merely smiled at him. It was a smile that said, 'Trust us, but not too much.' There were times when he seemed to know exactly what she was thinking. There were other times, strange, disturbing moments when he couldn't bear to look on his own daughter; couldn't bear to look into those magnificent, midnight eyes. They made him think of another Virginia. They made him bleed inside.

'Mind you behave,' he said again, 'and mind this house.'

Liz was impatient to leave. 'Stop nagging,' she chided. 'Give the girls their presents.'

Reaching into his pocket he drew out two cheques. 'I never know what to buy you,' he apologised. 'Your mother said you'd prefer money so you could buy clothes.'

The cheques were for a hundred pounds each. 'Thank you both,' Lianne cried, hugging them in turn. 'You could have used the money on the house, you know.'

Ginny merely smiled.

Mention of the house was enough to motivate Liz. 'Right then. We're off.' This house was Jack's private mountain. It took all their money and it came between them. To be honest, she wouldn't care if it was burned to the ground. 'Have a good time. We'll see you later.' She kissed each daughter in turn, then departed in a flurry, her high heels tapping out a tune on the solid floors.

Jack lingered a moment. 'We won't be too long, I expect,' he assured them.

Ginny wanted rid of him, but she had to agree with Lianne. He looked incredibly handsome. A real man. 'She'll go without you if you're not careful,' she said brightly. She wondered how she might kill him. Her heart was elated. Then it was filled with pain. Sometimes, at night when she lay in her bed, she harboured disturbing feelings towards her father. Sexual yearnings that some might claim were decidedly unhealthy.

'Go on, Dad,' Lianne ordered. 'We'll be all right.' Dave would be here any minute, she thought. And in front of her father she might not be able to hide their little secret.

Liz's voice echoed down the corridor. 'Jack! Are you coming or not?'

'Better go,' he said with a lopsided smile.

Like Liz, he gave them a quick kiss. 'Think on,' he said.

The sisters echoed his warning in loud unison: 'No candles. No fooling around. Behave yourself.'

Laughing out loud for the first time in weeks, he took his leave.

Lianne breathed a sigh of relief. 'Now they've gone out, Dave won't need to stay the night, will he?' she whispered. 'We can sneak out during the party instead.' The idea of Dave in her bed, with her parents only minutes away was too unnerving.

Ginny gave her a scathing look. 'Why are you whispering?'

'I didn't realise I was.'

'I hope you're not getting cold feet again!'

'Don't bully me.'

Grabbing her by the scruff of her neck, Ginny promised, 'I'll strangle you if you make a fool of me this time.' She propelled Lianne out of the hall. 'If we don't get a move on they'll be here before we're ready,' she grumbled. And the two of them went down the corridor at a run.

An hour later the first guest arrived. 'Hope you've got plenty of food?' Craig was a sixth former with an appetite like a gannet.

Lianne showed him the way to the great hall. When his avaricious eyes strayed to the tables, she told him firmly, 'Hands off the goodies until I say so.'

Ten minutes later the group turned up: a collection of scruffy, ambitious musicians from school, who immediately set about plugging in their equipment and rattling off a quick practice before everyone else arrived. By quarter to nine, the hall was filled. There were young men in jeans and sweatshirts, girls in mini skirts and others in long flowing dresses and wedge shoes.

'What a motley crew!' Ginny observed wryly.

Lianne thought the whole thing was marvellous and laid her presents at the foot of the stage. 'Open them together at the stroke of midnight!' someone shouted. And all thought that was a splendid idea.

Ginny's fellow looked sexy in tight-fitting trousers and open-necked shirt. He had not wanted to come, but Ginny was addictive. He could never say no to her.

When Amy Burton turned up, Ginny took Lianne aside. 'I thought I said you were not to ask that little cow?'

'It seemed unfair not to ask her,' Lianne protested.

Soon the party was in full swing. The music was loud and lively, splitting eardrums. Then it was soft and romantic, enticing couples on to the floor to smooch. There were other couples seated cross-legged on the ground, chatting, kissing, and generally having a great time. 'Where the hell is Dave Martin?' Ginny seemed more anxious than Lianne.

Hiding her disappointment, Lianne sipped at her orange juice. 'I expect he's changed his mind.'

Jack had rigged up an extension to the front-door bell. Attached to the rafter above the entrance and set against a tin background, for fire precaution, when the bell rang it rattled and sounded like all hell was let loose. It rang now. 'That could be him,' Lianne said hopefully.

'I thought you'd never answer,' Dave told her. 'I've been ringing this bell for ages. In another minute I might have broken down the door.'

Lianne thought it strange. 'The bell's been working all right until now.' She smiled, drawing him inside. 'Dad's pride will take a bashing when I tell him it's gone wrong.'

He gave her an envelope. 'Happy Birthday.'

'What is it?' Whatever it was she would love it, because he had bought it for her.

'Two tickets to a rock concert,' he explained. 'They're good for twelve months.'

She was delighted. 'How did you know?' Slade was her alltime favourite.

'I have my ways.' He bent his head. 'I do expect a kiss for them, though.'

The kiss was brief, and they were both embarrassed.

Halfway down the corridor he took her into his arms. 'Now can I have a proper kiss?' he murmured.

Suddenly she was overwhelmingly shy. 'We'd better get back before Ginny wonders where I am.'

He nibbled her ear. 'Let her wonder.' He had a strong dislike for Ginny Lucas. It seemed inconceivable that two such different girls could be sisters. 'You're not letting her bully you again, are you?'

'What do you mean?' In his arms she felt so safe. At night she went to sleep thinking about him. In the morning she couldn't wait to see him.

'I mean... you and me. The reason why she asked me to the party. Was it to get at you?'

'I wanted you here. I'd rather have you here than anyone else.'

'Do you love me, Lianne?'

'I think so.'

'That's only half an answer.'

'I don't know for sure if I love you, because I've never loved anyone else.' She ached for him. When he held her she wanted it never to end. If that was love, then she loved him with all her heart.

Ginny's voice was like a whip across them. 'Thought you'd got lost.' She scowled at Lianne and smiled at Dave. 'You're the last to arrive. Lianne was worried in case you'd changed your mind.'

With his arm round Lianne he nodded towards the source of the music. 'If you wouldn't mind, I'd like a few words with Lianne before we go in there.'

Her smile fell away. 'Sounds to me like you're not asking, but telling.'

'You've got it in one.'

Bristling with annoyance, she made herself smile. 'My! You really are an arrogant bastard.'

'Takes one to know one.'

Realising this could escalate into an all-out fight, Lianne intervened. 'Please, Ginny. We'll only be a minute.'

Ginny's face was like ice. 'Okay. But you do have other guests.' With that she angrily tossed her head and hurried away. He would pay for his arrogance, she promised herself. No one talked to her like that. Especially not in front of her little sister.

Lianne knew how vindictive Ginny could be. 'You've made a bad enemy,' she warned. 'Ginny won't take kindly to being humiliated like that.'

Swinging her round he took her by the shoulders and bent his face to hers. 'You just don't see it, do you?'

'What?'

'It wasn't me humiliating her. It was *her* humiliating *you*.'

'She doesn't mean to.'

'She does it all the time, Lianne. If you don't notice, others do.' He squared his shoulders. 'It makes me want to shake her... or you, for putting up with it!'

'Are you sorry you came?' She hoped he wasn't. She hoped Ginny hadn't spoiled everything.

He gazed at her in the half-light. There was a beautiful strength about him that made her gasp. 'No, I'm not sorry,' he whispered. 'How could I be sorry?'

She misunderstood him. 'I promise not to go back on my word this time.'

Placing a strong finger against her lips, he murmured, 'That's not why I'm here.' His smile gentled into her heart. 'Though I will confess I haven't stopped thinking about... well, you know... you and me.'

She blushed, hoping he couldn't see the colour rising. 'Me too.' She felt foolish, immature. There was less than two years between her and Ginny, yet Ginny had made love many times. 'I promise you I won't send you away this time.'

'Don't make promises,' he said lovingly. 'That way you're free to change your mind.'

He kissed her then. A long lingering kiss that tortured her senses. She would keep her promise. She wanted to. More than he could know.

For most of the evening, Ginny danced non-stop. When the food was announced, the musicians took a break and everyone flocked to the tables.

While Dave went to get food for himself and Lianne, Ginny took her to one side. 'You don't have to do it with him,' she said harshly. 'There are plenty of others who'd be glad to oblige.'

'I don't want anyone else. Especially not Old Tom.' She grimaced with disgust.

In a quick, spiteful movement, Ginny grabbed her by the arms. 'What's he got to do with anything?'

'I thought you knew?'

The eyes were probing, dark and dangerous. 'I think you'd better tell me.'

'The other day, I was sent to find him. Some joker had rolled a litter-bin on to the hockey-pitch and there was rubbish everywhere. He was in his hut. He knew about the party, and he said if I invited him, he'd bring some of his dirty pictures. He wanted the two of us to hide away somewhere and look at them.'

'Filthy bastard!'

Taking hold of Ginny's hands, Lianne shook her off. 'Thanks for the offer,' she said with sarcasm. 'You'll understand if I prefer Dave Martin.'

On two occasions Ginny had tried to seduce Dave herself, but he made it clear he wasn't interested. She hit back now. 'He might not be any good at it,' she said spitefully.

'Good enough for me.'

'You always were easy to please.' She then flounced off.

Dave returned empty handed. 'Are you all right?'

'Yes, why?'

He glanced to where Ginny was laughing with a group of young men. 'I just wondered, that's all.' He seemed awkward. 'She can be a real bitch, your sister.'

'I can handle her.' As much as anyone can, she thought.

'She seemed to be angry.' He glanced at Ginny once more. This time she returned his glance – a hard, sly glance that only convinced him of her nasty nature.

Made anxious by the look that passed between these two, Lianne asked jovially, 'Are you trying to starve me?'

He jerked his head round. 'Didn't hear that?'

'I thought you'd gone to get me some food?'

'There was a long queue,' he lied.

'I'll get it.' Something in the glint of his smiling eyes caught her attention. 'Are you really hungry?'

'Only for you.' His voice was soft, shamelessly intimate.

She wanted to speak, to say something witty, like Ginny would. But her heart was beating too fast, and the words got stuck in her throat.

He reached out and touched her hand. She couldn't even look at him. She felt herself being led away, and she followed, eagerly, as ready now as she would ever be.

They went out of the hall, down the corridor, and away from the living quarters. They didn't speak. They held hands, and hearts, and she felt closer to him than she had ever felt to anyone. She wasn't afraid. Not any more.

When they came to the bottom of the corridor, he turned the corner. There was a small door she had never even known was there. 'There has to be a back door under the stage,' he explained, pushing his way through, 'to get to the cables... electricity, that sort of thing.' Careful to lock the door behind them, he pressed his finger to his lips. 'Shh! Softly now.'

Big eyed and trembling, Lianne went on tiptoe. Once the door was closed she could hardly see. Everything was in shadow. Noises filtered through from the hall, muffled laughter, drifts of inaudible conversation. As the discolamps turned full circle, flickers of coloured light danced in and out. It was weird and cold. And scary.

As they made their way to the far side, they found themselves caught in a spider's web. In a panic the huge black spider scuttled towards them, falling down Lianne's face as she brushed away the sticky grey strands. Her scream pierced the air, at the very moment the music struck up.

Cleaning her face, Dave cushioned it between the palms of his hands. 'Okay?'

'Okay,' she answered, giggling foolishly.

He took off his coat and laid it down. With a gallant sweep of his arms, he offered, 'For you, my lady.' When she was seated, he made himself comfortable beside her. The music was deafening, a wild frenzy that rocked the stage above them. 'You'd think they'd play something more appropriate,' he whispered.

'Appropriate for what?'

'For us. You and me... our first time together.' He took hold of her hand and crushed it to his lips. 'You can't be so cruel as to deny me now?' As he spoke a purple beam lit up his face. There was a softness there. And a brute strength.

'Would you do it anyway? Even if I said I didn't want to?'

'You shouldn't have to ask that.'

'I'm sorry.'

'Don't be.' Leaning forward he wound his two arms round her body. 'You're so lovely.' As he kissed her, he gently pushed

194

back with his weight, until the two of them were lying flat on the ground, he straddling her, and she beneath him, looking up with trusting eyes. 'I won't hurt you,' he promised.

She smiled, echoing his own words. 'Don't make promises you can't keep.'

She had deliberately worn a loose wrap-around skirt that slipped on and off easily. She took it off now, rousing him every time she moved. Next came her briefs. From the breasts down she was naked. The cold was penetrating. The harsh hairs on his jacket pricked her skin, making her gasp.

In a moment he was totally naked. It wasn't enough. He needed to see her breasts, to touch them with the tip of his tongue. To feel them hardening as he hardened. To remember. To dream it again. Long after this evening was over. Snaking his hands behind her back he undid the flimsy brassière, skilfully, as though he had done it many times.

Lianne lay still, waiting, wondering how it would be. Her whole body ached with longing. He was so gentle, so right. His kisses were tender at first, then frantic, like the music. She kissed him, and held him, and loved him with all her young heart. When he entered her, the pain was crippling. Exquisite. She groaned aloud, pulling away at first, then cautiously pushing into him, her slim body writhing in his strong arms. So many sensations sped through her that she could hardly keep control. A breathtaking awareness blossomed inside her, opening from the roots of her soul, taking her into a dizzy spiral. Spinning. Spinning, sweet and breathless. She could hear herself moaning. Like an animal. Was that really her?

Suddenly the music erupted. So did she. Dave too. Spilling and throbbing into the corners of her self. Merging together. She cried out, clinging to him with all her strength. Suddenly she was laughing. 'I never thought it would be like that!'

Without warning the music stopped. Bright searching lights flooded the darkness, plucking them out, laying bare their nakedness for the world to see. There was a crescendo of clapping, rude remarks, lewd laughter. 'That was a great performance!' someone shouted. 'When do we get an encore?'

Squinting against the lights, Dave yelled something obscene. There was a burst of crude giggling.

Ginny's voice crept along the floorboards. 'I was wrong, sis!' she called out. 'He does it better than anyone I've ever had.'

Another burst of laughter, before the lights swung full circle. Horrified and in tears, Lianne saw a blur of faces peering at them from beneath the edge of the stage.

Ginny's was the most hideous. Filled with envy, she smiled wickedly, savouring every awful minute. 'How does it feel, now you're not a virgin any more?'

'*I hate you!*' Lianne could hear her own voice, high and screeching. Like a madwoman's.

Suddenly the music started and the faces disappeared. 'God almighty!' Dave was shocked. 'What kind of monster is she?' He was enraged. Not embarrassed. Virile young men were not prone to embarrassment.

Sobbing, Lianne grabbed her blouse and skirt. As she ran she managed to tie the skirt round her waist. The blouse was flung over her shoulders. Nobody saw her. Nobody cared enough.

Behind her she could hear Dave pleading, 'Wait! They don't matter! Don't let them spoil it!'

But it was already spoiled. 'Go away!' She didn't want him to, but how could he stay now? How could she face them?

In her room she cried until there were no more tears left. After a while she showered and crawled into bed. Exhausted, she fell asleep.

It was her mother who woke her. 'Are you feeling better, sweetheart?'

Confused, Lianne woke with a start. 'What time is it?' Her eyes swivelled to the clock on the bedside cabinet. It was quarter past two in the morning.

Liz touched the back of her hand to Lianne's forehead.

'Ginny said you left the party early… not well. How do you feel now?'

Desperate to get her wits together, Lianne played for a moment's time. The events of the evening were still blurred in her mind. All she knew was that she hated Ginny. Hated her with a ferocity she had never known before. 'I had a headache.' She looked up to see Jack standing in the doorway. 'But I'm fine now.'

'You had some lovely presents.'

Lianne couldn't hide her astonishment. 'How do you know that?' She had not even opened her presents. The last time she saw them they were piled at the foot of the stage.

Now it was Liz's turn to be astonished. 'Because I've seen them. Ginny was waiting for us when we came in.'

'*Ginny* showed you *my* presents?'

'Yes. That was all right, wasn't it?'

Coming to the bed, Jack gazed down on her. 'Did Ginny upset you?' He had a gut feeling that Lianne was lying. Her mouth was saying one thing, while her expression said another. Something had sent her running to her room, and it was *not* a headache.

She feigned surprise. 'What makes you think Ginny upset me?'

He gave a half-smile. 'Because I know her,' he said flatly.

Since the day she was born, he had felt a strong urge to protect Ginny. He blamed himself. By christening her with his grandmother's name, he had burdened his child; evoked an unspeakable evil. For too long he had made excuses for her. Turned a blind eye. Now, after two unexplained deaths, he had to be extra careful. At first he believed she would never hurt her sister. Now he wasn't so sure.

In the face of Lianne's continuing silence, he insisted, 'If Ginny spoiled the party, I want to know.'

Tempted to betrayal, Lianne opened her mouth to tell. But in spite of everything, she could not bring herself to do it.

Ginny was unbearably cruel, and there were times when she was so afraid of her sister that she hardly dared look at her. The fear was strong. The love was stronger. 'I've already told you,' she lied unconvincingly, 'I had a headache.'

Jack shrugged his shoulders, helpless against such blind loyalty. 'If you say so.'

Liz was not convinced. She had never liked Ginny. Even as a child in arms, she had frightened her. 'Don't cover up for her.'

'I'm not.' Yawning, she pulled the blanket over her head. 'Can I go to sleep now?'

Tired herself, Liz stood up. ''Night, then.'

Thankfully, Lianne turned over. ''Night, Mum.'

Later, when the house was quiet, she would go to Ginny's room. Her sister had a lot to answer for!

Dropping into the armchair, Liz took off her high heels. 'My feet feel like two balloons,' she moaned, rubbing her fingers over her toes. 'I'm getting too old to keep up with fashion. In future I'll stick to low heels.'

'Are we having a drink?' Jack didn't feel like sleep. He hadn't expected to come back and find Ginny waiting downstairs, and Lianne in her bed. There was something wrong.

'Not for me,' Liz answered. 'I had too many drinks over dinner. Anyway, I'm dog-tired.' She saw how disturbed he was. 'You don't believe her, do you?'

He poured himself a short brandy and brought it to the chair. Perched on the edge of the seat with his legs apart and his arms resting on his knees, he rolled the glass between his palms. 'She's lying,' he said, regarding Liz through narrowed eyes.

'Hmm! You haven't exactly set a good example in that department, have you?' She had only part-way forgiven him.

'I thought we'd agreed not to raise that issue again?'

'*You* agreed. But all right!' She raised her hands in protest. 'We'll put that aside for now.' Rolling down her stockings, she took them off and laid them on the back of her chair. 'Anyway, why would she lie?'

'You know why.'

'Because she's frightened, you mean?'

'Lianne's never been frightened of her sister.' Not like you, he thought.

'Why then?'

'Who knows? Your daughters are young women now. Young women have secrets.'

'They'll have to sort it themselves then, won't they?'

'You don't seem bothered.'

'I'm not.' She never pretended to be a perfect mother. 'I'm more bothered about you and me.'

'We're strong enough to get through.'

She came to kneel at his feet. 'Still love me, do you?'

He stroked his hand down her hair. 'Always,' he murmured, kissing her on the forehead.

'What will you do about your uncle?' She hadn't given up the idea that they might all still be friends.

'I would imagine they've gone.' He hoped they had. He hoped they would never again set eyes on him. Or Maureen Delaney.

'You should ring the hotel.'

He inwardly cringed. 'Don't start that again.'

'Do you want *me* to ring?'

'Forget it, Liz.'

'He means to give you a fortune.'

'I said forget it, Liz!'

'We could do with it. There's this house only half-renovated, and your daughters will soon be going to college. They'll need all sorts of help.'

'We'll manage. We always have.' He sipped at his brandy and wished he could turn back the clock. If he could turn it back over twenty years, how simple life might have been.

She stretched out her legs. 'Jack?'

'What now?'

Shocking him to his roots she asked in softer tones, 'Do you think Ginny killed your mother?'

The silence was like a physical presence.

He felt guilty. Did she really think Ginny had killed Katherine?

'I don't think I heard you right.' He couldn't believe what she'd said.

Turning to face him, Liz gripped his knees, her anxious gaze playing on his face. 'There's something very strange about her. She frightens me, Jack. Our daughter frightens me.'

Pushing her away he clambered out of the chair, mortified when his brandy glass slipped from his hand and made a small cut on her temple. 'Christ! I'm a clumsy bastard!' At once he fell to his knees. 'Keep still.' Taking out a serviette he'd picked up from the dinner table, he began mopping the trickle of blood.

He knew she was staring at him, and he felt threatened. He didn't like feeling threatened. 'You didn't mean what you said just now, did you?' he asked softly. 'About Ginny?'

Her voice was barely audible. 'I had a dream,' she revealed. 'It was so real, Jack, like it was actually happening.'

'What kind of dream?' Was it the same dream he had over and over? He mentally shook himself. No, how could it be?

'A big cold place, like a courtroom. Ginny, all alone in a big cage… bodies everywhere…' Horrified by her own mind she curled into a ball. 'I think I must be going mad.'

While she described the fragments of her dream, Jack relived it like it was yesterday: the courtroom, his grandmother alone in the stand… on trial for her life. And oh, the pictures that were handed round the jury. Awful pictures, of death, and torture, and human depravity. *And Liz had seen it!* Liz had tapped into his worst nightmares and seen it all! But it wasn't his grandmother she saw. It was Ginny.

He touched her and she looked up. 'What's happening to us?' A sob caught in her throat.

Forcing himself to smile he grabbed her by the arms and stood her up. 'We all have dreams,' he muttered. Dreams. Nightmares. Fragments of the past that are woven into our everyday lives. 'It was just a dream,' he promised.

Her stricken gaze lingered on his face. 'I don't want to lose you, Jack.'

Softly laughing he held her close. 'You're right,' he observed. 'You *have* had too much to drink.'

Relief washed through her. 'I expect you're right.'

'A good night's sleep – that's what you want, my girl! You go up. I'll check to see what kind of mess they've left in the hall.'

'They promised to clean it up.'

'I'll check anyway.' He was still concerned. Something had gone on here, and he needed to know.

He watched Liz go up the stairs, then he made his way to the great hall. Pleasantly surprised that they had kept their promise, he sat on the edge of the stage and lit a cigarette. 'They've left it tidy anyway,' he mused aloud. 'Nothing here to tell me what might have happened between those two.'

He smoked his cigarette, feeling calmer, feeling guilty. He had given strict instructions that there should be no smoking, no candles, no naked lights in this place, riddled with timber as it was. 'Shame on you,' he chided, stubbing the cigarette out on the hard timber flooring. 'A man should practise what he preaches.'

He stayed a moment longer. Alone with his thoughts. With his nightmares. I'm sorry I brought this down on your head, Liz, he thought. I should sell up. Take you away. Start a new life somewhere else. He jumped down from the stage. Who was he kidding? He was trapped. Imprisoned in a cage of his own making.

Liz was fast asleep. Seeing her lying there, curled up like a child, made him realise how vulnerable she was. 'I'll make it up to you, sweetheart,' he murmured, sliding in beside her. 'If I never do anything else in my life, I swear to God I'll make it all up to you.'

Restless, Lianne slept lightly. She had the awful feeling something terrible was about to happen, but didn't know what, or how to stop it. At the root of it all was Ginny.

She dreamed. Then she woke. She closed her eyes and ached for sleep, but it wouldn't come again. With her eyes wide open she saw herself and Ginny running down a long winding road. Someone was chasing them. Someone with murder in mind.

'Lianne? Are you awake?' A whisper. The figure, tall and slender, entered the room. 'Lianne?' Familiar now. Ginny.

'Go away.'

'I'm sorry.'

'No you're not.' Unforgiving, she turned away.

'Lianne!'

'*Go away*!' She could feel Ginny's warm breath on her face.

'He angered me. No one speaks to me like that.'

'I'm glad he put you in your place.'

'I wanted to humiliate him in the same way.'

Incensed, Lianne rolled round and sat up. The room was in shadow. She couldn't see. A slight movement drew her to where Ginny knelt beside the bed, just a heartbeat away.

'Don't be hard on me,' she whispered. 'You know what I'm like. Sometimes I do these spiteful things. Afterwards I'm sorry.' Her dark eyes were fathomless, sucking Lianne down. 'I really am sorry,' she murmured convincingly. 'Do you forgive me?'

'I should kill you.'

A quiet, merciless smile. 'You should. But you won't.'

'What do you want?'

'I had no right to open your birthday presents.'

'I would have been more surprised if you hadn't.' The sarcasm was biting.

'I didn't give you your present because it wasn't quite ready.' She sniggered. 'I've got it safely hidden away.'

'I don't want anything from you.'

'Please.'

The love between them was like a physical chain. Each resenting it. Each longing to be free.

Softer now. 'What is it?'

'Come and see.'

'Bring it here.'

'I can't.'

'Why not?'

'You'll see.' She switched on the bedside lamp. Her face alive with cunning, she rasped, 'Oh, Lianne, I do hope you like it.' Grabbing her sister's dressing gown from the chair she urged, 'Hurry up. And be quiet. We don't want to wake *them*.' Her gaze shifted towards the door. She was thinking of their parents. 'Later, I have a surprise for them as well.'

Struggling into her dressing gown, Lianne was suspicious. 'What kind of surprise?'

Playfully prodding her in the arm, Ginny chided, 'Listen to you! Anyone would think I was about to murder them.'

Mentally recalling Ginny's very words, Lianne was not convinced. 'I'll have to kill them.' That's what she had said.

Now it was Lianne's turn to threaten. 'I won't let you hurt them.'

'You take me too seriously.'

'Only because... sometimes...' She lowered her gaze.

'Sometimes what?'

Lianne's voice fell to a whisper. 'Sometimes you frighten me.'

There was a span of silence, during which Lianne dared not look up. Presently, Ginny's voice gentled into her thoughts. 'You'll make yourself a nervous wreck, worrying about nothing.'

Considering her sister's words, Lianne seemed a little reassured. Not content though. Never content. 'You don't mean to hurt them, then?'

'Like I said, you worry about nothing. You're all the same, you and them. Always worrying.' Her scheming smile gave nothing away. Lianne. Her parents. After tonight they would not have to worry about anything, ever again.

'Where is it?' Fastening her belt, Lianne slipped her feet into the cherry-red slippers. 'My present. Where've you hidden it?'

'I'll show you.' Impatient now, she led the way across the room to the door. 'You have to like it,' she whispered excitedly. Her voice took on a hard edge. 'I'll be upset if you don't like it. You see, I've been planning it for ages.'

A few moments later they were downstairs. Ginny opened the door to the cellars. 'Quiet now,' she warned. 'Every sound echoes.'

With only a pencil-torch to guide her, Ginny followed the familiar route. 'I've been down the cellars many times these last few weeks, so I know the way by heart.' Every now and then she would turn to make sure Lianne was following.

They went in silence: one exhilarated, the other apprehensive. In her heart Lianne had still not forgiven.

As they travelled deeper into the roots of the house, Lianne began to wish she had not agreed to come. 'Let's go back,' she urged. 'Show me in the morning.' The damp air seeped through her dressing gown, and the shadows followed their every step.

'Don't be a baby!'

'How much further?' She was born in this house, but never in her life had she been down the cellars. Once, her father told her it was like a labyrinth, a maze where you could easily get lost. Fear took hold of her. 'I want to go back.'

'We're almost there.'

As she spoke, they came into an opening. 'Wait a minute.' Taking a box of matches from her pocket she struck one and reached up. In preparation she had placed a candle on the ledge. She lit it now, and the shadows scuttled away. 'See?' Her voice was comforting. Like a mother's to a child. 'There's nothing to be frightened of.'

Unwilling to move, Lianne stared into every corner. The cavern was awesome. High stone walls dripping with condensation, their ancient formation making weird and wonderful shapes: of animals and men, and monsters.

As they continued, their feet were bathed in small pools of stinking water. The odour of something rotten filled the cavern from end to end. 'Why did you keep my present down here?' Lianne whispered. Down here, where no one could possibly hear, she felt the need to whisper, almost as if they were in a church. But this was no church. It was an unholy place.

Ginny's silence emphasised the sinister atmosphere.

They went through the cavern into a narrow place. 'There!' Ginny held the candle high. The shadows closed in. 'Do you see?'

Raising her eyes, Lianne followed the halo of light. As it moved slowly along the high ledge, it fell on one gruesome sight after another. Dozens of dead creatures all in a row, strung together by their tails and making a weird garland across the ledge. The walls beneath were spattered with blood, dark meandering stains that even the stone could not absorb.

As Lianne stared up through tearful eyes, the creatures stared down through dead, wide-open eyes, black pitiful things, stark with the agony they had endured. Lianne gasped with horror. 'Did *you* do that?' She didn't want to look on those poor tortured faces, but she couldn't tear her gaze away.

Ginny's voice murmured in her ear. 'Mice,' she hissed, 'rats... gerbils. It was me who broke into the science lab.'

'You're sick.' The words were emitted through clenched teeth, a great rage welling up inside her. 'Don't tell me you did this for me!' The muscles of her face worked in and out as she tried hard to control herself. 'Please, Ginny! Don't say you did this for me.' The thought was too shocking.

'Why would I do this for you?' She peered at Lianne's stricken face. In the half-light she saw what Dave Martin had seen, a lovely young woman with a nature as warm and generous as her heart. She saw it as weakness, and was angry. 'You say you're my friend, but you're not. You're just like *them*. You think I'm wicked and cruel.'

'I don't really think that.' It was love that spoke. Sadness too, for an unforgivable atrocity. 'Those poor creatures. What did they ever do to you?'

'Nothing.'

'Then... *why*?'

'I get lonely,' she snapped. 'The creatures keep me company. I didn't want to do it, but they would have run away.'

Lianne stretched out a hand. 'Now that you've shown them to me, we can go back?' She felt the need to humour her. 'I'll make you a cup of hot chocolate. How would you like that?' When Ginny shook her head in disbelief, she went on, 'I promise I won't tell what you've done here. But tomorrow morning I hope you will speak to Father yourself.' Her voice softened. 'You need help, Ginny. I know it now. You have to talk to someone.'

Ginny's laughter echoed round the walls. 'You want to go?' She clapped her hands together like an excited child. 'Did you really think this was your present?' she asked incredulously. 'No! No! Your present is through there.' Pointing to a small wooden door she would have taken Lianne with her. She was astonished when Lianne refused to budge. 'Don't you want to see it?'

'No, I don't want to see it.' The smile froze on her lips.

'It's a very special present.' The madness lit her eyes.

'You can show me tomorrow if you like. Right now, I want to go back.' Her instincts told her to play along, or be strung up there with the rest of the creatures.

Kissing her gently on the mouth, Ginny pleaded, 'Don't be frightened.'

A cold hand gripped Lianne's heart. 'I'm not frightened.' There was something terrible here. Something evil.

Taking Lianne's trembling hands into hers, Ginny pressed them close to her face. 'I wish I could believe you.' She was softly crying, the tears falling warm and sticky on Lianne's skin. 'You know I love you? More than anyone in the world.'

'And I love you.'

'Will you really come and see tomorrow?'

'I've said so, haven't I?'

'Yes.' A long deep sigh. 'You've said so.'

'Can we go back now?'

'If you like.' Casting a nervous glance to the small door, she said in a tight little voice, 'You'd better go and boil the kettle. Make my chocolate in Father's mug… the big blue one.'

'Aren't you coming too?'

'In a minute.' She glanced at the small wooden door once more. 'I have to make sure your present is safe.'

'I won't know the way out.' She felt trapped, as though she were buried alive. Her heart was beating fast and her lungs felt as though they were being squeezed by two giant hands.

'Here.' Thrusting the candle into her fist, Ginny told her, 'I don't need it. I can find my way blindfold.'

'If you're sure?' She wasn't about to argue. She wanted to get out of this place. And never come back.

Ginny gave no answer. Instead she walked away.

When she could no longer see her, Lianne called out, 'A minute, then? I'll have your chocolate ready… in Daddy's mug, just as you asked.' She couldn't see the logic behind that, but then Ginny was not given to logic.

From somewhere behind her came the sound of a door closing. The sound bounced round the cavern, echoing from the walls and putting the fear of God in her. 'I'm leaving you here,' she called out, hoping Ginny might still change her mind and come with her.

The silence was eerie.

Apprehensive, she retraced her steps, her eyes peeled for the stairway. 'Daddy has to know what you've done,' she muttered under her breath. 'If you don't tell him in the morning, then I will!'

Ginny softly closed the door behind her. In the darkness she took two steps to the right, until her leg met a hard boulder.

With a sigh of relief she reached down, her long manicured fingers scuttling along the stone like a monster spider. When the fingertips alighted on a small box, she bent forward. Holding the box securely between her two hands, she opened it and withdrew the match. When the match was struck and the flicker of light gave some relief in the darkness, she went carefully forward.

Darkness followed in her wake.

Wedged in the wall at the far side of the room were four candles. After lighting each in turn, she sat cross-legged on the ground, her beautiful dark eyes drawn forwards. 'I couldn't get her to come,' she said. 'She did promise to come and see you tomorrow though.' In the candlelight, her smile was never more beautiful, her words never more sinister. 'But... tomorrow will be too late.'

The darkness played in and out of the candlelight.

She sighed impatiently. 'You haven't got much to say, have you?'

The candlelight flickered. Shadows moved, closing in.

'I know I promised she would be here,' Ginny apologised, 'and I did try.' She laughed. 'At first it was only a ruse to get you into this house. If I hadn't said she would be here, that she wanted to see the dirty pictures... even wanted you to mate with her...' The idea made her chuckle. 'If I hadn't said all those things, you would never have been enticed, would you?' Tapping her nose knowingly she whispered, 'You forget I know what a cunning old fox you are.'

Anger hardened her voice. 'We were all right, weren't we, you and me? I let you touch me, didn't I? I looked at your dirty pictures and I let you touch me.' Picking up a small stone she slammed it at the wall, shaking her head in a rage, the words tumbling out in a breathless rush. 'Why did you have to spoil it all? Why did you have to make improper suggestions to *her*? Wasn't I enough for you?' With each word her voice heightened, until she realised she might be heard, even as far down as this. 'Shh!' Pressing her fingers to her lips she glanced round, smiling again, her mood swiftly changed. 'We don't want them to hear us, do we?'

Quiet now. Nothing left to say.

From somewhere inside the wall a rat could be heard scuttling along. Cocking a thumb in the direction of the noise, she chuckled. 'That must be the one that got away.'

The noise continued for a moment. When it ceased the silence was unbearable. 'Got to go,' she said brightly. 'Can't stay chatting with you all night.'

Getting up, she groaned. 'This ground is so damp.' She rubbed her knees and wiped her hand across the back of her jeans. 'I expect you feel it more than me,' she remarked casually. 'After all, you've been down here a few days now.'

Somewhere in the distance the moisture from the walls made a rhythmic sound as it dripped to the stone floor, drip, drip, drip.

'It's lucky you've got no family, or you might have been missed.'

One of the candles flickered and died. 'Bugger it!' After relighting it, she plucked it from its safe place and went to the corner of the room. Here she slipped her hand into a crevice and withdrew a sheaf of papers. 'I can't leave these here,' she explained. 'Mustn't be careless. The old lady was careless and look where it got her.' She caressed them as though they were a lover. 'They might be safer hidden in the bakery.' Out of the corner of her eye she gave him an intimate little smile. 'No one knows I've got them, except you,' she whispered, wagging a chastising finger.

A thought occurred to her. 'Would you like to see them?'

Cocking her ear as though waiting for an answer, she let the moment pass before replying. 'All right. But you must promise not to tell anyone.'

She fell to her knees. 'I haven't shown them to anyone else,' she said coveting the papers.

When they were spread on the ground, she cried excitedly, 'Look there!' Pointing a shaking finger at the first photograph, she explained, 'That's my great-grandmother… Virginia Louis. Did you know I was named after her?' She smiled proudly, waving her beautifully manicured fingers over each picture in turn. 'And do you see these other people?'

Again she waited for an answer. When none came, she frowned. 'Of course, you couldn't possibly know.' Her voice fell to a whisper. 'These people were bad. My great-grandmother was right to kill them.'

Sniggering, she carefully folded the papers. 'Americans don't hang their murderers, you know. They burn them to a crisp in the electric chair.' Hugging the papers close to her breast she rocked back and forth. 'I have her blood in me. They didn't tell me, but I always knew there was something. I'm glad I made it my business to find out.' Her eyes flashed hatred. '*They* would never have told me.' Her whole body stiffened as she stared at the door. 'They tried to keep the truth from me.' Her voice shaking with emotion, she went on, 'Now they're trying to keep her money from me. That's why I have to punish them, do you see? They've been bad too. And my sister. Lying. Pretending.' She turned away, the dark eyes awash with tears. 'I won't let them rob me!'

Again she cocked her ear as though intently listening. 'That's right,' she said, 'I don't have to tell you.'

Down there, in that closed cavern, the air was rank. The darkness lurked all around, momentarily held back by a feeble flicker of candlelight. There was something else too. An evil so powerful it consumed everything normal.

Leaning forward, Ginny sniffed the air. 'You do stink!' she protested. 'Don't you ever wash?'

She chuckled at her own stupidity. 'Of course, you can't, can you? There's no running water. And how could I carry a bowl of soapy water down here? That's a stupid idea!'

Raising the candle she regarded her guest. 'You haven't got much to say, have you?' she complained. 'Cat got your tongue?'

The silence angered her. 'All right. Sulk if you like.' At once she was apologetic. 'I suppose you're wondering when you'll be let out of here?'

Raising the candle she came closer. The face stared back at her. 'You know I can't let you go, so don't look at me like that.' She smacked the back of his hand. 'Serves you right for being a dirty old man.'

She stared a moment longer, soaking the image into herself, so she could recall it for all time.

From his hard stone seat, Old Tom stared back with accusing eyes. His cap was pulled hard down over his eyes, showing only the merest whisper of grey hair at either side. His skin hung in a multitude of wrinkles, yellowing now, sagging with a dead weight. Tiny rivulets of murky liquid escaped from the corners of his mouth and eyes, gently trickling, like the moisture down the walls.

Dressed in his best grey suit, the suit he was married in many years before, he made a macabre sight. His shocked and protruding eyes belied the grim smile, created by Ginny, and held in place with two little stones either side of his mouth. His gnarled hands were primly folded on his lap, and his legs casually crossed. He might have been waiting for tea. The truth was, he had been waiting for Lianne.

One side of his face was marred by congealed blood. It narrowed to a long thin trail down his neck and over his shoulder. 'I'm sorry your suit was spoiled,' she murmured. 'Some people don't know their own strength.' Beside him lay the wedge of wood that had spattered his brains.

A glimmer of compassion moved her. She held his hand. 'I have to go now.' Reaching down she kissed him full on the mouth. When he wobbled she righted him. 'Sorry,' she said with a naughty little giggle, 'didn't mean to get you excited.'

In the candlelight his eyes shone like two bright marbles.

Blowing out three candles she took the fourth with her. Before closing the door, she told him, 'Lianne won't come down here again.' Hatred marbled her voice. 'Still, I expect you'll all see each other in hell.'

Deeply troubled, Lianne was waiting at the kitchen door. 'Whatever have you been doing all this time?' she whispered harshly, ushering Ginny into the kitchen.

'I told you. I've been guarding your present.' She snorted angrily. 'At least it's better than that awful scarf you bought for *me*.'

'Sit here, at the table, while I get your chocolate.' Pulling out a chair, Lianne waited for her to be seated. 'I've already boiled the kettle.'

'I want it in Father's mug.'

'He won't like it.' She reboiled the kettle, scooped two spoons of chocolate into the mugs and poured on the hot water. Taking the mugs to the table she put one before Ginny. The other she carried to her own place opposite Ginny, from where she could watch her every expression. 'Why don't you want the chocolate in your own mug?'

'Because this one belongs to the head of the house.' Raising the mug she greedily sipped from it, sighing with satisfaction as the hot liquid slithered down her throat. Kissing Old Tom had put a nasty taste in her mouth, and she needed to wash it away.

Lianne had a feeling she was being laughed at. 'I still don't understand what you mean,' she said lamely.

'I mean exactly what I say.' Tapping the side of the mug, she spoke in a slow methodical manner, as though addressing an idiot. 'This mug belongs to the head of this household, doesn't it?'

Shifting her gaze to the large blue earthenware mug, Lianne nodded. 'I know that much,' she replied patiently. 'What I don't know is why you wanted your chocolate in it. What's wrong with your own china mug?'

Clicking her teeth, Ginny dropped her head to her hands and stared at the table. 'You really are thick,' she grumbled.

Lianne was hurt. 'That's an unkind thing to say.'

'Then don't be so bloody stupid!' Looking up, Ginny met her gaze and held it.

Convinced that Ginny meant to have an argument, Lianne scraped back her chair and stood up. 'I'm going to bed.' She felt somehow used. She was also desperately anxious about Ginny's state of mind. All the same, there was little she could do until the morning, and the last thing she wanted at this unearthly hour was a fight.

'Aw, I'm sorry, sis.' Catching hold of Lianne's hand, Ginny pulled her back to the chair. 'Sit down. Finish your chocolate, and I promise I won't be spiteful.'

Lianne sipped at the hot liquid, her gaze intent on Ginny's face. 'You will talk to Daddy in the morning, won't you?' She couldn't get the sight of those poor creatures out of her mind. This time she had no intention of letting Ginny get away with it. 'If you don't tell him what you've done, I will.'

'Don't worry. I'll tell him.' He won't hear me, but I'll tell him anyway, she thought.

'Promise.'

Ginny laid a hand across her breast. 'Cross my heart.'

Lianne took another sip. The chocolate was getting cold. Something else was playing on her mind. 'You shouldn't have watched me and Dave. And to tell the others... oh, Ginny, that was just hateful.'

'I won't do it again.' Because there will never be another time, she vowed silently.

'Next time we'll go somewhere you can't find us.'

Ginny laughed aloud, instantly alarmed that the sound might travel. 'Shh!' The two of them glanced to the ceiling. 'We mustn't wake *them*.' It warmed her cold heart to think *they* would never wake again.

'It'll take more than you laughing to wake them,' Lianne reminded her. 'Our mum could sleep through an earthquake, and Daddy was dog-tired even before he went out.'

'So?' Digging into her jeans pocket, she took out a packet of Players and the box of matches brought from the cellar. Lighting a cigarette she took a deep drag and offered it to

Lianne. When it was refused she said churlishly, 'Oh, I forgot, you don't have any bad habits, do you?'

'Enough, I suppose.'

Regarding her through slit eyes and a haze of smoke, Ginny asked pointedly, 'So you'd like there to be another time, then? With Dave, I mean?'

Blushing pink, Lianne lowered her head. Wondering how to answer, she concentrated on the swirling dark liquid in her cup. She felt angry. Embarrassed too. Ginny had a way of touching the dark places where secrets lived.

Ginny revelled in her sister's embarrassment. 'Seems like the cat's got *everyone's* tongue,' she teased. 'Answer me, sis. Either you want there to be a next time or you don't. Which is it?'

There was no escape. 'I want there to be a next time.'

'He was that good, eh?' Just a flicker of envy. But it didn't matter any more. In the morning the slate would be wiped clean.

The pretty eyes were upturned now. The blush deepened. 'I think I love him.'

For what seemed an age Ginny drew on her cigarette. 'Does he love you?' she asked, blowing the smoke out through her nose.

'Maybe.'

'What kind of an answer is that?'

Lianne shrugged her shoulders. 'He says he does.'

'Hmm.' Another long drag on the cigarette. A slurp of chocolate, then she dipped the cigarette into the cooling liquid. It made a comforting, sizzling sound. 'Did he use a rubber?'

Lianne reeled. 'A rubber?'

'A French letter… prick sheath… call it what you like. Did he use one?'

'I don't know.'

'So he could have planted a baby inside you?'

The colour drained from Lianne's face.

'I shouldn't worry about it, though.' Ginny had her own sinister reasons for comforting her. 'He probably did use one. I mean, he's got a great career lined up for himself. He won't want to be lumbered with some bawling brat, will he?'

Suddenly Lianne's whole world was turned upside down. Suppose it was true? Just suppose she really did have Dave's baby growing inside her? Visions of her parents looked tall in her mind. Please don't let it be true. 'You don't really think he's made me pregnant, do you?'

'No, of course not.' She hadn't reckoned on the possibility of killing two birds with one stone. The idea amused her enormously.

A moment while each grappled with disturbing thoughts.

'You know those red shoes?'

Thrown by the sudden change of subject, Lianne took a moment to adjust her thinking. Mentally shaking off her dilemma, she injected a tone of normality into her voice. 'The high-heeled ones with the ankle-strap?'

'Hmn. Can I have them?' All things considered, she could easily just take them. After tomorrow, neither Lianne nor her parents would be in a position to complain. But taking Lianne's shoes without permission, well, it did seem a very impolite thing to do.

'You mean borrow them?'

She quietly smiled. 'If you like.'

Lianne didn't hesitate. ''Course you can,' she said, 'as long as they come back clean and polished. The last time you borrowed my scarf, it was returned covered in mud and grass.' She leaned forward, looking Ginny in the eye. 'Anyone would think you'd been lying in a field.'

'Stuart's fault,' she said. 'He couldn't wait until we got to the barn.'

'That sounds more like you than him.'

Grinning with pleasure, she whispered cuttingly, 'From what I saw of you with Dave, you're not much different.'

'I hope I am.'

215

'Cow!' Pushing back her chair she stood up, yawning and stretching. 'It's been a long day. Time we were both in bed.' Until the whole household was fast asleep, she couldn't put her plan into motion. The sooner it was done the better.

'Wait for me.' In a minute, Lianne had taken the cups to the sink, where she filled them with hot water. 'Chocolate makes such a mess,' she remarked, rubbing her finger round the inside of the rim.

'Never mind that.' Impatient now, Ginny switched off the light. 'And be quiet, or you'll wake *them*.'

Before they parted company on the upstairs landing, Ginny had one more favour to ask. 'Can I have your long black coat as well?'

'I said you should have got one instead of that awful brown leather thing.'

'Don't be silly!' Ginny replied indignantly. 'I love my leather coat.'

'So why do you want my black one?'

Sauntering to her own room, Ginny took her time answering. 'It's more fitting for the occasion.'

'What occasion?'

'Can I have it?'

'Only if you tell me what the occasion is.'

Again she made Lianne wait for an answer. As she closed her door, she murmured, 'I need it for a funeral.'

Straining her ears, Lianne daren't call out too loud. 'What did you say?'

The door softly closed. The lock turned, and Lianne knew she was dismissed. 'It's no good you sulking,' she murmured, entering her own room, 'I haven't forgotten what you did to those creatures. In the morning, we'll see what Daddy has to say about it.'

Jack had lain awake a long time. He heard the girls moving about downstairs, and he heard them come up to bed. It wasn't unusual for them to be wandering about, and he rarely took them to task over it. At least they were talking to each other, and not at each other's throats.

Mumbling, Liz stirred and turned towards him. Her leg was soft and smooth against his thigh. Her hair tickled his armpit, making him smile.

Kissing her gently on the forehead he whispered, 'Go to sleep, sweetheart.'

'*You* go to sleep, for goodness' sake.' She groaned from deep inside. 'You're keeping me awake with your fidgeting.'

'Sorry.'

'So you should be.'

Her leg slithered over his, waking a desire in him. He kissed her again, this time on the mouth. 'Do you want to make love?'

'I want to go to sleep,' she said, irritated, slapping him with the flat of her hand on his chest.

Bone-weary, he closed his eyes, praying for sleep, wishing he had mapped his life in a different way. He couldn't rest. He couldn't forget. And, because Liz had her leg across his, he couldn't move without disturbing her again. His nose began to itch and he couldn't scratch it. Liz was sleeping like a baby. He glanced at her in the half-light. She was lying on her side, mouth open, gently snoring, her nose twitching curiously with every snore. One of her eyebrows was dishevelled. With a tingling shock he realised how ugly it was. How jagged and hairy.

Suddenly the situation seemed ludicrous. Laughter bubbled up inside. He squeezed his lips together and bit his tongue, trying desperately to control the giggles. Christ! He couldn't believe it. Here he was, in the middle of some kind of nightmare, feeling like the world was about to fall down and crush him, and he was taken by a fit of the giggles. He couldn't hold it any longer. It began like a small slim spiral in the pit of his stomach, then it grew and grew until he was giggling like someone demented.

In a minute Liz was bolt upright in bed, glaring at him through red-rimmed eyes. 'What the hell's wrong with you?'

Swinging himself out of bed, he put on his robe. 'Go back to sleep.' His fit of giggles was over, but his smile was devilishly handsome. 'I'm going down to get a drink.'

Rubbing her eyes she yawned noisily. 'Must you?'

Hopeful, he returned to bed and sat beside her. 'I don't suppose there's any chance of me having my wicked way with you?'

'No chance.'

He nodded, seeming to accept she was not in the mood.

'What time is it?'

He peered at the bedside clock. 'After two.'

'What woke you?'

'I haven't been to sleep.'

She stroked his face. 'What's wrong, Jack?'

Lowering his gaze he toyed with the button on her nightgown. 'Everything.' He sounded beaten.

'Your mother?'

'Sort of.' It wasn't just Katherine. It was her reason for coming here, the way she was returning home. The past. Ginny. Cyrus. Maureen. Everything.

'Why don't you ring your uncle?'

He sounded incredulous. 'I can't do that.'

'Why not?'

Suddenly he was lonely. Lonely for his childhood, for his mother, his grandmother. Missing America for the first time in years. Hating this house. Wishing he had never been born. Like a drowning man he could see his entire life going before him. 'Help me, Liz,' he murmured. 'I feel like a rabbit down a hole with the dogs about to close in.'

Liz didn't know how to help. 'They're family, Jack,' she insisted. 'Hating won't mend things.' She tugged at his sleeve. 'Ring him!'

He shook his head.

'Please. For all our sakes.'

'I can't, Liz. You don't know what you're asking.' With that he went out of the room and down the stairs.

When he returned five minutes later, carrying two glasses, Liz met him with a sheepish smile. 'They've gone,' she said. 'I rang the hotel. The night clerk said your uncle checked out yesterday morning.'

Relief tempered his anger. It was as though a great weight was lifted from him. 'You shouldn't have done that, Liz,' he told her sternly, 'but maybe we can get on with our lives now.' Holding out one of the glasses, he said, 'Brandy. Drink it down.'

'I see.' She took a sip and pulled a face. 'Trying to knock me out, eh?'

Placing his own glass on the bedside cabinet he took hers and put it alongside. 'Now that we're awake...' His green eyes sparkled mischievously.

Closing one eye, she peered at him through the other, a playful look on her pretty face. She didn't speak. Instead she reached out her arm and switched off the light. For the next few minutes there was a little teasing, a little giggling, subdued cries of pleasure, and then silence. Contented. While they slept the sleep of the innocent.

Ginny bided her time. She had it all planned. In fact she'd had it all planned ever since Katherine Louis looked up at her from the doorway. Still dressed in jeans and sweatshirt, she stood by the window. Outside the wind had gained momentum. For weeks now, Liz had been asking Jack to secure the loose television cable. Up until now he had not found the time, and so it was blown in every direction, clattering against Ginny's window like a great fist wanting to be let in.

'Soon,' she kept murmuring, 'soon.' Her avaricious eyes swept the sky. The eyes and the sky looked the same: a beautiful vast stretch of dark velvet, interspersed with scintillating diamonds. One was unspeakably beautiful. The other unspeakably wicked.

Like a caged lioness she walked the floor, then she sat a while, and walked, and schemed. There was a kind of ethereal beauty about her face, a strange unearthly charisma that throbbed and glowed in the soft lamplight.

'It's time,' she whispered, stripping off her outdoor clothes. In a moment the effect was complete. In her nightgown, with her thick auburn hair roughed up, she looked for all the world as if she had just woken from a deep sleep. A final swift glance in the mirror, a smile of congratulation, and she was ready.

Opening the bedside drawer, she took out the same box of matches she had brought from the cellar, a wodge of cotton-wool, and a small bottle of liquid. That done, she went about her wicked deed.

First stop, Lianne's room.

Here she went straight to the bed, took the top off the bottle and soaked the cotton-wool with the liquid. Gently now, she pressed the cotton-wool to Lianne's nose and mouth. Exhausted and soothed by the hot chocolate, Lianne stirred only slightly. One final gossamer kiss to her sister's mouth, a whispered goodbye, and it was done. Softly she took the red shoes and long black coat from the wardrobe, before setting fire to the other clothes.

Lingering for just a moment, she watched the flames curl and caress. She felt the heat and grew excited by it. When the bags and shoes began smouldering, emitting a grey acrid smoke, she felt her throat contracting and knew she would have to hurry. Pressing the doors shut, she checked to see that the smoke was wafting from beneath the doors. Satisfied, she crept from the room.

Carrying the red shoes and the long black coat, she quickened her steps to her parents' room. Before entering, she laid the coat over the banister, and placed the shoes beneath. These things were precious. They were hers now.

This time she was more cautious. If Lianne had caught her creeping about, it would not have caused a stir. She and Lianne entered each other's rooms at any time of the day or night. But she had never once been in her parents' room while they were there.

In each other's arms and out to the world, neither was aware of the intruder. Pressing the cotton-wool to her mother's nose first, Ginny froze to the spot when Jack suddenly opened his eyes and called out, 'Don't go in! For God's sake don't go in!' There was terror in his face, tears glistening in his eyes.

Liz stirred, reaching out to comfort. 'Shh!' With strong merciless fingers, Ginny crushed the cotton-wool to her face and she was silent.

As quickly as Jack had opened his eyes he closed them again. Emitting a heart-rending sob he rolled over, away from her, his head in the pillow, making it more difficult for her to reach his mouth. When he began to struggle in his sleep, she held the cotton-wool to his face a moment longer. 'It doesn't matter whether you die now or later,' she said cruelly.

He finally lay very still, seeming to accept death, as though it was a just punishment.

Deeply satisfied, she made sure the curtains were blazing before closing the door and making her way downstairs.

In the kitchen she sat at the table, smoking a cigarette and wondering at which moment should she raise the alarm. Twice she picked up the telephone and twice she replaced it. 'Mustn't be too eager,' she chided herself. 'By the time the fire engine gets here, I want to be sure there's no hope left.' She laughed. 'Have to be careful, though,' she said, wagging a finger at the empty air. 'Have to be very careful I'm not caught in it. That would never do. I want to enjoy my grandmother's money... travelling. Gorgeous men.' She sighed, filled with a terrible pleasure, waving her arms about as if she had an audience. 'After the grieving, I can have anything I want. Go anywhere I choose.' Her insane laughter echoed from the walls.

Going to the foot of the stairs she looked up. As yet there was no sign that the fire had taken a real hold. She sniffed the air. 'Whew!' The air was already tainted with the unmistakable smell of burning. 'A few more minutes,' she giggled, 'then I really should call for help.' But she was in no hurry. Better to be sure than sorry, she thought. Softly whistling, she returned to the kitchen and boiled the kettle. 'Get your story right, Ginny,' she told herself. 'You couldn't sleep, so you came down to the kitchen to make yourself a drink.'

Mimicking a man's voice, she put herself through an inquisition. 'And what time was this?'

Turning on the tears, she answered, 'I can't remember... two... half past.' The tears became sobs. 'I can't believe it! I should have been able to save them.'

The man was sympathetic, the voice breaking with emotion. 'It's all right. Come on now... let's get you into the ambulance.'

The sobs intensified. Her acting was faultless. She congratulated herself. 'Virginia Lucas!' Throwing her arms wide, she imagined her names in lights. 'The newly discovered acting talent of the century.' Collapsing in a fit of giggles, she took a moment to recover, before setting the scene. First make certain the kettle had boiled. Now, make the tea. Pour a cup. Drink a good measure of it. Set the chair at an angle from the table. Knock it over as she ran. She went through the motions, taking quite a time over it. 'Panic,' she muttered. 'You smelled the smoke... realised there was a fire, and you panicked.'

While Ginny was setting the scene, Dave Martin strode down the drive towards the house. He had to make her see it didn't matter, or he would lose her for good. He stopped, looked up at the house. But how? If her father caught him here, he'd have every right to kick his arse out of it.

As he stared at the bedroom window, wondering which one was Lianne's, he couldn't quite make out what was wrong. He stared a minute longer. The window was closed, but the curtains were being blown about. He looked closer. In the background he could see the lights, short flickering bursts of colour. His mind exploded with realisation. As he sped towards the house, he yelled at the top of his voice, *'Fire! Lianne!'*

Enacting her gruesome task, Ginny didn't hear him pounding on the door. She raised the telephone receiver to her ear and dialled. Outside he was frantic, hammering and screaming. Inside, the fire had taken hold. Smoke filled the stairway. The sound of wood crackling seemed to be splitting the house apart. Composed, she waited for the voice at the other end. When it came she began screaming.

'Help! Someone help! There's a fire!' When the person at the other end tried to calm her, to extract her name and address, she blubbered and protested, and was so caught up in her own performance that the terror became real.

Eventually, she gave her address and was told to get out of the house at once, that help was on its way. Grabbing the coat and shoes, she ran into the hallway. It was almost impossible to see by this time. Smoke billowed down from above. The bulbs in the overhead lights were popping, and the stairway was already smouldering. From all around came the sound of wood splintering and crackling. 'Sounds like bonfire night,' she chuckled.

She was still chuckling when the door caved in and Dave Martin stood there, staring at her with the look of a wild man. Something in her face, the guilt, the lingering smile, made him suspicious. Almost without thinking he whispered with horror, 'What have you done?'

'Leave them!' she screamed. 'Get out of my house!'

Pushing her aside, he bounded up the stairs. With a speed born of desperation, Ginny went after him, snatching at his clothes, grappling with him, trying frantically to pull him away. 'It's too late!' she screamed. 'She's dead. They're all dead!'

Each time he threw her off, she came back at him like something demented. In the end he proved to be the stronger. Running down the landing he kicked open the doors. Long tongues of fire spat out at him. Incessantly he shouted her name: *'Lianne!'*

Jack felt as though he were in some kind of nightmare. He was choking. So dazed he could hardly think he raised his head. The whole room was alight. He closed his eyes and stared again. His sight was blurred, his tongue so swollen it seemed to fill the whole of his mouth. *'For Christ's sake! Liz!'* He reached for her. Realising they were both about to die, he found a strength from somewhere. Barely able to stand, he half-carried, half-dragged her to the door. He couldn't open it. For all his determination he could not open it. His senses failing, he called out, his arms cradling Liz as the two of them sank to the floor.

Suddenly there was help. Dave had heard the feeble cry, and was leading them along the landing. With his hand feeling the rail as he went, he guided them safely away. The smoke was blinding. Fire was spreading fast now, infecting every surface, swallowing the house whole. 'Where is she?' he begged. 'Lianne... which room?'

Pointing along the corridor, Jack told him, 'There.' Echoes of the past filled him with terror. Catching hold of Dave's sleeve, he kept him a moment longer. 'Ginny?' He needed to know.

Before he broke away, the look on Dave's face told him everything.

As Dave ran into the inferno, Jack pressed Liz close to his heart. 'We'll make it, sweetheart,' he murmured. She didn't stir.

As he neared the stairway he felt a presence behind him. He swung round but couldn't see; the smoke billowed and rolled, and his eyes ran with tears. The first name that came to his lips was 'Mother?' There was a soft, insane cackle of laughter. In that moment he knew. 'Ginny!' He felt the push of a hard strong hand in the centre of his back. The banister gave way and there was no saving himself.

As he fell, the laughter followed him. All he could remember was holding on to Liz as they fell through the air. And the laughter. The same laughter he had heard once before. *In his worst nightmare.*

Realising she had allowed panic to overtake reason, Ginny fled into the night. Dave told how he suspected she might have started the fire. He also told how, while carrying Lianne to safety, he believed he saw Ginny push her parents through the banister. He couldn't be sure because of the density of smoke, but he heard her laughing. That much he would never forget.

Part 2

...and Seek

8

On a blistering hot June day in 1982, Eddie Laing nosed his car through the streets of New York. Normally it would have taken him only ten minutes to get from Central Park to the Louis apartment in the heart of Manhattan. Today, he had been stuck in traffic for the best part of an hour. 'What the hell's going on?' Winding the window down, he leaned out, far enough for the cab-driver to hear him above the din.

The round-faced driver spat out his chewing-gum. 'Peace march.' Without another word he wound up his window, and concentrated on picking his teeth with his nail.

Ten minutes late, and suffering a head like two after a night on the town, Eddie glanced at the road in front. The sidewalks were jam-packed, the traffic brought to a halt by the masses of people surging down the road. There were some carrying banners and others loudly chanting. The rhythm of voices and the general uprising noise was deafening. 'Jesus!' Winding up the window, Eddie slunk down in his seat. 'Some peace march,' he grumbled. 'More like the start of World War Three.'

He discovered later that there were almost a million people taking part in what was one of America's biggest marches. For now though, he idled away the time by examining his nose in the mirror and considering how he should make an appointment with a surgeon. 'Think what a snip here and there would do for your ego,' he chuckled, twisting his nose and imagining it a different shape. A thought suddenly occurred to him, and it was a sobering one. As long as the guy didn't let the knife slip, he wryly observed, casting a wary eye to his trouser flies. That would put an end to his love life for sure. He wrinkled his face and stared forlornly in the mirror. Some love life, which at the present time was absolutely zilch!

Recalling the blonde he took home last night brought the smile back to his face. He had plans, and rolled his eyes with anticipated pleasure.

Eddie Laing always had plans. The smile evaporated when he remembered how the same blonde had sent him packing with only a peck on the cheek for his troubles. No use having plans if they never came to anything. Last night there had been one fantastic moment when he really believed he had it made. For the first time in ages he had felt like he was at the top of the world. But it didn't last long and now, after another swift examination of the nose in the mirror, he felt thoroughly miserable. Who in their right mind would want to wake up next to that? he thought woefully.

The line of marchers seemed never-ending. 'You'd have thought they'd have the sense to shut this street off to motorists,' the cab-driver yelled. So far he had managed to keep his temper. After all, while the meter was ticking, he was making money, so why should he care?

Now, though, his fare was legging it up the street and he was spitting fire. 'You'd better run, you smart-arse, because if I ever get my hands on you, you'll wish you'd never been born!' He glared at Eddie as though it was his fault. 'Son of a bitch!' he growled menacingly. 'Would *you* be a cab-driver?'

Maureen poured a healthy measure of brandy into Cyrus' glass. She would have stopped then, only he placed his hand over hers and held it there until his glass was half-full. 'It helps me to think,' he argued.

'Sure yer just an old drunkard,' she teased. Her love for Katherine's brother was obvious. Gesturing to the ornate French clock on the mantelpiece, she remarked with disgust, 'He's late again.'

Cyrus beckoned her to the window. 'Have you seen out here?'

She stretched her neck to see over the sill. The street below was teeming with people. 'Peace march,' she said. 'Oh! That reminds me, will ye be wanting grilled fish or boiled eggs for breakfast?'

He had long given up trying to fathom her thinking. Instead he took her as she was, and thought himself fortunate to have such a good woman. 'Maureen, will you listen?'

'I'm listening.' She knew what was on his mind, for it was on hers also, and had been ever since Eddie Laing had contacted Cyrus last evening.

'What news do you think he'll bring?'

She regarded him awhile, thinking how unlike his sister he was, in looks and nature. 'If ye want him to bring news that Jack has forgiven us... that he wants to come home, then I'm afraid it'll be bad news.' There was no point beating about the bush.

'How can you be so certain?' There was sorrow in his voice, and a great deal of regret.

'Oh, Cyrus! Will ye never face the truth?' Seating herself in the red leather chair, she gazed at him with compassion. 'Jack can never forget, and neither can we. I wish to God Katherine had not gone after him, but she did, and now all our lives are turned upside down.'

He sighed, a deep long sigh that betrayed his pain. 'One of the things I regret most of all is never having a son.'

She smiled, remembering how dear that dream had been to him. 'So now ye want Jack to be that son, is that it?'

He took her hand, and held it tight. 'You know how angry and afraid I was when Katherine said she meant to find him?'

Her smile was understanding. 'Sure don't I know what a fuss ye made?' she chided. 'But it's all different now. That's what yer thinking, ain't it? That's what ye've been thinking ever since ye saw him, only ye've not had the heart to come right out and say it.'

'I want him back. Katherine wanted him back. She was right and I was wrong. In the end love tells, and we have to follow our instincts.' He leaned back in the chair. Since Katherine's untimely death he had come to see things the way she saw them. 'I put Eddie Laing back on his trail because I want to know his every move. I need to know he's all right.' He hesitated, his mind going back over the years. 'I think it would be too painful if he should disappear yet again.' He looked away. 'Or if there should be any more tragic accidents.'

Maureen had always been able to read his mind. 'Yer thinking of the girl, aren't ye?' Jack's daughter had been on her mind also. 'And the swimming instructress. And Katherine.'

In that first moment, when she'd glanced up to see Jack's daughters seated on the stairs, Maureen had seen the same look in the girl's eyes as she had seen in her great-grandmother's. The same look as... No! She could not let the thought materialise. 'Badness runs in her blood,' she said softly.

'She's very beautiful.'

'And evil?'

He hung his head, searching for the answer. There was only one. 'I don't want to believe it,' he said regretfully, 'but yes. I'm afraid she is... evil.'

'Yer also afraid she was the one who caused Katherine's death?'

'Yes.'

'Yer afraid she may kill again?'

He looked up, and his eyes were desolate. There was no need for him to answer. It was there, in his gaze, in his trembling hands.

'Was it wise to tell the solicitor that Jack must inherit the bulk of Katherine's estate?'

'I've already told you.' He seemed astonished that he should have to explain again. 'You know how Katherine meant to change her will in Jack's favour anyway.' Wondering why she should be so concerned, he asked, 'Are you discontented with what she left you?'

'Of course not.' She bit her lip, betraying her anxiety in that familiar way. 'I'm deeply concerned about the letter sent to Jack by yer solicitor. That letter informs Jack that he's Katherine's main beneficiary. If the letter fell into the wrong hands...'

'Virginia, you mean?'

'Just a thought.' Now that her point was made and he seemed to be considering it, her mind moved on. In a more jovial mood, she got out of the chair. 'Yer man will be here in a minute, sure he will. I'll away and make a good strong pot of coffee.' She smiled mischievously. 'It'll take the smell of brandy from yer breath.' No sooner had she finished speaking than the door bell rang. 'There! What did I tell yer?'

Eddie was full of apologies. 'Sorry I'm late,' he said sheepishly.

Gesturing for him to sit down, Cyrus got straight to the point. 'You have something to report?'

Without hesitation, Eddie undid his briefcase and took out his dog-eared notebook. 'It isn't good news, I'm afraid.'

Both men turned when Maureen muttered, 'I knew it!'

'Please, Maureen.' Cyrus was still master in his own house. 'Coffee, if you please.'

While she went away in a huff, he impatiently pressed Eddie. 'I'm waiting.'

Taking a moment to gather his thoughts, Eddie couldn't help but recall the last time he was here, in this very room, in this very chair, talking to the late Mrs Katherine Louis about the very same man. 'There was a fire,' he began. 'The house was gutted...'

At once Cyrus was on his feet. 'My *nephew's* house?'

Eddie nodded, his face telling a reluctant story.

'How bad? Dear God, what happened? The girls? Were you told about the girls? Virginia! What about Virginia!' He fell backwards into the settee, calling Maureen's name as he fell.

Maureen was not far away. In fact she was listening at the door. In a minute she was at Cyrus' side. 'It's all right.' Handing him the brandy glass, she ordered, 'Sit still now. Let the man tell yer in his own good time.' Seating herself on the settee beside Cyrus, she asked Eddie one question, before allowing him to continue. 'Was anyone killed?' Her heart stopped when Eddie nodded.

It lifted again when he went on, 'The dead man was a Mr Tom Wright. Apparently he was janitor at the school.' Once the worst was out, he began to relax a little. It was always an ordeal coming into a place like this, talking to rich people like these. They enjoyed a lifestyle ordinary mortals could only ever dream about. One day though. One day he would have such a place, God willing.

Cyrus' voice cut through his thoughts. 'Mr Laing!'

Putting on his most authoritative air, he told them the whole story. Of how the fire was already raging through the house by the time help got there. He explained how a young man by the name of Dave Martin had fought his way through the flames and smoke to get to the youngest daughter. 'Thanks to his courageous action, the young woman escaped serious injury, though the two of them did inhale a quantity of smoke and so were detained in hospital for a while.'

He thumbed through his notebook before glancing up, his face set in a serious expression. 'Unfortunately your nephew and his wife were not so fortunate.'

'What are you trying to say?' Cyrus was on his feet, standing over him. 'Out with it, man.'

'I haven't got all the details yet, but according to my source, your nephew and his wife fell from the upper level. The woman has second-degree burns to her back and legs. Your nephew suffered burns too... not so serious, but he broke both legs, amongst other serious injuries.'

Shocked to the core, Cyrus continued to stare at him. When he felt Maureen's hand on the back of his hand, he quietly sat beside her, wiping his hands down his face, one word on his lips: 'Virginia.'

'Will they recover?' Maureen's voice was incredibly calm.

'I'm assured yes, they will.'

'I see. And the youngest daughter? You say she escaped serious injury? With the house gutted, and her parents in hospital, where is she?'

Eddie consulted his notes once more. 'I have it on good authority that she's all right. She's staying with the Martin family.'

'Have you had them checked out?'

'I have. You'll be pleased to know they're a fine, respectable family.'

Cyrus wanted to know about the other one. 'The eldest daughter. Is she staying with the Martin family too?'

Here, Eddie found himself out of his depth. He searched for a kind way to put it, but there was none. Instead, he took a newspaper cutting from the notebook and handed it to Cyrus. 'I'm sorry,' he said. He watched the two, heads together, reading the cutting, and his heart went out to them.

When Cyrus looked up, he was a man haunted. 'I want you to do something for me,' he murmured. 'I hope you will not refuse.'

Apprehensive as to what he might be letting himself in for, Eddie was nevertheless curious. 'I can't agree or refuse,' he said cautiously, 'until I know what it is you have in mind.'

A short time later, Eddie drove home. The streets were clear now, and the traffic was flowing as freely as it ever did in New York. Whoever said money talks was right, he mused. There wasn't a man alive who could turn down an offer like that. The lights changed. Someone bipped a horn behind him. 'All right! All right!' He was in a foul mood.

Angrily jutting one finger in the air, he surged forward, oblivious to the curses that rained down on him. Eddie was preoccupied with Cyrus Louis and his ill-fated family. 'Jinxed, the lot of them,' he muttered. The sooner this one was over, the easier he would sleep at night.

Maureen watched Cyrus from the doorway.

Leaning over the table he read the caption again and again. 'I had hoped you were wrong,' he said, as she came to stand over him.

'I hoped so too,' she said, 'but I saw it in her eyes.'

Drawing her gaze to the headlines, she read them again: 'LOCAL COUPLE FIGHT FOR LIFE AFTER MURDER ATTEMPT. DAUGHTER COMMITTED TO ASYLUM.'

9

Mrs Martin had been meaning to raise the issue for days, but until this Friday morning she had not been absolutely certain. She was certain now. 'When you've seen Dave off, I wonder if you and I could have a little talk, dear?'

She always called Lianne 'dear'. It was her way of showing affection. Lianne had been living with them for over three months now, and in spite of her earlier reservations when Dave suggested bringing her here to live, Mrs Martin had come to love her like a daughter.

Apprehensive, Lianne promised she would be right back. 'Woman talk, I expect,' she told Dave as he kissed her goodbye. 'I'm sure there's nothing to worry about.' She knew it had been coming, and now she didn't know how to deal with it.

Holding her a little longer than was necessary, Dave murmured in her hair, 'Don't let her bully you. Her bark is worse than her bite.' He held her at arm's length, regarding her small face with delight. The pretty green eyes shone with health, as the smile came more readily to her features. 'I can't believe how much better you are,' he remarked proudly. 'When I first brought you to this house you were in a shocking state, thin and ill, just out of hospital and pining for your family.' He shook his head with disbelief. 'Oh, Lianne, I'm so lucky to have you.'

Blushing with pleasure, she told him, 'It's me that's the lucky one. I don't know what I would have done without you.' She brushed away a tear. 'Your parents too. I can't thank them enough.'

'I'm glad you and Mum get on so well.'

'She's been very good to me. They both have.'

Sensing her dilemma, he hooked his fingers under her chin and raised her face to his. 'But you'd rather be with your *own* parents, is that it?' He was mortified when she flinched at his innocent remark. 'It's all right,' he whispered. 'I do understand.'

Taking hold of his wrist, she raised it up and turned back bis cuff. The time on his watch was five minutes to eight. 'You'd better hurry, or you'll be late.'

'I'd rather spend the day with you, than driving a van about the roads.' He would rather spend the day with Lianne than do anything at all, he thought. 'But a man has to earn a wage,' he joked. 'How else can he afford a honeymoon?'

'I didn't know you were planning on getting married.' She knew very well what he had in mind. It was like a little game between them. He hinted. She pretended not to notice. It would be easy to trap him, but she didn't want him that way. Besides, she knew something he didn't.

'I don't tell you everything,' he declared with a wink. Only because 'everything' was her. Only because without her, his life would be nothing. He was afraid if she knew how desperately he loved her, she might be frightened away. Lianne had been through so much. She was still weak and vulnerable, and he did not want to burden her.

Lianne frowned. 'You talk as if you're not going on to college in September.'

Taken aback by her remark, he brushed it aside. 'Who knows?' he declared with a wide grin. 'I might prefer to be a van driver than a doctor.'

'Don't joke, Dave.' If he didn't fulfil his ambitions, she would always blame herself.

'Who's joking?' he said disarmingly. Grabbing her to him, he threatened, 'Give us a kiss, or I'll refuse to budge. I'll be late. The boss will get rid of me. And I won't have any money to take you out on Saturday nights.'

'That's blackmail!' She felt safe and warm in his arms.

'Of course!' he declared, kissing her full on the mouth.

The kiss lasted so long it took her breath away. When he released her, they gazed into each other's eyes and their love was stronger than ever. 'Love you,' she whispered.

'No you don't,' he teased. 'You're just after my money.'

'Get off to work.'

'Oh! A bully as well, eh?' He swung her round, leaving her gasping for breath while he jumped into the Transit. 'See you later,' he said, and waved all the way down the street.

Mrs Martin turned from the window, a warm smile lighting her homely features, as Lianne came into the kitchen. 'You two are so good together,' she said.

'We love each other,' Lianne replied simply.

'Sit down, Lianne.' Mrs Martin gestured to one of the ladder-back chairs beside the oak table. 'I've just made a fresh brew of tea. Fancy a cup?'

It was the last thing she wanted, but she didn't have the heart to refuse. 'I'll get it,' she offered, moving across the kitchen. She could feel the older woman's kindly eyes on her. It was a peculiar feeling.

'It's all right. You sit down, and I'll do the honours.'

Without further ado, Mrs Martin set the tray. She prided herself on serving tea as it should be served, not thrown together. As always, the tray was meticulously prepared: first the cups and saucers, then the sugar bowl, complete with silver-coated teaspoon. The china biscuit barrel, filled with butterdrops, and placed at just the right angle on the corner of the tray. Next the freshly filled teapot, first rinsed twice with hot water before the tea was spooned in. Finally, the kettle boiling and bubbling while the water tumbled over the tea leaves. Such a fuss. Such a pleasure. With the delightful Mrs Martin chatting all the way through.

Usually Lianne felt so comfortable in this kitchen. With its big, bright interior, pretty tiled floor and white units, it uplifted the spirit. On a day like today, with the early July sun pouring through the window, gilding the roses in the curtains, Mrs Martin's kitchen was like an oasis in a desert. If it hadn't been for the ordeal she knew was to come, Lianne would have felt relaxed. Instead she was like a cat on hot bricks.

'You're looking peaky, dear.' Mrs Martin poured the tea, and pushed Lianne's cup along the table. 'Drink it down while it's hot,' she urged. 'It'll do you good.'

There was a short and uncomfortable span of silence, while each sipped tea and contemplated the other. 'Would you like a biscuit, dear?'

Lianne shook her head. If Mrs Martin was about to throw her out, why didn't she get on with it?

With great deliberation Mrs Martin picked up the biscuit barrel, took out a butterdrop, placed it on a small china plate and put it in front of Lianne. 'Just in case you feel peckish,' she said pointedly. 'I noticed you didn't eat any breakfast.'

Another span of silence, during which Lianne reluctantly sipped her tea while Mrs Martin crunched noisily on the butterdrop, each loath to raise the issue that was on both their minds. Each praying the other would speak first.

Suddenly they were speaking together.

'I'm sorry, dear…' Mrs Martin started.

'You know, don't you?' Lianne demanded, unable to stand the suspense any longer. Red with embarrassment, she looked down at the table.

'Yes, dear.' The older woman's voice was kindly as ever. 'I *do* know,' she said softly. 'I would like to help, if you'll let me.'

Pushing the teacup away, Lianne leaned forward, wringing her hands on the table, her gaze downcast, as she murmured ashamedly, 'I don't know what to do.'

Mrs Martin was astonished. 'Why! You'll get married. *That*'s what you'll do.'

'I can't ask him to do that. He's too young. We're both too young.' She looked up, her pretty green eyes anxious. She felt incredibly alone, unsure of what the future held. But this much she did know: she would not jeopardise Dave's career. 'What about college?' she demanded. 'You know he's all set for medical school.'

'Don't you think that's for him to decide?'

'If we did get married, where would we go? How would we live?' She had gone through the whole thing in her own mind, over and over. 'I don't want you to tell him,' she pleaded. 'I have to be the one to do that… when I feel the time is right.'

'Answer me, dear. Are you happy here, in this house with us?'

Lianne's heart turned over. 'I have no right to be happy.' With her parents in hospital and her sister in a mental institution, she could see nothing ahead but heartache.

'Look at me, dear.'

Lianne raised her eyes. They were awash with tears. In her sorry heart there was crippling pain, and a terrible anger. Also a strength she never knew she had. Dave and his family had done enough. How could she ask them to do even more?

'Are you content here, with us?'

Lianne nodded. As content as she would ever be again, she thought.

'And do you want to have the child… yours and David's?'

Her face lit in a smile. 'Oh, yes!' This child was hers and Dave's, made with love, and growing strong inside her. It was a bright, glowing light in the middle of darkness.

Mrs Martin was satisfied. 'That's all I need to know,' she said. Coming round the table she wound her chubby arms round Lianne's shoulders. Hugging her tight, she declared, 'It's settled, then. You're to be a mother. I'm to have a grandchild, and this will be your home for as long as you want it.' Anticipating Lianne's protest, she told her sternly, 'As for Dave's career, there is no reason why he can't still go to college… on to medical school if that's what he really wants. Though I suspect he would want to take a job, and support you and the baby.'

Already Lianne was wondering how she might persuade him to her way of thinking. She said, 'How can I persuade him not to give up his career?'

Mrs Martin made a sly little face. 'Don't underestimate yourself. I've an idea he'll listen to what you have to say.' Nudging Lianne, she grinned broadly. 'My son might be a stubborn bugger when he wants, but he adores you. Besides, I have great faith in you, dear.'

'You don't think we're too young to be married?'

'Not a bit of it! If you're right for each other, age doesn't matter a jot. Mr Martin and I were in our teens when we wed, and as you can see, we've come to no harm.' She returned to the subject of the baby. 'You'll need to see a doctor, dear. You can't neglect these things, especially as it's your first one.' She lowered her voice to a whisper. 'How far are you? Three, four months?' She instinctively glanced to Lianne's stomach. It was suspiciously flat. 'I must say, you've covered it well, dear.'

'It happened at the party,' Lianne confessed. 'I'm about three and a half months.'

'However did you manage to hide it? If I hadn't heard you being sick in the mornings, I might never have guessed.'

'You'd be surprised what a tight pantie-girdle and loose-fitting clothes will do for the figure,' Lianne explained.

'You'll have to tell him soon, dear.'

Lianne's eyes clouded over. 'I know. I'll have to tell my parents too.' Not Ginny, she thought, I can't tell her. For the briefest moment she suspected that Ginny might already know.

Suddenly it all came flooding back: the creatures in the cellar; the discovery of Old Tom and the idea that Ginny had killed him with her own bare hands. The fire. Her parents at death's door. Amy Burton on the witness-stand, saying how she had actually seen Ginny swim to the other end of the pool, just before the teacher was drowned. Ginny had denied nothing, and now she was locked away. It was all a nightmare.

'I don't want to talk any more,' she said now. 'I have to go and see my parents.'

Mrs Martin understood Lianne's pain. What she didn't understand was why she shut everyone out of the tragedy. 'Why won't you ever let Dave go with you to the hospital, dear? He would be such a comfort to you.'

Lianne was adamant. 'I'm better on my own.' On her own she could talk to them, say things that no one else could ever understand. On her own, she could share their suffering. 'I'll be back in a few hours,' she said. 'They never let me stay long.'

'I'm sure it's for the good, dear.'

'I suppose so. I've got another duty as well.' Good God! Why did she say it like that? Another duty? As though visiting her parents had also become a duty?

Paying particular attention, waiting for her to finish what she started, Mrs Martin said, 'What duty, dear?'

Lianne felt her face growing hot with shame. 'Nothing to worry about. It's just that I promised Mum I'd keep an eye on the bakery.'

'I thought your father wanted old Fred to take care of all that?'

'He did. And Fred's doing a really good job.'

Mrs Martin understood. 'But your mother wants you to keep an eye on it, anyway, eh?' She tapped the side of her nose. 'When it comes to the important things in life, us women don't tend to trust anyone,' she whispered.

Both women were thinking of how Lianne had tried to hide her pregnancy. Both women were glad to have shared such an important secret.

'I'm sure Mum does trust old Fred, but she's bound to ask me today, so I'd better call in at the bakery on my way to the hospital,' she said, 'just to make sure everything is all right.'

'Okay, dear. Mind you take a key. I have to go into town. I'll probably be back before you, but just to be sure, eh?'

When Lianne left the room, Mrs Martin's heart went with her. It's a good job she's made of strong stuff, she thought as she nibbled a butterdrop. Many another would have buckled under the weight of it all.

An hour later, Lianne left the house. In a straight blue skirt and butterscotch blouse, she looked stunning. Her short, fair hair was washed and bouncy, and her green eyes shone like an ocean in the sunlight.

241

'Morning, lovely.' A nasty little man with an unfortunate tendency to spread malicious gossip, Mark Robbins had been the postman round these parts for many years. He was late as usual. 'How are you?' he asked, with a sickly grin.

'I'm fine, thanks,' Lianne answered, hurrying by. As she went down the street she could feel his beady eyes on her. 'Sly little bugger!' she grumbled, knowing he wasn't the slightest bit interested in how she was. What he really meant to say was, 'How are your parents after your sister tried to burn them to death? And what about her? Is it right what they say? That she's completely crazy? And do they really keep her in a straitjacket?'

At the bottom of the street, she turned. The postman was still following her progress. In a fit of rage, she lost control. 'I shouldn't look at me for too long!' she yelled, startling him. 'How do you know *I'm* not the crazy one? How do you know they haven't locked my sister away when it should be *me* they put in a straitjacket?'

Mrs Lorrimer, from number four, came out of her front gate. Realising what was going on, she said, 'Don't let him rile you. Don't give him the satisfaction.'

Lianne was still bristling. 'It was the way he stared at me,' she murmured. 'Saying one thing and meaning another.'

'I'm afraid there will always be people like him.' Like everyone else, she knew of the Lucas scandal. She was also one of the many that loathed the one sister, and pitied the other. 'It won't be easy,' she said, 'but you will have to deal with it.'

They parted company then, the older woman to her shopping, and Lianne to the bakery. It was quite a walk, down the street, along the main road and down the hill towards Heath and Reach. It took her fifteen minutes at a brisk pace.

Fred was in the office. 'Thought you might call in again,' he said, wedging the pen behind his wrinkled ear. 'You can tell your mother everything is shipshape. The order book is healthy. Money duly banked, and if you look down there…' leading her to the window, he pointed a gnarled old finger to the bakery floor, 'you'll see the ovens are all producing, and the men are hard at work.'

Letting her gaze rove from one end of the bakery to the other, Lianne felt more alone than she had ever been. In her mind's eye she could see her father, dressed, like the others, in white overalls and peaked cap. She could see him walking up and down, carrying his precious ledger, checking this, checking that, loading pallets with crusty brown loaves, and counting the big currant teacakes into the trays. He was smiling. Now he was angry because the ovens had gone wrong again. Then he was climbing the steps towards her.

For a moment she needed to be quiet. The pain clogged her throat and the tears burned deep inside. But she wouldn't let them pour out. She wished she could, for it might open that hard, agonising fist inside her. Would it never end? Would life ever be normal again? In the end, what was normal?

'Got a lot on yer mind, eh?' Old Fred was wise enough to know she had come out worse than anyone.

Her sad eyes belied the smile painted on her lips. 'Oh, I was just thinking,' she confided. She had always liked this old man. He was a good friend to her father. Loyal and trustworthy.

'And what were that then, eh?' His toothless smile put her in mind of his faithful old dog.

'I was just thinking how some things never change,' she mused aloud. 'The house is burned down. My parents are just back from the brink of death, and my only sister is branded insane. But here, in this old bakery, time seems to have stood still.' In a strange way she didn't altogether understand, but it was a comforting thing.

'How are they all?' He could guess how they were. They were scarred for life, in more ways than one.

'Daddy's very moody. He's in a lot of pain still, because of his neck, mostly. I spoke to the doctor yesterday about Mum. He says the burns on her back are healing well.'

Slowly nodding his head up and down, he considered for a minute before asking in a wary voice, 'What about your sister?'

Lianne's face fell. 'I've had permission to see her again. I'm going at the weekend.' A shaft of fear stabbed through her. She still suffered nightmares about the last and only time they had let her see Ginny.

Fred knew, because he was one of the first she had told. His voice betrayed the concern he felt. 'And are you taking your young man with you next time?'

'Dave says he won't let me go without him.' She had argued, afraid of how Ginny might react. There was a terrible resentment between those two: Dave because he was protecting his sweetheart, Ginny because she had been rejected by him and couldn't forgive.

'And what about you?'

She stared at him through big, surprised eyes. 'Me?' The surprise was replaced by pleasure. 'Nobody ever asks about me.'

'Well, old Fred's asking, so tell me, young lady, how are you coping?'

Gulping back the emotion, she whispered brokenly, 'Oh Fred, I do miss them so.' She dropped her gaze, closing her eyes in anguish. 'Why did it have to happen?'

He had no answers. But her plight caught at his old heart. 'Can an ugly old bugger like me give yer a hug?'

'Please.'

He put out his arms and she went to him. He was soft and old, his jacket was rough to her face and he smelled of flour and nutmeg. She felt like a child again. 'Ginny and I never knew our grandfathers,' she murmured.

He looked into her pretty green eyes, his smiling face uplifted in a multitude of cavernous wrinkles. 'If you ever feel the need of a grandfather,' he told her, 'I'm yer man.'

He held her a moment longer, though his mind had moved on to other things, like the phone call he had to make with regard to a big order from the Bull Hotel in Leighton Buzzard. There was an urgent delivery to Buckingham this morning, and it was late already. A batch of currant buns were ruined when a rat found its way into the stores and left its calling card. They would have to be replaced, and time was short. With all this playing on his mind, his eyes wandered towards the window. The girl was in no hurry to be released. He could feel the weariness in her, the heartache that a body could never speak about to another. 'Be brave, young 'un,' he murmured.

There was a whispered reply, so soft he couldn't make it out. Straining his ears, he heard it again. 'What's that yer say, me darling?' he asked.

Lianne heard it too. 'It wasn't me,' she murmured, gently pushing away with the flat of her hands. With a fast-beating heart, she listened with him.

The faint whisper was like a teasing breeze, or the rush of a skirt as it swished by: *'Kill him… Old Tom watching… Kill him!'*

The old man gasped. 'What in God's name?' He looked confused. Horrified. 'I must be going mad,' he said, rubbing his old eyes.

Lianne also. 'What did you hear?' she asked softly.

He felt a little foolish. The ovens were drumming in the background, and the sound of men chatting filtered up between them. He forced a little grin. 'Did *you* hear anything just then?'

'No,' she lied. The voice was as real to her as it had been to him. 'I'll have to go,' she said, 'or I'll be late.'

Before she left, they talked about finance, and orders, and he reported how he had had to send one of the vans in to be fitted with a complete new exhaust line. 'It's all written down,' he said, handing her the office ledgers. 'The accountant spent the entire day here on Wednesday. Very pleased, he were. Said I were doing a grand job. It's all in order.' Opening the filing cabinet he urged, 'See for yourself.'

Lianne graciously declined. 'I'll leave it to the accountant,' she said. 'After all, I expect Daddy pays him an absolute fortune.'

She thanked him for everything and hurried away.

As she turned the corner out of sight, the old man took a swig of brandy from his secret bottle. 'I know what I heard,' he told the wall. 'It was a voice. A soft, beautiful voice, like I've never heard before.' He took another swig, before making the sign of the cross on himself. Putting the bottle away he went downstairs. 'Shan't be sorry when the responsibility's lifted from these old shoulders,' he muttered. Glancing behind him, he quickened his step.

Lianne tried to shut out the voice. The harder she tried the louder it echoed in her mind. 'I heard you, Ginny,' she whispered. 'Please! Don't torment me.'

'Lovely day,' the bus conductor announced as she boarded. 'Shame some of us have to work.'

She bought her ticket, and chose to sit at the top of the bus, right in front, so she could see where she was going. That was important to her now. Once upon a time she would have sat anywhere: at the back; in the middle; behind one of the posts. Now, though, after all that had happened, she would fight her way to the front, where she could look out of the window and see the road ahead. She couldn't explain it. She just felt safer. As though she might see the enemy coming from a way off, instead of being taken by surprise. The journey from Leighton Buzzard to Aylesbury took just under an hour. They stopped several times to pick up and deposit passengers, and much to everyone's frustration, the bus was delayed by roadworks on the main route.

Lianne got off at the corner, just a step away from the hospital gates. As usual the foyer was busy, with people going back and forth, porters with trolleys, visitors carrying huge bouquets or baskets of fruit, and the few fortunate patients who were allowed a little walk down the corridors.

'Is it all right for me to go straight up?' she asked at the desk. In the earlier weeks when she came here, Lianne was sometimes asked to wait until the doctor attended one or both of her parents. Badly injured and close to death, they were being closely monitored in Intensive Care. Now, though, they had been moved to private wards, and visiting was easier.

'You can go in.' The nurse was too busy to look up, and too tired to smile.

With Jack in the main wing, and Liz in the burns unit at the far end of the hospital, Lianne had developed a visiting pattern. On Mondays she would see her father first, and alternate the turns each day. Today was Friday, so it was her father's turn.

From the moment the doctor left, Jack did not take his eyes off the door, because he knew that at any minute Lianne would walk through. He wished it could be Ginny, but sadly, that was not possible. He blamed himself. Though he could never admit it to anyone, least of all Lianne or Liz, he loved Ginny more than anyone. She was cold natured where Lianne was warm. She was extraordinarily beautiful where Lianne was merely pretty. Ginny hated. Lianne loved. Of the two, Lianne was the stronger. Ginny was weak and flawed, and like any parent he believed it was all his fault. Somewhere along the way he had failed her. That was why he had to love her the most.

Lianne opened the door. The sight of her father lying there was now all too familiar. On his back, with both legs in traction and his body twisted at a peculiar angle to allow for the brace around his neck. 'Hello, sweetheart.' He couldn't even move his head. His eyes followed her progress to the bed. 'You're late.'

Leaning over to kiss him tenderly, she explained, 'There were roadworks.' She had brought a novel for him to read. She laid it on the bedside cabinet and sat down beside him. 'When will they take the plaster off?' Every day she asked, and every day his answer was the same: 'When they're ready.' That was his answer now.

His green eyes closed in pain, as he tried to turn. He sucked in a long breath, and held it for a minute. Lianne did not intervene. She knew he would cope. When he was composed, he voiced the anxieties that plagued him. 'Have you seen Ginny? How is she? How are they treating her?' A tear trickled out of one corner of his left eye. 'Does she really know what she's done?'

Lianne reached out to pick up his unbandaged hand. Raising it to her face, she caressed it there. 'You forget,' she reminded him, 'so far, I've only been allowed to see her once. But I've had a reply back from the authorities, and I can see her again, this weekend coming.' She stroked his thick dark hair, gently pushing it back from his forehead. 'I've already told you what she was like the last time.' The memory was shocking. 'She was fine, doing well, and filled with remorse,' she lied.

The truth was, Ginny didn't say a single word the whole time her sister was there. Instead she sat in the chair and stared out the window, her beautiful dark eyes haunted. Whenever Lianne spoke, she would snatch her head round and stare at her, as though she would like to rip out her throat. When, in a startling move, she lashed out at Lianne, with her fingers crooked like the claws of an animal, the warden quickly intervened and took her away.

'When you see her...' The tear grew plump and round, slithering to the pillow.

'Yes, Daddy?'

'Never mind.' How could he ask her to relay what was on his mind? That would be too cruel. 'Have you seen your mother?'

'Not yet. I'm going straight after.'

He smiled, and winced when it hurt. 'They've promised to take me in a wheelchair when I'm out of plaster,' he told her. 'The nurses are very good. They carry little messages between us, and they tell me how well she's doing. They even let me use the phone once. It was good to hear your mother's voice.' He smiled with pleasure. 'But she sounded strange, kind of muffled.' He pointed to his neck. 'Moving is hell. Even to speak into a phone.' He was quiet for a minute. 'She shouldn't have done this,' he groaned. 'Why would she do such a thing?'

'Do you want me to tell her anything?'

'Tell her she must be brave. Tell her not to hate herself for what she did to me and your mother. We've forgiven her. Tell her that.'

Lianne felt a little rush of anger. 'I didn't mean Ginny.'

He rolled his eyes to the ceiling, his mouth set in a grim line. 'Sorry. You can tell your mother that I love her, and miss her. It will be good to see her with my own eyes.'

'I'll give Ginny your message, too.' She wanted to make amends for being angry.

'If you like.' He fleetingly touched her hand. 'Are you happy with Dave's family?'

Lianne smiled at that. He was interested in her after all. 'They're very good to me,' she said.

'Have you decided about going back to school after the summer?'

'I won't be going back.' It was on the tip of her tongue to tell him about the baby.

'You're looking for a job, is that it?'

'Would you mind very much?'

He considered for a while, before replying in a soft, almost inaudible voice, 'Lying here, you get to think a lot.' The nightmare never ended. 'Who am I to say what you should do with your life?'

'You're my father. Ginny's too.' The question spilled out without her even realising: 'Is she really insane?'

He turned his eyes towards her. There was such sadness there that it squeezed his heart. 'I want you to go now, sweetheart,' he said. And he hated himself.

'Are you tired?' He looked tired, haunted. Like Ginny, she thought. 'Maybe I shouldn't come to see you every day,' she reluctantly suggested.

His eyes flickered with horror. 'No! I want you to come and see me, every single day.' When she was here he knew she was safe. When she was away from him he could never be sure.

'If you only knew how I watch that door every morning,' he revealed. As if to allay her suspicions, he changed the subject.

'Remember to tell your mother... keep herself beautiful for me.'

'I will.'

She kissed him and pressed her face close to his. No more words. It was all said.

The doctor had a moment to spare. 'Your father's doing very well,' he assured her. 'Tomorrow we're taking the plaster off, and after that he'll be doing physiotherapy to strengthen the muscles.'

Lianne was delighted. 'How long before he can come out?' She would have said, come home. But they had no home.

'Now, now, don't be too hasty.' He liked this young woman. In spite of everything, she always had a bright smile for the staff. 'Your father's legs were shattered. We had to use pins just to hold the bones together. Oh, he will walk again, probably even without much of a limp. But it won't happen overnight.' Rubbing his chin, he said consideringly, 'Taking into account the damage to his spine, a month, maybe longer. Each patient is different.'

'Will he be crippled?'

The doctor could at least be honest. 'No, he won't be crippled. But, as I've already explained, although thankfully none of the damage is permanent, a full recovery won't happen overnight.'

Her mother's specialist had a very different story: 'Your mother suffered second-degree burns to the whole of her back and legs. She'll recover, but I'm afraid the scars will always be with her.'

A short time later, Lianne walked through the glass-topped tunnel that led to the new burns unit. In the stark, white room, she sat at her mother's bedside, watching while she slept, still not able to believe that this catastrophe had fallen on her family. Liz looked so pretty, so still and quiet in her empty slumber. While the tragedy was unfolding, she had been cosseted in the arms of her man. Unlike Jack, who was conscious throughout, she was spared the trauma of living through every terrible moment.

'Lovely, isn't she?' The nurse came in softly. 'Like a child,' she said. 'So small and delicate.' She checked the dressings and changed the drip and still Liz slept on. 'Try not to disturb her,' she asked. 'She needs all the sleep she can get.'

After the nurse had gone, Lianne silently regarded her mother. 'Like a child,' she repeated softly. Until just recently, Liz had been drip-fed, and as a result had grown very thin. She had only just begun eating solids again, but the high cheekbones were still prominent, and the arms were pathetically small. With her pale, flawless skin and shining brown hair she looked years younger than Lianne remembered: not at all like the mother who yelled at them to come and get their breakfast, or put their shoes away, or drop their dirty clothes in the linen bin.

Suddenly, it was too much to bear. Leaning forward, she folded her arms on the blanket and laid her head down. When Liz winced in her sleep, she whispered brokenly, 'Forgive me, Mum. Please... forgive me.' She didn't know why, but she felt it was all her fault.

Lying on her stomach, Liz appeared at first glance to be unhurt. Her face and arms were clean and glowing. It was only when the nurse lifted the blankets to check her that Lianne saw her mother's lower neck and entire back swathed in bandages. She could only imagine the raw flesh beneath.

Talking as though to herself, Lianne revealed how Mrs Martin had got her a part-time job at the newsagent's, and how Mr Martin said they should get a discount off their newspapers now. She told how Dave had done so well in his temporary job as a driver for the local garden centre, that they had given him a new van.

'Bigger than the bakery vans,' she said proudly. 'He's earning a good wage, and he really enjoys the work.' Careful not to betray the secret that only she and now Mrs Martin knew, she said anxiously, 'I think he means to give up the idea of college, but I won't let him do that. He has it in him to make a fine doctor. It would be a sin and a shame if he threw it away.'

After a while, she grew tired of talking to herself. Taking the notepad and pen out of the bedside cabinet, she scribbled a note and propped it up on the fruit bowl where her mother would be able to read it:

Hello, Mum,

I didn't want to wake you, so I'll see you tomorrow.

I've been to the bakery again, and everything is all right. Fred says the accountant visited, and that he was very pleased.

Daddy sends his love, and so do I.

Miss you Mum. See you tomorrow.

Lianne.

xxx

As she leaned over to kiss her, she whispered, 'I'm so sorry, Mum. It was me that made Ginny angry. If only I'd known what she meant to do, I might have been able to stop her.' At the back of her mind was the knowledge that once Ginny made up her mind, *no one* could stop her. Still, she somehow felt responsible.

When the door closed quietly behind Lianne, Liz opened her eyes. 'Not your fault,' she said. 'It's *his* fault, and mine... for creating a monster.' Too afraid to think, she closed her eyes and sank into a deep, replenishing sleep.

On Friday evenings, Mrs Martin watched the television. Her husband paid his once-a-week visit to the local pub, where he played darts, drank a slow pint and caught up with men's gossip – mostly soccer, work, and the state of the nation.

Lianne and Dave walked in the lazy heat alongside the canal, talking lovers' talk, and planning a future. 'I hope you don't want me to get down on one knee,' he said, drawing her into the shade of a tree, 'but I wondered if you might like to get married?'

Lianne was taken aback. Half-expecting him to raise the idea of marriage, she thought she had prepared herself for it, when in fact she was knocked over. 'Are you serious?' she laughed. 'You really want us to get married?'

'Wouldn't ask you otherwise.' Parting her lips with the tips of his fingers, he put his mouth to hers and tenderly kissed her.

When he drew away, his hand remained on her face, gently stroking, caressing. 'I won't take no for an answer,' he whispered, his cocoa-coloured eyes smiling into hers. 'I know all the old arguments... that we're too young, or we have no money. We love each other, that's all that matters. The rest will follow.' He leaned forward, so close he could touch his lips to hers without even moving. 'You do love me, don't you?'

'You know I do.'

'No argument then.'

Lianne had to be certain. 'Everything you said... about us being too young, and having no money. It's true just the same.'

'Not insurmountable,' he declared, with a firm shake of the head. 'As for being too young, we'll just have to grow older a bit quicker. And we won't be poor for long, because I'll work hard to get us the things we need.' Anticipating her next argument, he went on, 'I'm sure Mum will let us stay there until we have our own place.' He grew excited, afraid to lose her. 'If you don't like the idea of living with the in-laws, I'll make enquiries about places to rent.'

She had to admire him. 'You've obviously thought it through.'

'You bet I have. I won't risk losing you. I don't want anyone else. I never will.' Putting both his hands on her shoulders, he held her so hard she couldn't move. 'I love you, Lianne.'

'I love you too.' She wondered how she could tell him that she was carrying his child. Should she tell him now? Later? Would he feel trapped? Would he hate the idea? Would it only serve to make him all the more determined to work, rather than study? In that precious moment, when he looked at her with such intensity, wanting her to say yes, willing her to give all, she could not meet his gaze.

His heart fell like a stone inside him. 'Tell me,' he urged. 'There's something else on your mind, isn't there? Tell me, Lianne.'

The two things uppermost in her mind were the baby, and college. She chose to keep one to herself, and reveal the other. 'I would never marry you if it meant your giving up the idea of being a doctor.'

He reeled back as though she had slapped him in the face. 'Then you're making things impossible,' he argued. 'I can't go to college, and earn a wage to keep us as well.'

'Then we'll wait until you leave college.'

Horrified, he stared her out. 'You're talking years!'

'I know.' She also knew she had done the right thing in keeping quiet about the baby.

His smile was a bitter one. 'Are you really prepared to wait that long?'

'If I have to.' Somehow she would manage, God willing.

'I see.' He began walking, waiting for her to follow. 'You say you love me, but you don't mind waiting five... maybe six years for us to marry?'

She was almost running to keep up with him. 'If that's how long it takes.'

'What if I say I don't want to go to college? What if I tell you I had already changed my mind about being a doctor?'

'I wouldn't believe you.'

They walked home in silence, angry with each other, angry with themselves. 'Think about it,' he told her, as they went into the house. 'If you love me enough, you'll let me make the choice.'

Lianne was considering her answer when Mrs Martin called out from the living-room. 'Come in here, you two,' she said. 'I've been on my own too long, and I feel like a chin-wag.'

Dave gave Lianne a quick kiss. 'Sorry,' he said.

'So am I,' she replied. 'I don't mean to be bossy.' Then, to his frustration, she muttered, 'But I meant every word I said. Give up college, and you give up me.' In her heart she knew he still wanted to be a doctor. If he let that go for her, she would never forgive herself.

On the first Sunday in July, Lianne went to see Ginny.

Dave insisted on accompanying her. 'After what happened last time, I want to be there,' he told her.

Lianne didn't argue. Instead she merely asked that he be careful not to antagonise Ginny with his presence. 'She was never happy about me being with you,' she confessed, 'so if you'd stay in the background, I'd be grateful.' She would be more than grateful, she thought. She would be safe.

Mr Martin made the generous gesture of offering them his precious Hillman Avenger for the day. 'And mind you don't scratch it,' he warned.

Dave was shocked but delighted. 'I passed my driving test ten months ago, and you've never once let me borrow your car,' he declared. 'What's so different now?'

His father studied him through proud eyes. 'Because you've had the good sense to bring home a young woman like Lianne,' he said, giving her a warm smile, 'and she'll make certain you return my car unscratched.' He then opened out his newspaper and returned to his reading. As they went out the door he called to them, 'No canoodling in the back, mind. And wipe your feet before you step on my carpets. They cost me five bob at Halfords.'

'He's a fusspot, but his heart's in the right place,' Mrs Martin remarked as she saw them off. Dipping into her purse, she gave Dave a couple of pounds. 'Make sure you don't run out of petrol,' she told him. To Lianne she gave a parting kiss. 'Don't you worry,' she murmured, 'things have a way of straightening themselves out.'

Lianne knew what she meant. She meant the baby. And Dave. And Ginny too. She meant, 'Take care. Don't let her hurt you. And don't be afraid of the future.' In that moment, Lianne loved her dearly. But she wanted her own mother. However kind and thoughtful others might be, there was no real substitute for your own flesh-and-blood mother.

The car ran smoothly all the way. Along the Leighton Road and out towards Buckingham. Through the little market town, and on to the outskirts. The journey from home to the clinic took an hour; now they were travelling up the drive, and there it was, looming before them in the brilliant sunshine, a vast building of Victorian design, with rambling gardens and a wide imposing entrance.

'Don't be nervous.' For most of the journey, Dave had been quiet, concentrating hard on the road, and getting used to his father's car.

Now, as the miles were covered and they drew closer, he felt more relaxed. Taking one hand from the steering wheel, he gripped her small fingers in his. 'I'll be with you every step of the way.'

Lianne, too, had been deep in thought, with little to say. Now, though, there it was, standing before them like Judgement Day, a place where the mentally disturbed were housed, a place unjustly feared by outsiders.

Reliving the last time she was here, Lianne could feel herself trembling. 'I'm not nervous!' she snapped. 'Why should I be nervous of seeing my own sister?' She glared at him, not knowing how to tell him she was afraid.

Dave wasn't offended by her sharp tongue. Though he sensed the deep ties between these two, he had never really understood it. Lianne was soft and loving, while Ginny was hard and cruel. They could not be more different. Yet there was a unique bond between them that left everyone on the outside. 'I didn't mean to suggest you were nervous of seeing Ginny,' he lied. 'I just thought you might be worried about going inside, that's all.' He squeezed her hand. 'It won't be like last time,' he promised. 'She won't want to hurt you.' She'd better not try, he thought, or she'll answer to me!

'You're right,' Lianne admitted. 'I *am* a little nervous. And I had no right to snap at you like that.'

He turned into the car park and slowed to a halt. Wrenching on the brake handle, he switched off the motor and leaned over to kiss her. 'Friends?' he asked sheepishly.

Her pretty face broke into a grin. 'Friends!' she said. They got out of the car and walked hand-in-hand through the car park, up the wide steps to the front door and over to the desk. 'We've come to see my sister,' Lianne announced.

The nurse on reception remembered her from the last time. It wasn't unusual for a patient to attack their loved ones in such a violent manner, but this young woman had been extra good with her sister, gentle and caring, wanting only to be with her. It was always sad when a meeting ended in violence.

She thumbed through the appointments ledger. 'Virginia Lucas... and you are Lianne?'Her smile was brighter than a summer's day. 'And this must be David Martin, the young man you rang about?' Whenever the arrangements were changed, there was always a procedure to follow. Lianne had to let them know if she was bringing a second visitor.

While the nurse filled out the necessary forms, Lianne felt the need to question her. 'Is Ginny all right?'

The woman scribbled faster. She had a lot of work to do and it was already eleven thirty. 'She's a great deal better,' she answered, without looking up.

'Is she looking forward to seeing me?' Her voice broke with anxiety. You never knew how Ginny's mind was working.

Swinging the form round, the nurse handed her the pen. 'Sign please. The young man too.'

While they signed, she made a brief phone call. By the time the pen and form were returned, another nurse had appeared to accompany them. She was a gentle giant with huge feet and lipstick smudged all over her teeth, and she chatted as they walked. 'Your sister is so much better,' she said. 'She's working out in the gym… under supervision of course. It's an innovation for us. Physical exercise helps to calm the mind. That's the theory, and I must say it does seem to work.'

She led them down yet another corridor. It was lined with windows through which the sun poured in. 'Of course there are some patients who would not benefit from that kind of exercise. Some are sadly too ill to cope with that level of therapy. Others might be very strong, extremely violent people who could pick up a weight and crush your head with it.' She gave them a smile which was meant to put them at ease. 'Fortunately there are few of that nature in *this* establishment.'

Lianne flinched as they were led into the day-room. It was in this very room that Ginny had attacked her. 'Will you be staying with us?' she asked the nurse.

'Not actually inside the room. We won't be far away, and we'll be able to see everything that goes on.'

Lianne looked puzzled. 'If you're not in the room, how can you see what's going on?'

The gentle giant smiled. 'See that watercolour?' She pointed to a painting of swans on a lake. Her voice dipped to an intimate whisper. 'We'll be looking through that.'

Dave was fascinated. 'James Bond stuff, eh? I've heard of things like that, but I've never heard of a two-way painting before. I always thought they used a two-way mirror?'

Placing her fingers on her lips she murmured, 'Shh. I'm not really supposed to have told you.' Her eyes turned to Lianne. 'Only you had a bad time on the last visit, and I wanted to put your mind at rest.'

'Thank you.' Lianne was glad she had told her. 'Does Ginny know?'

The smile stiffened, and the voice became authoritative. 'No, she doesn't. And you must not say anything.' She waved her arm round the room. It was a pleasant room, overlooking the garden, and contained a number of comfortable-looking armchairs. 'Sit where you like,' she said. 'Someone will be along with refreshments in a while.' Then she hurried from the room.

There were two armchairs set opposite each other. Lianne sat in one. Dave sat in the other. 'I'll move when she comes in,' he confided.

Another nurse arrived with the refreshment trolley. Lianne had a strong cup of coffee, while Dave had a soft drink. Neither of them really wanted a drink, but it seemed impolite to refuse.

'You heard what the nurse said,' Dave remarked, holding Lianne's hand. 'She said Ginny was so much better.'

'I'll believe it when I see it.' Lianne glanced up at the painting. 'Do you believe her?' she whispered. 'It seems just like a painting to me.'

He shrugged. 'Who knows?' he said. 'It seems like a good idea though, don't you think?'

'A bit sneaky.' In fact the idea had angered her. It seemed like a gross intrusion of privacy. 'But I expect you're right. Maybe it's a better idea than having someone standing over us, like they did last time.' She knew her sister better than most. Ginny was proud and independent. Maybe it was the presence of a guard that had provoked the attack.

A tall, slim woman in a bright blue cardigan entered the room. 'Hello,' she said, shaking hands with each of them. 'Ginny will be here any minute.' Addressing herself solely to Lianne she said, 'I just wanted a quick word before you see her.'

Lianne had met her before. Dr White was Ginny's psychotherapist. 'She's all right, isn't she?'

The doctor strolled to the door. Lianne followed. 'Ginny is coming along fine,' she said. 'She's responding to the new treatment. Beginning to talk at last.'

'How long will it take for her to get better?' Ginny *had* to get better. Please God, don't let her spend the rest of her life in here!

The doctor gazed out of the window, gathering her thoughts, in the way that doctors do. Treading the thin line between telling the truth and dashing any hopes, or creating hope by fabricating a little white lie. It was a difficult balancing act.

'That's not for any of us to say,' she replied tactfully. 'No two patients are the same. I'm afraid your sister has withdrawn into herself. She's a lost soul at the moment, and until we can bring her out of herself, we have no way of getting to the root of it all.'

'Will this new treatment bring her out of herself?'

'I'm not God,' she answered with a wry little smile. 'I'm merely a psychotherapist. However, I do have high hopes for your sister's full recovery. In time.' Realising that her assurances meant little, she laid a comforting hand on Lianne's shoulder. 'Trust me,' she said simply. 'Your sister is in the best hands. When she comes, you'll see how much she's improved since the last time.'

She was right.

When, a few moments later, Ginny came into the room accompanied by a middle-aged and formidable-looking nurse, Lianne could hardly believe her eyes. There was a calmness about her that immediately put Lianne's mind at rest, and she was smiling. Dark, beautiful eyes glowed with pleasure as they rested on her sister's eager face. 'Hello, Lianne,' she said, and even her voice was smiling.

Lianne choked back the tears. 'Oh, Ginny! You do look so much better. You *do*!' She would have run to her, hugged her close like she used to. Only she still wasn't sure. She wasn't sure of her sister. She wasn't sure of herself. And the memory of what happened last time seemed to come between them.

The nurse ushered her forward. 'There you are, Ginny. Here's your sister to see you.' She made no move to leave.

Ginny gave her a withering glance. 'I won't hurt her,' she said pointedly. The previous incident was on all their minds.

The nurse's smile was bright. 'Of course you won't!' She stood like some great tree, loath to uproot herself.

It was only when Lianne said that Dr White thought it was all right for them to be alone that she visibly relaxed. 'I'll leave you to it then,' she said. 'I won't be too far away. Call if you want me.' Her eyes bored into Lianne's. So did the warning.

In a moment the nurse had joined her companion. Closeted in the next room, they monitored the scene. 'I still don't trust her,' one said. 'Virginia Lucas is a devious bugger... slit your throat soon as look at you, I reckon.'

'Then she has no right being in there without one of us alongside.'

'Orders. They give 'em and we jump.'

The other nurse watched for a while. She saw how Dave moved to another chair at the back of the room, his whole attention riveted on Ginny. He was neither relaxed, nor listening to what was being said. Instead he was perched right on the edge of his chair, as though expecting to leap up at any second.

'He doesn't trust her.' The quiet remark filtered through their thoughts. 'I don't expect for one minute he's here because he wants to be.' A gracious smile as she gazed on Lianne's face. 'He's here to look after his sweetheart, and who can blame him?'

'We see it all in here, don't we, eh?' She shivered. 'I don't think I've ever seen this before though.' Pointing to Lianne, she muttered, 'There's Good.' Pointing to Ginny, she whispered, 'And there's Evil.'

The big woman gave her a sideways glance. 'Nobody's all good, or all evil. Anyway, you shouldn't be talking like that.' Funny, though, because she had been thinking exactly the same.

'Do you reckon she'd go for her sister again?'

'If she does, we'll be ready.'

Impatience. 'But do you think she *will*... go for her?'

The gentle giant shook her great head. 'I don't think so.' But she had serious reservations.

'I still think they were wrong not to have one of us in there with her.'

'Doesn't matter what we think.'

'But it should! What if she suddenly throws a fit, and we can't get to her in time?' She drew in a sharp, hissing breath. 'What if this time she... *kills*?'

'Then it won't be on *our* conscience.'

'That's callous.'

'Not callous: sensible. If it was up to me, we'd go in and stay there until the meeting was over. But the decision has been made not to stand guard. It's a wrong decision I grant you, but it's not up to us. You and me are general dogsbodies, paid to nurse the sick, and to be honest, I'm thankful that the more frightening decisions don't fall on our narrow shoulders.'

The other one looked at her companion's shoulders, and gave a little titter. 'What! You could carry the whole building on them shoulders,' she said with admiration.

But the big nurse seemed not to hear. Intent on the activities in the adjoining room, she whispered, 'Did you see that? Oh, I don't like the look of that.' There was no need to whisper, because they could not be heard. But there was something unsettling about watching people when they didn't know they were being watched. Something irreverent, like talking in church.

Ginny was out of her chair, leaning over Dave. She was softly laughing, murmuring into his ear, making him hate her, making him love her. Her voice was uplifted in mock sing-song: 'Little Jack Horner sat in the corner.'

'I thought you and Lianne would want to talk.' He would have drawn away but she was positioned in such a way that she had him pinned there.

Kissing him lingeringly on the forehead, she looked from him to Lianne, and back again. The other two were unsure how to react. Dave kept his eyes on Lianne, sending out messages of love and reassurance. Lianne stood up, ready to intervene, praying Ginny would not react violently. 'Do you want Dave to wait outside?' she asked hopefully.

Ginny whispered to him, 'You didn't have to hide over here. Why didn't you sit next to me? I would have liked that.'

Lianne's voice was like the crack of a whip. 'Ginny!'

Now she turned, dark eyes innocent. 'No, I don't want him to wait outside,' she answered. 'I'm glad he came. I can't thank him enough for bringing you to see me.' Touching his collar, she leaned over him again. 'Do you think I smell nice?' She dipped her face, touching her hair against his cheek. 'Do you think I'm still beautiful?'

'What I think,' he said firmly, 'is that you should go and sit with Lianne. After all, it's not *me* that's come to see you.' Anger fused his gaze with hers.

Incensed, she raised her hand to slap him, but he caught her wrist and walked her back to her chair. At that moment the door opened, and in walked the gentle giant. 'Is everything all right?' she asked innocently.

Calmer now, wanting to control the situation as always, Ginny's smile was disarming. 'Everything is wonderful. Thank you.' She stared at Lianne, then at Dave, softly pleading, as she turned again to the nurse. 'Surely you don't mean to send them away?'

'No.' The big woman knew how to play the game. 'Not yet. But they will have to leave soon. You know the rules… half an hour at a time.' She then addressed herself to Lianne. 'You still have a good ten minutes.' It would be the longest ten minutes of her life. There were times when she doubted her own capabilities. This was such a time.

Her companion was right, though. Mostly this clinic was full of sick people, poor tortured souls who had lost their way and were trying to find it again. The same could not be said of Virginia Lucas. Here in this room with her, there was a terrible sense of evil. Powerful. Destructive. Never in her whole career had she felt it so strongly.

Lianne sensed it too. She felt Ginny's smile on her. She saw it shift to Dave and she felt the danger. 'I think it might be as well if you did wait outside for me,' she told him.

'No way!' He strode across the room to stand beside her. 'I'm not leaving this room without you.'

The nurse intervened. 'It might be as well if you left them together,' she said reluctantly. 'Sisters are a special breed. They always have a lot to say to each other.' There was no doubting the hostility emanating from Ginny.

Dave was adamant. 'You'll have to throw me out.' He knew why Lianne wanted him to leave. Ginny had manipulated her, just as she always did.

Delighting in the upset she had caused, Ginny found herself regarding Lianne in a different, more detailed way. Realisation dawned. Her gaze opened with astonishment, and suddenly her whole mood changed. She pleaded with Lianne. 'It's my fault. Let him stay.'

Lianne looked at the nurse, realising with a little shock that it was up to her.

'I promise to behave,' Ginny said.

She seemed contrite enough. Lianne was convinced. The nurse was not quite so certain but decided to play along. 'Ten minutes, that's all.'

Dave resumed his seat. Lianne too. 'Why do you have to be so hateful?' she asked.

Ginny lay back in her chair. 'I don't want to stay in here,' she said sulkily. 'I *won't* stay in here.'

Lianne believed the correct way to deal with her was to be firm. 'Get better, then,' she said, 'and they might let you come home.'

Ginny's smile was wicked. 'I haven't got a home.' She glanced at Dave. 'Unless you want me to come and live with you and the Martin family?'

Dave gave her a hard look. 'Afraid not,' he said quietly. 'There wouldn't be room anyway.'

Rebuffed, she turned to Lianne, her next words meant only for her sister's ears. 'Are they dead?'

Lianne was dumbfounded. 'I won't talk to you about them.'

'Would you believe me if I said I was sorry?'

Choking on the hard lump that straddled her throat, Lianne cried, 'Oh, Ginny! I hope you are.' If only it could be true. If only Ginny really was sorry. 'The sooner you realise what a terrible thing you've done, the sooner you'll get better.'

The silence descended, swallowing them.

After a while, Ginny spoke again. Defiant. Totally convincing. 'It wasn't me, you know.'

Lianne was confused. 'Are you saying you didn't set fire to the house?'

In the next room the tension was electric.

Sitting forward in her chair, Ginny stared at Lianne through wild eyes. She looked like someone demented. 'Oh, yes. I did that,' she confessed softly. Her eyes closed, and she seemed to be going through anguish. 'I had to.'

'Why?' This was the first time Ginny had spoken to her about the fire. 'You could have killed them. And me. You nearly killed me. If it hadn't been for Dave, I wouldn't be here now.'

'So they're not dead?'

'No, thank God.'

Ginny's face fell, and then it was beaming with happiness. 'Oh, Lianne! I'm so glad. I never wanted to hurt them, or you. How could I have wanted to hurt you?'

Lianne sighed, a long deep sigh that came from her soul. 'I have to believe you,' she murmured. Then she realised what Ginny had said earlier. 'A minute ago, you said you didn't do it, and now you're saying you did.' She shook her head, concentrating, while she waited for Ginny's explanation. 'What are you telling me?'

'I did light the fire.' There was a glow in Ginny's eyes, as she recalled the flames licking up the curtains, and the three of them lying helpless... until Dave raised the alarm. She forced herself not to look at him. If she were to turn now he would see the venom in her eyes. She couldn't risk that. If her plans were to come right she needed him on her side.

'I don't know what you mean.'

'I didn't kill Old Tom,' she lied.

Dave spoke out. There was disbelief in his voice, and in his heart. 'Why didn't you say that in the courtroom?'

'Yes!' Lianne continued. 'If you didn't kill Old Tom, then you didn't kill *anyone*. It would have made all the difference.' There was something here she didn't understand. 'Why, Ginny? Why didn't you tell them?' For one incredible minute she actually believed her.

Ginny's laugh was sinister, her voice almost inaudible as she accused, 'I didn't tell, because I couldn't.' Her eyes narrowed with loathing. '*You* should know.'

Unable to hear her mutterings, Dave insisted, 'It's unbelievable! Why would you let them accuse you of murder if you didn't do it?' He was challenging her.

'Because they would never have believed me.' She smiled secretly at Lianne. 'Tell him,' she urged. 'Tell him why they would never have believed me.'

The big nurse came in then. 'Time to leave,' she said. 'I'm sorry.'

She remained at the door to count them out. Dave stood up first. 'Look after yourself,' he told Ginny. It was a foolish thing to say, because he knew she above all others would look after herself. But he had to say something, and it was as good as anything else. Certainly as good as 'I'm delighted to see how well you look'. He had seen her on that night. She had clawed at him, fought with him, and tried every way possible to stop him

266

from saving her own family. He wouldn't forget that in a hurry. Not in a lifetime, he wouldn't.

As Lianne made to leave, Ginny caught her in a tight embrace. 'I do love you,' she whispered, 'and I'm glad you came.' She had that uncanny knack of looking directly through Lianne's eyes. Through her soul.

'I'm glad, too,' Lianne said, wishing Ginny wouldn't squeeze her so hard. It was difficult to breathe.

'They think I'm insane, but I'm not.'

'I know you're not.' Lianne couldn't help but wonder, though, and she felt ashamed. 'Of course you're not insane!'

'They think I am.' Dark eyes slanted sideways, towards the nurse. 'They've sectioned me, haven't they?'

'I don't know what you're trying to say, Ginny.'

Ginny squeezed her harder, making her go pink in the face. 'The will!' she hissed. '*You*'ll have to lay claim to the money on my behalf. Then, when I'm out of here, you can give the money to me.' She pressed her face so close that she was almost kissing her. 'Don't try and cheat me.' Something in Lianne's expression alarmed her. 'There *is* a will, isn't there? Dad's had a letter, hasn't he? You wrote and told me so.'

Lianne nodded, then, keeping her own voice as low as Ginny's, 'Apparently Grandmother didn't have time to change her will, and everything was left to Cyrus. But he's put a great deal of money into an account, in Daddy's name. It's there for when he and Mum get well again.'

'*If* they get well again.'

Hating the look on Ginny's face, Lianne pulled away. 'They *will* get well again,' she declared angrily. 'The doctors have promised.' Her voice rose in panic, causing the others to move towards them.

Dave stepped forward to take her away. 'Goodbye, Ginny,' he said. 'No doubt we'll see you again.' Much as he loathed the idea, he knew Lianne would want to come again. Whatever Ginny did or said, Lianne felt in duty bound to forgive and love her.

But Ginny had the parting word. 'You can't make room for *me* in your little love nest!' she yelled out after them. 'But you'll have to make room for the bastard!'

When, white faced and shaken, they both turned, she laughed cruelly. 'I've got better eyes than you have, Dave Martin. You've made my sister pregnant, and you didn't even know.'

Her voice faded as she was dragged away between the two nurses. But it echoed down the corridor, bouncing off the walls and telling the world of their shame.

Dave looked down on Lianne's white upturned face, and he knew it was the truth. He didn't say anything. Instead he took her in his arms and held her close. Words alone could never have said as much.

They broke the news over tea. Although it was no surprise to Mrs Martin, her husband was shocked. 'What the hell were you thinking of?' He stared at each of them in turn. 'You're just kids! Hardly got the nappy stains off your arses!' He scraped back his chair, and stormed out of the room.

'Give him time,' Mrs Martin murmured, sipping her tea with deliberation. 'Once he's got used to the idea he'll be back.'

A moment later he returned. He sat down and spread his hands on the table. There was an awkward moment, during which he stared at his son without saying a word. He glanced at his wife, and he shook his head. Then he spoke to Lianne, whose fists were nervously clenched under the table. 'I'm sorry,' he said. 'It was a shock. I don't know how to deal with it.'

Sensible as ever, Mrs Martin said firmly, 'The way to deal with it is to talk it through. First of all, you're right. They *are* very young.' She smiled at him, and he knew what she was thinking. 'But we were not much older when we got married.'

'You weren't pregnant though.'

'And Lianne is, eh?' She smiled broadly at her. 'The most important thing is... do you and Dave want to keep this baby?'

When all three looked at her with horror, she nodded her head, and went on in a quiet, sobering voice. 'All right. So now there are more practical things to be discussed... like where will you live? And whether Dave wants to work or go to college...'

Dave had given it a great deal of thought, and though the passion to be a doctor was still strong in his blood, he had a greater passion: Lianne, and the baby she was carrying. 'I'll do what's best for my family,' he answered.

'I understand that, son,' his father said. 'But wouldn't it be better to think long-term? There's nothing wrong with driving a van. It's a respectable way to earn a living, and I'm sure there are those who would never want to do anything else. But you have it in you to be a doctor.' His voice dropped to a plea. 'Don't throw that away.'

There was a brief silence while everyone reflected on his words.

Dave was thinking of Lianne.

She was thinking of him.

Suddenly, her wise words rose above her thoughts. 'Dave knows how I feel,' she said. 'I can't let him turn his back on medical school.' She gazed at him with a love only the two of them understood. 'Promise them,' she said softly, 'and I'll go along with anything else you want.'

There was another brief moment when Dave turned the whole matter over in his mind. At length he said, 'I can't lose you. If it's at all possible, I'll carry on with my studies.'

Mrs Martin cried into her handkerchief. Her husband leaped out of his chair to shake his son's hand. 'We'll *make* it possible!' he cried. Then he hugged Lianne, and called for a celebration. 'There's a baby on the way, and a wedding to plan,' he laughed. And Lianne's heart soared with joy.

Amidst the excitement, Ginny was momentarily forgotten. At that very moment she was lying on her bed, staring up at the stark white ceiling and making her devious plans. Wicked, selfish plans. Plans coldly designed to cast a dark shadow over Lianne's happiness.

10

On 22nd August, Jack was released from hospital. 'I have to come back twice a week for therapy,' he told Liz, 'but I won't neglect you, I promise.' He was sat beside her bed, one leg bent comfortably at the knee, the other stretched out awkwardly. His crutches were propped against the wall.

Sitting up in bed, Liz made a pretty picture. She was wearing a blue silk nightie and had taken the trouble to put on some lipstick. 'You look good, Jack,' she told him. Her manner was a little strained. She had something on her mind and didn't know how to say it. It had to do with Ginny. Always Ginny.

'You don't seem your usual self,' he remarked, peering curiously at her serious face.

'Neither do you, Jack,' she said without looking at him. 'But then it's not surprising when we've both been to hell and back.'

He laid his hand over hers but she pulled it away. 'All right,' he snapped. 'What is it?'

She remained silent. How could she tell him she never again wanted to lay eyes on her own daughter? As a mother, how could she even *think* it?

'Is it because we have to live over the bakery for a while?' He grimaced when she still remained silent. 'It's only until we get ourselves sorted,' he said. 'Then you can choose a house... not as grand or large as the one we had, but maybe you'd prefer that.'

She raised her gaze to his. 'Why are you doing it?'

'What? Living over the bakery?'

She flashed anger. 'You know very well I'm not talking about the bakery! I'm talking about Lianne. Why are you doing it to her?'

He looked away, tapping his plastered foot against the bed leg. Then he replied impatiently, 'She's too young, for Christ's sake!'

'Too young to be a wife, you mean?' She gave a small laugh. 'Well, she's not too young to be a mother, is she? With a baby due in four months, all she wants is to get married so the baby isn't born illegitimate.'

'She doesn't need my blessing.'

'Of course she does!' Slapping him on the arm, she spat the words out. 'She needs both our names on the form. You know that, bugger you!'

'She doesn't need to marry him. I've already told her she can live with us. Her *and* the baby.'

'Do I have an opinion on that?'

'That goes without saying.'

'Then you'd better know this: if Lianne and the baby come to live with you, I certainly won't.'

He stared disbelievingly at her. 'You're talking out of your arse.' Then, 'I don't know what you want,' he said painfully.

'It isn't what *I* want. It's what Dave and Lianne want, and they want you to give them your blessing so they can get married.' She was blood-angry and it showed. 'You've led that girl a merry dance, Jack, and now I'm leading you one. Go and see her, or when I get out of here, so help me, I'll find myself a place to stay, and to hell with you!'

'So! It's them or you, is it?'

'Looks that way.'

'I'll go round tonight.' His smile was devastating. 'She shall have her father's blessing, if that's what you want. I'll even be proud while I walk her down the aisle. How's that?'

'That's all she wants, Jack. Thank you.' She even afforded him a fleeting kiss on the mouth.

The nurse came in to change her dressings. It was a slow, painful business. The wounds were healing now, but there had been complications.

Jack waited until the curtains were drawn back, and the nurse gone. 'Have they said when you can leave?'

'When the infection's cleared away. A week, they said, maybe two.' If it hadn't been for that, she might have made it out of here before Jack. In a way she was glad she had not. 'Don't bother coming to see me tonight,' she suggested. 'Spend a little time with Lianne. She'll be so pleased.'

'I believe we have another daughter,' he reminded her sternly. 'Or aren't you interested?'

Again she remained silent. No, she wasn't interested. And no, as far as she was concerned, she did not have another daughter.

'So you can't forgive her?'

'Can you?' Her tone was one of disgust.

He stood up and balanced himself on the crutches. '*Someone* has to forgive her,' he answered flatly. 'I would have thought a mother could understand that more than most.'

She was glad when he went, making his way down the ward with surprising agility. 'I'm sorry, Jack,' she murmured. Ginny was evil through and through. She wanted them dead. She admitted that on the witness stand. How could she forget? A cold chill rippled through her. She hasn't finished with us yet. If you can't see that now, you never will.

The doctor was beside her when she looked round. 'Oh!' She was startled. 'I didn't realise you were there.'

A man of about Jack's age, with bright blue eyes and a ready smile, Mike Pearson had taken a fancy to Liz. During their many hours of consultation, he had got to know her well enough to realise that she was vulnerable, and open to suggestion. 'How are you today?' he asked in his most professional manner.

'Wonderful,' she answered with a twinkle in her eye. 'Aren't I always?'

He examined her back, and touched her with the utmost tenderness. He dropped her nightie and whispered in her ear as he straightened up. 'I could get struck off for what I'm thinking.'

'Please don't,' she answered softly. 'We should never have started it. I'm still in love with Jack. Whatever problems we have, we'll sort them out.'

Lifting her hand, he pretended to be taking her pulse. 'I'm here if you need me,' he told her quietly. 'Remember that.'

'You've been a good friend,' she said. 'I won't forget.'

He rubbed his finger suggestively over the palm of her hand. 'More than a friend, I hope.'

He held her hand, and she took comfort from it. Her life was upside down. Her feelings were torn apart, and it was good to have a safety net. That was Mike Pearson. Her safety net.

The sister had seen him at Liz's bedside, and came hurrying over. 'This is the impatient one,' she said, grinning at Liz. 'Every day it's "When can I go home?" ' She tutted, folding her arms, and glanced at the doctor. 'Anyone would think she wanted rid of us.'

He gazed down on Liz, and for a moment she was terrified that he might be indiscreet. Instead he took her clipboard from the foot of the bed, and made a note on it. His parting words left her unsettled. 'Then she'll have to be patient, won't she? We all have to learn patience. Take me, for instance... the most patient man in the world. When I want something, I usually get it.'

Lianne looked beautiful. The bump on her stomach was cleverly camouflaged by the empire line of her cream satin gown, and the pale high-heeled shoes gave her a delicate countenance. With her fair hair and green eyes, she looked like a china doll. Jack walked her down the aisle as promised. He smiled when his eyes encountered Dave, looking impossibly handsome in his new dark blue suit. He smiled throughout the hour-long service, and he beamed when Lianne turned to look at him. The truth was, he had come to accept the situation.

Liz stood beside him, quiet and lovely. 'You were right,' he told her through the veil on her hat brim. 'They do make a delightful couple.'

'I'm glad,' she said. 'Lianne deserves to be happy.'

The love fled from her heart when he whispered in her ear, 'Doesn't Ginny look lovely?'

Liz followed his gaze. Ginny was standing beside Jack, her dark eyes intent on Lianne and Dave. On her other side was a female official from the clinic. 'I moved heaven and earth to get her here,' Jack said. 'But then, she's doing so well, how could they refuse?'

Ginny pretended not to notice that she was being discussed. She stood tall and straight, aristocratic almost. Her glowing beauty and commanding presence had already caught the eye of one of Dave's friends, an amiable young man by the name of Luke Morrison. He and Dave had met at the open-day for the college course. That was a week ago, and they had hit it off straight away. Luke was a bit of a loner, articulate and extremely intelligent, except where women were concerned. He had a habit of choosing the wrong kind, and ending up with his heart broken. He was attracted to Ginny from the minute he saw her walk by, and now he couldn't keep his eyes off her.

Ginny revelled in his adoration. She felt good. Jack had bought her a very expensive cream-coloured two-piece, with a long straight skirt and a fitted jacket. The choice of colour was hers. Chosen deliberately to rival her sister's wedding gown. 'Doesn't Lianne make a lovely bride?' she said, looking at her mother.

Liz nodded and turned away. She couldn't bring herself to speak.

Lianne was in a world of her own. Dave was beside her and she was not afraid.

The vicar's voice gentled into her mind: 'I now pronounce you man and wife.' Dave took her in his arms and kissed her. In that very precious moment the child inside her moved, and her world was filled with sunshine.

In the vestry at the back of the altar, they signed the register, and talked and laughed, and it seemed like no time at all before they were retracing their steps down the aisle. They walked through a sea of smiles: the smiles of people wishing them well; her mother softly crying; her father genuinely proud.

Only one face stood out from the crowd. One face that was not smiling, but was scrutinising her with dark cruel eyes, eyes filled with envy, and with something else. Something she could not easily recognise. 'I wish you had been my bridesmaid, Ginny,' she told her as she passed. But Ginny's face remained impassive.

Refusing to allow anything to spoil their day, Lianne linked her arm with Dave's, and walked out of the church into the sunshine and a hail of confetti. 'I love you, Mrs Martin!' Dave cried as they ran to the car. Inside the car he kissed her again, holding her so tight that she thought he would never let go. In her happy heart she *prayed* he would never let go. As the wedding car pulled away, Lianne glanced out of the back window. She watched her parents get into the second car. They still carried the marks of their ordeal, her father now reduced to one crutch, her mother stiff-backed, still afraid. But they were alive, she thought. Thank God they were still alive.

Ginny was with them. Striking as ever. Better now. But not well enough to bear the responsibility of being bridesmaid. That was a great pity, because Lianne had wanted no one else.

The hotel laid on a splendid meal. Everyone was satisfied, and later, when the music struck up and the evening wore on, people danced across the floor, occasionally stopping to wish the happy couple well and to have yet another look at the wonderful presents set out on the long table.

'I'm a lucky bloke to have such a lovely wife,' Dave said, dancing with Lianne. 'There isn't a man in this room who doesn't envy me.'

Lianne looked up at him, thankful that her long thick lashes had grown to fringe her eyes as before. Her smile revealed the depth of her love. 'What? You mean they all want a fat wife, with swollen ankles and a skin problem?' Lianne was in too good a mood to worry about the side effects of being pregnant, but she did like to tease.

'Away with you, woman!' he said, gently swinging her round until she squealed. 'Even with your fat belly, swollen ankles and spots... you're still the best-looking bird in the place.'

It did Liz's heart good to see them so happy. 'I remember when we were like that,' she said, her sorry eyes turned to Jack. Visions of Mike Pearson flooded her mind. He was a rogue, refreshingly uncomplicated, wanting her with no strings attached.

Jack sidled closer, clinking his glass with hers. 'It doesn't have to be a memory,' he murmured. 'I love you just the same. Nothing's changed.' But Liz had changed, although he couldn't see it. She was more distant. Growing more afraid.

'You're wrong, Jack,' she said soulfully. 'Things *have* changed. You... me. Everything.' She wished it wasn't so. Oh, if only she could turn the clock back, things might have been very different.

'Are you saying you don't love me any more?' Suddenly Jack was attentive. If he lost Liz he had lost it all. She meant everything to him.

Liz couldn't look him in the eye. 'I don't know *what* I'm saying,' she confessed. 'I'm all mixed up. Since I came out of hospital, I can't seem to think straight.' Her smile spoke volumes. 'I do love you though, Jack,' she said. 'You need never doubt that.' It was his passion for Ginny she couldn't cope with. And her own inability to love her daughter, even a little.

The music slowed to a ballad. Without a word he took her in his arms and drew her on to the floor. His steps were clumsy, making him self-conscious. 'I'm still having trouble managing without the crutches,' he told her, 'but it's been so long since we danced together.'

As they moved round the floor, they made a handsome couple. Jack, tall and straight, cut a dashing figure. Liz, too, was over the worst of her injuries and looked lovely in a black dress and silver jewellery. They danced close, she with her face against his shoulder, and he with his arms round her waist. 'I think I want to make love with you,' he whispered in her ear.

His ardour made her smile. It was the old Jack talking. 'I'll have to get on top then,' she replied softly. 'My back's still much too sensitive to take your weight.'

Lianne felt proud. 'Don't they look right together?' she said to Dave. 'Next week they're going to look at one of those new houses along Leighton Road.' Her eyes shone with love. 'Oh, Dave, I'm so glad they're home.'

Dave was glad, too. 'I'm glad your father had a change of heart about us.' He had the feeling there was a bit of jealousy there. But then he supposed every man was a little jealous where his daughter was concerned.

Ginny, too, watched her parents dance for a while. 'They're very attractive, don't you think?' She glanced at the woman beside her, wondering how to be rid of her without raising suspicion. She had her eye on Luke Morrison, who in turn had been watching her all evening. She had an insatiable desire to lay writhing beneath him, under the stars.

The female official nodded. 'They certainly are an attractive couple,' she said, 'and not doing too badly, considering.' Realising what she had said, she quickly clammed up. There was nothing to be gained by reminding this young woman of the pain she had put her parents through.

The music stopped. Jack took Liz back to the bar. Dave and Lianne retired to a corner, where they talked softly and gazed into each other's eyes.

When the music started up again, Luke took the opportunity to ask Ginny for a dance. She in turn took the opportunity to pause on the way, and inform her father that he really ought to have a word with the official. 'After all, you and Mother will want to know what progress I'm making.'

As she and Luke went out through the french doors, the music changed to a slower tempo. Glancing back, Ginny was

277

pleased to see her father take the official on to the floor, where he gave her the treat of her life by dancing close and swaying her ample body to the rhythm.

As he danced into view he caught sight of Ginny and winked at her. She took that to mean she should go and enjoy herself while she had the chance.

'I'm a bit the worse for drink,' Luke told her, as they came out on to the verandah. 'Whisky is one of my weaknesses. The other is women.' He laughed in her face and she startled him by poking the length of her tongue into his mouth. Before he could get his breath, she pushed him against the balcony wall and was ripping off his jacket. 'Bloody Hell!' he giggled, fighting to keep his balance. 'You're a fast worker.'

She was on him with a frenzy, her mouth covering every inch of his face, her hands all over him. Now his trouser zip was open and she was fumbling inside. 'Anybody would think you were desperate,' he chuckled.

She didn't answer. She was too busy trying to persuade him to harden. Nothing seemed to help. Not his hand on her naked breast, nor when her kissing moved from his face to his penis. He didn't even respond when she took off her briefs and opened herself to him. 'Christ! What's the matter with me?' Frustrated, he pushed his finger in and out of her, hoping to revive a semblance of passion. 'It's the drink! It's always the same when I've had too much to drink!' He hung his head and looked like a little boy lost. 'I'm sorry,' he moaned. 'I'm bloody useless.'

Throbbing with a desperate need for him, she stared at him in disbelief. 'You're right,' she snarled. 'You *are* useless. And you're no good to me.'

It happened with such speed he didn't even have time to scream. Suddenly he was toppling over the balcony, falling through the air like a rag doll. There was a sickening sound, like air being punched from a bag. A gushing sigh. And an eerie silence.

When she looked down he was staring up at her, his eyes wide open and glazed with shock. His body was twisted into a grotesque shape, impaled on the railings, pumping blood into the fishpond and turning the water a dirty shade of crimson. She smiled at him. Then she slowly fastened her blouse, made herself look respectable, and returned to the hall. The music was still playing. Her companion was talking to Liz, and everything seemed quite normal. As no one seemed to be taking the slightest notice of her, she sauntered over to the bar and got herself a cocktail.

Liz saw her come back. And she recognised the evil delight on her face. 'Where have you been?' she muttered beneath her breath. 'What wickedness have you been up to?'

At nine fifteen, Ginny said her goodbyes. Her minder took Jack aside. 'I'm delighted with the way she's joined in.'

Jack kissed his daughter. 'We have to look forward,' he told her.

Liz stood back. 'I expect we'll see you soon,' she said. What she thought was, I don't care if I never see you again.

Lianne hugged her hard. 'Oh Ginny, I'm so thrilled you came to my wedding. It wouldn't have been the same without you.'

Ten minutes after Ginny and the minder departed, Dave and Lianne left for home. 'I'll make it up to you for not having a honeymoon,' he promised in the cab. 'With my first salary we'll cruise to Mexico.'

'I'd rather spend a fortnight in Weymouth,' she laughed, 'playing with Junior on the sands.'

'It'll be at least five years before I draw a salary,' he pointed out, tenderly stroking the bump on her belly. 'We may have half a dozen by then.'

'We'd better not,' she told him. 'I won't argue with the idea of one more, but if you want half a dozen, you can have them yourself. See how you like being a carthorse.' She then kissed him, and thought herself lucky to have such a wonderful future.

'You're right,' he said. 'One more, that would be nice. Besides, children are expensive I'm told, and we've got a few debts to pay along the way. If it hadn't been for Mum and Dad providing for us, college would have been an impossibility.'

A thought suddenly occurred to Lianne. 'What happened to your friend?' she asked. 'Luke, isn't it?'

He laughed aloud. 'Would you believe it? I forgot all about him.' He cast his mind back to when they left the hotel. 'Funny though, he wasn't around when we left.'

Lianne put his mind at rest. 'From what you tell me, he's probably entertaining some woman or other.'

Dave relaxed. 'That's where he'll be, right enough,' he agreed. 'Hidden away, charming some poor unsuspecting female.'

The house lights were on as they came in. 'It's a wonder the fuses don't blow,' Lianne chuckled. 'It's like Blackpool illuminations in here.'

Dave ran around switching the main lights off. 'It's *Dad* who'll blow a fuse,' he said. 'He nearly had a fit when the last electricity bill came in.' He carried her up the stairs. 'I hope you're not going to be so extravagant. Not like Mum. She has this idea that there are burglars watching her every move, ready to empty the house the minute she goes out.'

He stopped talking when she kissed him. 'As far as I'm concerned,' she said softly, 'your mum can do no wrong. I think it was very clever of her to let your dad have too much tipple. That way she could persuade him to stay over at the hotel… so we could have our honeymoon night all alone.'

He agreed. 'With a bit of luck she might persuade him to stay tomorrow as well. That way we can have *two* honeymoon nights.'

When he laid her on the bed, Lianne feigned shyness. 'Are you saying you want your wicked way with me twice over?'

His answer was to take off his clothes and stand before her, naked and magnificent. 'I'm yours if you want me,' he said cheekily.

She wanted him. Then, and twice more before the night was over.

In the morning he rolled over.

'Sorry about the bump,' she said.

'No problem,' he told her. 'I would never let anything come between us.'

Her gaze fell to his large penis, standing bold and erect. 'Are you sure?' she laughed. And soon the two of them were helpless in a fit of the giggles.

The short honeymoon ended when Dave's parents arrived home, just as they were having their breakfast. Mrs Martin was in tears. 'I'm sorry, son,' she said, 'but there's been a terrible accident.'

While his father took him to one side, Mrs Martin confided in Lianne. 'I shouldn't really tell you in your condition, but you'll find out soon enough, because the police are questioning everyone who was at the reception.'

Lianne was suddenly afraid. Her mind went straight to her parents. And Ginny. Always Ginny. 'What's happened? Tell me. Please.' She could be strong. Life had taught her to be strong.

Mrs Martin saw the strength in Lianne's eyes. She told her, as gently as she could. 'It's that nice young man... Luke Morrison. They say he got drunk and fell from the balcony.' She heard Dave cry out, and lowered her voice to a whisper. 'One of the waiters found him when he opened the curtains in the dining-room.' She drew in a long breath, as if to brace herself. 'He's dead,' she whispered. 'Dave's friend is dead.'

Just as Mrs Martin predicted, the police arrived soon after. Dave and Lianne told them only what they knew. That yes, he had seemed to be drinking rather a lot. 'I did have a word with him about it,' Dave revealed, 'but he held his drink well, and seemed to be capable enough. He arrived in a taxi, and no doubt intended going home the same way.'

Lianne found it too distressing, but the officers were gentle. 'Did you see him go out on to the balcony?' they asked. She told them no, she hadn't seen him for some time. 'I was with Dave. We were dancing.' And all the while they talked with her, she thought of Ginny. She had seen the way they looked at each other. The way he seemed attracted to her. She had seen how Ginny seemed to encourage him. Ginny. Always Ginny.

Seeming satisfied, the officers went, leaving behind them a sadder household. Lianne clung to Dave as they sat and talked. 'You mustn't let it cast too dark a shadow over your special day,' Mrs Martin pleaded.

Lianne smiled sadly. It was too late. How could they feel happy when such a terrible thing had happened? Again she thought of Ginny. All her life, when things went wrong and her happiness was spoiled, it was always Ginny.

She silently chided herself. Don't be unfair, she thought. It wasn't Ginny this time. The young man died because of an accident. But there was something. *Something!* Ginny. Always Ginny.

An inquest was held. The verdict was as everyone expected.

'Death by misadventure.' The coroner's voice echoed across the courtroom. The unfortunate young man had drunk too much alcohol. After going out to the balcony he became confused. Judging by the disarray of his clothing, it appeared he attempted to relieve himself, lost his balance and fell to his death.

At the inquest, only one person silently refuted the verdict. Liz believed that somehow Ginny was at the root of Luke Morrison's death. Yet she had no logical reason to uphold that belief. She had no proof. It was just an instinct. A terrible gnawing instinct; born out of evil, and kept alive by terror. Even now, so long after Ginny had tried to murder her, that same terror threatened to destroy her.

Jack could bear it no longer. 'It's been a month now, and I still can't get through to you. What in God's name's the matter with you? I thought you wanted a house. I thought you couldn't get away from the bakery soon enough?' He had on his coat, ready for the second time in a week to go viewing houses. And, for the second time, she had refused to go. 'For Christ's sake, Liz, when are we going to get our lives together?'

'I'm not ready to leave here yet.' She hated living above the bakery. The constant humming from the ovens and the sound of the vans revving up of a morning got on her nerves. She was sick of the smells that filtered into every room, smells of baking, cakes, buns, doughnuts and fresh bread. All easily recognisable to her. Smells of home, and family. Smells that at one time she would have enjoyed. Now they wafted round her like the bars of a prison. 'You go,' she said. 'I don't feel up to it.'

Something in her voice calmed him. He regarded her then, his quiet gaze roving her face with compassion, noting the dark lines beneath her eyes, and the sad droop of her mouth. 'What did the doctor say when you saw him yesterday?' he said, coming over to her. 'You were so quiet when you came back. I can't know what's on your mind if you don't talk.' He stroked her hair like he used to. 'There isn't a problem, is there? I mean, the doctor didn't say anything to worry you?'

She raised her stricken eyes to his. She was thinking of Ginny. For weeks she had thought of nothing else. 'That boy,' she murmured, 'what happened to him, Jack?'

Drawing back as though she had slapped him, he muttered angrily, 'What are you getting at?'

His face told its own story. 'My God!' she exclaimed. 'I'm not the only one who thinks Ginny had something to do with it. *You* think so too, don't you?'

'Are you insane?' Rage coloured his features. 'How can you even think that? Ginny was in sight the whole time.'

'No she wasn't.' Liz was on her feet now, driven by the conviction that he too believed Ginny had killed that young man. 'She was out on the balcony too... it must have been at the same time as Luke Morrison.'

Liz was convinced. 'You know what I'm saying is the truth. You know she killed that poor young man, but you won't admit it.' She turned away. 'I can't believe you'd want to protect her.'

'She's so much better,' he said brokenly. 'Don't do this to her, Liz.'

'Open your eyes, Jack! Can't you see the evil in your own daughter? Must you always make excuses for her?' Memories came flooding back. They had never really been far away, just lurking in the back of her mind, like some nasty slimy creature. There was no holding back now. 'You're protecting her again, just like you've always protected her! Even as a baby; when she took her vicious temper out on Lianne; when she deliberately broke things; when the kitten Lianne brought home was found hanging in Ginny's wardrobe; even when she admitted the most awful atrocities, you would always make excuses for her.'

'She was a sick girl. Any father would do the same.' It was the past that had produced a monster like Ginny. He had kept the past alive by giving her his grandmother's name. He had to make amends for that. 'I know I should have been stricter... punished her.' How could he punish her? It was he who made her what she was, and it was he who must be punished. Ginny was bad. She couldn't help herself. 'But she didn't kill Luke Morrison.'

'Why not? She killed that poor old caretaker, didn't she?'

'No! Why would she want to kill a harmless old man?'

'She admitted it, for God's sake!'

'Because she was sick. But she's so much better.' He was pleading for himself, for his family. For their future together. 'You heard what the nurse said... Ginny's been very ill, but she's getting better all the time. If she can put it behind her, why can't we? We have to give her a chance, Liz. If we don't, who else will?'

'She's had all the chances I can give her.' The very idea of having Ginny under the same roof filled her with horror. She turned to him, appealing to his love for her. 'You know what she's done, yet you blindly adore her.' The envy coloured her eyes, filling her veins with malice. 'You love her more than you love me, or Lianne. Even your own mother. Why, Jack? Tell me why?'

His voice came out in a whisper. 'I don't love her more than you,' he said. 'How can you think that?' If only she knew. If only she could read his mind at that moment, she would see why he was so bound by the past. She might understand why he had to protect Ginny, come what may.

Then his eyes filled with pain. 'You're right,' he admitted. 'I know I should turn my back on her, but I can't. I won't! I couldn't live with myself if I deserted my own flesh and blood.'

There was nothing left to say. With her shoulders hunched and her arms folded in defiance, she kept her back to him.

He touched her ever so gently, kissing her neck with the softness of his lips. It was soft and moist on her skin. 'I want you to come with me,' he pleaded. 'Please, Liz. Let's settle this once and for all.' His heart was breaking. He felt like ending it all.

She began to melt. He could do that to her. One touch, one kiss and she crumbled at the knees. 'Come with you… where?'

'To Ginny. I know she'll be able to explain.'

Liz swung round, eyes blazing, as she told him in a trembling voice, 'I don't want to hear her lies. I don't want to see her. I don't even want to be in the same room as her.' She pushed him away. '*You* go to her if you want. *You* listen to her lies.' Her voice took on a hardness he had never heard before. 'Go to her, then. It's up to you. But I'll tell you this, Jack. If you do go to her, if you walk out that door… I swear to God, I won't be here when you get back.'

'Please, Liz!' His whole world was falling apart and he didn't know how to hold it together.

'Don't go, Jack. Let's move right away from here.' In her ignorance she believed it was the only way. 'Just go.'

'Come with me now. Later, I promise we'll talk it through.'

It was all over now. 'Just go.'

He waited a moment, before putting on his jacket. 'I can't leave it like this. I have to talk to her.'

'It's up to you.' Her voice was softer now, giving him false hope.

'You won't tell the police, will you Liz? About Ginny… and Luke Morrison,' he pleaded. 'Let me talk to her first.'

'No, I won't tell the police.' She wasn't strong enough to carry such a burden. 'I'll leave that to you.'

She heard him go, and a part of her went with him. 'Goodbye, Jack.' Staring out of the window into the fading daylight, she let the tears flow.

When her heart was quiet, she made a phone call. It was the saddest one she would ever make. Afterwards, she sat on the edge of the bed. Their bed. A new and expensive bed. A lonely bed, where they had made love just a few times since he brought her from the hospital. The distant sound of a vehicle coming down the street sent her running to the window. She imagined it was Jack come home. It wasn't.

'I will always love you, Jack,' she whispered, 'but I need to know if I can live without you. Without them.' She gave a sad little smile. In the hospital she had had time to think. They had talked a lot. She wasn't sure she could do it, but now she knew she had to. She fingered the photograph of the two of them, young and carefree. Before their lives were shattered. *Before Ginny.*

A few moments later she packed a suitcase and left a note for him. It read:

> I'm sorry it had to end like this, Jack. I thought we might be able to work it out, but it's not possible. Ginny will always come between us. And I will always be afraid.
>
> Please, Jack. Don't come looking for me. Let me be alone for a time. Later, if I think there is

hope, I'll be back. But it has to be my decision. If you try and follow me, there will be no going back for either of us.

Don't worry. I'll be all right. I promise.

Don't hate me.

Liz

xxx

I have a way out, she thought, but I never thought I would take it.

By the time she reached the bottom of the street, a faint autumn mist was creeping up, and the darkness was relieved only by the garish halo of light from the street lamp.

As she approached the car, the man swung out of his seat. Wasting no time he took the suitcase from her and laid it in the back. 'You're doing the right thing,' he said. In the half-light his face looked different.

She turned to gaze on the old bakery, with its ancient doors and fat little chimneys. 'I have no choice,' she told the night. '*They* made the decision for me.'

He waited for her to climb into the seat, then he closed the door, before returning to his own side. He shifted the car into gear, and let it roll gently forward.

Liz leaned back in her seat. The sound of the engine, purring as it took her away, was oddly comforting.

11

On this Friday evening, just as on every other Friday evening since her mother disappeared some two months back, Lianne went to see her father.

She found him sitting where he always sat, above the empty bakery, staring out of the window, watching for Liz. It was pitiful to see him. 'Do you think she'll ever come back?' he asked. His question was addressed to Dave. He didn't abandon his vigil. Instead he looked at Dave's reflection in the window, waiting for his reply, as though it might be his salvation.

'I don't know,' Dave answered truthfully, 'but you can't spend all your days looking out of the window, hoping she'll show.'

Jack gave him a withering glance. 'I'll wait a lifetime if I have to,' he said.

Dave was thankful when Lianne came in from the kitchen. 'I've made the tea and set out the cakes I bought,' she said. 'Would you fetch it in?' She pointed to her huge stomach. 'One kick from this little bundle and the whole lot is likely to end up across the floor.'

Relieved to get out from Jack's scrutinising gaze, he leaped out of his chair and almost ran into the kitchen. He even had the good sense to hide in there while father and daughter talked. Or at least while Lianne talked, and Jack pretended to listen.

'You shouldn't have sold the bakery,' she said regretfully. 'It was your only livelihood. What will you do now?'

He suddenly spun round on his heel and gave her a wonderful smile. 'I'm absolutely starving,' he declared giving her a brief hug. 'Where are these cakes I've been hearing about?'

On hearing Jack in a more sociable mood, Dave came in with the tray. 'At your service,' he said jovially. He almost dropped the tray when he saw Jack's face. It was drawn and haggard, and his trousers hung on him like two baggy sacks. His concerned gaze went to Lianne. It wasn't Jack so much that he worried about. It was his own lovely wife. The baby was due any day now, and it was heavy going.

As though reading Dave's thoughts, Jack asked, 'Well? When are you going to make me a grandfather?' He injected delight into his voice, but in truth he wasn't looking forward to a new face in the family. Not without Liz beside him to share the experience.

'Soon.' Handing him a cup of tea and a slice of walnut cake, Lianne explained, 'I've had three false alarms already.' She could hardly sit back on the seat for the size of her stomach. 'I shan't be sorry to drop this little lot, I can tell you.' She felt disgustingly fat. Her ankles were like balloons; the baby was lying on her bladder, and she was passing water every few minutes.

Jack looked at her then, at her bright pretty eyes and cheery demeanour. His façade of merriment slipped away and he was filled with immense regrets. 'I wish your mother was here,' he said, choking back the emotion.

'So do I,' she said, scrambling out of the chair to hug him. 'But she isn't. You are, though, and I can't tell you how happy that makes me.'

'Where is she?' He could feel her arms round his neck, and he clung to her like a drowning man. 'Why doesn't she come home?' He raised his sorry eyes to Dave, telling him what he had said a million times already. 'I've searched high and low for her. It's like she's vanished from the face of the earth.'

'It's a well-known fact,' Dave said limply. 'You can't find someone who doesn't want to be found.' He was never sure what to say, or how to deal with this heartbreaking situation.

Sensing Lianne's distress, Jack plucked her arms from round his shoulders. 'Sit down, woman!' he ordered jokingly. 'I've finished blubbering.'

She sat down, but regarded him constantly while they ate. 'You still haven't answered my question,' she said presently. 'What *will* you do now that you've sold the bakery?'

'I haven't really thought about it,' he said. 'I've got until the day after tomorrow to vacate, so I'd better make a plan of sorts, I suppose.' He ruminated on the issue. 'Maybe I'll take to the high road. Be a gypsy.'

She frowned. 'Look for Mum, you mean?'

'I didn't say that.'

'You didn't have to.'

He took a bite out of his cake. 'Actually, I've been thinking about you and Ginny,' he said with a full mouth. 'I have an idea.'

Dave didn't like the sound of that. 'What kind of idea?'

Jack was wise enough not to pursue it. 'Something and nothing,' he answered. 'The bakery brought a good price. I have more than enough for my own needs.' He winked at Lianne. 'I just want to do right by my children, that's all.' By Ginny. He wanted to do right by *Ginny*.

Sensing that he was about to lapse into one of his uncomfortable silences, Lianne pressed him on the one subject he would talk about for hours on end. 'Why don't you go and see Ginny? You'll be pleased to hear she's a trustee now. There's talk of her being allowed home soon.'

'I know.' He looked from one to the other, feeling guilty. Feeling naked. 'I should go and see her, but I'm not very good company just yet.' He couldn't forget the last time he had gone to see Ginny. She told him a few truths he would rather not know. And when he got home Liz was gone. Since then he had hardly gone out, hoping she would come back. Praying he had not lost her for ever. For the first time in his life, he resented the hold Ginny had on him. It didn't make him turn away from her though. It only made him feel he had to protect her all the more. 'I'm aware she's close to being released.'

Lianne peered at him curiously. 'How do you know that? *I* only found out during visiting last weekend.' Her face lit up.

'Did you go and see her?'

'No.'

'Then how did you find out?'

He dug a letter out of his trouser pocket and handed it to her. 'I got this today.'

Lianne read the letter aloud:

Dear Dad,

Why haven't you been to see me? I know we argued the last time, but you said things that hurt. So did I, and I'm sorry. You must know how much I need you. I watch for you every day.

I've been tempted to run away, but that would only make things worse. They would just catch me and lock me up again. Then I might never get out of here.

I must be very careful, you see. I've been made trustee, and yesterday the doctor said that all my new tests were very good. It won't be too long now before they let me home for a while.

I have to get away from here. I can't bear not to see you.

What's happening? I know something is happening. I saw it in Lianne's face when she came to see me. She wouldn't admit it, but I knew. I could always read her mind.

It's Mother, isn't it? She's gone away.

Don't worry. I'll find her. Then everything will be all right.

Ginny.

'It'll take her a while to adjust. It won't be easy.' Jack's mind ran rampant. What if Liz came home? What then? What if she didn't come home? Oh, but Ginny had promised to find her. No! You mustn't let her do that. The doctors thought Ginny was almost normal. They don't know. Only he knew. *Ginny could never be normal.*

Dave was thinking of the more practical side of Ginny's eventual rehabilitation. 'I suppose she'll have to work. I know she was destined for higher things, but I should imagine all that's changed, hasn't it? Like you say, it won't be easy for her.'

Lianne was more positive. 'Ginny might be coming home,' she said. 'That's all that matters.'

While they finished their tea and cakes, the conversation shifted this way and that. They talked about not having decided on a name for the baby; about whether the new owners of the bakery might start it up again or convert it into a home; they chatted about what Jack might do with the furniture, and that brought them on to another matter.

'I only wish I had somewhere to store it,' Lianne remarked. 'I hope to have a home of my own one day.'

Dave didn't like the dark oak furniture. He thought it was too old-fashioned. 'When we do get our own home,' he told her, 'I hope I can take you to the big stores and let you buy what you want.'

'I see.' Jack was on to it. 'So! You don't like my taste in furniture! I daresay Liz would have chosen something very different, but I was out of hospital before her, and it had to be done quickly.'

'Oh no!' Dave was mortified he might have offended. 'I didn't mean it like that. I only meant that, well, what looks good in an old bakery might not suit a modern house.'

'A modern house, eh? Like the ones at the top of Leighton Road, you mean?'

Lianne and Dave looked at each other with amusement. Lianne sighed dreamily. 'If only!' she declared. 'With Dave still in his first year, it'll be ages before we can buy our own place. Even then, our money won't stretch to one of those posh places.'

'Still,' Jack probed deeper, 'you're cosy enough where you are for the time being.'

Draining the dregs of her teacup, she answered in a worried tone, 'For the time being, yes we are. Dave's parents have been very good to us. It's thanks to them he's been able to take up college, and they've made sure we haven't gone short. But Dave's father is due to take early retirement, and they want to move to the coast. They'll have to sell their house here, to buy another. So we're having to think hard.' She smiled. 'We'll sort it, though, so there's no need for you to worry.' They had never asked him to help. And he had not offered. They understood.

A short time later they left. The December air was bitingly cold. Inside the car it was soon warm and cosy. Feeling more relaxed now, Dave chatted about his mock exams, about how he might ask his dad for a loan to buy a little car of their own; and the baby. 'I wonder if it'll be a boy or a girl?' he said. 'If it's a girl I hope it's just like you, and if it's a boy, I hope he's strong and handsome like me.' The two of them laughed, enjoying each other's company. The moments flew and soon the car was turning into their road.

'It'll be a boy,' Lianne decided, as he got out of the car and came to the open door.

'How do you know that?' He peered in at her.

'Because the little bugger's just as impatient as you are. Get me to the hospital, or I'll have it here and now in your father's back seat.'

His eyes grew like two big balloons. His mouth moved, but nothing came out. When she gave a cry, he panicked, running on the spot, not knowing which way to turn. 'Hold on!' he yelled. 'Hold on!' He kicked her door shut and ran round the car, missed his footing, and fell in the gutter. 'Hold on!' Then he leaped into the car, slammed the door on the tip of his finger, shot off up the road with such speed that he sent her backwards into the seat with her legs in the air. 'Hold on!' he kept yelling. He was still yelling when they wheeled Lianne into the hospital.

Torn, bleeding and dishevelled, he ran after them, looking as though it was he who needed the trolley.

At ten minutes to midnight, Lianne gave birth to a son.

Filled with wonder, Dave stayed with her throughout. 'He's beautiful,' he said brokenly, holding her hand. 'A son!' He couldn't believe the miracle he'd just seen. The tears flowed, but he didn't care. 'Oh, Lianne, I love you so much.' They held each other and talked until, exhausted, she fell asleep.

Outside, the others waited patiently. 'It's a boy!' Dave shouted as he came through the door. 'We've got a son!'

His parents were jubilant.

Jack hung his head. 'Is she all right? Can I see her?'

'She's sleeping now,' Dave told him, 'but we can come back in the morning.'

Taking hold of the young man's hand, Jack congratulated him. 'Mind you take good care of them,' he said. Then he walked away. To think. To dream. In his heart he knew it was all over for him.

'I feel so sorry for him.' Mrs Martin saw how haggard he was. She saw the weary stoop of his shoulders as he went away, and her heart went out to him. 'He misses his wife so much, poor man. How could she leave like that? And with her daughter pregnant?'

Mr Martin also had an opinion. 'Who knows what goes on in a woman's mind?' he said grimly. 'And who are we to judge?'

12

It was Christmas morning. Snow had poured from the skies all night long. It was still fluttering down when Lianne opened the bedroom curtains. 'Dave, get up! It's a white Christmas!' When he grunted and turned over, she threw herself at him. 'Get up!' she cried. 'I want you to see.'

He leaned up on one elbow, squinting through the window at the early morning brightness. 'What time is it?'

Throwing the covers off him, she dragged him out of bed. 'Never mind what time it is,' she said. 'Come and look out of the window.'

While he hobbled, half-asleep, to stare at the snow and shiver, Lianne collected the child from its cradle. 'Look there, little man,' she murmured in his ear, 'a white Christmas, just for you.'

Dave turned to look at the two of them. His wife and his son. 'Happy Christmas,' he said, drawing them into his embrace. 'Even if I have been dragged out of a nice warm bed.'

Lianne was overwhelmed by it all. 'I'm so happy,' she said. Mingling with the joy was a sense of loss. A dark shadow crossed her smile as she said sadly, 'I wish Mum would come home.'

'She will,' he promised. 'As soon as she finds out about this little fellow, wild horses won't keep her away.' If he could have just one wish, it would be that Liz might come home to put Lianne's mind at rest.

'It's eight o'clock.' Lianne glanced at the bedside clock. 'I'd better feed him.' She bent her head to sniff at his nappy. 'Better change him too,' she said wryly. 'He's done a packet.'

Dave gave them each a kiss. 'Now that I'm out of bed I might as well go down and get breakfast.' He felt the need to remind her. 'What with all the practice I've had these last few days, I've got to be quite a dab hand at cooking.'

'Won't hurt you,' she told him, balancing the baby on one arm while she dug his toiletries out of the drawer. 'I don't suppose you've got to be such a dab hand that you could get breakfast for *everyone*?' She chuckled. 'You wouldn't know, because you sleep like a dead thing, but your son kept me awake half the night. I don't think your mum and dad got much sleep either. I haven't heard them get up yet, and it would be nice if they could have a lie-in, don't you think?'

'No sooner said than done,' he said, with a servile flourish. 'I shall cook a breakfast the likes of which you have never seen before.'

Still shivering, he dressed quickly, hopping about like a thing demented as he tried to get into his trousers. 'Christ, it's cold! My arse has got goosebumps the size of strawberries.'

'Don't be crude in front of your son,' she chastised with a smile. 'And no peeking at the presents!' she called out as he went from the room.

'Would I ever?' he said cheekily, rushing back in to kiss the two of them. 'You two are the best present I could ever have.'

And she could never love him more than she did at that moment.

At five minutes past nine he shouted from the bottom of the stairs, 'Breakfast is served! Come and get it while it's hot!'

Lianne had fed and settled the baby, and he was sleeping soundly. She and Dave's parents entered the kitchen together. They couldn't believe their eyes. The kitchen table was fully extended, and covered with one of Mrs Martin's best gingham cloths. All of her best vegetable dishes were set out: one filled with fried potatoes; another with fat juicy sausages; yet another with curled and blackened bacon; and a fourth was running over with scrambled eggs. Her best china set was set out too. And a dish of preserve, and a plate piled high with toast.

'God almighty, son!' Mr Martin was the first to recover. 'We're not royalty.'

'No, you're not,' Dave agreed, ushering them to the table. 'You're my family. Worth more than royalty to me.'

It was a splendid breakfast, and the women didn't even have to move a muscle, except to eat. Mr Martin got into the spirit of things, and helped his son to wait at table. 'But don't think I mean to make a habit of it,' he warned his wife. 'It's my extra Christmas present to you, that's all.'

Afterwards they went into the sitting-room and opened their presents beneath the tree. Lianne was thrilled to have a wooden jewellery box, complete with a beautiful cameo brooch; Dave got the electric typewriter he wanted; Mrs Martin was thrilled when she saw the dressing gown that had been in Mason's front window for a week; and her husband was as pleased as always with two new sweaters and a pair of socks. 'You forgot the Y fronts,' he joked. There was a burst of laughter when Mrs Martin presented him with a pack of five.

Baby got his name. 'We thought about calling him after all the men in his life... his daddy and his two grandaddies,' Lianne explained. 'In the end we thought David Neville Jack Martin was too much of a mouthful, so we've decided to give him just one name. David, after his daddy.'

Mr Martin was thrilled. 'It's a good name,' he said, 'or I wouldn't have given it to my own son.' They drank a toast to the new male of the line, and afterwards set about the washing up.

'I'm glad your father agreed to come for dinner this evening,' Mrs Martin said. 'It'll be a real family gathering.'

'Thank you for asking him,' Lianne murmured, and gave her a grateful hug. 'He's been such a hermit since Mum went. I didn't think he'd accept, but he's really looking forward to it.'

'That's good.' Mrs Martin rolled up her sleeves and got out the cooking utensils. 'Better get on,' she said. 'There's a lot to do.'

'And you won't be short of help,' Lianne answered, taking out the dish for the trifle. 'Now then, is it red jelly, or orange?' She felt elated at the idea of her father sitting down to a

Christmas dinner with them. 'Do you realise, there'll be three generations round this table tonight?'

Dave put his arm round her. 'You're right,' he said, lovingly squeezing her. 'Something to remember.'

As they looked forward to the evening, no one there could have seen the horror that was to come.

At quarter to eight, Jack arrived. Lianne had been watching for him out of the sitting-room window. The minute she saw his van pull into the kerb, she flew to the front door. 'I was afraid you might change your mind,' she said running down the path to greet him.

He was more like his old self than she had seen him in a long time. His smile was warm, his manner easy, and he was walking with only the slightest limp. 'I've been looking forward to tonight,' he said. 'Why would I want to change my mind?' He draped an arm round her shoulder while they returned to the house.

Lianne shivered. 'Brr! Let's get in out of the cold.'

She didn't see him glance furtively back at the van. Nor did she suspect that they were being watched. He hadn't brought presents, either for her or his new grandson. In her excitement she didn't realise. It wouldn't have mattered to her anyway.

Just as they were about to sit down to dinner, Jack made a speech that was to change their lives. 'For the both of you,' he said, handing Dave an envelope, addressed to him and Lianne. He made no mention of the baby. 'I haven't been much of a father,' he apologised, looking at Lianne, 'but I hope this will make up for it.'

Everyone waited while Dave opened the envelope. 'I don't understand!' Taking out a small bunch of shiny new keys, he held them up for Lianne to see.

'These are the keys to your new home,' Jack explained, with a broad smile. The best is yet to come he thought, crossing his fingers, and hoping they would not refuse.

Intrigued, Lianne turned the keys over to read the attached label. 'Number Four, Greenlands, Leighton Road.' Her face coloured with surprise. 'That's the new development!'

There was a moment of utter disbelief, then a burst of excitement, while everyone talked at once. Jack said he had been wondering what to buy his daughter and her family for Christmas. 'When they told me you were thinking of moving to the coast, I knew what I had to do,' he told Mr Martin.

Dave's parents were thrilled, and relieved. 'Though we would have helped them to rent a place,' they explained, 'it will put our minds at rest to know they have a home of their own.'

Dave was delighted, too, though a little embarrassed. 'We'll pay you back,' he declared. 'As soon as I'm earning, we'll pay back every penny.' He was not deterred, even when Jack told him it was a gift, not a loan.

Lianne could hardly believe it. She had only one reservation. 'Are you sure you can afford it?'

'I wouldn't have done it if I couldn't afford it,' he said. 'I told you... I got top price for the bakery. What would I do with all that money?'

Laughing, Lianne threw her arms round his neck. 'It's a wonderful surprise,' she laughed. 'When can we go and see it?'

'Soon.' He glanced at Mrs Martin. He might need her before the night was over. 'We mustn't let this wonderful dinner spoil,' he said cunningly.

As the meat was served he decided it was time for him to make his next move. 'I have another surprise,' he told them, smiling particularly at Mrs Martin. Before they could respond, he stood up and pushed away his chair. 'If you'll excuse me, it'll only take a minute.' Again before anyone could say anything, he hurried out of the room, leaving them bewildered but intrigued.

It seemed no time at all before he returned.

Ginny was with him.

Extraordinarily calm, she let her dark gaze rest on each of them in turn. 'Hello, everyone,' she murmured. 'I told Father he shouldn't bring me along, but he insisted you wouldn't mind.'

Lianne ran to her. ''Course we don't mind,' she chided. 'Oh, Ginny, are you home for good?'

'I have to report back twice a week, but yes, I'm home for good.'

For a moment they quietly held each other. Ginny thinking how Lianne had got herself a nice little nest here. She deliberately averted her eyes from Dave. She would have him, she decided, vehemently recalling how he had refused her in the past. That was something she could not easily accept. At some time in the future, when his guard was down, she would have her way with him. Right now, there were other, more urgent matters on her mind, such as finding her mother, and getting rid of her parents and her hands on a certain amount of money that should be hers. Oh yes! She would destroy this little family, with their little ideas. The prospect made her smile inside.

They were halfway through their meal when Jack appealed to Mr Martin. 'You said you meant to help Lianne and Dave with renting a property,' he remarked casually. 'I've already contacted several estate agents about rented properties, and they tell me they're few and far between. In fact, they've got nothing at all on their books just now.' He took a deliberate bite of the succulent apple pie. He wasn't a lover of pastry but he made a good show of enjoying it. 'Best I've ever tasted,' he told Mrs Martin.

'So? You've decided to take a rented property after all?' her husband asked with some surprise. 'Lianne said you had ideas about travelling?'

'Oh, it isn't for me!' he answered, feigning astonishment. 'It's for Ginny. One of the release conditions is that she has a stable environment.' He hung his head. 'Of course I did wrong in selling the bakery. If I hadn't done that, there would be no problem.' He smiled at Dave and Lianne. 'But then I wouldn't have been able to buy you that beautiful house, would I?'

Mrs Martin had an idea. 'Why doesn't Ginny move in with Dave and Lianne? It's a big house, and I'm sure it wouldn't be long before you found something to suit Ginny better.'

The suggestion might have provoked an interesting reaction, but the knock on the door stalled any discussion. 'I'll go.' Embarrassed by the turn of events, Mr Martin made his getaway.

At first when he opened the door he didn't recognise the woman standing there. 'Is Jack here?' she asked. And only then did he realise. 'Why! It's Mrs Lucas, isn't it?' It was a shock. A bit like seeing a ghost from the past. 'Come inside,' he invited. 'It's bitter cold out there.'

She made no move. 'Could you please tell him there's someone to see him?' Her voice dropped to a whisper. 'Don't say who it is, will you?'

Instinct urged him to look up and down the street. There was no one about, just Jack's van, and another, darker car parked a short distance away. 'I'll tell him,' he agreed. 'Won't you at least come into the hallway, in the warm?' She shook her head and he hurried away, politely leaving the door ajar.

She waited patiently. In a moment Jack appeared, confused and curious. He stood at the door and stared down on her. 'You want to see me?' he queried. Slowly his eyes grew accustomed to the half-light. His face opened in astonishment. '*Liz!*' He almost fell down the steps, his disbelieving eyes crinkling to a smile. 'My God, it's really you!'

'I had to come back,' she said. 'I had to be sure.' Her voice was flat and accusing, halting him in his tracks.

'Sure?' He was puzzled. 'Sure about what?'

'Ginny.' Her eyes raked his face. '*You.* And I had to be sure, about *these!*' She thrust a sheaf of cuttings at him. 'I came back to the bakery. When you weren't there, I had an idea where I might find you. You see, Jack, I haven't been too far away. All this time I've been near enough to watch your every move. I know it all now. *They* told me. But I didn't believe them. When you weren't at the bakery, I searched around... looking for anything that would help me to know the truth. I found these... hideous things, hidden in one of the old ovens. Who put them there, Jack? Was it her? Please, Jack... tell me it was her.'

He didn't have to look at the cuttings. He knew them by heart. 'Yes. She must have put them there,' he said, not surprised. 'I want you to come home,' he pleaded. 'The bakery's sold, but we can find a new place, you and me... and Ginny.'

She was devastated. 'I was wrong to come back,' she said bitterly. 'You'll never put me before her.' She stared at him with such pain that he could almost feel it. 'You're never going to tell me the truth either, are you, Jack?'

When he didn't answer, she flung the cuttings to the ground, where they lay very still, grotesque against the pure white snow. 'Goodbye, Jack,' she muttered. 'This time I won't be back.'

As she went quickly down the path he ran after her. 'Don't leave me again,' he pleaded. 'I need you. *Liz for God's sake help me!*'

As he pursued her down the street, neither of them saw the shadowy figure slip away. It smiled menacingly before sliding into the van. It took the stolen keys from its pocket, and thrust them into the ignition. For a moment the silence was awesome. Long slim fingers with crimson tips. One quick twist and the engine started. The van shot forward at screaming speed.

In that split second, Jack turned. And he knew. *'No! Ginny!'* His scream exploded into the night. There was no time for thought. No time to save himself. With the strength of a bull, he launched himself at Liz. Taken by surprise she thought he was attacking her, and fought like a tiger. She was no match for him. He threw her aside as if she was a rag doll in that moment the van careered into him. He jerked forward, high in the air, before falling down across the windscreen. Bloodied and hurting, he stared at her through the windscreen. She was laughing at him. Hating him. *Hating him!*

Losing his grip, he slithered to the ground, the soft tissue of his face colliding with the hard surface. His cheekbone split open. He heard the wheels screeching as she went after Liz. *'Run, Liz!'* he was shouting. The noise was only in his head. He couldn't shout. His life was ebbing away.

Suddenly everyone was out on the street. Lianne, on her knees beside her father. 'Don't die.' The words fell away as she cried, 'Please Daddy… don't… please…' From the corner of her eye she could see her mother, running, stumbling now, almost beneath the wheels of the van. Unable to look, she clung to her father, holding him to her, his blood running down her arms, spoiling her new white blouse. In her confused mind she thought of Ginny. Where was she? Their father was dying. *Where was she?*

Ginny spoiled everything.

Dave threw himself at the van again and again, until his clothes were torn to shreds and his skin erupting. There was someone else too. A man. Trying to get to Liz. Trying to save her. Suddenly there was a thud and Liz went down. The van recoiled on impact. This was his chance. Wrenching open the back doors he clambered in, clinging on by his fingertips when the van surged forward. He could hear laughter. Wild insane laughter.

Without warning she turned on him.

Lunging over the seat, she made for his throat. She had a saw-edged knife. In his mind's eye he remembered it before, on the dining-room table, lodged in the turkey's groin.

The van veered dangerously from side to side as they struggled. He feared every minute would be his last. Losing his balance, he fell backwards, spreadeagled against the driver's seat. She raised the knife to his throat. The blade glinted in the light from the street lamp. The van jerked and crashed, splintering the wall, sending the bricks crashing through the windscreen. She fell sideways and lay there, very still, very beautiful, staring up at him, the smile fixed on her face. The knife embedded deep in her heart.

'It could have been me!' Horror shot through him. And still she smiled at him. Such beauty. Such evil. Gone now.

Sleeping.

Heartbroken and deeply shocked, Lianne was led away by her husband. In the distance the ambulance siren could be heard. The police had arrived within minutes of Mr Martin's call.

Twisted and broken, Jack lay in Liz's arms. He had only minutes, he knew that. 'I'm sorry, sweetheart,' he murmured.

'There you go again,' she said through her tears, through her pain. 'Always saying you're sorry.'

'Take care of her.'

Thinking he meant Lianne, she answered, 'I promise.'

The smile slid from her face at his next words. 'I know you've always been afraid of her. Please don't punish her, Liz. It isn't her fault. It's mine.' His eyes closed and he was quiet.

Leaning closer she persisted, 'Why, Jack? Why is it your fault?' How could she let it end this way? How could she go on, not knowing? She had to be sure. 'What they told me – was it true?'

His handsome, easy smile broke her heart. 'All true,' he whispered.

'What, about Ginny?' Her voice fell to a whisper. 'Did she really kill those people?' In her heart she knew the answer.

He stared for a while, his senses going fast now. 'Ginny... grandmother. *Insane.*' His voice shook with emotion.

'Did Ginny kill Old Tom?'

A nod.

'The young man, Luke Morrison?' She hesitated. 'Your own mother?'

A nod.

'May God forgive her,' she whispered.

Suddenly afraid, he gripped her hand, his dark eyes paling. He stared at her for a long minute, a solitary tear running down his face. 'Sorry, sweetheart.' He smiled that slow easy smile she'd always loved. 'There you go again...' he whispered. 'Saying sorry.' Soft laughter, much like Ginny's. His voice faltered and he was gone.

In pain from the injuries she'd suffered, Liz closed her eyes, trying to shut out the things he had told her.

Eddie Laing had returned some days ago. He came to her then, his slow American drawl soothing her frayed senses. 'I said you shouldn't come back.' Gently, he pulled her to him. 'You were safe in their house, with them. With me.' There was an intimacy in his manner. A warmth she desperately needed. 'Cyrus Louis warned you. He knew all along.' He grimaced with disgust. 'They *all* knew.'

Empty of emotion, she leaned on him. Together they watched them take Jack and his daughter away. Her voice was little more than a whisper. 'All those years I watched her grow. And all the time...' Her mind reeled in shock. 'Oh Ginny!'

As the ambulance pulled away, taking father and daughter, Eddie said, 'The old woman went to the chair, God rest her soul, but at least his daughter won't suffer.'

He walked her away. 'It's best you don't think too long on all of this,' he suggested kindly, 'for your own peace of mind.'

The events made sensational headlines around the globe: 'TWENTY YEARS ON, MASS MURDER AGAIN.'

The story took many forms, some exaggerated, others indulging in graphic horror. But the story was the same underneath. It had been more than twenty years since Virginia Lucas' great-grandmother had killed some fourteen people.

The horror was over. The wealthy Louis family went into hiding, hoping the world might forget, praying too that they would find a measure of peace. Now history had repeated itself. The articles went on to describe how Jack had died. It told of the daughters, Lianne, and Virginia... 'the mad one'... 'the killer'.

The funeral of father and daughter took place in a small market town situated in the heart of rural England. Reporters flocked from all over the world. Ordinary people too. Kind sorry people who grieved for the family. And the ghouls who fed like parasites on the weaknesses of others.

Seven years later, the family gathered again. This time there were no reporters. No strangers. Other, more sensational stories had superseded the gruesome tale of Virginia Lucas. The church this time was situated in a pretty hamlet on the Yorkshire Moors. The occasion was a christening.

The vicar was a kindly man who knew nothing of the family's background. All he knew was that Dr Martin's daughter was being christened. When all the preliminaries were done, he held the child to the font. As the holy water tumbled down her forehead, the words rang out: 'In the name of the Father, the Son, and the Holy Spirit, I anoint this child... Elizabeth Lianne Martin.'

When the baptism was over, the family returned to the big old cottage where they had stayed for the past week. This was Dave and Lianne's home. It was a delightful stone-built place, with rambling roses round the door, and July clematis growing up the walls. The cottage came with the position of local doctor, taken up by Dave just a year ago. There were five bedrooms in all: enough to provide one for Cyrus and Maureen, who had recently wed; another for Mr and Mrs Martin; one for Liz; and the small one at the front for Eddie Laing.

As a temporary measure, the large room at the back of the house accommodated Dave, Lianne and their two children. David was seven now. Normally he slept in his own room. But while Eddie Laing occupied it, the boy reluctantly agreed to sleep in his parents' room: 'I'm not sleeping in the cot with Elizabeth!' he said, making the kind of face that might turn the milk sour.

He needn't have worried, because Dave brought the boy's own little bed in, and tucked it in the corner. After that there was no argument.

'It's such a beautiful day,' Lianne said. 'I thought we ought to have our tea outside.'

They had a wonderful tea. Mrs Martin had baked a whole pile of scones. Irish Maureen had made blackberry jam from the fruit she had picked along the lanes in the week they had been here. Lianne had been getting ready for the christening for days now, and the table did her proud.

'Ye'll all have to come and stay with us in New York, sure ye will,' Maureen told the boy. 'How would ye like that, eh?'

Now that he was about to have his own room back, he was in no hurry to leave it again. 'If I do, can I bring my own bed?'

Maureen was boggle-eyed. 'Sure, ye'll never get it on the plane!'

'I won't come then, thank you. But you can take Elizabeth, 'cause she cries all the time.' When everyone laughed, he made one of his best sour faces, and fled across the lawn to torment the pet Labrador.

Eddie Laing stood up. 'I sincerely hope young David will change his mind about coming to the States,' he said, smiling down on Liz, 'because this lovely lady has finally agreed to be my wife, and we want you all at our wedding.'

Everyone cheered and drank their health, and Liz blushed like a schoolgirl.

The next morning, while the others were still in bed, Lianne and her mother had a heart-to-heart.

'You don't mind me marrying again, do you, sweetheart?' Liz asked.

'Does he make you happy?' Lianne murmured, shushing the child in her arms.

'Yes, he does.'

'Then I'm really pleased for you.' She sealed her approval with a kiss, and put the child into its pram.

Soon it was time to go. First to leave were the Martins. 'Take care of yourselves,' they said, and waved all the way down the lane.

In no time at all, the taxi arrived to take the others to the airport. At the terminal they had time for a cup of tea. 'Are you all right?' Eddie asked Liz, when the others had gone to freshen up. 'You were very quiet in the taxi.'

'Just thinking,' she answered. 'Memories, you know.'

'All in the past now,' he assured her softly. 'We have a future to plan.'

'I know,' she said, 'and we'll make it a good one.' In her heart, Liz knew that to be true. Besides, it was what Jack would have wanted. She rummaged in her bag for a tissue. The bag had been a birthday gift from Jack.

'Jeeze!' Eddie remarked. 'That looks years old. Remind me to get you a new one.'

'I'll keep you to that,' she told him.

He squeezed her hand. Suddenly she felt at peace. It was a good feeling.

Lianne came running into her son's room. 'It's all right, sweetheart,' she said, calming him down. 'You had a bad dream. Mummy's here now. Shh! It's all right.' She held him, until he felt limp in her arms, then she gently slid him between the sheets and covered him over.

As she made to stand up he opened his troubled eyes. 'Bad people don't go to heaven, do they?'

Lianne stroked his forehead. You're a funny little thing, she thought, but she soothed him with reassuring words. 'There are no bad people here. Nothing for you to worry about, sweetheart.' He seemed content, and she stayed by his bed until he was sleeping peacefully.

Afterwards she went to the window and looked out at a starry sky. She recalled her son's words. No, sweetheart, she thought. There is no heaven for bad people. No heaven. No hell. Only the dark place between. Shivering, she closed the curtains and shut out the night.

Dave was awake, leaning up on one elbow, and waiting for her to come back. 'Is he all right now?'

'He's asleep.' Taking off her robe, she checked the baby. 'She sleeps like an old woman,' Lianne chuckled.

She shivered as she climbed into bed. 'Cuddle me,' she pleaded. 'I'm cold.'

The cuddle became a kiss. The kiss grew passionate, and soon they were in the throes of lovemaking.

The lovemaking ended. The love remained. And all was well.

We hope you enjoyed this book.

For an exclusive preview of your next thrilling J.T. Brindle book read on or click here.

Or for more information, click one of the links below:

J.T. Brindle

More books in the Talisman sequence

An invitation from the publisher

Read on for a preview of

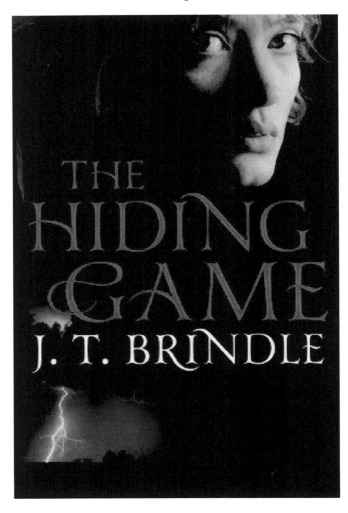

THE
HIDING
GAME

J. T. BRINDLE

He had seen it with his own eyes, heard the awful screams, but nobody would believe him. Is Mike Peterson losing his mind? The doctors certainly think so and Mike is confined to a psychiatric unit.

Three years later, life has changed irrevocably for the Peterson family. The children will never forgive their father for shattering the family, his wife has built herself a successful career.

But now Mike is coming home...

Part 1

August 1980

Out of the Darkness…

1

'I'm cold.' Inexplicably afraid, the boy shivered. 'I want to go home.'

Mike glanced up at the sky. Only a minute ago the sun was blazing down. Suddenly, the clouds were gathering; the air strangely chilled. There was a sense of danger all around. 'It's getting dark.' He looked at his watch; it was just gone three. 'Must be a storm on the way. Come on, son, we'd best pack up and make our way home.'

'I'll just give the ducks these leftovers.' It was a shame to waste them and the birds seemed so hungry.

Mike nodded. 'Sure. But don't be too long about it.'

While the boy gathered the stale sandwiches, Mike packed the picnic basket, his thoughts going back over the past few days. Lately, he had been so on edge, there were times when it put a strain on his relationship with Kerry.

The picnic had been a great idea. Kerry was right, as always. He and his son needed some time to themselves. They needed time to get to know each other. Ever since Jack had been born, Mike had devoted himself to building a successful business so he could provide for his family. It meant sacrifices. It meant working every minute God sent and, worse than that, it meant neglecting the ones he loved most. He had not realised the cost. He had not seen how it was taking over his life and swallowing everything in its wake. Now, Jack was five years old, and he hardly knew the boy.

He looked at his son and pride filled his chest. Jack had a look of him, especially the eyes, brown and serious; right now they were gazing out across the pond, watching the ducks scurrying for the bread. Ruffling his hair, Mike reminded him, 'Time to go, son.'

Scrambling up, Jack looked scared. 'Why is it so dark?'

Strapping the picnic bag over his shoulder, Mike led him by the hand. 'It's just a storm. Don't worry.' He didn't want to frighten him. But it was a strange sky, darker now, pressing down. Such cold, eerie silence. It was like nothing he had ever experienced.

As they approached the car, he heard someone call his name. 'Mike! Mike Peterson!'

Swinging round, he saw a woman and for a moment she was just another stranger. Then, as she ran up to him, he couldn't believe his eyes. '*Rosie!* Rosie Sharman, after all these years.'

Still slim and attractive, the years had been kind to Rosie; her long auburn hair shone, and her skin was like that of a child. But then she couldn't be very old; when he last saw her she wasn't much more than a child. Seeing her now, the memories flooded back – along with the guilt.

Dropping the picnic bag he grabbed her as she ran into his arms. She felt soft and warm against him. 'How long has it been?' he asked, reluctantly releasing her.

'Fifteen years,' she reminded him with a grin. 'And you don't look a day older than you did then.'

'Liar!' Flattered, he laughed out loud. 'I'm thirty-eight and look ninety.' Pressure of work aged a man before his time.

Rosie quietly observed him. 'Rubbish,' she said. 'You're as handsome as ever,' and in a move that startled him she kissed him soundly on the mouth. 'I recognised you straightaway,' she said. 'The turn of your head... the way you walk. I knew it was you.' Her thoughts flew back over the years. As if she could ever forget! In their young, carefree days, there was a time when Mike Peterson had been her whole life.

'You look well, Rosie.' Over the years he had often wondered about her. Did she still think of him? Did she cherish the wonderful times they'd had together? Did she have a new man? Married? Children? Was she a career woman? It was always at night when he thought about her. Always after he and Kerry had made love. 'It's great to see you.' She still had that uncanny way of making him feel good. 'But what are you doing here?' he asked. 'Do you live around these parts?' Life was a funny thing, he thought; after they had parted all those years ago, he was sure he would never see her again.

Avoiding his question, she brought her attention to Jack who was shifting impatiently from one foot to the other. 'Is this your son?' Her voice was soft, her green eyes smiling on him. 'Of course,' she answered her own question. 'Anyone can see he's your son.' She introduced herself. 'I'm Rosie. What's your name?'

'Jack.'

'Hello, Jack.' She held out her hand and laughed when he hesitated. 'I'm told I can be a bit overwhelming but I promise I don't bite.'

Allowing her to shake his hand, Jack remained silent.

For a long moment she smiled into Mike's eyes, started to say something, and then, with a proud gesture, swung away. 'This is *my* son.' Half turning, she urged a boy to come forward. 'Luke, come and meet an old friend.'

Mike had not noticed the boy standing behind her. Rosie had a son! It didn't seem right somehow.

'Hi, Luke.' Mike guessed he was about fifteen. He was tall and good-looking, with brown hair and eyes of a paler shade than his mother's.

The skies began to rumble. 'I reckon we're in for a drenching,' Mike said. 'That's why we packed up – just as we were enjoying our picnic. Isn't that right, Jack?' Smiling down on the boy, he drew him closer. Where was Rosie's husband? he wondered.

Rosie read his mind. 'If you're curious about my other half, he's not here.' She gave no explanation.

'So you *are* married then?'

Leaning forward, she said softly, 'You didn't think I could love you for ever, did you? Life has to go on, Mike.'

Mortified that she should have misunderstood, Mike actually blushed. 'I didn't mean... I was curious, that's all.'

A mischievous smile put him at ease. 'Look, Mike. Seeing as your picnic was spoiled, why don't we all go for a drink and a bite to eat? Luke and I are in no hurry to get back.'

He was tempted, but before agreeing he turned to Jack. 'What do you think, son? Are you hungry?'

A hesitant nod was all Mike needed. 'OK. Everyone into the car.'

As they loaded up, Rosie turned to glance at him, and the years seemed to roll away. With the memories came a sense of nervousness and, for a fleeting moment, Mike wondered if he was doing the right thing.

Just a few minutes away, the inn was a welcome sanctuary. The moment Mike drew into the forecourt, the heavens opened. Making a run for it, the four of them burst in through the door, shaking the rain from their clothes and laughing.

Before directing them to the family room, the landlord took their order. 'One coffee, a pint of lager… two lemonades, and four chicken salad sandwiches.'

'Don't forget the crisps,' Rosie reminded him, 'and plenty of mayonnaise on my sandwich.' Rosie was partial to mayonnaise.

'I'll be as quick as I can with the sandwiches,' the landlord said, 'but what with the rain and everything, there's been a rush on.' He wasn't complaining though. The more people, the bigger the orders, and the bigger the orders, the more profit. 'Sit yourselves down. I'll have your drinks here in no time at all.'

Settling at a table by the window, Mike glanced out. 'Good God! Look at that!' The rain was lashing down, the wind so violent it was bending the trees almost to the ground. 'It's as well we came here, Jack,' he said, 'or we might have been blown off the road.' On the other hand, it might not be wise to linger here too long. The lanes were narrow and might soon be impassable.

The drinks arrived. Jack's attention was on a young couple nearby. 'Look at that,' he exclaimed. 'What's that game?'

'It's called table football,' Rosie's son explained. 'When they've finished, I'll show you how to play if you like.' When Jack seemed excited at the prospect, Luke grinned from ear to ear. 'I'll give you a head start,' he promised. 'We'll play best out of three.'

Rosie laughed. 'You against the boy? That's not fair. Besides, he probably won't even be able to reach the table.'

Jack was indignant. 'Yes I will!'

'If not, I'm sure the landlord will find him a box to stand on.' Luke had it all worked out.

Jack was sold on the idea. 'Can I, Daddy? Please.'

'What about your sandwiches? They'll be here any minute.' He wasn't sure whether he wanted to be left alone with Rosie.

'I'm not hungry now.' Jack's appetite seemed to have disappeared.

'Might as well say yes,' Rosie laughed, 'or we'll get no peace.' Unlike Mike, she yearned for the two of them to be left alone. She and Mike had unfinished business. *He* may have forgotten, she thought bitterly, but she hadn't.

Mike relented. 'One game then, and only if that young couple finish their game before your sandwiches arrive.'

Rosie regarded the couple. 'Poor little buggers,' she commented wryly. 'By the looks of them, I'd say they were on the run.'

Mike was intrigued. 'What makes you say that?'

'Come on, Mike. You've only got to look at them. The girl is what? Fifteen, sixteen? She's about the age I was when we first met.' She let that sink in before going on, 'The boy isn't much older, and the pair of them are filthy.' Pointing to two grubby rucksacks leaning against the table leg, she muttered, 'Travelling light. And they're thin as rakes. I shouldn't be surprised if they haven't eaten for days.'

Mike gestured to the tray of sandwiches and drinks close by. 'Looks to me like they're not short of money.'

'They're probably sleeping rough at night and begging on the streets during the day.' She laughed. 'Some of these beggars are better off than any of us.'

'What d'you reckon they're running from?'

Rosie shrugged. 'Who knows? Bad parents? Violent background? They could have been abused in some way. They might even have been brought up by the authorities, and now they've been turned out to make their own way in life.'

'If you ask me, they're just enjoying themselves. I can't see they're any thinner or scruffier than other kids of that age.' He didn't share her obsession with the couple.

Rosie was adamant. 'No, Mike. They're running from something, or somebody. All the signs are there. And look how they keep glancing towards the door – look at the eyes, how haunted they are.' She shook her head decisively. 'No, if you ask me, there isn't a soul in the world who gives a monkey's where they are, or what happens to them.'

'How can you be so sure?'

Meeting his gaze, she said quietly, 'Trust me, Mike. I know about these things.'

The young couple finished their game and left the table hand in hand. The two boys rushed across the room, and Mike resigned himself to a lengthy stay. Raising his glass, he laughed nervously. 'Well, here's to you, Rosie.'

Rosie looked across at Mike's son. 'You've got a good kid there, Mike.'

Taking a gulp of his drink, Mike was quiet for a moment, before answering, 'Yeah, he's a good kid. Trouble is, I'm not a good father.'

'I don't believe that.'

'I have a daughter too. Susie's three years old. She's a good kid also but I'm so busy working, I hardly see them.'

'What about your wife?' She had to know everything.

'Kerry?' A smile crossed his features. 'She's the best thing that ever happened to me – apart from the kids of course.' Not realising how his comment had shocked and hurt her, he looked to where Jack was scrambling on to a small crate. 'Look at that. By hook or by crook, eh?'

Laughing, Rosie made another toast. 'Here's to being young and foolish.'

'And not giving a sod!'

Clinking glasses, Rosie regarded him thoughtfully. 'We were young and foolish once,' she said carefully, 'and you didn't give a sod, either.'

Embarrassed, he looked away, pretending to concentrate on what the boys were doing, but he could feel her eyes burning on his face. Suddenly, he felt threatened.

Swigging back the last of her drink, Rosie said sweetly, 'I wouldn't mind a rum and coke.'

He stared at her. 'I thought you didn't drink spirits.' After all these years, he hadn't forgotten.

'Times change.' Her smile betrayed how pleased she was that he had remembered.

Unsettled, he swung out of his chair. 'Rum and coke it is then. Keep an eye on Jack for me, will you?' When she nodded, he hurried away; thinking the sooner he got out of here the better.

'The old magic is still there,' he muttered. 'She's still a looker... and she still sets me trembling. But don't flatter yourself, Mike old son. A lot of water's gone under the bridge since you and Rosie rolled in the hay.' His expression became grim. 'Put it behind you,' he told himself sternly. 'For *all* your sakes.'

Chasing from one end of the bar to the other, the landlord was at his wits' end. 'I'll be with you in a minute,' he told Mike. 'It's like bedlam in here!' In his hurry to be rid of one customer he spilled a pint of beer over him. 'Sorry, mate,' he said, and got a mouthful of abuse for his trouble.

Looking over his shoulder, Mike saw that Rosie had gone to supervise the boys' game. For a long moment he watched, wondering about her, trying to guess how she had come to be here, in this area, so far away from where they had grown up – and so close to where he had chosen to settle down.

Feeling the need for a breath of fresh air, and realising he might not get served for some time yet, Mike went outside.

The wind seemed to be settling and the sun was once again trying to struggle through. He walked along the side of the inn and down towards the gardens at the back.

At first he couldn't quite make out what the sounds were. Gruff, breathless sounds, almost like those of an animal in distress. Concerned, he looked about. The sounds were coming from the spinney. Quickly, he made his way there, peering between the trees as he went.

The sounds got louder – behind him now. He swung round, and there, only yards away, he saw them. Spreadeagled in the undergrowth, the young couple were blissfully unaware that he could see them.

Outstretched on the ground, her hair matted with leaves and debris, the girl's long legs were tightly wrapped round the young man's thighs, her arms about his body, keeping him there, trapping him to her. The young man, body low and head high, thrust in and out of her with brutal force.

The sounds Mike had heard were cries of pleasure, and pain. Being so close and seeing them together like this, his own heart beat faster. 'Jesus!' Into his mind came an image of himself and Rosie. It was almost more than he could bear.

Much as he wanted to tear himself away, his curiosity kept him rooted to the spot. He watched them clawing at each other, and recalled how it was when you were that young. He wondered why Kerry had never given herself in the same way Rosie had; why she always seemed to hold back at the crucial point. Now, shamelessly watching these kids, he felt the need for that kind of love again.

Filled with regrets, he hurried away and returned to a quieter bar. He remembered how it had been between himself and Rosie. She was like that girl out there in the shrubbery, exciting and demanding, insatiable. But not his Kerry. She was different.

But he wouldn't blame her for that. No two women were the same, thank God. Kerry was a lady, while Rosie had been a wild thing. He had been wild too, as he recalled. But that was when they were young and rebellious. Now, he was a family man, older and wiser. He had other things to occupy his mind – bills to pay, responsibilities that came with growing up. He had a beautiful wife and two adorable children. When he and Kerry made love it was always good, and he wouldn't change her for the world.

He told himself all these things, and still could not rid himself of a nagging feeling that he was missing out.

He made his way back to the table, where Rosie and the boys, who'd finished with the table football, were waiting. 'I was beginning to think you'd run out on me,' she said, her bright eyes twinkling. 'We've eaten most of the sandwiches.'

'The weather seems to have changed for the better,' Mike said. 'Jack and I should be making our way home.' He offered to give her and Luke a lift back and was greatly relieved when she declined.

'No need, thanks all the same,' she said. 'But I would like to see you again. We've had so little time to talk.'

Mike was wary. 'I don't have much free time,' he said. 'But if ever I do, you'll find me and Jack picnicking down by the river.' He wanted to say he thought it better if they never saw each other again, but some sixth sense warned him to humour her. So, against his better judgement, he unwisely encouraged her.

She smiled at him. 'I'll look forward to that.'

Jack was ready to leave. 'I don't like that game,' he said sulkily. 'It's no good.'

Luke grinned. 'That's because I beat you every time.'

Luke's triumphant smirk turned to a scowl when Rosie remarked, 'Jack seems to have got the hang of it now, so don't count on winning next time.' Glancing at Mike, she murmured, 'You won't forget me, will you? When you have that moment of free time?'

Smiling, he made no reply. Somehow he thought it wiser. Not because of her, but because of the overwhelming feelings rising inside himself. Feelings of want... lust. Feelings that had lain dormant all this time – until she had appeared. It was disturbing.

Outside, she kissed him. 'Remember how it was between us?' she whispered. 'Shame it had to end.' Her fingers wandered to his thigh, tenderly touching him. Sending shivers down his spine.

He drew away. 'It was good seeing you, and if we don't meet again, take care of yourself.'

They went their separate ways; Rosie and her son headed back towards the river, while Mike and Jack walked towards the car.

'Will we see them again?' Jack wanted to know.

Opening the car door, Mike ushered him inside. 'I don't think so, son.' Rosie was dangerous. She got inside him like no other woman ever could.

They had gone only a short way when the rain started again. 'Is the storm coming back, Daddy?' Jack was nervous.

Mike peered through the rain-spattered window. 'Let's hope not.' Switching on the windscreen wipers, he settled back in his seat. 'I think the worst is over,' Instinctively, his hand went to his mouth. Rosie's kiss still burned his lips. 'We'll soon be home, son. Just sit tight.'

The journey was a nightmare. The rain defied the wipers and blurred his vision. 'I'll have to pull over for a while,' he told Jack. 'I know this lane like the back of my hand but I can't see a damned thing now.' Sighing, he leaned against the steering wheel, his mind ticking over, wondering what to do for the best. 'But don't you worry,' he assured the frightened boy. 'We'll be all right.' All the same, he had a feeling the worst was yet to come.

Just as he feared, the storm came back with a vengeance. Howling wind rocked the car and dark clouds turned day into night. Rain fell in torrents, battering the car and pummelling the ground until the grass verges became slithering mud banks.

When the car began sliding towards the ditch, Mike knew it was time to get out of there.

He scrambled out of the car and dragged Jack after him. 'Hold on tight, son,' he told him. 'We'll have to go back.' Reasoning that the inn would be the safest place, he headed back down the lane, battling against the wind and carrying Jack in his arms. 'Don't be frightened!' He had to shout to be heard. 'We'll be all right, don't worry!'

If the lines were not down, he intended calling Kerry from the inn. He didn't want her to worry. And Rosie, he thought, was she all right? Did she and Luke get home before the storm returned?

Cursing himself for bringing Rosie to mind, he hugged Jack close to him, wrapping his arms tighter about the small, shivering frame. 'We can't be too far away.' But, to tell the truth, he had lost all sense of direction and had no idea which way he was headed.

Jack's voice invaded his thoughts. 'Daddy! Look!' Holding on to his father, the boy pointed towards the field.

At first, Mike couldn't see anything, then, peering through the blinding rain, he saw the shadowy figures. It was the young couple. 'Hey!' Relieved when he realised his sense of direction had not deserted him altogether, he yelled again, 'Hey, you two!' The wind carried his voice away.

They didn't hear him. Instead they kept going, hand in hand across the field and up towards the top of the hill. 'You'd do best to stick to the road!' he yelled out again, but still they appeared not to have heard. 'I hope they know what they're doing,' he muttered.

The wind was buffeting so fiercely he could hardly keep a foothold; branches were cracking from the trees and falling all around them. Then, with a suddenness that sent him stumbling forwards, the wind fell and the rain eased off. He could breathe again. 'Thank God!' But where were they? Nothing around them seemed familiar.

Something was very wrong.

After the noise and confusion, the silence was awesome. The air was unbelievably cloying; Mike felt as if he was choking. 'What the hell's going on?' He was no coward but now, caught up in this strange experience, he was afraid.

Jack sensed it. 'Daddy, what's happening?'

'I think it's over,' he murmured, but deep down he knew it wasn't.

He looked up to see the clouds clearing to reveal wide, amazing skies of brilliant blue. From some way behind, a solitary sheet of lightning daggered to the ground, splitting a tree wide open, where only minutes before he had trodden.

Following on the heels of that one came a second, nearer strike. The impact shook them both, making Mike cry out. 'Jesus!' The ripple of air became a terrifying force, throwing them to the ground. And, as they fell, with debris crashing all around, Mike wondered if it was the end of the world.

Trapped beneath the branches of a tree, Jack was sobbing, his arms reaching out to his father. 'Hold on, son!' Pitting his strength against the weight of the tree and the strange force of the air, Mike managed to grab the boy's arms before he himself was pinned by the legs. 'I'll get you out, son,' he promised but, without help, he knew it would be no easy thing.

Suddenly he felt the undercurrent sucking at his body, tugging at Jack, pulling him out of his grasp. Terrified, the boy stared up at him, his small fingers groping to hold on. Again, the eerie silence descended, striking new horror into Mike's heart; with all his strength, he clutched at Jack's wrists, his scream shattering the silence, 'Don't let go! For God's sake… don't let go!' Something bad was happening, and they were right in the eye of it.

The undercurrent grew stronger: loose branches, enormous in size, were tossed about like matchsticks, spinning through the air as if some huge hand had snatched them up and sent them at unbelievable speed across the field, towards the young couple… into the soft, shivering light.

Mike felt weightless, helpless in the face of what was happening, but still he would not let go of Jack, not even if his arms were torn from their sockets.

While the wind screamed and the heavens shifted, Mike quietly prayed. He could feel himself losing the fight; the mighty tree which held them was beginning to lift, freeing them – to what?

Dear God above, he was losing Jack… 'Noooo…' His cry stretched through the air. He tightened his grip, holding on, even while the two of them were dragged out, skin and sinew torn as their helpless bodies scraped along the rough bark; shoes and socks were stripped away, clothing and hope shredded as they were drawn, inch by inch, from their sanctuary.

Suddenly, a terrible coldness enveloped them, and the quietness after such fury fell about them like a blessing. With the weight of the tree lifted from them, Mike found he could move. But his limbs were numb and stiff, wet with his own blood and Jack's. Jack was lying face up, his stricken eyes staring out towards the field.

Mike followed his gaze.

He could see the young couple standing hand in hand, unsure, hesitating. Then they began to run, first one way, then another. It was as if an invisible wall held them trapped.

The air was bitter-cold now, deathly quiet with a strange kind of beauty. Mike knew instinctively it was life-threatening. The power that had destroyed was still there, quieter now, beneath the surface, sharing the very air he breathed,

'Daddy, I'm frightened.' White-faced and trembling, Jack clung on.

Mike kept his eyes on the couple, who were still in his sights. Hopelessly disorientated, they continued to run about, confused and frightened. 'Make your way back here!' Mike called out, but his voice was thin and empty, almost as though he didn't exist.

In that moment of incredible calm, he saw the youths driven apart; arms outstretched and calling to each other, they were carried away. Terrified, yet strangely intrigued, Mike watched as they were raised above the earth, spinning, gently at first, and then so fast he could not make them out at all. But he heard their screams; awful, shocking screams that made him tremble.

Like a great moving canvas, the sky seemed to roll back and take them into itself. One minute they were there, and then they were gone.

Mike had seen it with his own eyes but he couldn't believe it. The sky had swallowed them up!

Silent and disbelieving, Mike and Jack held on to each other, fearing that if they were seen to move, they, too, would be sucked into oblivion.

Some hours later, mercifully unconscious, they were found. 'God Almighty, they're lucky to be alive!' Hacking them free, the firemen stood back for the medical team to do its job.

As they were lifted into the waiting ambulance, somebody remarked, 'The poor devils look as if they've been through hell and back.'

Only Mike and Jack knew the truth of that.

2

Seated on the steps of the camper van, Rosie lifted her gaze towards the seafront. From the high vantage point, she could just make out the shape of West Bay harbour as a ring of lights and, further down, the many colourful boats bobbing on the water. 'It's lovely here,' she sighed. 'I think I could settle here.'

Lying in his bunk, Luke heard her sigh and turned his head. For a long moment, he stared at his mother, thinking how beautiful she was, with the moonlight playing on her long auburn hair and those pretty green eyes that could light the world with a smile. But they weren't smiling now. Instead they were sad and faraway. He hated it when she was like that.

'Why are we here?' His intrusive voice startled her. Clambering off his bunk, he pushed past her down the steps. 'I never wanted to come here,' he complained. 'Neither did Eddie. It was *you*. Eddie brought you here, and now you don't want to go. I heard what you said just now, about settling here.'

'It's not polite to eavesdrop.'

Incensed, he stood before her, legs astride, deliberately blocking her view of the harbour. 'It was to see *him*, wasn't it? You made Eddie bring you here just so you could see that Peterson bloke.'

Rosie didn't look up. 'He's an old friend.'

'Hmh! An old lover, you mean.'

'All right, an old lover.'

'I thought you said it was all a long time ago.'

'That's right.'

'So why did you want to see him?'

'None of your business.'

'What if I was to tell Eddie?'

'Tell him if that's what you want,' she said with false bravado. Eddie had a vicious temper.

'Why is Peterson so important?'

Looking up, Rosie took stock of her son. Tall and gangly, he bore little resemblance to Mike, except for the unkempt brown hair that no comb could tame. But in many ways he reminded her of Mike – when he smiled, that swinging, easy way he walked. He had the same square chin too. Oh, yes, he was his father's son, in more ways than one. But she didn't want to tell him, not yet. The time wasn't right.

'What makes you think he's important?'

Answering one question with another was a coward's way but she had no choice.

Luke shrugged impatiently. 'If he isn't, why can't we leave?'

'We will.'

'When?'

'When I'm good and ready.' She had things to do here. Important things that had waited too long.

'Eddie doesn't want to stay either.'

'He can go when he likes. And so can you!' Angry, she tossed her head, eyes blazing up at him. 'You've two strong arms and you can find work at the drop of a hat, so you've no need of me.' No sooner were the words out than she regretted them. 'I'm sorry, son.' Opening her arms, she invited him to sit beside her. 'It's the Irish temper.' Laughing, she hugged him close. 'Sometimes my tongue runs away with my head.'

Distressed, he sat on the step beside her. 'I know I can earn a wage and I could manage if I had to. But you wouldn't really want me to go away, would you?'

'You know I wouldn't.' She gave him a stern glance. 'But I do love it here and I'm not ready to go yet.'

'OK, Mum.' Everything was all right again. He had stepped over the mark and meant never to do it again.

'So you'll stop going on about me leaving – for a while anyway?'

'I won't say another word, honest.'

She flicked his hair back from his forehead, the way she used to when he was a child. 'I'm sorry, Luke. I shouldn't have snapped at you like that. Only I don't want you nagging me.' Just then her gaze fell on a lone figure making its way towards them. In a low, sorry voice she added, 'I get enough aggravation from *him!*'

Luke's mood darkened. 'I'm going for a walk,' he said, and before she could reply, he was gone, making his way down the other path, away from the approaching man, towards the open fields.

'Don't go too far!' she called after him. 'You never know who's lurking about.'

'Leave him alone. The boy's old enough to take care of himself,' growled Eddie Johnson. He and Rosie had been partners for some years now, sometimes loving, sometimes hating. Lately, their relationship was strained to the point of breaking. He didn't want to lose her but Rosie did not care one way or the other.

Springing up, she stood on the lower step so he would not tower above her. 'You've been drinking again.' She eyed him with contempt.

'Been celebrating.' A squarely built man, with fair hair and close-set dark eyes, he had a high opinion of himself. 'The harbourmaster's taken me on as lookout.'

'Then he's a fool.'

'Don't be so bloody daft, woman. I'll not be drinking on the job.'

'Only before and after, eh?'

He laughed, rocking on his feet. 'You cheeky bugger!' He caught her to him. 'I'm feeling randy.'

'Are you now?' Laughing in his face, she taunted, 'The state you're in, I shouldn't think you could make him stand up long enough.'

'Long enough to satisfy you.'

Disgusted, she pushed him away. 'I don't think so. But I'm sure you could find yourself a whore to satisfy.'

As she turned to enter the camper van, he slid his hands over her thighs, gripping her so tightly she couldn't move.

'You're looking really lovely tonight, Rosie.' He swung her round. 'Why would I want a whore when I've got you?'

Angered, she slapped his face and he retaliated by crushing her to him. 'I came back half an hour since to tell you my good news, and you were nowhere to be seen.' Frowning, he added, 'These past weeks that seems to be happening a lot – I come back and you're not here. I don't like it, Rosie. Where were you tonight, for instance?'

'I went for a walk.'

'I missed you.' He kissed the back of her neck. 'I *always* miss you.'

'I'm tired, Eddie.' Again, she tried to pull away. But it was no use.

'I waited for you but you were gone a long time.'

'I walked across the fields, all the way into town.'

'Do you miss *me* when I'm away?'

'You know I do.' He had a mean, ruthless streak; she thought it best not to antagonise him.

'I got worried,' he murmured, 'thought you might be seeing another man.' Raising his face, he gave a long sigh. 'If you ever did that to me, Rosie, *I'd have to kill him.*'

Rosie knew he was capable of such a thing. 'I'm not seeing anybody.' When you hunt with beasts, she thought, you have to be just as cunning. And she was. 'I've always been faithful to you, Eddie.' Not in her *heart* though. In her heart and mind, she had always loved Mike, always dreamed of getting back with him. Now, because of what had happened, it would take that much longer. But she could wait. She had waited a lifetime already. All the same, knowing that Mike had fathered two children by another woman made her boil inside. Jealousy was an ugly, dangerous thing.

'Don't fight me.' Pushing her down on to the steps, Eddie kissed her, a long, brutal kiss that bruised her lips. 'Let's do it here.' Red-faced and excited, he tore at her clothes.

Rosie did not resist, though shame coloured her face. 'Not out here,' she chided. 'Luke could come back at any minute.'

'So what?'

'We should go inside.'

Unzipping his trousers, he held her there. 'I can't wait,' he groaned. 'You've really got me going now. And *you* want it as much as I do, I can tell.' Raising her skirt, he took her right there, across the camper steps.

It was quick and frenzied, and he was right, Rosie had wanted it too. Seeing Mike again, and knowing he was out of her reach for a while, had left her on edge. Eddie was small consolation, but it wasn't Eddie she was making love to; it was Mike – Mike who was invading her body, Mike whose arms held her tight; *Mike* whom she meant to have, by fair means or foul.

Luke heard them from some distance away and he knew from past experience that they were having sex. It was never love; it never could be. Eddie was a beast who had to satisfy his lust, and Rosie was just Rosie, indomitable and exuberant. She believed life was for living, and Eddie had to be tolerated.

Ever since that other man had come into their lives some time ago, Rosie had been different, quieter somehow, and oddly distant. Sadder too, and that wasn't like her. There was something about Mike Peterson that bothered Luke. His mother had a secret, and she kept it close. But he would find out. He had his ways.

Dismayed and thoughtful, he stood by the great oak tree and watched them for a while. His mother was spreadeagled on the steps, legs apart and feet touching the ground. Thrusting in and out on top of her, Eddie held her arms above her head, pressing the backs of her small hands into the rim of the camper van door. He cried out in bliss when Rosie arched into him.

Unable to watch any longer, Luke turned away, and as he did so, he heard Eddie give a long, shuddering sigh. At the same time Rosie uttered a name, the name Luke had on his mind at that very moment: *'Mike!'* In a moment of ecstasy, the name sprang from her lips, and Luke knew she would be punished.

'Bitch!' yelled Eddie. He dragged her up the steps and into the camper van. 'You lying bitch!' Digging his fingers into her flesh, he drew her up to face him. 'So it's Mike, is it? And where is he, this Mike?'

Fearful for her life, Rosie stammered, 'I don't know what you're talking about.'

'Liar!' He flung her across the camper van and then pulled her up again by the hair. He pressed his face close to hers, his voice grating. 'You'd better talk or I swear to God I'll do for the pair of you.'

Wiping the blood from her nose, Rosie was defiant. 'I don't know anybody called Mike.'

Another hard slap made her buckle at the knees. 'I mean it, Rosie. If I can't have you, nobody else will. I'll see to that.'

She didn't answer. Instead she turned her eyes upwards to look at his face, ugly and distorted with fury. In that moment she knew him better than she ever imagined. 'If I can't have you, nobody else will,' he had warned. *That was how she felt about Mike.*

Again he grabbed her, raising her to him by sliding her up against the wall. 'You've been seeing him, haven't you? All this time! And again tonight when I couldn't find you – you were with him, weren't you?'

Hating him, Rosie stayed silent.

A vicious slap across the mouth brought a fresh spurt of blood. Rosie raised her head as if about to answer, then spat in his face. Incensed, he held her away from him, bunched his fist and brought it crashing down against her temple. With a cry she slumped to the floor and he raised his foot to kick her.

'Leave her alone!' Luke burst through the door and without any thought for his own safety launched himself at Eddie. There was a vicious scuffle and for a time it seemed as if the boy's anger was more than a match for the man's strength. But after a few minutes, Luke was hurt and bleeding, and Eddie was triumphant.

Taking the boy by the scruff of his neck, Eddie asked softly, 'Tell me where I can find him or I swear I'll tie you both up and set fire to the place.'

'You wouldn't!'

Laughing, he shook his head. 'If you think that, you don't know me.'

Realising he was crazy enough to carry out his threat, Luke wondered if he should tell. Why should *he* care about Mike Peterson anyway? Nothing was the same any more. His mother was even talking about settling here, when their plans had always been to travel, to be free, see as much of the world as they could. He didn't know she had been scouring the country for *him*. Mike Peterson was all she cared about now, so why not let Eddie finish him off? The idea was tempting.

'Well? I'm waiting!'

It was on the tip of his tongue to tell Eddie that Mike Peterson was now in a mental hospital, and had been since the night they had first met him. But then he thought of his mother and how she would feel, knowing he had betrayed her, and changed his mind. 'His name is Mike Peterson,' he answered sullenly. 'And it's no good asking me any more, because I don't know.'

Eddie's answer was to smash his fist into Luke's face. 'Maybe that will loosen your tongue.'

'You can hit me again if you like, but I still won't know any more than I've told you.' He remembered his mother's courage and could not be less than she was.

Taken aback, Eddie hesitated. He had known Luke since he was a small boy, and knew him well enough to recognise that he might be telling the truth. 'Mike Peterson, you say?'

Luke nodded. 'That's all she's ever told me.'

Hard-faced, Eddie nodded. 'I'll find the bastard,' he rasped, 'and when I do, he won't be a threat any more.' With murder in mind he stamped out of the camper van.

Luke tended his mother. After a splash of cold water and a few minutes to recover, she managed to sit up in his arms.

'Where is he?'

Luke remained silent.

'Luke! What did you tell him?' Tugging at his sleeve, she made him face her. 'Please, Luke. I need to know.'

Looking down at her cut and bruised face, Luke felt ashamed. 'I didn't tell him where he was if that's what you're worried about.' Anger betrayed itself in his voice. 'I nearly did though.'

'So what *did* you tell him?' Wincing with pain, she drew herself up to sit in the chair, her eyes pleading with him to tell her the truth.

'His name, that's all. He's gone to find him.' The enormity of it all suddenly dawned on him. 'He won't kill him, will he?' Murder! A thing like that would touch them all.

Rosie leaned forward to rest her hands on his shoulders, her eyes wide with fear. 'You know what he's like. We have to stop him.'

Luke looked at her defiantly. 'Why should I stop him?'

'What do you mean?'

'Ever since that day when we met Mike Peterson at the river, you've changed. You always seem to be miles away... thinking about him. You take off and don't tell anybody where you go.' His voice stiffened. 'I followed you... the other night, when you thought I was nowhere about.'

'You had no right.'

'I know where you go.' His voice shook. 'I know what you do.'

'I have nothing to be ashamed of.'

Luke shrugged her off. 'Sitting outside a mental hospital like some sort of vulture, watching his wife come and go. I saw you creeping round the building, peering through windows, trying to catch a glimpse of him.'

'That's enough, Luke. I don't want to hear any more.'

'If you ask me, it should be *you* in there because you're as mad as he is.'

Rosie smiled. 'I'm in love, that's all. I've always loved him.'

Luke leaped up, his face warped with anger. 'You don't understand, do you? He's not yours to love!'

'Oh, but he is.'

There was a pause then, as these two looked at each other, a wealth of love between them; a love confused by all that Rosie knew, and Luke could only imagine.

'You'll find out one day,' Rosie said, 'so you might as well know now.' Pausing, she took a deep, invigorating breath. 'You have to understand… how it was…' Rosie's courage almost deserted her, but she had always known the moment for truth would come.

'What are you trying to say, Mum?' Like a prisoner waiting to be executed, Luke wanted it over.

'Mike Peterson is your father.'

For a long, agonising moment, he stared at her, eyes wide with disbelief. He saw the truth on her face but could not accept it. 'He can't be my father. You told me he was dead!'

'I lied to protect you.'

Grey with shock, Luke turned on his heel and ran into the night. Behind him, he could hear his mother's frantic cry, 'Eddie wants to kill your father. You've got to stop him!'

Painfully, Rosie pulled herself out of the chair and staggered to the water bowl where she sponged her face and neck, and wiped away the blood. 'Got to find him.' Mumbling to herself, she buttoned her blouse. Catching sight of her dishevelled self in the mirror, she was deeply shocked. 'I can't let him hurt Mike.' Without Mike she was nothing.

A moment later, she left the camper van and disappeared into the darkness.

The quickest way from West Bay to Bridport was on foot.

After leaving the camper van, Eddie had followed the ancient route through the spinney, across the meadow, and along the narrow footpath that ran alongside the river. The only light was the soft haze of moonlight above, and even that was muted by the tall trees.

Filled with murderous thoughts, he pressed on towards Bridport where he would find the nearest pub and begin his search. He suspected Rosie and Peterson must have been meeting in Bridport, and that was where he would find him, he was sure. Bridport was a small place; everybody knew everybody else. Someone was certain to know Mike Peterson.

He grinned. 'He needs to be taught a lesson… they *both* do. Nobody takes my woman.'

He leapt the stile and clambered over the gate – but his feet never touched the ground.

Stealing up behind him, the figure was stealthy, silent as the night and indistinguishable from the trees all around. Quick, agile fingers curled round a chunk of branch and, raising it high, brought it crashing down on Eddie's skull with a nauseating crunch. The terrified scream of a night creature sent the animals scurrying for cover and from somewhere in the distance came the sound of voices.

Satisfied, the figure went softly away.

In the ensuing silence, the broken body settled. Caught by its feet it hung upside down from the top rung of the gate, its eyes wide open, staring after the furtive figure.

There was no backward glance. The escape was swift and sly, and soon, save for those accusing eyes, it was as if nothing had happened.

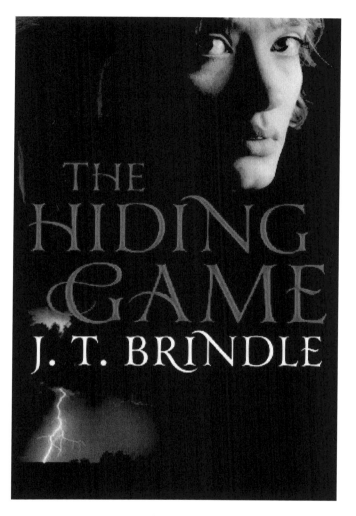

Available now

About this Book

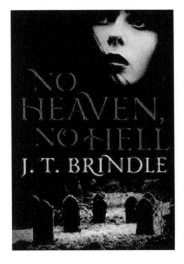

Virginia is the living image of her great-grandmother. She has the same presence, the same outstanding beauty. But behind her smile lies a terrible secret.

One by one her family die – first her grandmother, then her aunt, then her father. Only her loving sister Lianne is spared.

It seems that Virginia has inherited not only her great-grandmother's name and looks, but also the unspeakable evil that took her to the grave....

Also by this Author

THE TALISMAN SEQUENCE

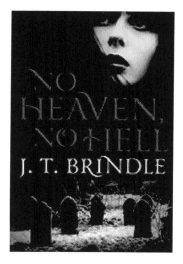

No Heaven, No Hell

Virginia is the living image of her great-grandmother. She has the same presence, the same outstanding beauty. But behind her smile lies a terrible secret.

One by one her family die – first her grandmother, then her aunt, then her father. Only her loving sister Lianne is spared.

It seems that Virginia has inherited not only her great-grandmother's name and looks, but also the unspeakable evil that took her to the grave....

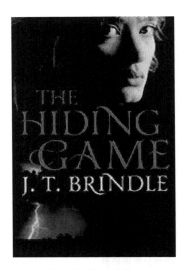

The Hiding Game

He had seen it with his own eyes, heard the awful screams, but nobody would believe him. Is Mike Peterson losing his mind? The doctors certainly think so and Mike is confined to a psychiatric unit.

Three years later, life has changed irrevocably for the Peterson family. The children will never forgive their father for shattering the family, his wife has built herself a successful career.

But now Mike is coming home...

The Hiding Game is available here.

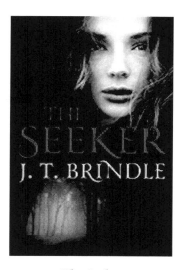

The Seeker

She is known as the woman on Bluebell Hill, a beautiful, ghostly figure haunting the lanes surrounding a remote rural inn, searching for something, or someone.

One moment the road is clear, the next she appears from nowhere; a squeal of brakes, a sickening thud and she vanishes as mysteriously as she appeared.

David Walters is a contented family man, until she singles him out.

Vowing to find out more about this mysterious, troubled apparition, Walters stumbles on an age-old secret – one that will endanger the lives of everyone he loves.

The Seeker is available here.

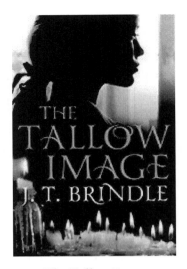

The Tallow Image

1880: Hauntingly beautiful Rebecca Norman is condemned to die. As she awaits the hangman, she fashions two crude dolls from candle tallow.

Over a century later, one of the dolls falls into the hands of young, newly married Cathy Slater. Under its malign influence, Cathy beings to change, tormented by emotions she does not understand and cannot control.

Only one person can help her – a frail old woman who has waited with dread for an ancient evil to surface…

The Tallow Image is available here.

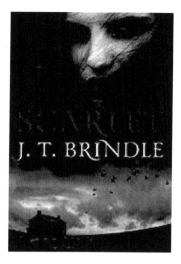

Scarlet

On a fateful winter's day in 1937, 18-year-old Cassie Thornton boards the Queen Mary and sets sail for England. Her mission: to find the mysterious Scarlet Pengally, the mother who abandoned her many years ago.

Her search leads to the West Country, to the dark, forbidding edifice of Greystone House, where Scarlet was born, home to generations of Pengallys. Yet it is also home to an unspoken dread, epicenter of a haunting tragedy – a desperate love and dark vengeance that has plagued the family for generations.

The key to it all is Scarlet. And Cassie must find her – for now the family's curse is threatening her own young life…

Scarlet is available here.

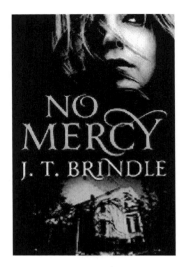

No Mercy

Many years ago, Thornton Place had been a magnificent sight. Now the isolated mansion is almost derelict; a bewitching, foreboding place. Yet it is Ellie Armstrong's home, the house her father had been hired to renovate. And – still grieving over the recent death of her mother – Ellie has learned to love it.

As winter draws in, the shadows cast by Thornton Place's sinister past lengthen. But Ellie is oblivious. She has found love. A love that is hypnotically powerful – and fatally compelling.

No Mercy is available here.